SOULS
IN THE
STARS

ALSO BY SARA JANE TRIGLIA

CHILDREN'S BOOKS

The Littlest Magnolia

SHORT STORIES

The Origins of Raine
Jumping Caspian

SOULS IN THE STARS

SARA JANE TRIGLIA

Snowfire Publishing
Visit our website at www.snowfirepublishing.com
Edited by Nick Hodgson and Donna West
Cover design by Get Covers
Interior design by Lorna Reid

PRINT ISBN: 979-8-9904830-0-2
EBOOK ISBN: 979-8-9904830-1-9

Made in the United States of America
First Edition June 2024

For twelve-year-old me,
I'm sorry it took so long.

If you would like to know if this novel contains any topics that might concern you, please check the back of this book for details.

N
W E
S
The Mysterious North
Non-Alliance Territory
Mines
Portal of Gifts
Water sources
Nostalgia Forest
Verve
Helio Territory
Smallholding
The Valley
Darning
Halcyon
Sub Rosa Island

PART I

INFINITE

1

Ever since my brother caught the curse, form-death was all I could think about. I was told that spiritual people regarded death as freeing—*the letting go of worldly flesh in order to free the untethered soul* or some crap like that. It sounded nice when phrased that way, but it didn't stop the rock from crushing my stomach. The thought of my little brother dying and leaving his form was terrifying, not freeing. I didn't care if I knew where he was going after death; I wanted him to stay with me. But I had no choice, and I had to get over it. That's what a spiritual person would have done, anyway: let go and surrender.

"I found something on the village border," Kailas said, breaking my spiraling thoughts. "Wanna see?"

Across the room from me, my best friend was sprawled on a sofa chair, his long legs dangling over the armrest. Kailas had a knack for showing me things I didn't care to see. From a box with a lost chick inside of it (he was feeding it bugs) to a rusty tractor part he had found in a cornfield (it was useless) to a map he said would lead us to hidden treasure (he had drawn it himself). We had been best friends for our whole lives, so I guessed his show-you-something outings came with the territory, but I was too tired to move.

"What is it this time?" I huffed.

He swung his legs so that he was sitting and looked me straight in the eye. "You could at least pretend to be interested."

I twirled the ends of my long, blonde hair. "I don't wanna move. Weeding kicked my butt this morning. Couldn't you just tell me what it is?" The couch felt nice. My shoulders and spine had already relaxed into the cushion.

He jumped up. "All right, you lazy turd, get up." He extended his callused hand out to me.

I didn't want to, but fresh air sounded better than my dismal thoughts, so I reluctantly threw my hand onto his, and he pulled me off the couch.

For what felt like an eternity, we hiked through our farming village, cutting through town center and many grasslands filled with cacti. That was Smallholding, our village: dry and desert-like. When I was about to start complaining about the heat, we came to a standstill in a field of taller-than-my-head grass.

I looked around. "Grass. Wow, this is great," I uttered in my most sarcastic tone. "If I were a hungry goat."

Shaking his head at me, Kailas stepped forward and created an opening, revealing a thin trail that I assumed was made by wild deer. At the end of the path, I spotted something but couldn't make it out from the distance. I stepped through Kailas's opening and made my way toward the thing as he followed close behind.

The ground changed from dirt to black tar. A paved road sliced its way through the field. The road was clear of debris, which told me that Halcyon workers still used it. Parked on the side of the road was a rusted red truck covered in grime. It must have been sitting there for the better part of a decade.

"Is this the road to Halcyon?" I asked Kailas, knowing he couldn't answer. That was private information for delivery drivers only. Halcyon was our island's hub and reserved for only the most spiritual people.

"No, but it's a road to somewhere." He headed to the passenger side door and yanked it open. "Get in!"

"It won't work."

"Bay, just get in." He groaned, holding the door.

I scoffed, made a stink face, and hopped into the truck. For someone who sort of knew how to fix up cars, Kailas could be clueless. There was no way a rusted old truck was going to work.

Stop complaining. Spiritual people don't complain, I told myself. *It wouldn't kill you to be positive.*

He slammed the door shut and made his way to the driver's side. Once in, he lowered the visor, and a set of keys fell into his lap.

"Let's see who's right." He picked up the keys, selected one, and inserted it into the ignition. He turned the key, and the engine roared.

My eyes widened, and I stared at him in disbelief, laughing awkwardly in the way people do when they're pleasantly surprised. I hadn't driven anywhere since the war began when I was five. Kailas drove in a Halcyon vehicle weekly to make the crop and water deliveries.

"See?" A triumphant smile escaped his lips as he put the transmission into gear. The truck pulled forward, and we turned onto the road.

"I'm amazed," I said more positively. "Where are we going?" The land slid by us as I rolled the window open to stick my head out into the cool breeze. It looked like we were leaving Smallholding, which was forbidden.

"Our moms used to take us up the mountain to a forest. Remember?"

Somewhere deep in my mind, a memory unlocked— miniature versions of Kailas and me running through a crisp forest, climbing tall trees, and pretending to be wild behemoths.

I longed for those simple, carefree days. Yet they were so long ago they seemed like a dream.

I pulled my head back into the truck. "We can't go there."

"Why not?" He took his eyes from the road to look at me.

"Well, for one: we don't know where it is." It was only logical; we couldn't go somewhere we didn't know how to get to. Yet I could feel I was being difficult. I was about to get away from the place I had been trapped in for thirteen years. For a seventeen-year-old, that was the majority of my life. I didn't know why I was challenging him when I so desperately wanted to leave Smallholding—even if just for the day.

"I was there a month ago, with Masculines, for work stuff."

I gave him a doubtful frown. "And it's safe?"

"Of course."

There were only a handful of green trees in Smallholding, nothing like the crisp air and adventurous energy of the woods. It would be wrong to go, of course, but fun. I let go of my reservations and settled into the seat, welcoming the distraction from my brother's looming form-death.

The trees blurred by the windows as wind stirred about wildly in the cab. Pushing my hair out of my face, I decided to tie it in a ponytail. Then I scavenged the truck to see what I could find. I studied the interior, searching for clues. It was clean. No wallet, no boots, no belongings. The seats were wiped clean. The dash hadn't collected a layer of dust. The fuel gauge read FULL. I didn't know much about vehicles, but wouldn't the battery have been dead if the truck had sat immobile for years? That's when it hit me. This must have been Kailas's truck or a truck he had found and worked on. I peeked over at him as he focused on the road. *What is he up to?*

We wound up the mountain for a while longer. The farther we went, the more debris filled the road; fallen trees and decaying leaves were strewn along both sides. Tree roots had burst through the pavement, forcing Kailas to zigzag around them. At one point, I turned the dial on the radio, but nothing played except static. The grasslands changed to a forest of trees. When a canopy of branches cast shadows on us, I knew we had arrived. Kailas parked in a patch of dirt, and we bounded from the truck.

As my feet hit the soil, an immediate sense of relief overtook me—something different, something new, and something that wasn't day-in and day-out on the stark farm. No cacti or hay-like grass in sight, only greenery. There was a moistness to the air and in my lungs that I had forgotten existed in the world. Taking in a refreshing breath, I let it fill my soul. This was exactly what I needed.

We rushed into the forest of trees and let them swallow us. Hours passed like minutes as we raced through the woods and played like children. We swung from vines, wrestled in leaves, and acted foolishly juvenile. If I was with anyone else I might have been embarrassed, but this was Kailas. I could be myself with him. He had known me my whole life, knew my scars and accepted my weirdness. He was also a big geek himself, so he couldn't say much.

Using a log as a balance beam, I walked across a patch of hairy, carpet-like green moss. Squatting, I slid my fingers across it and scanned the area, searching for a stream.

"No river," Kailas said. "It mists here, but that's all."

Our island was short on water sources, and there was nothing I wouldn't do to find one for Smallholding.

I leapt off the log to find the tallest nola tree I had ever seen standing before me. *I have to reach the top,* I thought. Grasping the rainbow colored bark, I made it about forty feet high when climbing to the top was looking a little too ambitious. So, Kailas joined me and sat beside me on a thick branch, and we watched the forest come alive—birds calling on the branches above, cotton ball-like creatures bouncing along the dirt below, and wind rushing by the tree.

With our legs dangling off the branch, a lock of Kailas's black hair fell into his face. He was handsome, but I hardly looked at him in that way—at least, not until recently. Ever since he turned eighteen and grew his hair out, something changed. I lowered my head and rested it on his shoulder. It was the safest I had felt in forever, and I softened into a tranquil state.

In a flash, a flying object cut through the air, catching my attention. I raised my head off Kailas's shoulder.

"Oh shoot, I lost it," a man's voice rang through the forest.

"Maybe try hitting your mark and you won't lose it next time," shouted a second voice, that of a woman.

From behind a patch of trees, a figure materialized—a tall, fit young man with short, brown hair, and light skin. He wore a pair of thick-framed glasses, carried a bow, and wore a quiver on his back.

I looked at Kailas, curious about what he made of the man. His expression was stern. The man hadn't spotted us and most likely wouldn't from our high position in the tree, so long as we didn't make a sound.

The man picked up the flying object that had landed on the ground. At first it was unclear, but then, as it came into focus, I saw it: an arrow. He whisked the arrow over his head and tucked it into the quiver on his back. That's when the young woman walked into sight, out of a patch of dense forest. Wearing a beige dress that trailed behind her in the wind, she strode confidently toward the man. Around her neck dangled a long, brown-beaded necklace, adorned with a weighty golden gem. She carried an auburn leather knapsack on her back. Her skin was pale, as if she had never been in the sun. The detail that stood out about her the most, though, was her hair. It wasn't long, only past her shoulders, but it was blue. A soft, teal blue with thin, sporadic white streaks.

I had no idea that people with hair of such colors existed in the world. The woman was gorgeous. No, that wasn't the right word. She was *divine*.

"Halcyons," Kailas whispered.

I had seen Masculines, the town's military men, but I had never seen a Halcyon—the island's most spiritual people.

I couldn't help but stare at this mesmerizing blue-haired young woman.

When she took a step forward a bush blocked my view of her, so I scooted sideways to get a better look. I repositioned my hand but missed the branch entirely. My heart dropped into my stomach as I fell forward and slipped from the tree.

2

I*'m about to die.* A thought had never hit me so hard. As I slipped from the branch and fell headfirst, reality smacked me in the face.

With my eyes shut tight and my heart in my throat, I gritted my teeth. Gritted my teeth? Shouldn't I have been dead? *Why am I not dead?*

Opening my eyes, I found the world upside-down. Headfirst, and with the sky at my feet, somehow, some way out of my control, I floated in the air. Blood pulsed through my head as some outside force had me in its hold. Nothing made any sense, but I was alive. Slowly, the world turned upright, and I could feel the blood drain from my ears. With my feet back under me, I hovered about twenty feet above the hard ground that was supposed to kill me.

A single leaf fell from the tree above. It swayed side to side, passing my face on its way down. I held my hand out, and the leaf landed gently in my palm. Below me, Kailas climbed down the tree and planted his feet on the forest floor as he eyed up the Halcyon man. The two of them stared at me but with entirely different expressions. Kailas was fascinated; the man wasn't.

I let the leaf go.

Farther back, behind Kailas, the teal-haired woman looked straight at me, her eyes bright blue. Her hands faced out, glowing the same teal shade as her hair. Without my controlling it, my body drifted over the men and toward the woman, lowering itself toward the ground. My feet landed on the forest floor before her as gravity returned to me with its weighty force.

By some miracle, I had fallen forty feet and lived. I looked at the woman standing before me. She was even more stunning up close; her teal eyes shone so brightly I wasn't sure if they were glowing or simply vivid blue. With such radiant features, I must have appeared bland standing beside her. She was a *real* spiritual person from the most spiritual town on the island.

"Are you all right?" she asked with a strong, clear voice.

I nodded and dizzily wobbled on my feet while she looked me over.

My eyes trained on her little and pointed ears. "Yeah," I told her, pulling my gaze to her face. I couldn't concentrate. Maybe it was the blood rushing back to my head.

Kailas embraced me from behind. I turned to him, pulling him in close.

The Halcyon man approached the three of us, taking his place at the woman's side.

"I can't believe you're okay. I mean, I thought..." Kailas glanced at the blue-haired young woman. "Thank you, I think. You did this, right?"

The Halcyons exchanged a long and silent look.

"Don't mention it," the woman said. She turned on her heel and headed away, gesturing for us to follow. "We have a place up here we're calling home for now. You're welcome to come with us while you gather your bearings."

"Thanks," Kailas said as we shadowed her. "I think we know our way, but I have a few questions for you."

"I have a question for you too."

"Okay, shoot."

"Where are you guys from?"

"Oh, uh, Smallholding," Kailas answered.

"I've never met anyone from there."

"Well, now you have. You know who I've never met before? A person who can catch people with their eyes." Kailas couldn't hold his tongue. But that was fine because I hoped he would do all the talking. *Be confident*, I told myself. *Spiritual people are confident.* Still, I couldn't help but sink into my meekness. I wished I could be more like them.

"Well, you need to get out more… uh… what should I call you?" the young woman asked.

"Kailas." He nodded. "And you?"

"I'm Blue," she answered, "and that's my boyfriend, Sterling."

Kailas scoffed. "Blue… Really?"

Sterling turned and looked straight at Kailas. "You got a problem with her name?"

Kailas clicked his tongue. "No, it's a great name. Also, a fantastic color."

"I'm Bay," I offered, trying to save Kailas.

"Like the body of water," Kailas added. That was Kailas: completely himself with people he had just met. While he sometimes came off as rude, I still envied that quality about him. The being himself part.

The conversation died as we hiked through the forest with nothing but the sound of crunching leaves under our feet. Blue and Sterling walked a few paces ahead of us, but I wasn't exactly sure why we were still following them. I thought we were waiting for Kailas to ask his questions, but no one spoke. The sun shone on us at an angle through the distant branches. It was getting late, and the day would soon close.

The four of us had traveled about a mile when Blue and Sterling stopped at our presumed destination: a twenty-foot-high teepee made from logs, branches, vines, pine needles, and other plants. It wasn't huge; the four of us could probably fit inside, but not comfortably. I sized up Sterling. He was a husky guy with broad shoulders; he certainly had the strength to put it together.

"Did you make this?" Kailas asked, taking the words from my mouth.

Blue entered the teepee and knelt to sort through her belongings—a sack, a map, and some other things I didn't get a good look at. She removed a red apple from her bag and slipped a pocketknife from her bag. She made her way out of the structure and stood near us.

To our right, a log rose from the ground and glided through the air toward the teepee. It settled into the structure, piling on top of the other logs. Of course. Blue had built the teepee, not Sterling. I suspected he hadn't lifted a finger.

Kailas backed away from the teepee. "That's a nifty trick."

Holding the apple, Blue cut off a slice with her pocketknife and placed the piece into her mouth. As she chewed, she appeared unfazed by Kailas's comment.

"Where'd you get the apple?" I asked.

"Brought it with us."

"Brought it with you… from Halcyon?"

Blue leered at me as if trying to decide something. "Yeah."

"Leaving town is against the law," Kailas remarked from beside me.

"Leaving Smallholding is against the law too."

"Touché," Kailas replied. "But you have guards patrolling your borders; we don't. You must have used your superpower to get out of there unseen."

Blue smirked at him. "You're right. I used my gift." She emphasized the word "gift" as if to correct his terminology.

"Why would you leave Halcyon?" I asked. Becoming a

citizen was next to impossible unless you were born there. Since only the most spiritual people lived there, it was bound to be a serene place. Not to mention the countless meals and all the water you could possibly drink.

"It's complicated," Blue replied, looking to Sterling.

"Apples are hard to come by." Kailas nodded at Blue. "I haven't seen one in ages."

She eyed the apple. "Apples are in abundance in Halcyon." She slid the last slice into her mouth, the fruit crunching between her teeth. She closed the pocketknife, guided it back into its home in her bag, and tossed the core into the forest.

"Why are you all the way out here? There's nothing up in these woods," Kailas pressed.

Sterling moved next to Blue. "We could ask you the same thing."

"It was me. I haven't left Smallholding since the war," I offered, my voice small and meek with unease. "I had to get out of there for a bit. Kailas works in transportation with Halcyon, so he knows the roads."

Sterling nodded in understanding as Kailas stepped toward the teepee, testing out the logs, checking for sturdiness.

Brushing the dirt off her dress, Blue let out a breathy sigh. "We're leaving Halcyon for good," she told us. "We had to get out of there too."

Kailas drew his focus back to Blue. "Halcyon surveys this part of the island. They'll find you in a matter of weeks if you even survive that long. I can tell that your rations are dwindling. How long have you been in this forest? A day or two? You're better off going back to Halcyon, where your food and water are in abundance. Anyway, ten miles that way, and you run into River Clan territory."

Something Kailas said caught Blue's attention, and her

eyes widened. "Ten miles *that way*?" she inquired, pointing in the direction Kailas mentioned.

He moved closer to her. "Ten miles around the curve of the mountain, there are hundreds of savages waiting to fight to the death to protect their land from being stolen by Halcyons like you."

Blue gazed toward the River Clan territory. She turned to Sterling, who looked serious. Making some kind of silent agreement, they both went into the teepee. Swiftly, they packed up their belongings, slung them over their shoulders, and returned to us.

"Good luck in Smallholding," Blue said and tossed her arm in the air.

The teepee disassembled as she left. Branches, logs, and vines spread out in the air, scattering along the trail. Each dismantled piece found a place in the woods where it was camouflaged, leaving no trace of the teepee behind.

Kailas chased after them. "Uh, that's the way *toward* the River Clan."

"You should be getting back to your farm village," Blue said.

Kailas scoffed. "Wait, you *want* to find the River Clan? Are you insane? They'll take one look at you and shoot an arrow through your neck."

Blue went on marching forward, Sterling keeping pace with her.

I walked alongside Kailas, watching the scene unfold.

"I can stop an arrow before it hits me," Blue said evenly.

"Can you stop a hundred arrows? Hold off an army?" Kailas retorted. "I mean, I know you've got your big, strong boyfriend to protect you, but you'll only get him killed too."

That's when Sterling stopped—the two of us freezing behind him—and faced Kailas, who took a single step back.

Sterling spoke into Kailas's eyes. "Since you know everything, why don't you enlighten us on the River Clan?"

Blue waited paces ahead, still facing the path.

"Would love to," Kailas began, clearing his throat. "I don't know what Halcyon tells you about the River Clan. I also don't know how long you've been on Sub Rosa Island, but I've lived here my entire life. Even before the war, the River Clan didn't want our kind on the island. They believed we were mutants. They despised us. Many bloody battles were fought between us, but no one ever won.

"Eventually, the River Clan claimed the island's west side, leaving us with the center and east. We agreed never to set foot on their side, knowing that if we did, they would kill us dead." Kailas drew in a deep breath. "They lived up to that promise. There's a cemetery outside Smallholding dedicated to those people—hundreds of graves." He called forward, saying his last sentence louder so Blue could hear him. "I don't know you, but I don't want you to be another body in their cemetery."

Blue unfroze herself and turned toward us, purposefully striding to Kailas and pausing a foot from his face. A second of silence passed before she gave him a questionable smile. "Are you done with your little speech now?"

Kailas pulled back as he shrugged. "Well, yeah."

"The Helio aren't savages. They're connected beings who live as one with One," Blue began. "They found this island first and have had more than half of the island stolen from them, and they're rightfully protective of what little they have left. As higher beings, they have a sense we don't have; they feel energy. They may look at my flesh and want to shoot an arrow, but they will recognize my soul and embrace me," she declared. "And what's more, what you just recited are false myths, completely untrue and unfair assumptions about the Helio."

Kailas leered at her, baffled. After a second, he asked, "Do you seriously believe that?"

I spoke up. "She has a point. I mean, they don't refer to themselves as the River Clan—that's the name we came up with since they control the island's largest water source. How much do we honestly know about the Helio besides what their enemies have told us?"

However, I knew more about them than I let on. I had requested Helio lessons from Gemma, my spiritual guide. When settlers first came to the island, they thought they could civilize the Helio. Gemma was hired as a teacher and communication specialist. She interacted with a subgroup of Helio to establish a relationship and with hopes of building a school. That's when Gemma, and her former colleagues, translated the Helio language. The school was never built, and war raged instead, but their language was never lost. However, Helio was a forbidden tongue in Smallholding, never to be spoken again. I would be a traitor if anyone heard me speak it.

Kailas looked at us. "I guess if Blue can float things, it's possible the River Clan aren't savages." He directed his attention to me next. "But I'm still not taking my chances. I'm going back to the truck and heading home. It's getting late, anyway, and someone will notice we're missing. Are you coming?"

I agreed.

For the mile-long trek back to the truck, the four of us walked in two groups: Blue with Sterling up front and Kailas and me trailing behind. I wanted to ask Blue the questions plaguing my mind. When would I ever have this opportunity to meet a Halcyon again? When the parked truck, where we would part ways, came into view, I quickened my pace and caught up to Blue.

"Before you go," I started, feeling more like myself—

skeptical yet curious—"I have to know: why did you have to get away from Halcyon?"

With a sigh, Blue tucked a strand of teal hair behind her ear and replied, "I lived there for ten years. It's not what you might think. People are…" She glanced at Sterling, searching for the right words.

"People aren't as genuine as they make themselves out to be," he said, finishing Blue's sentence.

"I see the truck," Kailas called out. "Ready to go, Bay?"

"I guess. I just…" I was about to ask to stay awhile longer when something on Sterling's bow caught my eye. I moved in to get a better look. "Where'd you get your bow?"

"I found it yesterday; in these woods, actually." He shrugged. "I figured it got lost during the war."

I ran my fingers over the carvings on the handle. "This bow isn't old enough to have withstood the wars. It's not weathered. No moss or mold."

"Maybe one of the Masculines lost it during a survey?" Sterling looked around.

"Don't you know?" Kailas asked in a hushed voice, surveying the area. "Masculines don't use bows."

That's when I felt it—a slight shift in the air. I listened to my instincts and dropped to the ground just as an arrow whizzed over my head. It struck the tree behind me, the fletching protruding from the bark. I didn't wait for the next one to come. I maneuvered behind a wide tree. There hadn't been a second to look for Kailas, but my mind went to him.

On the ground, I pressed my back against the trunk. Arrows rained through the air like a meteor shower. To my right, Kailas crouched behind a tree about three yards away. Any relief in his safety was fleeting as I realized it was as temporary as mine. Many arrows stuck out of his tree, with new ones lodging into it at every second. We locked eyes, and

I knew he felt as helpless as I did. None of the fighting skills we had learned were useful—not in real combat. I had never been a strong fighter anyway.

Kailas pointed behind me, and I turned to find Blue standing in the middle of a war zone, arrows coming at her head-on. She stood tall, with her palms facing out as if an invisible forcefield protected her. Each time an arrow flew at her, it soared through the air, slowed, and then dropped to the ground. Blue now had a collection at her feet, but something told me that if she lost her concentration, she would be done for.

I searched my mind for some way I could help. I scanned the area around me, willing an idea to surface and make me useful. Nothing came to me. Soon whoever was attacking us would be upon us. It wouldn't be long before they reached us and sent the final blow through our hearts. I hoped it would be quick and painless. I hoped they would do it with reverence.

That's when I heard a voice call out. It was in Helio. It took me a moment to translate as I hadn't heard it spoken by anyone except Gemma. I thought it said, "Bows down." Were they laying down their bows? Surrendering? But why? Blue hadn't moved from her spot when the arrows ceased like waves in an ocean gone flat. A cool gust of wind whispered through the forest, lifting Blue's beige dress from the soil and waving it out behind her. Her essence was suddenly apparent—her pale skin, soft features, feminine energy; a delicate yet thorny rose.

At that moment, Sterling dropped his bow and charged out from behind a nearby tree, his feet flinging dirt up into the air behind him. He sprinted to Blue as fast as he could. It took only five seconds for him to reach her, but he made it with no time to spare. Raising his forearm, he took the brunt of a heavy blow that was intended for Blue's skull.

A teenage Helio male—his skin celadon green, his hair

and beard lilac-gray—towered over him, grasping a large wooden staff. His oversized eyes showed no visible pupils; instead, his eyes were a blue-green painted galaxy of stars. In between his eyebrows, on his forehead, lay a tiny oval opening that radiated a white light.

The Helio barreled forward violently, his shoulders rushing Sterling's upper body, knocking him to the dirt. While Sterling was down, the man tried to kick his side, but Sterling grabbed his ankle and pulled. As the man crashed onto his back, his staff whacked the ground, billowing up a cloud of dirt. In a flash, they were both on their feet again, and the fight ensued.

In the distance, Blue climbed a towering nola tree, unscathed. I turned to the tree where Kailas had taken refuge, but he wasn't there. Rising to my feet, I rapidly scanned the area for him as my heart raced. When I rounded my tree, a Helio woman materialized and punched me hard in the face. I stumbled back as intense pain radiated up my nose. For one second, I allowed myself to study her—one second was all I could afford.

The woman was about the same size as me, slightly taller. She had the same features as the Helio man, except her purple-gray hair was longer, just grazing her shoulders, and wildly wavy. A shark-tooth necklace hung over her chest. She wore a creme halter top and brown long skirt made from what appeared to be jute fibers. She twisted her body toward mine, her irisless eyes hard to read. But even then, I knew this would be a fight for my life.

I blocked a blow to my right, then to my left. Then she threw me on the dirt before I could understand how she did it. The air knocked out of my lungs. I lay with my back on the hard ground and her sitting on my chest, my shoulders pinned by her knees.

I knew how to get out of this hold thanks to my practice with Gemma's mate. I pulled my hips up into a bridge, pushing my opponent's momentum forward. As her palms landed on the ground, I grabbed her arm and pulled it toward me. Her mount weakened, and I rolled to the left, pushing her off me.

Within a second, we were both on our feet. The Helio woman was fast, much faster than me, and difficult to evade. I wouldn't be able to elude her. This fight wouldn't end unless one of us ended it, which meant I needed to take her down. But how?

That's when she lunged forward and grabbed onto my shirt, attempting to pull me to the ground. As my weight fell forward, I freed my arms and rolled over her.

When I landed, I swung to punch her in the face. But she blocked my punch, grabbed my arm, and pulled it down. Next, she twisted my elbow. In an instant, I was in an arm-bar—and there was no tapping out. I tried to pull my legs up to shove her away, but it was no use. I screamed in pain as she pushed to break my arm. Then, suddenly, I was free.

Gasping for breath, I crawled backward and pressed my spine against a nearby tree, shaking the pain out of my arm. Kailas was there, fighting the woman, while Sterling fought three Helio teenagers at once. From up in the tree, Blue used her magic to chuck rocks, sticks, massive logs, whatever she could find at the men attacking a weakened Sterling. To my right, a young Helio man lay unconscious, or maybe dead.

That's when I spotted her: a toddler Helio girl. She couldn't have been more than two years old, with shoulder-length green hair and wearing the Helio version of a diaper. She stood alone, scraping a rock across the rainbow bark of a nola tree, oblivious to the mayhem around her. From the corner of my eye, I saw a large tree trunk soar through the air. It crashed on the forest floor, barreling in the direction of Sterling and the Helio men, but also on course to hit the little girl.

A vine dropped directly in front of Sterling; he grabbed it and it raised him into the tree branches just as the trunk barreled by. The three Helio men leapt over it, but one didn't jump high enough, and it barreled into him. The impact barely slowed the tree.

I sprinted toward the little girl, who was unaware that an enormous trunk was about to crush her.

3

As I closed in on the girl, the trunk closed in on me. I made it to her just in time to lift her to my chest and leap into the aerial prop roots of the nola tree for protection. I landed inside, shielding her in my lap just as the log crashed violently into the roots. The brutal impact shook the branches, and loose leaves showered down on us from above. The once threatening force of nature now sat harmless at the foot of the nola.

The Helio girl on my lap was unscathed but whimpering; startled yet alive. I took a second to catch my breath, then maneuvered through the roots and carefully climbed out. The battling had stopped. Kailas, Sterling, the three teenage Helio, and the young Helio woman stood still. Their eyes were locked on us.

An adult Helio woman and an elderly man came from the woods. They had the same green skin, lilac-gray or green hair, and irisless, green-blue galaxy-like eyes as the others. The man carried a tall wooden staff with elaborate carvings and a golden crystal mounted on the top. His beard was as gray and wild as those on the rest of the men.

The woman rushed toward me with outstretched arms and wide eyes. She must have been the girl's mother. As the woman reached us, I held the girl out to her, and she snatched her up. I couldn't miss her gigantic, pregnant belly under her dress. Without meeting my eyes, she stomped off with the girl on her hip, grumbling something in Helio. Maybe scolding the little girl for wandering off, maybe cursing me; I couldn't be sure because the words were unintelligible. By her attitude, it seemed she had missed the whole show. Had she not seen me save her daughter? Risk my own life? Did she despise our kind so deeply that the only form of gratitude she could show was to not murder me?

I stood facing the Helio as I assessed Kailas, who seemed to be fine besides a minor flesh wound on his cheek. The older Helio man said something in their language that sounded like their farewell greeting. Then the three teenage men headed over to the unconscious man. One of them picked him up, slung him over his shoulders, smacked his rear end, and laughed. The woman with the shark-tooth necklace grimaced at me, faced her clan, and took steps to meet them. As she passed Kailas, she spat on the ground by his feet. They collected their arrows from the trees as well as Sterling's bow, then the four young men, the shark-tooth woman, and the older couple with the toddler girl headed away from us.

Don't be afraid, I reminded myself. *Fear is unspiritual. Be brave.*

I should have just let them go, but with their backs toward us, I took in a breath for courage and uttered the words, *"Mi ho'o lenaba."* As soon as they left my lips, I wished I could take them back. It was so unlike me to speak up like that—so foreign.

I hoped to have said something anodyne, but for all I knew I had sealed our fate by acutely offending them. "We are not your enemy" was what I wanted to say, but my Helio was rusty at best.

The older man, presumably their chief, stopped in his tracks. He swiveled his body around to address me with his staff erected in front of him.

"*Mi ho lenaba, ni hoa mo Helio?*" he asked authoritatively. *Don't be afraid, don't give into fear.*

"I learned Helio to understand your side of the story," I said in Helio, feeling Kailas's presence next to me. His shoulder brushed against mine. He never knew that I could speak Helio.

"Don't come to these parts. You rescued Mara, so we spared you. We're even now," he said in Helio, as well as another sentence I didn't understand, and then he stomped his staff on the dirt.

"I thought this was open territory," I replied. "Your land starts ten miles—"

The man shook his head angrily. "We found this island first and we will go where we like. It's all ours!"

Blue was next to me now. She placed her arm on my shoulder and whispered in my ear. "Ask them if they can feel my energy. Tell them I come peacefully and with reverence. Ask them to *see* me."

I shook my head in disagreement. What she wanted me to translate was too far out of context with the conversation.

"She," the Helio man said in his language, pointing to Blue. "She is unusual. She's mutated and can make things move to her will. Why?"

I looked to Blue. "They're asking about your gift. They want to know why you can do what you do."

Blue gazed directly at the Helio and said in my language, "Please allow me to join your clan. I'm enlightened. My partner is too." She gestured to Sterling. "We want to join you, to learn."

She looked at me intently, waiting for me to translate, but I hesitated. She was the most spiritual person I had ever met, so I should have trusted her, but it had the potential of going terribly wrong. I didn't even know the translation for some of the words she had used. As I contemplated what to do, Kailas spoke up.

"You're kidding, right?" he scoffed in disbelief. "Can't you tell by the flying arrows aimed at your head? They're not exactly rolling out the welcome mat."

"They were defending their side of the island," Blue retorted. "We're talking now, aren't we?"

"We don't even know what they're saying. They could be talking about eradicating your mutant magic by slicing off your head."

"Maybe we should go," Sterling said softly, looking at Blue. "Maybe we're in over our heads here."

Blue turned away from him to look at me. "What are they saying?"

My eyes met each of theirs. The Helio grew impatient with us wasting their time. "They said we shouldn't be here, the island is theirs, and they want to know why you have mutant powers."

"Please tell them what I said," she pleaded. "Please."

I exhaled, glancing at the clan. Against my better judgment, I tried my best to translate. "She says she's…" What was the translation for enlightened? "Um… special and well aware. She wants to learn your customs. She asks to join your clan."

The young woman with the shark-tooth necklace stomped in protest. Her response was of repulsion, of hatred. The young men chuckled; the one holding the unconscious man on his shoulders seemed uninterested and exhausted from holding his large friend. The pregnant woman with the toddler girl walked off to show her daughter some flowers on the ground.

"You are not Helio," the man replied, lifting his staff. "Never will you be."

The Helio at once turned away and walked in the opposite direction. The woman picked up the toddler girl, holding a bouquet of pink flowers, and followed behind them.

Blue's eyes searched me for an answer.

"You will never be Helio," I told her. "That's what he said. I'm sorry. We need to go before they change their mind about sparing us."

Blue wrinkled her face, shook her head, and then marched after the clan. Before she was upon them, Sterling caught up to her and wrapped his arms around her. As he held her back, she screamed after the Helio, begging them to return. But they were gone, too far off in the trees to see her. She fell to the ground, weeping and murmuring to Sterling. Blue's desperation was palpable and I could almost feel it in my own heart.

Kailas approached me and locked me in a hug. His palm caressed my back, smoothing out my hair. We stayed there for some time, soaking in each other's presence. Then slowly, we pulled away and made eye contact.

"This didn't go to plan," Kailas said. "I wanted to give you a good day. A break from the farm. Not almost get you killed… twice."

I exhaled. "Well, thanks for trying." I ran my fingers along a scrape on Kailas's cheek.

"When did you learn to speak River Clan?" he asked.

"I thought you might ask about that."

"Is that why you get three hours with Gemma? Instead of two?"

"Maybe."

"How do you say, 'It's a good day…for your funeral' in Helio?"

"Helios are twice your size."

"It's not the size of the man, but the fight he's got inside of him."

I shook off his remark. "I can't believe we actually met Helios. Talked to them. Fought them."

"Crazy, right?"

As the adrenaline wore off, I rubbed my sore arm. "Terrifying," I told him.

"Beats that time a behemoth wandered onto your farm."

"Yeah." Suddenly I was tired.

"Yeah."

It took awhile, but eventually, Sterling persuaded Blue not to pursue the Helio. Blue was comatose—broken by the Helio's rejection. I wanted to ask her about it, but I wasn't sure how.

"We're heading back to Smallholding," Kailas told them. "You guys need a ride somewhere?"

Blue and Sterling exchanged glances. Sterling nodded. "Back to Halcyon."

"All right," Kailas replied. "Hop in the bed."

The first half of the ride was dead quiet. Maybe it was shock, maybe it was something else. I gazed out the window for a long while, watching the trees blur by in rapid flashes. As we exited the forest area and made our way back to the desert grasslands, there was a heaviness in my heart—the dread of going back to Smallholding. Back where my brother, Ash, was dying of a curse.

"Hey, Blue," Kailas called out, "how come you didn't use your eyes to pick up those guys and throw them halfway across the island?"

I turned, glancing through the rear window at Blue and Sterling sitting in the bed of the truck. Blue's teal hair whipped in the wind, her back pressed against the side of the bed. Her formerly bright eyes were dull with defeat. She somberly peeked up at Sterling, sitting opposite her, but she didn't speak.

"She can only control objects without freewill. She can't control humans who have bodily autonomy and freedom of choice," Sterling told us, his answer barely audible as it came through the rear window.

Kailas contemplated this. "But what about Bay? When she fell out of the tree? I'm pretty sure she's human," he said, eyeing me.

"Bay was falling. She didn't have freewill in that moment. It was different," Sterling answered almost robotically. It was obvious he was drained and merely answering Kailas's questions to appease him.

"Hmm," Kailas replied. "Interesting. How come—" I nudged his side with my elbow and when he looked at me I shook my head at him. It wasn't the time for jarring questions. Blue was upset, and Sterling was obviously worn out. Kailas understood my message and ceased his prodding.

We were about a quarter mile from Smallholding's entrance when the truck came to a squealing stop. Through the smudged windshield, I took in the radiant image of the valley. While our village was hot, dry, and sometimes unbearably barren, the one thing it did have was a view. The wide-open spaces made for unobscured sights. Diverse shades of pink and orange lit up the clouds as the sun began its descent into the ocean. The sea traded its natural deep sapphire for violet. Halcyon's buildings were tiny, pale dots in the otherwise brown-and-green blanketed valley.

The driver's side door opened and I glanced over to see Kailas exiting the truck. He told Blue and Sterling to stay put, then came around and unbolted my door. His hand extended to me, and I placed my palm onto his as he guided me out of the truck. The soles of my feet landed on the warm pavement, the tar already cooling. Kailas kept his grasp on my hand and led me away from the truck.

Tall grass stood behind us, but a clearing allowed a full panorama of the center of Sub Rosa Island. The sky was fiery and magnificent, the sunset in its full glory. It was magic hour.

"Hey," Kailas said softly.

I peeled my eyes away from the dreamy dusk sky to face him. With our bodies parallel, he gave me a tender smile and then held my face in his palms. My skin tingled as he stroked my cheeks with his thumbs. Something inside me stirred, and a chill ran up the back of my neck. He leaned in toward me and held me tight in his arms, my head landing in his chest.

We stayed there while the sun dipped below the horizon. With my eyes closed, I couldn't see it, but I could feel it— secure, loved, whole. I wondered if he felt the same. Then he pulled back.

"Will you be okay walking home by yourself?" he asked. "I still have to drop these guys off."

"I think I can manage." I said. "Will I see you tomorrow?"

"You can count on it."

I gave him a smile, and then turned and headed toward our village.

"Oh, hey," Kailas called out. I stopped and faced him. "Happy early birthday." *Oh, right, my birthday is tomorrow.*

"Thanks."

With a raise of his eyebrows, he pivoted and headed toward the truck.

The thought crossed my mind to say goodbye to Blue and Sterling, but my legs didn't carry me there. I wasn't sure why I didn't go. Maybe I was too drained to gather the wits for parting words. Maybe it was because I wanted the day to be over. But, really, I think it was because I had an inkling that I'd see them again.

I made it to Smallholding just as the charcoal sky darkened to black. The heavy clouds made for a starless night.

As Kailas had said earlier, there were no Masculines guarding Smallholding. It was seamless to come and go, even though it was technically against the law. As I passed under a trellis—the village boundary—I wondered why I hadn't left more often.

4

In my dream, I levitated in a twilight sky high above my farm. It was a cloudless day, which allowed me to see the entire shape of the island. The ocean stretched out before me for a thousand miles. I wasn't afraid of the fact that I was floating; my brain had accepted it in the way that we accept strange things in dreams. Out in the distance, hovering at the same height as me, I spotted something. As it approached me, it grew, and by the time it reached me, it was my size.

It was a person, or so it seemed. They appeared to have a human form, but the head wasn't human at all. The head was a moon—gray, with many craters. Their moon head also held a face with bright green eyes. They wore a boysenberry robe adorned with luminous charms. As they extended their human-appearing hands out to me, they held a sparkling red light in their palms. Somehow, I understood that this moon person was offering me the light.

A deafening thunderbolt interrupted us and a fiery blaze blasted into the distant sky. As it flamed, it shot high into the stars until it was out of the atmosphere. A rocket ship. I directed my gaze back to the moon person, but they had vanished. Whatever force was keeping me in the sky ripped out from beneath me, and I dropped toward the sea, screaming.

"Hey." Someone shook me. "Wake up."

I shot upright and grabbed my chest, gasping for air. My

eight-year-old brother, Ash, stared at me with a puzzled face. I had slept in his room that night to be near him while he was still in his form.

"You were freaking out in your sleep," he told me.

"Weird dream," I explained.

"About what?"

"Outer space, I think. I met a moon person."

"Were there aliens?"

I shook my head. "Sorry."

He crossed his arms over his chest. "Aliens would've been better."

I pushed the sheets from my leg. "How are you feeling?" I placed my hand on his forehead. He was burning.

"Fine," he replied, as I ran my fingers through his golden blond hair. "How are you?" *He* wanted to know how *I* was doing.

"Good," I said. I had my health. I was good. Then I glanced at the window and realized the sun was already up. "Did I oversleep?"

"A little."

"You should've woken me." I poked him in his skinny belly. He giggled, but then his laughter slowly turned into a wheeze. *Don't be scared, be spiritual. Form-death is freeing.*

"It's your birthday, you should take the day off."

"I don't get days off, kid." I smirked.

Rising from Ash's warm bed, I wrapped myself in my tattered bathrobe and headed for the hallway. As I passed my mother's room, I stepped carefully to avoid the creaky floorboard, not wanting to wake her from a dream that was no doubt more pleasant than her reality. I made it to the washroom—if I could even call it that, since there was no plumbing. Instead, a ceramic bowl rested in the sink with our family's allotment of rinsing water for the week. I cupped the liquid in my palms, then splashed the coolness on my face.

Drops dripped down my chin while alarming thoughts about yesterday crept into my mind. As the dependable one in our family, I had no room for anxiousness, so I shoved it back down.

"Bay!" It was my mother's distressed shout.

I locked eyes with myself in the mirror. My long, blonde hair hung past my waist and desperately needed washing; maybe even brushing. The tangles were so dense a bird might mistake it for its nest. There wasn't enough water to wash it, though. I considered cutting it short, in the name of practicality—but I *liked* my long hair. Wasn't I still allowed to have things that had no practical use?

A crash came from the living room, drawing my attention from the mirror. Using the scrunchy on my wrist, I tied my hair into a low, messy bun and let out a breathy exhale. Hesitantly, I left the solace of the washroom and made my way to the living area, where I found my mother looking more distraught than usual—pillows, blankets, and other knick-knacks were scattered across the hardwood. She frantically rummaged through the contents of a large wicker basket.

"Have you seen my carving knives?" she asked, focused on her search.

"I used them to make a whistle. They're in the tool chest… where they belong."

"The tool chest," she mumbled and marched to the chest on the far side of the room. She threw the lid open and pulled her dark brown hair into a ponytail to search.

"What are you making?" I asked.

"Ash wants a toy," she replied.

For a split second, I had thought she remembered my birthday and was going to make me something. Anything.

"*Toy*." I repeated the unusual word, rolling the sound off my tongue to see if it elicited a memory. "What's a *toy*?"

"Things children used to play with," she said absently. "You used to play with them; old trucks and dolls."

A blurry memory of a doll came to me. For a second, I could almost see its face, but the image faded as quickly as it came. "How does Ash know what a toy is?"

"I don't know."

I drew a long breath. "You need anything else?"

"No." She lifted the kit with the carving knives from the chest, marveling at it as if it were hidden treasure.

I closed my bathrobe. "I'll get started on the farm then."

"That'd be great," my mother replied. She opened the kit and scrutinized the knives, inspecting them as she ran her fingers along the handles, satisfied to have found them.

In my room, I dressed, exchanging my bathrobe for work clothes: a pair of old, worn jeans and a white, long-sleeve shirt. Removing the elastic from my hair, I allowed the locks to drape down my body. Hovering over my brush on the dresser, I contemplated if it was worth the hassle to tame the nest, then spent a while working through the mats.

Using a mirror, I braided the hair on the side of my head. Then I smiled, pleased with myself, because it was the nicest I had looked in a while. A nice birthday look. The style reminded me of my stepfather, as he was the one who used to fix my hair. It was my signature hairdo before his form-death.

After I had fastened my hair, I sat on the bed and slipped on my leather boots. The left one had a hole at the toe where the seams had ripped over the years. I meant to sew them, but I seldom had energy left at the end of my day for sewing. It wasn't a problem, though, as I didn't *need* to wear boots. Living on a tropical island where it was always warm, boots were more of a preference than a necessity. Some days, I did the farming barefoot or in sandals, but I found I could get more done faster without worrying about centipedes biting my feet or cutting my toes off with a shovel.

In the kitchen, I drank a glass of water from the allotment keg, and browsed through the produce on the counter. We had various fruits from the farm and trading with the neighbors: papayas, a couple moldy mangos, and a rack of bananas. I picked a banana and peeled one of the sides. As the skin folded down, a dozen ants and a cockroach crawled out of it. I dropped the banana and squished the little black ants with a rag. The cockroach scurried into a crack in the counter before I could get it.

I hated when bugs got to our food. I tossed the banana into the compost outside and searched for anything that wasn't insect-ridden. The papaya was clean.

After breakfast, I retrieved a glass of water for Ash and placed it on his bedside table. For good measure, I also brought him a bugless banana for if he got hungry. Seeing how dreary his bedroom was, I decided to do something about it.

In our yard, I cut lavender, with their purple corollas and gray-green leaves, and made a miniature bouquet. With a single lavender pinched between my fingers, I spun it slowly and watched the petals twirl. Something about the rhythm of it comforted me. There was a time when Ash used to pick me flowers, but not anymore. No. Going outside was against the rules for him, but it wasn't like he was strong enough to walk anyway.

I placed the flowers in a vase on Ash's bedside table as he flipped through a comic book. He only had four of them, and they must have been getting dull. Too weak to walk or do much besides lie in bed, he had little ways to keep himself occupied. It had been weeks since he had left the house, and I was forgetting what it was like when he was healthy; how he used to run about in the overgrown grass, catching lizards, and chasing butterflies.

I brushed his blond hair away from his eyes and felt his sweat cling to my palm. He looked up at me and then reached into the vase and plucked a single flower out. Holding it out to me, he said, "For you. For your birthday."

This small act felt like a piece of Ash had been revived. I smiled and tucked the lavender into my hair. As I glanced at my brother, an unwanted question crossed my mind—who would last longer, the flower or Ash?

I grabbed my brown leather satchel, opening the flap to check if it had everything I needed for my day: my three eight-inch balanced throwing knives, a flask for water, a kit of dried fruit, a tincture of healing clay and herbs, and the whistle I had carved with my mother's knives. I removed the whistle.

"I hear you want a toy," I said to Ash.

"I don't know. I don't care." He shrugged. "It's Mom; she wants me to have a toy."

"Oh, she does, does she?" I had figured that much.

"Yeah." He let out a hacking cough that left black mist in the air that slowly settled onto the bedding. When he was finished, he cleared his throat and said, "I think she's freaked out that my form is dying."

Yeah, she is, I wanted to say. But it wouldn't have been helpful. I wiped the black residue off the sheets.

"She'll be fine," I said instead. I didn't actually believe it, but the white lie would help him feel better.

"If she's not, will you take care of her?"

"You know it."

He wriggled under his sheets. With a huff, he sat up and fluffed his flat pillow. As he exhaled, he wiped sweat from his forehead.

"It's hot in here, huh?"

Of course it was hot. It was always hot, especially in that

sunbaked house. The air was as stale as a tomb, and I could feel perspiration piling up on the back of my neck.

"I'm used to it." He pushed the sheet off his legs.

"I could fan you if you want."

"You have work to do."

"I have some time." I grabbed a straw fan from his bedside table.

Ash suffered from Hackle, an incurable curse that stole the breath of the frail. My mother and I were immune to catching it, but we had no idea why—none of us who were immune knew why. It was rumored that the curse was accidentally conjured when the Spiritual World War began. Some type of physical manifestation of the bad energy it created. A theory was that those who were immune were lighthearted souls with no negative energy for the curse to latch onto. But witnessing the curse attack my innocent brother—and not me or my mother—was proof that theory was bogus.

The curse's signature symptom was a cough that expelled a black cloud-like breath. The lungs were what the curse attacked, and in the final day, the victims lost their voice and will to live. Nothing a young boy should ever have to experience if you asked me.

"I wonder what form I'll take next," my brother thought out loud, folding one arm over the other. Ash didn't seem fazed by his approaching form-death. He seemed to be okay with it. I guessed kids were naturally more spiritual—more spiritual than me anyway.

"Maybe you'll be human."

"I don't want to be human." He wrinkled his brow.

"What do you want to be then?"

"I don't know." His eyes shifted around as he thought about it, then, when he landed on a decision, he looked straight at me. "Something that can fly."

I raised my eyes brows and nodded. "That sounds fun." Our casual conversation about his form-death made me feel like it was a natural phase of life. Nothing to be afraid of. *Everything will be okay.*

"I'll soar across the sky." He raised his arms out to his sides as if he were soaring.

"You'd make a great bird."

"Eagle." He grinned, pleased with his choice, then lowered his hands.

As I fanned Ash, I desperately tried to be there with him—to remember every freckle on his face. More than anything, though, I tried to memorize his soul so I could recognize it again. Maybe even see him in another form.

I held out my fist to him. "I made you something." Hidden inside my hand was the whistle I had carved.

With wide eyes, Ash grinned again and I blossomed open my fingers to reveal the whistle. When he saw it, his face fell flat to a frown.

"A stick," he said, trying not to sound too disappointed. "Thank you?"

I couldn't help but laugh. "It's a whistle." I put it into his hands and pointed to the mouthpiece. He delicately raised the whistle to his lips and blew into it, making a loud, shrill sound.

"It's to call me when I'm out on the farm. If you need something, you blow into this. I'll hear you and come running."

"Wow, thanks. You gave me a present on your birthday." I wasn't sure if he was asking me or telling me.

"I love you," I told him as I tousled his hair. He flattened it back down and looked up at me sourly, but then softened.

"Love you back."

This is how I will remember him.

5

I crossed the dirt-covered yard where my mother sat on a tree stump, carving a square piece of wood. Her eyes were bloodshot, and her armpits were dark with sweat. I avoided talking to her so I could get to work before the sun rose too high.

In the yard, a few throwing knives stuck out of a tree—my target tree. I had carved a bullseye into it years before. On my way to the farm, I yanked a knife out and carried it with me. As I reached the beginning of the field, I turned and eyed up the target a few yards away. I hurled the knife at the tree, and it soared through the air and sunk into the bark. It wasn't a bullseye, but it was close enough.

Each step toward the broccoli field was cumbersome. I dreaded the heat, the sweat, and the physical exhaustion of farm work. Before my stepfather's form-death, I didn't mind working the crops. Actually, it might sound crazy, but I sort of liked it.

As a child, I couldn't wait for summer so I could pick the strawberries, run through the fields of corn, and climb up the mulberry trees. It was freeing and fun and wonderful. I sat in the branches of the mulberry trees until the sun went down, stuffing my face with their delicious offerings. I would come home for dinner with my lips and hands stained purple. My stepfather would joke that I looked like I had eaten alien brains.

After he died, the burden of carrying the farm was too weighty for a teenager to bear. It was my mother's farm technically, but everyone in the village knew she had all but checked out. So, lots of people came to help out, but with all the work that needed to be done, it never felt like enough. Really, I should have been grateful just to have food, but I couldn't help my dismal feelings.

The view before me had once been verdant, but now it was predominantly brown and stark. Smallholding sat relatively high on the mountain, and we could see the ocean and Halcyon. Many miles out to the east sat a mossy green mountain with high peaks and valleys. The lush color of it meant one thing: water. During our most smoldering days in Smallholding, I fantasized about hiking into that valley, where I imagined raging waterfalls and mountain streams. But I knew I would never make it there without a Masculine scooping me up and throwing me into isolation.

I met my first Masculine when I was thirteen, one of them having been sent to Smallholding to install our holograph machine. His appearance startled me at first, because he had a tattoo in the middle of his forehead of a black circle with an infinity symbol in the middle. Later, I would come to know that symbol as the Halcyon emblem. The Masculine wore black linen pants and a brown linen draw-string shirt, and he seemed to never smile. He was also barefoot—the standard in Halcyon. Though as a soldier, I thought it would have been smarter for Masculines to wear combat boots.

We kept the holograph machine in our village center, where it ran off solar panels. It was placed there in case Mother Quinn, Halcyon's leader, wanted to relay messages to us. Yet she had never done that. The only time I had seen her was in a short clip in one of the Soul Tracing episodes.

Moving on with the day, the rest of my morning was spent

weeding the broccoli garden. I was the only one working that patch as Brutus, the farm manager my mother appointed, had everyone else focused on harvesting the corn. Surrounding the broccoli garden grew weeds taller than my head—the same grass that Kailas's truck was hiding in. It was my job to loosen the deep roots of the plants with a pickax. The dry soil made the feat near impossible, and it was the worst job in the world. I thought I would die from heat exhaustion every single time I did it.

Pausing for a water break, I saw a doe munching on a lemon tree down the way. I found a rock and chucked it toward the deer. It landed by the deer's front hooves, and she darted off. The remainder of the herd emerged from their hiding spots and galloped down the gulch. There were so many of them it appeared as if the ground were crawling.

The sun reached the spot directly above me, indicating that it was time to make my way to my spiritual guide for my daily lesson. After Smallholding was established, it was decided that all children would be taught by a spiritual guide from years eight to eighteen. With only twelve children of those ages living in our village, we were each assigned a specific part of the day to visit Gemma, our guide. My allotted time was the highest point of the sun, since I was a farm worker and had to take a break during the heat of the day anyway. Before I headed her way, I rinsed off, changed clothing, and removed my boots, leaving them on the porch, I walked to her house in sandals.

Gemma's house was an old cottage that was seasonally adorned with assorted flowers. I wasn't sure of their proper names. They stood knee length from the ground and showed hundreds of tiny yellow petals. Others were similar in shape but with purple blooms. Gemma used portions of her allotted water to feed her garden. Otherwise, her yard would have been as dead and ugly as everyone else's.

I didn't need to knock; Gemma swung the door open as I approached. She wore a charming, floral-printed dress, with her naturally red and curly hair flowing by her shoulders. Her smile was not only genuine but also healing and nurturing. At times, Gemma felt more like my mother than my actual mother.

"Welcome back," she said as she embraced me. Being in her presence lifted my mood. She was a ray of sunshine, and I soaked in her positive energy. She was perfect. "Your hair. It's beautiful. I haven't seen you wear it like that in ages," she noted.

"Thank you," I said, stepping into her home. She pressed the door shut behind me, and we began down the hallway. I longed to tell her about my encounter with the Helio. The things we could have discussed and figured out together. There was no doubt in my mind that if anyone could find peace with the Helio, it would be her. But I had to protect Kailas. And Sterling and Blue. So, I swallowed all the words that sat on my tongue.

"Have you given some thought to what we discussed during our last meeting?" She gestured for me to head to the meditation room at the end of the hall. Except Gemma didn't usually call it meditation. She called it *mind-break*, because she looked at it as a break from our minds.

"I have." It would have been impossible to not have given it thought. It was a milestone in my spiritual journey. We entered the meditation room and I lowered myself onto one of the many sitting pillows on the floor.

"And?" Gemma asked.

"And I think I'm ready," I said, then cleared my throat. "I'm ready."

"Good."

We folded our legs into the lotus position.

"When will we do it?" I asked, closing my eyes and taking in a full breath, preparing for our regular mind-break.

"Right now."

Except for the faint sounds of birds through the open windows, the room fell silent. The hot air was still, and sweat dripped down my neck. The darkness that filled my sight morphed into shades of red as light was cast through my eyelids. Inhaling deeply through my nose, I held the breath. My form used the oxygen to fuel my cells. My heart pumped, strong and steady. As I exhaled, I silently thanked the trees for lending me oxygen.

"One," Gemma began, "we ask if it's in the good of all, that our sister be given the opportunity to learn the lessons you wish to teach her. We ask that you set her forth on her spiritual test, so she can best understand her place in this mysterious world."

The room disappeared, and I allowed my mind to go blank. I was no longer bound by space or time as I traveled through the veins of my own body. My heartbeat was a profound sound in my ears. Gemma's breaths were faint in the distance as I drifted further into awareness, into One. Then there was nothing. Nothing but uncut darkness and a bit of eye static. Then, out of the dark: a vibrant, sparkling red ball of light. Just like the one in my dream.

"All right." Gemma's voice cut through the meditation and the red ball of light vanished. "That went well." My eyes fluttered opened. "I hope you'll be given some learning experiences."

"I do as well," I said, feeling connected and whole.

"Are you ready to move on?"

I gave her a nod.

Gemma gracefully rose to her feet. I did the same as I shadowed her into the next living space. A brightly lit room with oversized windows and a white table in the center filled my eyes. It was the classroom. Here I learned my alphabet, reading, languages, correct human interaction, peacemaking, mathematics, the basic history of humankind, and the science of life. Gemma was not only a wonderful and brilliant spiritual guide but also a wise and patient academic teacher.

Outside, in the yard, was where her mate had taught Kailas and me how to fight. Well, he taught Kailas how to fight—I never took well to the whole fighting thing and was better at the evading part. Evading I could do. As a small person it came more naturally.

"Do you know what today is?" Gemma asked as she settled into her seat at the table.

I shook my head.

"Today marks your eighteenth year in this form."

"Oh, right." *How could I forget again?*

"This is your last class with me."

I had forgotten about that too. "Already?" I asked, my heart feeling heavy.

She motioned for me to sit. "But we have one last thing to accomplish."

I settled into the wooden chair opposite her, breathing slowly to calm my nerves.

"I want to see how much of what I taught you has taken place in your memory."

I pushed my hair back over my shoulder. I hadn't realized that this would be my final lesson with her, or that my memory would be tested. The blissful feeling I had achieved earlier wore away and in its place ballooned anxiousness.

"How?" I whispered.

"I'm sorry?"

I filled my lungs and repeated the word more loudly. "How?"

"I'll simply ask you a question." She opened a leather-bound notebook and glanced at the paper. "All you have to do is answer it."

She slid a sheet of a white paper and a pencil to me. I sat quietly in my chair, waiting for Gemma to ask me her question. I wasn't prepared, and I didn't want my lessons with Gemma to end. I looked forward to her classes more than almost anything.

"Okay," Gemma said, breaking my thoughts, "What is the history of human kind as it relates to Sub Rosa?"

"The history of humankind," I whispered to myself, taking a moment to gather my thoughts. "Do I start writing now?"

She gave me a nod and then wrote something in her book.

I began to write:

Thousands of years ago, humans appeared. After living wild with the animals for many years, we eventually invented language and tools that would separate us from the rest of the animal kingdom.

At some point, we became possessed by our minds. As we evolved, we lost our spiritual ways and disconnected from One, the source of all life. This disconnect caused us to live in our own deluded reality. It was a mass insanity.

As we reached our planet's carrying capacity, an island was discovered, but its location was kept secret. It's the island we live on today. They called it Sub Rosa. Here, a technological invention was made—a machine that traces the human soul at death. Through this invention, it was discovered that after the death of a human form, a soul is reborn into another human form, or any animal form.

This discovery was controversial and over the course of ten years, it created a string of spiritual wars that led to the Spiritual World War. Those who didn't believe in rebirth fought this discovery, claiming it was fabricated. The invention of the soul tracer was the beginning of the end. It sparked a division among people that couldn't withstand the Hackle curse, environmental changes, and resource scarcity. These stressors brought humanity over the edge.

During the most hostile times, Sub Rosa Island was blamed for inventing the soul tracer and ostracized as a punishment by our government. We were cut off from all imports, exports, and communication. Besides the documented history of our island, there's no way of knowing what is happening on the mainland, or even how many survive. With our island being thousands of miles away from the next shore, and all our vessels gone, we aren't able to voyage across the sea to find out. Thankfully, after several years, peace was found on Sub Rosa, and the war ended here.

After the war was over, we rebuilt a city-like town, Halcyon, in the valley of our island. It's guarded by military men called Masculines and is only open to the most spiritual people. Across the rest of Sub Rosa, there are communities who were accepted by Halcyon as part of a Peace Alliance, trading them goods for water. Today, we're salvaging what is left, and abiding by the Peace Laws set forth by Halcyon. Our village is part of this alliance, and we refer to ourselves as Smallholding.

I re-read my answer, checking for mistakes, and then placed my pencil down.

Gemma held her hand out for the paper and I passed it to her. Her eyes scanned each line as she read through my work.

"Thank you," she said, jotting something else in her book. Was that a good or a bad thing?

"Why didn't you go into more detail about Hackle?"

I cleared my throat. "Hackle is a curse that began spreading during the war. It's also known as the Black Breath. It killed almost a billion humans. Many are immune to the curse, but we have yet to uncover the reason for the immunity, a cause, or a cure. My stepfather died from it about nine years ago, and my eight-year-old brother has it now."

"That's right," she said. "Your brother's form-death is coming up."

I knew I couldn't let her in on my true feelings. She wouldn't get it. Gemma fully accepted everything that *is*, like a real spiritual person. Not like me.

"You must be excited for him."

"Yeah." I forced a smile.

"Still…" She returned a half smile. "He will be missed." She stood. "Bay—you've shown an understanding of what I have taught you. This includes comprehension, emotional intelligence, wisdom, and the means to communicate those ideas through language."

I nodded, unsure of what to expect.

"You're free to go." Gemma smashed the covers of her notebook together, startling me.

"Go?"

"We're finished," she said. "I've taught you all you need to know."

"I, um, I have a question… if that's okay."

"Sure."

"Um…why…" I struggled to think of something. "Why was Sub Rosa discovered so much later than the rest of the world? Why was it so hard to find?" I was grasping for a reason to stay.

"That's a good question." Gemma smiled, then placed a finger in the air. "And not an easy one to answer. I'm not sure anyone knows for sure, but there are many tales. Only our government and a select few were privy to where it was and how to find it."

I already knew that much. "Well, what do you think? Why was it so difficult to find?"

"Me?" She exhaled. "Well, I think there are some things

we don't get to know the answers to. It's our responsibility to learn to be okay with that."

Gemma rose to her feet and walked toward the front door. She wasn't going to let me stall. I stood and followed her through the hall. She stopped at the exit and turned to face me.

"Any other questions?" She was on to me.

"I guess not."

"One will be your teacher now. In life and through your dreams," she told me. "Don't forget the history of human kind. It will teach you about your own journey."

I exhaled loudly, wanting to protest, feeling unsettled as Gemma opened the door for me to leave. I admired the way she let go so effortlessly and controlled her emotions so steadily. *Why can't I be more like her?*

"There's a war going on inside all of us," she said as I reluctantly stepped outside. "One will be with you." Her words still hung in the air as the hinges shut.

I turned, facing the house. I stared at the mahogany door and slipped into nostalgia as I remembered my days spent crafting, learning breathing techniques, and playing with Gemma. Grappling with the pull to stay a child forever, I forced my legs to move.

I found my way to the village center to look for Kailas. I wanted to ask him how his trip to Halcyon went the previous night. He should have been done working with his dad by now. When I arrived, I found a couple of my neighbors setting up the holograph machine for a *Soul Tracing* broadcast. That was weird—it had been a long time since they broadcasted a soul tracing.

Kailas wasn't there, anyway, so I searched the dirt fields where we sometimes played games. I didn't see him there either. Maybe he had to make a delivery to Halcyon? Or maybe he was still at home? I ran to his house at the far end of

Smallholding. When I made it there, I knocked, but it took some time for Kailas's father to open the door. He wore a white cotton shirt covered in stains, and his face was puffy, as if he had just woken from sleep.

"Mr. Andrews. Is Kailas here?" I asked.

He wiped something from his mouth. "I haven't seen him since yesterday."

I thought about this. "He didn't come home last night?"

"That's right. The boy left me with the chores while he was out doing who knows what." I had never understood Mr. Andrews and the way he lived his life. So lonely, so angry, and so bitter. There had to be a reason why he was the way he was. But, it was lost to me.

I closed my eyes for a brief moment to collect myself and then reopened them. "Okay, thanks, Mr. Andrews."

I turned to walk away, beginning to panic as different scenarios ran through my mind. The old truck broke down, and Kailas was stuck somewhere in the valley. They ran into the River Clan again and were killed. They made it to Halcyon but when they arrived, the Masculines put them in isolation. He could be just fine and had slept under the stars to gain perspective that night. Going home to his father was something he was known to dread and avoid anyway.

"If you find him, tell him he better come home and do some work," Mr. Andrews called out to me.

"Sure," was all I said, and then I ran off to the village center to look again in case I had missed him.

Mr. Andrews' bad attitude had depleted my mental energy. I felt empty and tired and needed a break from the worry. So, when I reached the building, I took rest under a shady tree.

I folded my legs in the lotus position and rested my hands on my thighs. I closed my eyes, a fresh breath filled my lungs, and immediately the red glowing light was there. I wasn't sure why the light came to me again, but I kind of liked it. It was peaceful.

Kailas. *What happened to him? Where is he?*

The red light went out. A real spiritual person could enter a meditation in any circumstance, but not me. I had to know Kailas was all right, so I gave up and opened my eyes.

Sitting cross-legged in front me was Kailas. His blue eyes were open and peering into mine. *Is this real? Or did I somehow imagine him?* I smacked him in the shoulder.

"Ow! What was that for?" He was real.

I groaned. "Where've you been?"

"Aw. You were worried about me?"

"No."

He glanced over his shoulder, then back at me. "The truck broke down on my way home, so I slept in it and walked back this morning."

"Did you drop off the Halcyons?"

"At their gate."

"How's your…" I motioned to the gash on his cheek from yesterday's fight.

He put his hand on the scab. "Oh, that? It's nothing. I got into a fight with a behemoth."

I rolled my eyes. "No one will believe that."

"You think I can't take a behemoth?"

"I think… if you fought a behemoth, you'd know by being dead."

"Whatever. I can take a behemoth."

"Right."

"Even though you have no faith in me, I made this for you…" Kailas pulled something from his pocket—a bracelet made of twine adorning a small orange and purple shell. "Happy birthday."

"How in the world did you get a shell?" I asked, putting my wrist out so he could tie it on.

"Bribed a Masculine."

"Well, it's beautiful." I ran my fingertips along the surface of the shell. I hadn't seen one in so very long. "Thank you." Careful to be conscious, I looked into his eyes and got lost in them.

The moment was shattered by the sound of a crash coming from inside the village center. Curiously, we rose to our feet and made our way to the entry way. Peeking inside, we spotted a group of twenty or so of our Smallholding neighbors sitting on folding chairs, watching a holograph play. In the back, a father picked up a row of collapsed chairs that his son had apparently knocked over.

The holograph caught my eye; it was playing a *Soul Tracing* episode—a documentary that followed soul tracings and their reunions. This episode focused on a village on the south side of the island called Darning. Darning specialized in clothing, with their main job being the Masculine's uniforms, though they also traded with the outlying communities. I had exchanged produce with them for some of my linen clothing before.

When I met with Darning's village trader, Tory, I remembered her expressing to me her distaste for Halcyon. She was ancient, very wrinkled, and the veins in her hands were so predominate that they somehow unnerved me. The elder generation typically rejected the new way, so her distain wasn't surprising. As she handed me my newly made clothes, she told me, "Halcyon is only a basting stitch. They're only holding us together until something better comes along."

I spotted Tory in the *Soul Tracing* documentary. It caught my breath and I took a seat in an empty chair to watch. She looked scarily ill, emaciated and yellow. We watched as

Halcyons set up their machines at her home to trace her soul. She was frail, weak, and hooked up to wires. She held her daughter's hand as she passed away. My heart felt heavy and my hands slightly trembled, but I got them under control. Seconds later, a beacon of light emerged and the tracers followed it out the door.

The documentary cut off and a narrator explained that the tracing led to a six-month pregnant woman living in Halcyon. It was presumed that Tory's soul had merged into this woman's baby. The tracers couldn't reunite the souls, as they usually would, since it breached the Contract of Contradiction. No souls that were reincarnated as Halcyons were to be reunited with their past lives' loved ones. It caused conflict, and conflict was against one of the new Peace Laws. Usually, Halcyon would hold a celebratory reunion, but this tracing ended abruptly with no happy ending.

Before the episode ended, we were reminded of another *Soul Tracer* episode. One with a happier ending. A recap played of a middle-aged man who was reborn into a puppy. I remembered the episode, as it was the last one that had aired. The wife of the man was able to keep the dog as her own, and the reunion was a massive celebration in the middle of Halcyon. The footage replayed and I watched closely as it was all I had to construct what it might be like to live there.

Over time, soul tracings grew few and far between, and it had been over a year since I had seen one shown in the village center. Until now. There had never been a soul tracing in Smallholding. I was glad for that. The soul tracer had sparked a war that devastated the entire world and its people. For all I cared, they could throw that machine in the ocean and let it sink. Who were we, if we didn't learn from our past and move on from using this divisive invention?

Behind us, vans pulled into Smallholding, their brakes

squealing outside the village center. I went to the door, along with most everyone else, to see what the commotion was about. Three Masculines exited through the back hatch of each of the vans and purposefully walked toward the village center. Kailas and I glanced at one another warily. He ushered me out of the doorway, and we casually left the building.

"You ever see anything like this before?" I asked softly, as we made our way off the grounds.

Kailas took a swift look over his shoulder. "Never," he whispered.

We walked briskly and in silence for several minutes toward my house and came to a stop twenty yards from my porch. I stared in shocked disbelief.

Directly outside my door was a Masculine standing at attention and wearing the usual Masculine uniform: brown linen shirt, black linen pants, and the Halcyon emblem tattooed on his forehead.

The door was left wide open, and the man had his metal wand ready for use on his belt. I had never seen a Masculine guarding a home. Not once. The Halcyon vans had only come to Smallholding minutes before. How did he get there so fast?

Ash. What would they do with a little boy with Hackle?

They aren't as genuine as they make themselves out to be. Sterling's words echoed in my mind. That's when I heard it: the shrill sound of a whistle from inside the house.

Ash's whistle. First it was one long pitch, and then it repeated over and over again like a siren.

6

Kailas made his way up the stairs ahead of me and halted directly before the Masculine at my door. I forced myself to stop because my spur-of-the-moment plan was bad. I couldn't bulldoze a man twice my size. Kailas tried to walk through the open doorway, but the big Masculine shifted his body to block him.

"A Halcyon Official is conducting a private matter," the Masculine said, looking straight ahead.

"Private matter?" Kailas asked.

"The specifics of the matter are not your concern."

Kailas pointed at me. "She lives here."

The Masculine's eyes shifted to me and then back at Kailas. "I can't confirm that."

"She's Bay Lilly. This is the Lilly household. You know that, right?"

"No one is to enter. Direct orders."

"Orders? What orders?"

"I'm not at liberty to say."

"You're *not at liberty to say?*" Kailas let out an ironic laugh. "What *are* you at liberty to say?"

"I'm at liberty to *do* more than I can *say.*" The Masculine's demeanor changed. He was agitated by Kailas.

"Is that a threat?"

The Masculine moved his hand over the metal wand

dangling from his belt. "I have orders to remove anyone who won't remove themselves." His fingertips slowly wrapped around the handle of the wand.

Kailas stepped back. "Okay." He held his hands up. "We'll leave."

Leave? We can't leave. What about Ash?

Kailas turned away from the Masculine and our eyes met. He winked. In one swift movement, he whipped his body around and backhanded the Masculine square in the face. His other fist went hurtling into the Masculine's stomach. He hunched forward gasping, while Kailas snatched the wand from his belt. "Go," he yelled at me. But I hesitated. "Go!"

I ran through the door and jetted down the hall. I could hear Kailas and the Masculine going at it—moans and groans and smacks of fists. I came to Ash's door, but it was shut. It was never shut. Before I could hesitate, I turned the knob and the door swung open.

Ash was in bed, with several men in suits surrounding him. One man held a mask over Ash's mouth; it connected to a tube leading to a machine by his bed. Ash's eyes widened as he spotted me at the door. He pushed the mask away from his mouth so he could speak.

"Bay," he called. "Look. People from Halcyon are here. They're helping me."

I stepped through the doorway. The room wasn't the same place it had been earlier in the morning. It had been invaded. The men in the black suits kept their eyes on me. One of them heard Kailas's quarrel outside and ran out of the room.

"Helping you? I heard the whistle."

"Oh, no," he said, smacking his forehead. "I was showing these guys. I forgot you would come." He held up the whistle and there as black stain around the mouth piece.

"I'm just glad you're okay." I felt all eyes on me. "You're okay, right?"

"I guess." He shrugged, "My chest feels like an elephant is sitting on it." Then he let out a terrible cough that covered his hands in black Hackle mist.

A gasp came from one of the men. He probably hadn't seen Hackle in person before. I couldn't help but analyze the man: clean-shaven, puffy, about twenty pounds heavier than the people in our village. An Official. I had heard of them. They made the rules. I kind of hated them.

I pointed to the machine beside his bed. "Are you going to introduce me to the robot?"

"That's not a robot," Ash said, as if I were the dumbest person in the world.

"I'm surprised you don't know what…" one of the men began but then trailed off. His eyes fixed on my mother, who I realized was sitting at Ash's bedside.

She placed an index finger over her lips. When she saw me, she dropped her hand to her lap.

"Bay, can we speak outside?" she asked me softly.

That's when Kailas crashed through the door. Even though his hands were bound behind his back, he burst in as if he were about to kill someone. When he didn't see a battle, but instead a bunch of people in suits talking, he froze and looked around.

"Having a party?" he asked, with a nod at Ash.

"Something like that," Ash replied.

Kailas glanced over his shoulder at the Masculine restraining him. "I'm all right." The Masculine looked for permission from an Official before letting him go.

"Did my invite get lost?" Kailas asked, being almost entirely ignored.

"Bay, can we have that talk outside?" my mother insisted as she moved toward the door.

"Okay."

This wasn't about protecting my brother. She didn't protect him from harsh realities. She didn't protect me from them either. I had watched my stepfather die when I was only nine years old. The reason she wanted to step outside was because she knew whatever she was up to would start an argument.

We exited the room together and walked out to the front porch. The door was still propped open; no Masculines or Officials were around. We had total privacy. I breathed deeply, trying to relax, because I didn't want to overreact. I reminded myself that no matter what, everything would be all right, as it was meant to be. But I was triggered, and words poured out of me like molten-hot lava.

"So, you have me at the edge of my seat," I said. "What is this? A Hackle curse remedy trial that might keep him alive another week?"

She opened her mouth to reply, but I spoke over her. "You do know that instead of making him live a teensy bit longer, it could make him worse? He could develop a side effect. I heard the trials make patients get oozing sores. Sometimes, worse fevers. You'd have to live with knowing you caused Ash more pain than he's already in. And if you think for even a second that I would be the one to bandage his skin, NO! *YOU! You* would be the one tending to his scabs because I won't do it. I won't cause him more pain to keep him a week longer. I won't!"

I paced around the porch, my mind racing. I was fuming. I didn't know what I was so mad at—my mother, or my own conflicting feelings about Ash dying. Suddenly, my mind bounded to an opposite, more comforting, thought. "Or maybe," I said softly, more hopefully, "maybe it *will* work.

Maybe he won't die. Maybe he could live. He could run and play and be our Ashy again."

Hope, a flicker of hope, sparked in my heart. A smile escaped my lips as I glanced at my mother. She gazed at me with gentle eyes, the same face that had sung to me when I was a child. For the first time in years, I was her daughter. I longed for her to envelope me in her arms and find comfort. As if *she* were the one who looked after *me*. I mean, she was there, she did farm work, she showed up a lot of the time physically. But mentally and emotionally, she consistently checked out. I was about to hug her, to let her be my mother again, but then she spoke.

"I called Halcyon," she whispered. "I asked them to do a soul tracing on Ash."

All the optimism I had mustered up was sucked out of me like a vacuum. The pain of being neglected, emotionally abandoned, and dealing with my mother's insanity for years came surging up. A thought of Gemma popped into my mind. A memory, really. When she told me there was a war going on inside all of us. I think she was referencing this very battle between reacting on emotions, versus expressing them in a healthy way. But, I couldn't do it. I couldn't fight the anger.

"You did what?" I shouted. "Why would you do that? You know that invention is what caused the war."

"I don't care. Ash is my son," she cried.

"He's more than just your son," I said rigidly. "He's his own being, with his own soul journey."

"I know that."

"Do you know? Do you *really* know? Because you don't act like it," I yelled.

"I do know, but I grew up in a different time. I grew up believing different things."

"Ugh," I scoffed. "Go ahead, tell me all the older

generation excuses. Tell me you've lived longer and know better and are afraid of the new way."

"Bay," she pleaded.

"Mom"—I shook my head—"even if you do this… even if you track his soul and find it… What are you going to do with it? Hold it captive? If he's a human, will you fight to adopt him? If he's a dog, will you keep him as a pet?"

"I don't know." She rubbed her forehead with her fingers like she was getting a headache.

"Have you thought it through, Mom?"

Her eyes closed with her hands covering them. She had no answer.

"You know," I said, "once Ash leaves this form, he's no longer yours."

She opened her eyes and looked right at me. Her body tensed, "He *is* mine. He's my son!"

"Maybe." I shrugged. "Maybe he's your son when it's convenient for you. Where have you been these last months? Where were you when he was vomiting on himself and needed someone to clean him up? Where were you when he had nightmares and needed someone to sing him to sleep?" All of a sudden, I was screaming. "Where were you?"

She exhaled, dragging her palm along her face. "That's not fair."

"You're right, it's not fair." My throat grew tight; tears welled up in my eyes. "It's not fair that I had to be his de facto parent because you disappeared. Or that I had to manage the farm because you slept all day. Or that I had to miss *dozens* of sessions with Gemma because you couldn't handle life. I did it, Mom. I did all of it! You've never even said *thank you*. You never even noticed. You took it all for granted. And maybe"— I shook my head again—"Maybe, just maybe, I needed a mom too. I didn't have one. She died when I was five… when the war started. You haven't been the same since. It's like you went away. You're an empty shell."

My mother closed her eyes for a long moment. When she opened them again, she whispered, "I'm sorry. I'm *so* sorry. I've done my best. It may not seem like it to you, but I have. It takes every ounce of my strength just to get out of bed every morning." She sighed, and her shoulders slumped forward. "Then whatever I have left is used up fast, and I cannot go on. I don't know. Maybe something is wrong with me. All I know is that I'm doing my best, and that's all I can do. That's all I've got."

I almost understood it. I had moments when I felt that way, but how could she give into those feelings every single day? I wanted to understand her, but I didn't have the energy to try to get into her head. Part of me wanted to go on arguing with her, to continue to express my pain, but a bigger part of me craved peace. I didn't want to be angry. "Okay," I said, trying to let it go.

She held her arms out. For a brief moment I hesitated, but then I went in for it. I let her hold me. Her touch was warm and comforting, just as I remembered.

"I'm so sorry," she said, rubbing my back with her palm. I usually wasn't lachrymose, but I started crying just then. I let the tears fall, but only for a moment, and then I collected myself and pulled away. I had other pressing questions I needed answered before we headed back into Ash's room.

"Why are Masculines and Officials here? Why are they at the village center?"

"The Masculines are setting up living quarters for the science crew and Officials at the village center. They'll be living there while we wait," she answered.

"Wait for what?" I asked, but then the answer came to me.

"For Ash to die." I paused while it sank in that it would happen soon. Ash would die within days. "Then what?"

"A Masculine and a couple of science crew go and find his new form."

"To bring back to you?"

"That's right."

I paced, thinking. "What if they can't find the form?"

"That's what they're doing in there now. I guess there's a way to tell if a person is a good candidate or not. If he's not, they won't do it."

"So, there's a chance they'll leave and not trace his soul?" I asked.

"So far, he's been a good candidate," she said. "This is probably going to happen. You should accept it."

"And what if I don't?"

"Suffer through the resistance."

I hated when her generation used our mantras against us. But maybe she meant it. If I didn't accept what was happening, I would suffer by resisting it. Maybe she understood the new way after all. Yet she didn't value it enough to let Ash go. Maybe I didn't either.

Tracing Ash's soul was my mother's last effort to keep him. It would do no good for any of us. It would most likely only create more mental health issues for my mother. If Ash became a mouse, she would sit by his cage, watching him run on a wheel all day. It would bring no closure. It would bring nothing positive into any of our lives, especially Ash's. She would restrict him, hold him in place for his entire next life. His soul journey would halt.

When we walked back to the bedroom, I saw Kailas sitting next to Ash on his bed, reading him one of his favorite comic books. It was about a talking panda that fought the forces of evil.

The science crew or Officials, or whoever they were, began

rerunning tests. Ash was shirtless. He had tiny round things stuck to his chest with wires connecting each one to the machine. There were more on his forehead. The one in the middle had an antenna sticking out of it. The whole thing was ridiculous.

"Look," Ash pointed to the antenna. "I'm a narwhal."

"I see." I forced a smile because it all pained me.

I sat on the edge of his bed. His little feet made lumps in the blanket, and I rubbed them. Kailas went on reading the comic book, and Ash placed his attention back on the illustrations.

Glancing up at the man working the machine, I sized him up. It was a different person than earlier. This one had black hair. He was thinner than the others. He wore an intense expression on his face, his forehead wrinkled. His fingers fluttered on a touchscreen connected to the larger machine.

"What're you doing?" I asked, curious despite everything.

The black-haired man at the touchscreen shot his eyes at me and then quickly moved them back to the screen. He exhaled noisily, as if I bothered him with my question. "Attempting to explain the complexities of my work to a feeble-minded person wouldn't be a wise use of my time."

Kailas paused reading and folded the comic to look at the man. "What did you just say to her?"

The man took a break from his work to glance up at Kailas. He exhaled again and replied, "Nothing. I was about to explain it to the girl." Returning his eyes to the screen, he spoke again. "I'm—how do I say this simply? I'm attempting to predict the trajectory of the soul energy after form-death. You know, trying to see where it's going. If it's projected to go beyond the perimeters of our safety zone, we typically won't follow the soul energy. Meaning, if your brother's soul energy is going somewhere unsafe for the crew to travel, he won't be a viable candidate for our research."

"You can do that? Predict where the new form will be?" I asked.

"We're working on fine-tuning the accuracy. We typically receive a general area and, as we get closer to form-death, the location becomes more precise."

"What will I be?" Ash asked. "A bird? A wolf? Oh no, not a *girl*?" He wrinkled his nose at the last one.

"It doesn't work like that. We only predict location, not form type."

"Aw." Ash groaned, disappointed.

"Where's he heading?" Kailas asked.

"The calculations are incomplete. The closer we get to the death of this form, the clearer the prediction will be."

Ash's head hung low. My mother had most likely never asked him if he wanted the soul tracing. He seemed excited about it, but that didn't mean he actually was.

"Can I have a moment alone with my brother?"

The black-haired scientist took his eyes off the screen to look at me for longer than a second this time. "That's a joke, right? You don't expect me to leave."

"Not a joke." Kailas stood tall. "I'll escort you out."

The scientist grabbed his notebook and pen. "Two minutes. I'll be back in two minutes. Don't touch anything. And don't take any of the wires off."

"Yes, ma'am," I replied.

Kailas ushered the man and everyone else out of the room, including my mother, who protested for a second before leaving. He shut the door behind him.

I was still rubbing Ash's feet.

He reached and grabbed the lavender out of my hair, tucking it back into the vase with a tiny bit of water at the bottom. "It was droopy," he said softly.

"What do you think of all this?" I asked tenderly, unsure if he would tell me the truth.

He rubbed his eye. "I mean, it's cool. Not many people get to do this."

"Is that what Mom told you?"

"Yeah, but..." He shrugged. "It's true. Most people just die and don't get to be traced. It's ultra rare."

"You don't have to do this," I said. "I can make everyone leave."

"They can stay. I don't care."

"Are you sure? This is going to be a big moment for you. Do you want all these people here when it happens?"

He wrinkled his brow and went quiet, thinking. "Will *you* be here?"

"Of course," I said. "Of course I will be."

"Then I don't care who else is here." He half smiled. "Maybe we can still be together this way because they'll find my new form and bring it to you. But," he added thoughtfully, "I won't remember you, will I?"

"I don't think so. No one remembers past lives, even if they get their soul traced," I answered.

"But you'll know it's me. Maybe I'll be a dog, and we can play fetch."

"Maybe."

"Don't tie me up on a leash and leave me in the back yard like Ethan does to his dog. Take me for walks, and throw me a tennis ball."

"Got it. Walks and tennis balls."

The intense scientist swung open the door and eyed us up. "You didn't touch anything, did you?"

"No, ma'am," Ash said.

I smiled, but I felt like crying.

7

The following morning, the crowd returned to Ash's room, and the testing continued. I lay on the bed next to Ash and rubbed his head for the majority of the morning, only taking breaks to eat, drink, and go to the outhouse. The sun shone extra strong at midday, and the house was as hot as fire. The Officials removed their jackets; some changed into shorts and cotton tees. Kailas had to work the chores with his father, so he came and went throughout the day to check on us.

Our mother, true to her nature, disappeared and reappeared as she felt like it, though for a while, she sat with Ash and rubbed his back. I offered to fan him, but he didn't want it, saying he was cold. Someone brought us a bowl of rinsing water with a cloth. I soaked the fabric, wrung it out, and delicately patted his forehead with it. He pulled away at first, but then he relaxed and allowed me to do it.

During the afternoon, Ash and I set up a puzzle on a tray on his bed. We spent the better part of an hour piecing it together. The jigsaw was a painting of a meadow with maroon and cerulean flowers growing in the grass. In the sky above was a complete rainbow. It didn't make sense for it to be there, though, because the artist didn't paint rain.

Ash was usually better than me at puzzles, but he was weak and couldn't focus. I assembled most of it alone while he rested by my side. I got childishly aggravated when I couldn't get pieces to fit into what I thought were their right spots, forcing them in and bending the edges. Eventually, I yanked them out and sorted through the pieces more patiently until I got into a groove and started making progress. When the puzzle was finally assembled, I turned to Ash to show him, but he was sound asleep.

By suppertime, Ash was in a near-constant state of sleep. He sometimes drifted in and out of it but was hardly fully conscious. His face grew pale and yellow. He didn't talk, except to moan that his body hurt. The doctor gave him some strong pain medication to drink.

Ash was rapidly declining, and I wasn't ready. The walls closed in as the day went on. The air sucked from the room, leaving none to breathe. I couldn't stand to be in there for one more second. As the sky started to fade, I excused myself, passing on the responsibility of watching Ash to my mother so I could take time outside. When I made it through the front door, I hyperventilated. Air couldn't come to me fast enough; my lungs wouldn't fill despite my efforts. All I could think of was Ash's suffering, the agonizing look on his face. Staying in the house for the entire day with him was unbearable.

I wasn't sure I could deal with it, any of it. Seeing my brother this way made me sick. It reminded me of my stepfather's death: same symptoms, same pains, and same deterioration. Watching someone you love wither away is the most horrible experience a person can live through. The looming doom weighed on me, and the world grew too heavy to bear. It was all I could do to not collapse on the porch. When I didn't collapse, my legs fixed to run and carry me away instead. Disappearing, like my mother, seemed like the only viable option.

I couldn't do this. I couldn't watch my brother die. But

Ash wanted me to be there when it happened. He needed me. I told him I would be.

I froze as fear took hold of me. The torment threatened to swallow me whole and spit me out as half the person I had been. I couldn't be there for my brother, not like this. Not with depleted energy and crammed with fear. This was no good for me, and especially not for Ash. I needed to center myself and regain my strength. I steadied my breath by pausing and inhaling deeply for four seconds. Once my lungs finally filled, I exhaled through my mouth for eight seconds. I cleared my mind and blew the fear out of my form. I repeated this until I was okay enough to walk to the porch stairs and sit on a step.

I tried to think of something else, anything else. I looked to a tree top and watched as the wind blew like a whisper through the leaves. Mynah birds spread their wings and soared through the air before they landed on the branches. Below the tree, young children chased after each other in an innocent game of tag. Devastation pervaded my life, but the rest of the world existed untouched by it. The planet still spun even though it felt like it had stopped. Calmer now, I consciously filled my lungs a final time, then headed into the yard. The day was ending, and the giant ball of light lowered itself near the horizon.

The soft orange of the sky comforted me like a warm blanket on a cold day. I breathed in the serenity, pulling it into my form to refill my soul. This was what I needed to endure what was coming. I would be okay if I stopped resisting the situation and instead, fused myself with it. As I exhaled, I found it again—my strength.

I twisted my bracelet around my wrist as the pink sun hung low in the sky. In another ten minutes or so, it would set. From behind me came the sound of crunching leaves. I turned to find Kailas standing a yard away, watching me.

"You're back." I smiled softly.

"I'm sorry I had to go."

I stepped to meet him.

Reaching for my hand, he said, "It's busy in there. I think it's time." I took a look at the house. Then, holding hands, we headed up the stairs together.

When I reached Ash's room, every scientist, Official, and stranger hovered over him. His bed was surrounded, blocking my view. I nudged the crowd aside and made my way to my brother. He lay there still, his breathing labored, his face pale. There was a familiar look in his eye—the look he got when he scraped his knee or got stung by a bee. He was scared. As he looked at me, I was sure to smile, even though it was the last thing I felt like doing.

The science crew worked around him using the machine, but I paid them no attention. I focused on my brother. He reached for my hand, and when I gave it to him, he squeezed tight.

This was it. Ash was dying.

8

When Ash was six, he loved running around our farm pretending to be a wild behemoth. I would be the hunter and chase him down. Anytime I was close to catching him, he collapsed to the dirt and lay there with his eyes shut. He stayed totally still and played dead. He was bad at it, though, because no matter how hard he tried, small giggles squeaked out from the back of his throat. The first few times my brother did this, I let him get away with it. I played along by walking away and declaring that the behemoth had died in chase. Eventually, I got sick of his cheating and instead tickled him madly until he sprang up and begged me to stop, laughing wildly.

How I wished I could tickle him out of this.

Ash's breathing was shallow and small as he held onto my hand. Seeing him so unwell was painful, like my beating heart was being dragged through burning coals. My throat was on fire and I was ready to vomit, but I swallowed hard. I willed myself to get it together. This was my time to be strong.

Ash was exhausted. His eyes grew distant, and his face emptied of all color. I could see his will to live slowly leaving him like bathwater swirling down the drain. I wanted him to stay. I wanted him to be healthy and vibrant like he used to be. I didn't want this to be happening. Holding myself together turned impossible and I crumbled as tears welled in my eyes. I loved him. I loved him so much.

Cupping his face, I rubbed his cheeks with my thumbs. "I'm here. I'm here."

He nodded, his breaths so small his chest hardly rose.

My heart sank to my stomach as the helplessness took hold of me. I was willing to do anything to change this. I silently offered One a trade: *Take our farm, our house, our rations, our clothes, take everything and leave Ash. Take me and leave my brother.* I would have done anything to make it stop, to keep him.

With our eyes locked, the vibrant Ash I knew slowly faded as the light in his eyes dimmed. He fixed intensely on me in a way I had never seen before, as if he were slipping from the world and the only thing keeping him tethered was me. That's when I thought of the sunset. Maybe it could do for him what it had done for me.

"Ash," I managed to whisper. "The sun is setting. Wanna see?"

He clutched my hand and nodded. This would help him; this I could do. I just had to pull myself together and do it. I slid my arms under Ash to scoop him up and carry him outside, but the black-haired scientist placed his hand on me.

"You can't move him," he said.

I looked at him squarely. I had forgotten he was there.

"He has to remain hooked to the tracer."

My eyes wandered to the wires attached to Ash's form. They had removed the ones on his face, but the ones on his chest were still there.

"He needs to see the sunset," I told him, anger building inside me. This man wasn't welcome in my home. He was rude and wrong and had no right to tell me what to do. "This is my brother's life. I couldn't care less about your stupid machines."

"The tracing will fail if he's unhooked. Your mother signed the release form. You can't take him."

I wanted to shake the scrawny man, beat understanding into him. This was pivotal for Ash. He was dying. He needed to feel at peace, loved, and whole. Not scared. Not like a scientific experiment. Not like a lab rat for their research.

"Try and stop me." I leaned over to scoop up my little brother. A hand reached out and touched mine. I was about to punch the person when I realized it was Kailas.

"He can see the sunset through the window," he whispered, and he slid the curtain open next to Ash's bed. And there it was, orange and soft and soothing. I looked to Ash and for a moment, he smiled. Then his face fell flat, his eyes blinking long and slow. He was slipping away.

"Help me move the bed." I looked to the black-haired scientist. "Don't worry. We'll move the machines with it. This'll work."

He rolled his eyes and exhaled. "Fine."

The men and I lifted the frame and shifted Ash's bed to the center of the room, turning it so that he faced the window. The science crew rolled the machine alongside it. Once the bed was in place they gave us space, except for the ones operating the tracer. The warm light from the sun fell across Ash's bed. I crawled onto his mattress and curled up with him, holding his small hand in mine.

My mother knelt at his side and clutched his other hand, her lips kissing his fingers. She was struggling. I could see it in her face, but she held back her tears.

Ash turned his attention to the sun. He stared at it with a calming presence. He was okay. The sun tethered him now.

"Did you know that the sun never really sets?" I whispered, trying to comfort him. "It's only from our viewpoint that the sun comes and goes. It's actually a trick: the sun doesn't go anywhere." Ash kept his eyes on the sun, his body relaxed. I could see the fear leaving him. "If you were a star floating in space, you would see that the sun always shines. The fact that the sun sets and rises is only a relative truth… from our one perspective on this planet. The universal truth is that the sun shines eternally. It's infinite."

Ash rubbed his thumb along the creases of my palm, silent and still. He had found peace. The round sun lowered into the ocean, only half of it left in our view.

"That's just like us," I whispered. "It's like you. You're infinite. The sun will set on this life. This human form will die, but *you* will go on. That light inside you, your soul, it's infinite… just like the sun."

Ash slowly rubbed my palm. His gaze fixed on the sunset, a subtle smile on his lips. His eyes shut for seconds at a time before reopening. I rested my head on the pillow beside his ear. I didn't know why, but I began to sing. It was a senseless song the two of us made up one summer while we lay in the grass watching the clouds drift by.

> *Blue skies, green trees, yellow sun*
> *I like this colorful life*
> *Bad days, heartbreak, cloudy skies*
> *I don't like this dark life*
> *One cloud, two clouds, three clouds*
> *These are the clouds passing us by*
> *Blue skies, green trees, yellow sun*
> *I love this colorful life*

When the last note of our song ended, I glanced at Ash's thumb in my palm. He no longer rubbed my skin. My brother lay still, the weight of his fingers heavy in my hand. The room went silent, and my ears rang. I felt it in my bones. My little brother was gone.

"This is it!" a voice called out. "His soul is moving on. Prepare the projector."

The seconds passed like grains of sand falling through an hourglass—heavy, slow, and irrepressible. The sun had set and the room fell dark. I looked to my mother, who sat on the other side of the bed, staring blankly at the mattress. The crowd in the room stepped forward and surrounded us to get a closer look. Even though I didn't turn to see, I could feel their eyes on us. Their presence was unwanted and my skin crawled with violation. I looked to Ash to see if he was okay with the crowd, but he wasn't there anymore; his eyes were blank and empty. It didn't feel real. It was a bad dream I was about to wake up from.

Light sparked and a soft glow lit the room. An Official lit a gas lamp on the bedside table. Beside the light were Ash's wilting lavender flowers, still in their vase. The science crew busied themselves around us, working on their calculations. Kailas came to me, placing a hand on my shoulder. Usually his touch was welcome, but I didn't want anyone near me. He leaned forward and placed his fingers onto Ash's eyelids, closing them. I opened my mouth to say something, but only a small sound came out. *Don't be sad*, I reminded myself. *Don't be sad.*

"The projector is generating the visual. It's estimated to manifest above the form in approximately one minute."

The form. Did they mean my brother? My head was too heavy to lift off the pillow to see what they were talking about. *He's moving on to a new form. This is exciting,* I told myself. But it brought such little comfort. I lay in a stupor as everyone moved around me, tinkering with the machine, adjusting the wires on Ash's chest. I focused my gaze on my brother's hand in my palm. It was small and soft and vacant. My heart throbbed, stung by something painfully venomous. The poison spread throughout my veins and paralyzed me. The palpable pain pounded through my body as tears pushed their way out of me. As I lay there, unable to move, my mind left the room. I traveled through space and time and found myself in a memory.

***

My vibrant little brother and I were out on our farm. We followed the tire tracks in the dirt, surrounded by tall, swaying grass. We locked hands as we skipped down the road, singing one of our nonsensical, made-up songs. From the distance, we heard our mother calling us home for chores. We looked toward her voice, but neither of us wanted to go. So, we pretended not to hear her and instead ran off toward the mulberry tree. When we reached the trunk, I hoisted my brother into it and he sat in the branches picking the berries, plopping them into his mouth. He called them alien brains, just like our dad did, and then he laughed wildly, showing off his purple smile. This was over a year ago. Now, the memory only existed within me.

***

I returned to Ash's room. I didn't want to be there. It was empty, and wrong. It was all wrong. This wasn't how it was supposed to be. Ash deserved a full life. *Don't be sad. Form-death isn't sad.* Then, like a strong gust of wind, the *never agains* swept over me. Ash would never eat mulberries again, he would never laugh again, and he would never play again. He would never be with me again. Not really, not as Ash. The overwhelming grief dragged me down and I wasn't sure I would ever be the same. Whatever happened next with Ash's afterlife and with the tracing didn't numb the sting of losing what we had.

"Here comes the manifestation!" Somehow, I was able to

shift my head so I could see it. Above Ash's chest, a speck appeared—a tiny ball of golden light. It flickered like fire and revolved in place, like a miniature orbiting sun. The ball gradually grew bolder, brighter, and bigger with each rotation. I watched it, mesmerized by its beauty, as it swelled to the size of my head. Then it hovered in the air, scintillating.

A radiant, golden-yellow ball of light came to life before us all.

"Is this Ash?" I asked, my voice cracking. I didn't want them to know I was struggling with Ash's form-death. But how could I possibly fake being happy?

Jon, a gray-haired scientist, stood behind the ball of light with a wide grin on his face, marveling at the vision as if it were his own precious creation. "This is the manifestation of his soul energy. We call it the *soul orb*," he explained.

"So, it's not him?" I asked.

"It is. You have to understand; we cannot see soul energy. The machine makes the soul visible to the naked human eye, because we can only trace what we see, right?"

"I guess." I had more questions, but I didn't have the vigor to ask them. Unable to conjure a smile, I rested my head back on the pillow.

"How does the machine make his soul visible?" Kailas asked, taking steps toward Ash's soul orb. The light from it shone on his face.

"It's complicated."

"Why's he just floating there, Jon? Why isn't he moving?" my mother asked, anxious.

Jon directed his attention to her.

"It's in shock. This happens in most cases. It takes some time for the soul orb to be ready to move on. It's normal. Don't worry, Mom," Jon answered.

She nodded.

"What happens now?" I asked softly from the pillow.

"We prepare, and we wait," Jon said.

"What do we wait for?" Kailas asked.

"For the soul orb to move toward the new form. Then we follow it. After it enters the form, we collect it and give it to Mom," Jon said, looking over at my mother. "Our documenter will take some shots. There may be a reunion interview. Sometimes the families are invited to Halcyon for a ceremony by Mother Quinn. That's about it."

"What about Ash's form?" I asked.

"We need it for now; the soul is tethered to it. Once the soul orb moves on, you can do what you want with it. Halcyon doesn't usually participate in that end of things."

Realizing I wasn't going to have much time left with Ash's form, I lay there silently. People came and went and did their work, but I paid them no mind. It was hard not to drown in the insurmountable grief that swelled inside me. I couldn't go on like that. So, instead, I rested there, thinking of him eating alien brains and how wonderful he was at telling stories. I relived the times we had played behemoth versus hunter together and the hundreds of flowers he had plucked to give me as gifts.

A profound realization swept over me: having him in my life, even if only for eight years, was better than not having him at all. A smile surfaced as I thought of his soul and witnessed his life stream before my eyes. He had lived a good one. He was happy. We were lucky. I lifted his hand up to my lips and kissed it.

"I love you," I whispered.

Part of me waited to hear *I love you back*, but I knew it wouldn't come.

I took in a conscious breath and willed myself to rise, but my body didn't move. The paralysis still had hold of my limbs.

Even if I focused on my positive memories of Ash, the grief was still too heavy. And I was burdened by what would come next. I imagined waking each morning as an only child. Finding Ash's room empty every day. How could I live with this hole in my heart? I didn't know how to survive with such unbearable pain. I wasn't sure I could even rise from the bed, let alone live the rest of my life. Then something Gemma had once said sprang to my mind. *We don't have to know all of our future steps; we just have to take the next one.*

My next step was to sit. I only had to focus on sitting. I pulled myself up and sat straight on the bed. My head felt wobbly and heavy.

An Official approached me. "I have a few questions for you. Do you have a moment to talk?"

I opened my mouth to speak, but nothing came out. To my left, Jon typed at the machine, often glancing up at the soul orb as if waiting for something to happen.

"We can unhook the wires now. Bay, if you'd like to pull them off, be my guest," Jon said, looking up at me. "Bay?"

All I could do was shake my head. I steadied my breathing because it was getting away from me, too shallow and rapid.

Jon leaned over Ash and removed the wires from his chest. "Come back later, Roth," he whispered to the Official, who backed off.

I reached forward and pulled the covers over my brother, tucking him in. I didn't know why; it just felt right. With his eyes closed, he looked asleep. My mother moved to a chair next to the bed and stared at the golden ball of light as if in a trance. I wondered if she had run out of tears. I glanced up at the brilliant, golden-yellow orb as it sparkled and shined. It was either my brother or a science-made illusion; I couldn't be sure.

My next step was to—what? Breathe. Breathing was good.

So, I breathed. And breathed again. Once steadied, my next step was to get up. Without thinking about it too much, I swung my feet off the side of the bed and rose. I was okay. It was working. One thing at a time was manageable. Directly before my eyes hovered the sparkling orb. I half expected it to radiate warmth, like the sun, but it didn't. It had no temperature.

"What you said earlier was inaccurate," the black-haired scientist said, his words cutting through the tranquility. "The sun isn't infinite. Factually speaking, the sun is a gas-filled dwarf star that will eventually burn out. The latter part of your statement was also false, as research shows that we live in a finite universe. There's no evidence to suggest otherwise."

I slowly twisted my head to look at him. He had put on a pair of glasses and was still engrossed in his work. I doubted he had even glanced up from the screen when he spoke to me.

"What's your name?" I asked him.

"Dr. Phillip Grayer."

"Phillip..." I looked at his eyes as he worked at his touch screen. "My baby brother, who I love more than *anything* in the whole world, just died in my arms not even five minutes ago. So, now is really not a good time to tell me how inaccurate you *think* my last words to him were."

Phillip closed his eyes for a moment, then exhaled. Facing me, he said, "It's *Dr. Grayer*, and I stated impartial and irrefutable facts. I'm sorry if hearing them hurt your feelings." He pushed his glasses up the bridge of his nose and went back to his computer.

He had no idea what this felt like or how close I was to slipping out of reality. Articulating emotions was difficult enough, let alone trying to do it for someone as apathetic as him. There was no way for me to put my thoughts into words that his twisted logic would accept. I wouldn't let him unhinge me. I placed my gaze back on Ash's orb and tried to steady myself. My hands shook with unfamiliar mix of anxiety and anger.

Kailas wrapped his arms around me from behind. My eyes closed briefly as I allowed myself to melt into him, to find comfort. His warmth calmed me and I was ready for the next thing, but I didn't know what my next step was. I wanted to do a million things all at once: run away, be invisible, go somewhere to be alone, cry and scream, go back in time and change things, make the world stop moving. Most of those things weren't possible. I couldn't think of anything I could do physically to soothe myself. Even a mind-break seemed trivial and as though it would only make me feel worse. Maybe what I really needed was to keep busy by helping with the tracing.

"Why don't you guys give us the room? It's going to be a while, and there's nothing you can do now but wait. Get some air. We'll come and get you when it's ready," Jon said, motioning toward the door. I preferred him over the other science crew. He seemed to actually care.

I wanted to stay—to protect Ash—but he was gone. Wasn't he? How would I protect a ball of a light, anyway? I separated from Kailas and headed toward the door. Maybe some air would do me good. Kailas and my mother followed me out. Brutus, the farm manager and my mother's friend, came too, but I didn't realize he had been there at all.

My feet moved beneath me and somehow, I ended up in the kitchen. I drank a glass of water and picked at a bowl of wild rice and black beans that someone had made for me. Usually, I would have wolfed it down, but I had no appetite. As we settled in for supper, unfamiliar faces joined us at the table. They didn't appear to be science crew or Officials, but they weren't from Smallholding either.

One was a young woman, around my age. She had brown skin and black, curly hair shaved into a Mohawk. Her cheekbones were painted with orange and black spots, like those on a jaguar. She had deep-set eyes with dark, shimmery glitter on her eyelids. Sitting next to her was a man, probably twenty years old. He had an average build, tan skin, and short, sun-kissed brown hair. As I met eyes with him, he smiled, but I couldn't return it.

"So, who are you? You don't look like science crew," Kailas asked, shoving a fork full of food into his mouth.

"I'm Amur," the woman replied. "Definitely *not* a scientist. I'm here to document the soul tracing."

Kailas nodded, then pointed his fork at the man. "And you?"

"Nic"—he nodded at me—"and I'm here because I'm here."

Kailas took in a breath. "All right. Well, I'm Kailas, and this is Bay. The boy whose soul is being traced is her brother."

"We know," Amur said sympathetically. "We were in the back of the room when he passed. I'm so sorry for your loss."

I looked straight at her. I didn't want her to feel sorry for me. I didn't want to be in a situation where there was a reason to be sorry. "Thank you," I whispered. I didn't want her pity, yet it was nice to hear someone acknowledge the loss. Everyone was focused on the tracing as if Ash hadn't even gone through form-death.

"Your brother seemed like a cool kid," Nic said, his eyes on me, "Tell me about him."

I thought about Ash. "He loves to catch reptiles. His favorite part is letting the lizards crawl on his arms. He's always been gentle, naturally, without anyone needing to remind him to be. After he's done playing with one, he puts it down with such tender care. He loves chameleons the most. I mean, he *loved* chameleons. I guess he's past tense now. Excuse me."

I didn't feel like eating or talking and all of a sudden, I was logy. I found my way to the living room and lay on the couch. I must have fallen asleep shortly after my head hit the cushion because I began to dream.

9

I was outside in a forest. It was dusk. A wolf howled, sounding close. My eyes darted to the right and there sat the wolf, twenty-five feet away, its fur entirely gray, its eyes glowing gold. Before I could react, in a blur, the wolf unexplainably morphed into a young boy. I stalled for a moment as I recognized it was Ash. His medium-length, golden-blond hair fell into his freckled face as he stood there confused and dazed. When he spotted me, his worried expression softened into relief.

"Bay," he called out. And then he was sprinting toward me.

"Ash." I dashed to meet him.

The space between us was closing when he tripped over a protruding tree root and toppled forward. The moment his knees struck the ground, his body disintegrated into a million black beetles. Some of the beetles fell to the dirt, and the rest took wing out into the air. The flying ones drew to me like a magnet. Within seconds, they engulfed me. I collapsed to the forest floor, shouting in panic as I wiped my face, attempting to knock the bugs off to no avail. Realizing I had no hope of ridding myself of the dreadful things, I curled into the fetal position, shut my eyes, and surrendered.

Then, after a minute, the crawling stopped. I opened my eyes to find that every single one of the beetles had vanished.

In one swift move, I pushed myself to standing and took in my surroundings. I wasn't in the forest anymore. I was at the summit of the mountain. Above the clouds, my view was a sweeping panorama of the island on a bright clear, sunny day. I looked to my feet to find I was standing in a crater filled with red dirt.

A strange figure appeared about five yards away. The sight was so bizarre that I didn't believe it at first. It was a man in a spacesuit. He rebounded as he moved toward me in long, gravity-less strides. From the corner of my eye, something blurred across the sky. My gaze shot its way. It was a bird, an eagle. It spread its wings and majestically soared over my head, swooping down near me. It circled me as it lowered, eventually making its way to the ground before my feet. When its talons met the red dirt, it transformed into Ash.

He stood only a couple feet away, with a soft demeanor. He didn't say a word. Instead, he reached into his pocket and removed a sparkling ball of light; *his* sparkling ball of light. His soul orb. With care, he cradled it in his palms.

"Don't trust them," he whispered.

***

I lurched awake. My heart pounded. Panic swirled in my stomach. Something wasn't right. I marched down the hall to Ash's bedroom. Kailas dropped his fork on his plate and caught up with me. The door was shut. I reached for the knob, but it wouldn't turn. Locked. With my fist, I banged on the wooden door and it rattled in its frame.

"Let me in!" I yelled.

"Just a few more minutes." It was Phillip's voice.

Something was wrong. My gut was practically screaming at me. Kailas, Amur, Nic, and one of the Masculines stood beside me. I looked to Kailas.

"I need to get it in there," I told him.

"Are you sure? I mean, what could happen to him?"

"I'm sure."

"Okay." He sighed. "Let me go get something to pick the lock." He headed toward the kitchen. Nic immediately ran forward, shoulder first, barreling himself into the door. The lock broke, the door flung open, and Nic went tumbling through with it. I darted into the room and found Jon and Phillip huddled around Ash's sparkling orb, looking culpable.

"What's going on here?" I asked firmly, knowingly.

"Standard procedure," Phillip said. "No need to break through the door."

I walked deliberately to Ash's soul orb, looking at it closely, examining it. "Why'd you lock the door?" I asked.

"Privacy while we work," Phillip answered. "Any more questions?"

I glanced at the bed and saw they had pulled the blanket over Ash's head, covering him completely. My first instinct was to expose his face so he could breathe. My brain lagged behind reality. My brother was gone, a painful sting each time I remembered.

"You covered him," I whispered.

"Out of respect," Jon explained.

My eyes made their way back to the sparkling ball of yellow light. I engrossed myself in it, scrutinizing it, making sure it was as perfect as it had been before.

"It's okay." Kailas spoke from behind me. "I think everything's all right. I think maybe you're, you know, grieving."

Was I? Was I unnecessarily suspicious? Did I have a reason to think something was wrong besides my dream? Maybe I was used to caring for my brother and this was how I was coping. *Maybe I've gone crazy.*

But then I saw something, a glimmer on the edge of Ash's

orb. I moved closer, trying to get a better look. It was a light whitish purple sphere, nearly invisible. It was easy to miss, but once I noticed it, it was clear as day. The casing surrounded and enclosed the soul orb. I shifted my gaze to Phillip.

"What is that?" I asked firmly.

"What's what?"

Behind me, the room filled. Masculines, Officials, my mother, and Brutus came in to see what the fuss was about. Kailas, Amur, and Nic were still there too. I turned to face them.

"If you look closely at Ash's soul orb, you can see there's something around it that wasn't there before. It's like a bubble," I announced, hoping they wouldn't think I was crazy. They moved in closer, their eyes focusing on the soul orb. For a moment, everyone was silent as they analyzed it.

"I see it. It's kind of purple," Kailas announced.

Brutus agreed. Then one of the Masculines. Then, before long, the whole room had seen it.

"That's standard procedure," Phillip said defensively. "We always place a shield on the soul orb to protect it."

I looked to Amur. As someone who had documented soul tracings before, she should have known.

She moved her focus to the soul orb, then back to me. She bit her lip, mulling something over. Then she shook her head ever so slightly, confirming my suspicion. I wasn't quite sure what came over me. I grabbed Phillip's shirt and pushed him into the wall, shoving his back against it hard.

"What did you do to my brother?" I yelled, fire running through my veins.

"Nothing, this is standard—"

I yanked him away from the wall and rammed his weak, soft body against it again. "If you say, 'standard procedure' one more time I'm going to put your head through this wall," I threatened, my voice straining.

He shook his head fast, his eyes white-rimmed with fear.

"Dr. Grayer, what did you do to the soul orb?" an Official asked from behind me.

Realizing we had an audience, I let go of my grasp on Phillip and moved back.

He relaxed and stepped away from the wall.

Straightening out my shirt, I took a breath to calm myself.

"Nothing, sir," Phillip said. "He's fine."

I punched him square in the nose. His head recoiled and smacked the wall behind him. He held his face, blood dripping from his nostrils. My hand throbbed with pain, so I shook it out.

A spiritual person would never punch a scientist in the face. But who cares anymore? I decided I was done with these people. I didn't care what they thought of me. My brother was all that mattered.

"What's that bubble for?" I demanded an answer.

Phillip glanced around the room, cupping his nose, waiting for someone to come to his defense. "Can someone get me a towel?" he asked meagerly.

I grabbed the cloth I had used to moisten Ash's head and hurled it at him. It hit his chest and he caught it before it fell to the ground.

"Something's happening," Jon said from behind me.

Phillip rushed by me and made his way to the machine. With one hand holding the towel to his bleeding nose and the other tapping away on the screen, he worked at something, though I couldn't tell what it was.

"What're you doing?" I asked. When he didn't answer, I looked to Ash's soul orb. It shook violently above his form, rattling like an animal in a cage.

"It's not working," Jon said, his eyes fixed on the screen. I had no idea what he was talking about, or who he was talking to. "We need to let it go."

"Wait, hold on," Phillip yelled, typing like mad as blood dripped on the screen. "Just wait, I can do it."

"Do what?" I yelled.

"It's not going to work." Jon cried.

"No," Phillip yelled. "I'll get it!"

"It's too dangerous. You have to stop. Now!" Jon shouted.

"I'm too close."

Kailas rushed Phillip, pulling him away from the computer by his underarms. "He said stop," he yelled, holding Phillip's hands behind his back as he struggled to get to the machine.

I stood there useless, unsure of what to do and confused about what was happening. My mother did the same on the other side of the room and, for the first time, I understood her.

"Jon, want to clue us in on what's going on?" Kailas asked, holding Phillip still.

Jon rolled his chair, shifting over to Phillip's side of the machine, and typed. "I'm gonna turn it off," he told us.

"Don't!" Phillip cried, but Kailas smacked his head to shut him up.

"Turning *what* off?" I asked.

"It's a prototype. You were right; it's a type of casing that encapsulates soul orbs. We call it the *pod*."

I took a step toward him as he typed intently. "What's it for?"

"We're developing a method to make soul orbs dirigible, and the pod helps us do that."

"Dirigible?"

"You know, like steerable. We're trying to move soul orbs to our will. This way, we can enter it into a designated form. We've been waiting for the ideal specimen to test the device on, and your brother was it."

"Wait." I shook my head. "So you're saying that thing around Ash's orb can drive his soul around?"

"That's what it's supposed to do. So far, it's only holding him in place."

Phillip spoke up from behind Kailas's grasp. "Consider the possibilities of a dirigible soul. Once we can steer soul orbs, we can control our afterlives. We can choose our forms. It's a remarkable invention."

"So you never had any intention of tracing his soul," Kailas accused. "You had an ulterior plan all along."

"There's a team waiting with a pregnant guinea pig in Halcyon. We planned on placing his soul energy into the fetus."

Kailas shook his head in disgust. "You're trying to control things you have no business controlling."

"Science can do incredible—"

"I don't care about this. I don't care about *any* of this!" I shouted, cutting him off. "What I care about is Ash. What's going to happen to my brother?" I looked to Jon, who peeked at me from his touch screen. "What will happen to him?"

"Well, he's not going into that guinea pig," he said, wiping sweat from his forehead. He got back to the touch screen. After about a minute of typing rapidly, he slowed. A satisfied expression swept over his face, and he flipped down a blue switch on the side of the machine.

"All right…" He exhaled. "The pod is off. He can go on his natural trajectory. Time to prepare for the tracing."

A collective breath released from the room, and our eyes shifted to Ash's orb for confirmation. Gradually, it slowed until it stopped shaking altogether. I took a step closer and focused my eyes on it, and there it was: Phillip's pod.

"It's still there," I said so everyone could hear me.

"Hold on." Jon lifted the switch, typed on the screen, and flicked it back down. "It should be gone."

"Try again. It's still there, bud," one of the Officials called out.

I saw it too.

"Damn it. This doesn't make sense. Something's not right."

"The prototype isn't working," Phillip said, mostly to himself. "We can't steer it. Best we can do is hold it in place," he added, calculating something in his head.

"I turned off the prototype already, Phil. It has no power. How do I remove the pod?" Jon asked, rolling his neck.

"The fail-secure is on," Phillip said, and the room shifted its focus to him. Kailas let him go so he could speak.

"You mean fail-safe," an Official said.

"No, fail-secure. Fail-safe means when no power is applied a door is unlocked; fail-secure means when no power is applied a door is locked," Phillip explained.

"Care to elaborate?" Jon asked.

"I built the pod with a fail-secure. When the pod loses power, it locks around the soul orb. In order for the soul orb to move, you'll have to keep the power off, though. You'll have to remove the pod manually with the power from the key once the soul reaches the new form. I designed it to work with the key for maximum control."

"So, he's stuck in the pod?" I asked.

"Yes. And, I have to warn you, the window to unlock the pod will be short."

"What window?" Kailas asked.

"You'll have to wait to unlock it just before the soul orb is about to enter the new form. It was designed that way, but without the ability to steer, slow, or stop the soul orb, unlocking it will be difficult as the soul orb moves rapidly toward the end. Hence, the window will be short," Phillip said.

"What will happen to Ash's soul if we miss the window?" I asked.

"We've witnessed soul orbs redirect to secondary forms

when they're unable to enter their primary form, in instances such as stillbirth. We call the secondary forms *backups*. We can assume Ash's soul orb will redirect to a backup."

"Fine, then we follow the orb to the backup," I said.

"Once a soul orb redirects, it's more challenging to track. When the trajectory changes, the tracer becomes less accurate. The path gets fainter, like a carbon copy. A single redirection decreases the visual by thirty percent. If you can't see it to track it, you can't be there to open the fail-secure at the right time."

I let this sink in. My mind raced to find a solution, but I was so overwhelmed I couldn't think straight.

Kailas cleared his throat. "Just so I understand: you're saying Ash is trapped in that pod and we only have one chance to free him?"

Phillip nodded. "One, two chances max."

"What if we miss those chances?" Kailas asked.

I was scared of the answer.

"Hypothetically, if you fail to remove the pod, the soul orb would attempt to enter a backup form. If it can't enter the backup either, it will try another backup, so on and so forth… leaving it to bounce in-between forms without ever effectively entering one," Phillip said.

"So, Ash's soul would be lost forever… stuck in the in-between," Kailas replied

"If my hypothesis is correct."

"How could you do this to him?" Anger came on strong as I marched at Phillip, my fists tight at my sides. "Why would you do this?" I looked into his beady eyes.

He shrugged. "For science."

"Science," I scoffed. "For science!" I laughed absurdly because it was the most ridiculous thing I had ever heard. He had risked Ash's soul, a human soul, for *science*?

"Science has probably saved your life. Have you ever taken

antibiotics? Been hospitalized? In order to make discoveries there has to be sacrifices."

Dr. Phillip Grayer was a waste of my time. There was no talking to him, so I shook my head and went to Jon. There was still a chance I could save my brother. And that chance was getting me through how terrified I was.

"What can I do? Tell me how I can help," I said, ready to do anything.

"The soul orb isn't moving yet even with the pod turned off. We may have delayed its onset. I'm going to look at some of the codes Phil wrote and see what I'm dealing with. So, I don't need any help right now, but maybe you could help *her*," he said, nodding towards my mother who was hyperventilating in the corner, mid panic-attack.

10

"Mom, you're all right. Everything's going to be okay. Breathe." I inhaled deeply to remind her how to do it. On the exhale, I formed an O with my lips as the air came out. "Ash is going to be okay, I promise." We practiced breathing three more times, and with each breath she seemed to calm. I turned to face Kailas. "Can you take her to her bedroom and give her some water? Make her comfortable. Repeat what I said until she's calm?"

"Of course." He wrapped his arm around her upper back and guided her out of the room. Brutus followed.

With my mother out of the room, I was ready to get down to business. She couldn't handle what would happen next, even if she was the one who had caused it. I was the one who had to solve this. I accepted it. I would be the one to save Ash.

"If you're planning on coming with us on the tracing, you need to be ready at a moment's notice," Jon told me. "Once the soul orb starts moving, we have to jet."

With his suggestion, I went to my room and shut the door. As it latched, I felt it: the space, the fact that I was alone. If I were going to cry, scream into a pillow, fall apart, this was the time to do it, but it didn't come. I was too motivated to cry. Instead, I searched through my dresser and found an outfit to wear—black pants and a gray sleeveless shirt. Then I filled my satchel with dried fruit, my throwing knives, and healing clay and herbs.

I took a moment to take in my reflection in the mirror. My long, blonde hair waved out around my arms and passed the end of my shirt. I hadn't rinsed it in days and, as I ran my fingers through it, they got caught in a mat halfway down. Grabbing the brush, I worked out the knots and pulled my hair into a side braid. I stared into my eyes; they were beginning to look more blue than green. My form was thinner than I remembered it being.

A knock at my door snapped me away from my reflection. "Come in."

The door screeched open, and Nic stood on the other side of it. He surveyed the room. "Nice space," he said, only it wasn't very nice. The walls were covered in wooden-looking plastic laminate. The mattress sat on a frame with a wooden backboard. The only other piece of furniture was my dresser. I didn't own many things.

"I don't spend much time in here." I shrugged.

"Jon said he's almost ready."

With that, I slung my satchel around my shoulder, flung my braid out from under the strap, and headed out the door and into Ash's room. The only people left were Jon, Kailas, Amur, a scientist I hadn't met, one of the Officials, and a Masculine. Nic walked in behind me. Ash's orb glowed brightly in the middle of the room. Jon sat on a chair at the machine, but he wasn't looking at the screen; he was watching Ash's soul orb.

"Where'd everyone go?" I asked.

Jon looked at me. "I kicked them out." He exhaled loudly. "No need for them to be here. They were mostly spectators. It's my apology to you for letting Phil talk me into trying his experiment. In my defense, he told me he had permission from your mother first."

"Thank you. Where is Phil?" I asked.

"The Masculines escorted him and all non-essential personnel back to Halcyon."

"It's going to be just us for the tracing?" I asked, relieved he was gone.

"Looks like it," he said.

I glanced around the room. "I haven't met everyone."

"I think you met our artist and journalist, Amur. This is my partner, Terrance; he's a tech guy too. The Masculine over there is Rocky, and next to him is Roth, the Official. Then beside you is Nickel. I think everyone knows your name."

"Bay," I said anyway. I looked at Kailas. "Where's Brutus?"

"He left; went home to sleep."

"My mother?" I asked.

"She's in her bed, counting. Sometimes she gets up to pace," Kailas said.

"She does that when her attacks are bad."

"I know."

I directed my attention to Jon. "Did you figure out how to get him to move?"

"Can't you tell?" he replied, nodding at the soul orb.

Ash's bed was against the wall on the far end of the room. His orb was no longer over his form; now it floated in the middle of the room. The ball of light was as radiant as it had been before, the golden-yellow sparks drawing me in. Like fire, it was mesmerizing to stare at.

"He's not tethered to his form anymore?" I asked.

"Nope." Jon smiled. "And he moved a whole four feet toward the door."

"He's moving right now," Kailas said, "just very, very, slow."

I focused closely, trying to catch it moving, but it appeared to be staying still. "Is that normal?" I asked Jon. "For it to move so slowly?"

"Very normal. Souls speed up as they get closer to their new form."

As I stared at the glowing ball of light, a chuckle bubbled up in my belly and erupted out. I wasn't sure why I was laughing. Maybe I was hysterical or had gone crazy.

"That's supposed to be Ash?" I laughed. At first, everyone was quiet and looked at me uncomfortably. Then they started smiling. "Ash is a yellow ball of light? How's that even possible?"

"Science," Jon replied. "Science is not all bad."

I considered it. "Or maybe it's magic."

Terrance shrugged. "Potayto, potahto."

"No one says it the second way," Amur scoffed.

"Potahto," Rocky replied.

We all gazed at the orb of light that was my brother. "Where's he going?" I asked softly.

Jon motioned for me and, as I approached him, he held onto a tech device with handles on either end, a screen in the middle, and a button above and below the display. He handed it to me.

"Do you see this button?" he asked, pointing to one in the right-hand corner.

"Yeah."

"Press it."

I did as he said, and the screen lit up. For a split second, the Halcyon logo, a black infinity sign with a circle around it, appeared and then faded. Jon pointed to the soul orb. I followed his gaze and was astonished by what I saw. A glowing path of sparkly, golden-yellow dust came dazzling out of Ash's soul orb, creating a floating path that led straight out the door.

"That's Ash's soul path. It shows us where he's going. This is the soul tracer."

I looked at the big machine they had been working at all day, confused. "I thought *that* was the soul tracer," I said, pointing to it.

"That's the soul *projector*. It's what makes soul energy visible by creating the soul orb. The soul tracer is what we use to trace the orb." This was the gadget that had stirred up wars, division, and hatred. It had nearly ended civilization, and it was small enough to hold in my hands.

"If we lose sight of the path, there's a way to track it with software similar to the Global Positioning System, but I won't bore you with all of that. I'll be there to do the tedious science stuff. You can help navigate us in this terrain we aren't used to."

I didn't care what my job was; my only mission was to get Ash out of that pod.

"I'll help any way I can," I told him.

"This"—he held up a tiny metal thing that resembled a key except with a flat circle on its end instead of ridges—"is the fail-secure key. It'll only work when we're within five yards of the new form. The pod won't open until it has two specific things: five-yard proximity to its next form and energy from this key. It's not your traditional key and hole setup. The key can touch anywhere on the pod for it to work. However, it must have both—the proximity and the key—or it won't open. That's how Phil designed it: he wanted control over which form the soul orb entered, and this is how he intended to do it."

"I understand," I said. "Once Ash reaches the form, how much time will we have to unlock it?"

"I'm not sure. Ten, maybe twenty seconds."

"So, we can't miss our shot?"

"We can't, and we won't," Jon reassured me. That's when Ash's soul orb began to visibly move toward the exit, slowly.

"Looks like he's ready," Kailas announced.

"I know barefoot is a Halcyon thing," Jon said, "but we're all going to wear shoes for this. You've both got a pair, right?"

Kailas and I nodded.

After tying on our shoes, I trailed after the soul orb first, then the rest of the crew tagged along behind me. I took slow, careful steps as I followed Ash's orb down the hallway. By the time we reached the living room, it was moving steadily, inches at a time instead of fractions of inches. When the eight of us exited the house, I was reminded by the darkness that it was still night. It felt as if it should have been daylight. I had no clue what time it was.

"Soul orbs take the direct route. They don't need paved roads to travel, so we'll be getting ourselves into some thickets," Roth said, letting me hear his voice for the first time. As an Official of Halcyon, he was technically in charge and would dictate our decisions on this trip. Thus far, though, he had been silent.

"I have a machete, if it comes to that," Rocky, the Masculine, said. His hair was curly and black. His skin and eyes were brown. He was fit, muscular, and strong. I took a moment to stare at the Halcyon symbol tattooed on his forehead. I never understood why every Masculine had one.

Before us, Ash's orb was ultra-vibrant in contrast to the night, like a bright flashlight. It wouldn't be hard to track as long as we reached the form before sunrise. The moon's light was bright enough for us to see somewhat while we trudged along our path. The eight of us walked in a scattered group behind Ash's sparkling yellow orb. After such a stressful day, it was a calm night. The sky was clear of clouds, the stars were shining, it wasn't windy, and the temperature was just right.

"So, what's the plan?" Kailas asked. "Assuming we have one."

"Follow Ash's soul orb. Get to the form the same time he

does. Touch the pod with this key," Jon said, holding up the key. "The pod falls away, Ash is released, and he enters his new form. We take the new form to Tabby, Bay's mother. Then that's it, easy peasy, lemon squeezy."

"What are the rest of us here for?" Nic asked.

"Moral support," Kailas quipped.

"Speak for yourself. I'm here to document," Amur retorted.

"I'm here to facilitate," Roth called out, raising an arm.

"We all have a purpose, all right?" Jon said. "Don't worry about that."

Ash's soul orb traveled into a patch of thick, tall grass at the edge of our yard. We could see its light glowing at the tips of the grass. At the edge of the meadow, I turned to face my house, and something occurred to me.

"Wait," I called out. "Ash's form. It's just lying on his bed."

Jon, Roth, Terrance, and Rocky paused. Their faces expressed the same look. There was no time for my disruption, for my feelings.

Kailas waved them on. "You guys keep going, we'll catch up." Jon, Terrance, Roth, and Rocky did as he said, but Kailas, Nic, and Amur hung back to hear me out.

"And my mother," I pleaded to Kailas, turning to him, "She's in there having a panic attack, and I didn't even check on her before we left. Now she's alone in the house with Ash's dead form." I felt awful for not thinking of it sooner.

"It's all right." Kailas took a step toward me and pulled me in for a hug, my head landing against his warm, hard chest. "I'll go back and take care of everything. You keep going."

I pulled away from his chest to look at him.

"Don't worry about your mom. I got it."

No. I wanted him to come with me. I *needed* him to come with me. There had to be another way.

"Ash can't wait for you." Kailas pointed to the light of his orb getting farther away in the grass. Amur and Nic walked to the path Rocky had made and started heading down it. I knew then that I didn't have the time to find another option. *I'm going to have to do this without him.*

"Thank you," I whispered. Before I could change my mind, I jogged into the path after the crew and Ash's orb, leaving Kailas behind.

11

We walked mostly in silence. At about ten minutes in, I found myself silently talking to my brother, asking him not to take us down any gulches riddled with cacti, telling him how thirsty I was, reminding him to go slowly so we could keep up. His orb moved faster than it had at onset. We had to keep a quick pace to stay with him.

As we exited a brush, we came to a clearing. Before us sat several stone cottages. Besides the sound of insects, it was dead silent. The windows were dark. Ash's bright light moved between the houses, his path traced by a trail of sparkling, golden dust hovering three feet in the air. As the ball of light traveled the track it appeared to absorb the dust, leaving no trace behind.

This place was the village closest to our own, about a mile east of us. They called themselves Verve, a diminutive village of only thirty. They traded medical herbs, tinctures, and healing advice to Halcyon in exchange for food, water, and security.

All the members of Verve were elderly. They would soon die out, as they had no youth to reproduce. We had proposed welcoming them into Smallholding as a mutually beneficial exchange, but they declined our offer. They told us that they desired sanctuary from other humans.

Jon held the tracer, following it meticulously as the screen projected a blue light onto his face. We slowly walked amid the cottages as Ash made his way between them, floating angelically by them. The seven of us stepped gingerly so as not to wake anyone. We weren't looking to start a commotion. There would be no fight between us and the elderly.

However, there were resident Masculines assigned by Halcyon to protect the Verve citizens. I thought to communicate this to Jon, who seemed to be leading us, but I had the feeling he already knew. Anyway, I didn't want to make a whisper.

As we reached the far side of the village, Ash led us into another thicket of tall grass. Rocky took the lead from Jon and began hacking away at the tall weeds. The harsh sound of the blade against the grass felt contradictory to our last minutes of stealth. Once we were out of earshot of the village, the energy of the group shifted. We relaxed, taking more ponderous steps, allowing ourselves to breathe normally.

"Are we there yet?" Amur asked.

"Almost," Jon replied. "Getting close."

Amur slowed her pace to walk next to me and whispered, "On the walk back, do you mind if I ask you interview questions? What was it like to see your brother's soul orb? How it felt to be reunited with his new form? Things like that?"

"Sure." I nodded. "I haven't thought that far ahead."

"No need to prepare the answers, just wing it," she said.

"I mean, what it would be like to meet Ash's new form."

She shrugged. "Most people are thrilled. I'm sure you'll be too."

We walked a few steps in silence.

"Maybe you can help me with something," Amur said to me.

"With what?"

"I'm trying to decide if I should cut out the part about Grayer and the fail-secure in my documentary."

"Cut it? Like, pretend that monster never risked my brother's soul? Why would you ever cut it?"

"It's controversial, and it would get Grayer in some hot water."

"So?"

"You're right. It's the best part of the story so far, anyway."

"Best part?"

"It's suspenseful. People will love it."

Amur must be insane. Why would anyone love my brother getting trapped in a pod?

"No one will care about Phil," Nic said from ahead of us.

"And why's that?" Amur asked.

The group came to a halt. Nic bumped into Jon's back, and I bumped into Nic's. He glanced over his shoulder at me and then toward the front of the line again.

"What's the hold-up?" Nic called out.

"The soul orb stopped," Roth replied.

"We're there?" I asked, pushing through to the front. "Where's his new form?"

I moved Roth out of the way to find Ash's soul orb floating still in the tall grass. The trail of Ash's soul path was gone. I searched right and then left, looking for a bird's egg in a nest, a lizard sack, a pregnant something or other. Yet there was nothing, only six-foot-tall grass every which way.

"Jon, the key, we have only seconds!" I shouted.

"This isn't it," Jon yelled, looking at the tracer's display. I stepped closer to him and peeked over his shoulder at the device. The rest of the crew formed a circle around us. "Look," he said, pressing the touchscreen. A hologram projected above the device: an aerial map of the island using the GPS function. It took me a second to understand what I was looking at. Then

I saw it. Ash's soul path was no longer heading east; it had shifted directions and was now routed west.

"I don't get it," I said.

"We're too late. We missed the window. The first form must have been stillborn, or maybe a different soul entered it. I'm not sure."

"Isn't this our worst case scenario?" I asked, panicked.

Jon turned off the hologram. "We're going to have to reassess."

"Reassess?" I retorted. "The path will still be seventy percent visible. We're going to keep following Ash's orb, find his next form, unlock the thing, and let him free. Easy peasy, lemon squeezy, that's what you said." I looked to Jon for an answer, but Roth spoke instead.

"It's not that simple anymore, I'm afraid." I shifted my attention to him. "The soul orb is now headed outside our safe zone. River Clan territory. We don't have the authorization to travel there."

The reality of the situation sank in.

"So, the mission ends here," I said harshly, pointing an accusatory finger at Roth. "You're putting your imaginary rules above Ash's very real soul."

"Even if we look past the rules, the reality is that traveling to the west side of the island is a death wish. There are predators there, both human and animal. It's unknown territory; we wouldn't even know how to navigate it," Roth said evenly.

Ash's soul orb slowly rotated in the direction we had come from, inches at a time, just as it had at the house. We watched on in silence as a new trail of sparkling golden dust illuminated toward the west, outlining Ash's new path. It was less bright than the last one. At once, I understood what I had to do.

"I'm going, with or without you," I declared.

"You'll get yourself killed," Rocky warned.

"I don't care." I shrugged.

I took measured strides next to Ash's soul orb. I hadn't a clue as to how I would do it, but I was going to save him. I had to. I couldn't let him be lost in the in-between forever. The very thought of losing his soul made me sick to my stomach. Then a realization rose in me.

"I'll need the key, Jon," I said, glancing at him over my shoulder. If only Kailas had come with me. He would have taken my side, been my partner in this.

"I'll go with her," Nic said.

I turned toward him. I barely knew him.

"Me too," Amur said, taking a step toward me. We made eye contact and she added, "It'll be a great story. Assuming we live to tell it." Then the three of us looked to Roth.

"That's all fine and well," he said, "but you won't get very far without the tracer."

"Why wouldn't they have the tracer?" Terrance asked, looking at Jon.

"I can't advise my top scientists to go along on a death mission," Roth told them. "Everyone in Halcyon would have my head if something happened to you."

"What if a rogue Masculine knocked you out and it wasn't your choice?" Rocky asked from behind me.

Roth backed away with his hands up. "Then I guess it would be out of my hands. Who could blame me for that?"

"It's settled, then," Jon said, looking me in the eye. "We're going to free your brother."

The six of us looked at Roth in an understanding that this was off the record. Ash's orb was yards ahead of us. He wasn't going to wait. Those of us going ran ahead to catch up with my brother, leaving Roth behind.

"Nic has to stay," Roth called out. "That I can't get away with."

Nic turned to face him, then back at us. I was missing something, but I didn't care to figure it out.

"Fine," Nic said. We continued walking, but before we got more than a few yards away, he yelled, "Don't die."

During our walk with Ash's light, the five of us made a plan. Well, mostly Jon and Rocky made the plan. Jon mapped out my brother's existing path and confirmed that the form was deep in Helio territory. The good news was that Ash was to stay on a track by the ocean, which meant we would be able to drive along the old dirt roads. If we did that, we would only be on foot for about two miles; the other twenty would be in the vehicle. The only problem was that we didn't have a vehicle; not yet, anyway.

Rocky suggested we head back to Verve. The Masculines there had a van we could borrow. He made it sound more like we would be stealing it, but I let that detail go. Terrance had the idea to get ahead of Ash's orb, to drive past it on the road, instead of following behind. Since we could see where Ash was going, we had the opportunity to get there first. It would ensure us enough time to unlock the fail-secure with the key. The only bit of information I divulged was that I could speak some Helio. I didn't tell them of my encounter with them. I wasn't sure they would still want to help me if they knew how potentially lethal the Helio were.

Before we reached Verve, Jon approached me with the key. He had tied it to a long piece of twine. "Here," he said, holding it out to me. "You should carry this."

I thanked him, and Amur volunteered to tie it around my neck like a pendant. It dangled loosely on my chest, right above my heart. Soon we crouched along on the tree line before Verve. To the right of us sat the stone cottages, still quiet and serene. To the left, the Masculines' van was parked in the cut grass near a dirt road. Rocky explained that Masculines there were instructed to place their keys in a magnetic lock box behind the left front tire. Rocky didn't explain why. I thought maybe it was because their linen pants had no pockets.

We made the preparations to go in for the vehicle: We would dash to the van. Rocky would grab the key from under the wheel and hop into the driver seat. The rest of us were to slide open the van door and jump in the back. When Rocky gave the signal, we made a break for it. I rocketed and within seconds, I was at the van. As I closed in on the sliding van door, a figure appeared beside me. I pulled back, thinking it was a Masculine, but it was Nic. *Nic?*

I climbed into the van and Nic jumped in behind me and slid the door shut. The rear of the van had two benches bolted to either side. Amur, Jon, and Terrance settled on the far bench. I took a seat opposite them, and Nic sat next to me. Rocky put the van in "drive," and we were off.

There wasn't much to hold onto, so, as he pulled the van forward, our bodies fell back. I pushed into Nic, and he put his arm out to support me.

"Here they come," Rocky said, looking into the side-view mirror. "See ya later, boys," he cackled. He seemed to enjoy pulling one over on the Verve Masculines. We sped down the bumpy dirt road, and I held onto the bench.

"We're passing Ash," Rocky called out.

I hunched forward to look through the windshield. Ash was ahead of us to the right of the road. His soul orb shone brightly, moving leisurely, while Rocky pushed forty miles per hour. We blew by him, leaving him in our dust. Something felt wrong about not staying with him, but it was the most logical thing to do.

"Don't worry, he'll catch up," Jon said, reading my mind.

"Made a great escape?" Amur motioned to Nic. I repositioned my body to face him, eyeing him up and wondering the same.

Terrance added, "Shouldn't you be halfway back to Halcyon with Roth by now?"

Nic shrugged. "Nah. Roth decided to let me come."

"Uh-huh, yeah, I'm sure that's what happened," Amur mused.

Jon pulled the tracer out of his pack and pressed on the hologram, which projected in the middle of the van.

"We're here," he said, pointing to a green dot on the map. "This is where we're going." He traced his finger on the yellow line that was Ash's soul path. It was growing dull and harder to see than the first. "The path has faded because of the redirect, but we can make do. We'll ride along the shore for as long as we can, then park and cut inland about here. We'll have to hike the rest of the way."

"It's an hour's drive," Rocky called out. "If you want some shut eye, I'd do it now."

I should have been tired, but my adrenaline kept me from sleep. The only one who decided to take a nap was Terrance. He sat in the passenger seat, reclined, and was snoring in less than three minutes. After awhile of travel, I opened my satchel and took out my flask. Being conservative, I only took a sip.

Jon wrote something in a notebook as Amur and Nic talked about Halcyon—people I didn't know, references I didn't understand. I was once again among Halcyons. This was my chance to get to know them and ask my questions about the town, but I didn't care about that anymore.

"Hey," Rocky said from the wheel, "what if the kid comes back as a River Clan baby?"

"That'd suck," Nic commented.

"Actually, that'd be epic," Amur said, her eyes brainstorming.

"I'd imagine the probability of that happening is low. There are more animals on that side of the island than there are River Clan," Jon said, looking up from his book. "But if it does happen, we'll cross that bridge when we get there." He looked at me.

I tried to put the disturbing thought out of my head but the pregnant Helio mother came to my mind. What if it was her? My hands tingled and fear stirred inside of me, threatening to paralyze me. *No. I can't be frozen by fear. Not now. Control your thoughts. Deep breaths.* I willed my mind to be empty. With some effort, my thoughts quieted and I reached the state that can be felt just before sleep.

"What about you?" Amur asked, looking at me.

My focus was brought back to the van. "Huh?"

"What's your favorite food?"

"Oh." I was so out of it, I couldn't produce an answer. "I don't think I have one."

"What kind of person doesn't have a favorite food?" Nic asked.

I shrugged. "My kind?"

"One of my favorites is sushi," Amur offered. "Do you like fish?"

"No." I never had it.

"What about breakfast? You like eggs?" she asked.

Smallholding was too far from the ocean for fish, and even though we tried to, we couldn't get our hands on any hens for their eggs. "Papaya, I guess. I like papaya," I answered.

"Papaya?" Amur asked. "Of all things… papaya?"

"It's easy to grow. If pruned right, it's not too high to pick. It's hydrating. The seeds are good for salad dressing, and the skin can be composted."

They stared at me blankly, as if I had answered wrong.

"Okay, papaya then," Amur said. "But once you try chicken soup with a side of guacamole and a nice, warm baguette, you'll change your mind." Chicken? They ate chicken? Halcyon had outlawed hunting mammals as part of their compassion initiative. In Smallholding, we had herds of hundred-pound deer eating away at our crops, destroying our fields. But hunting them would have meant losing Halcyon. If we lost Halcyon, we lost our water. I guessed birds were still fair game to them.

"What is—" I began, but then Rocky hit the brakes, and the van came to a screeching stop. I fell sideways off the bench and landed on my shoulder on the floor.

"Rocky?" Jon yelled. He fell off his bench as well, his pack spilling its contents all over the floor.

"Sorry," Rocky called out. "Everyone all right?"

We looked around at one another.

"I busted my ass, but we're fine," Jon called out as he picked up his things.

"The road is blocked," Rocky told us, unbuckling his seat belt. "No way around." He and Terrance climbed back into the rear of the van with us.

He slid the van door open, and we poured out of it onto the road and into the moonlight. The air was humid and balmy, especially compared to where we started up on the mountain. As I walked around the hood of the van, I saw the fallen tree that blocked our path. Its trunk was as wide as the van, making it the most massive tree I had ever seen. Then I took a sweeping glance around me; there were hundreds more of that same type of tree surrounding us—an entire forest of them.

Riding in the back of the windowless van, I had missed watching the landscape transform. We were no longer in the stark desert region of the island, but the lush jungle part—the part of the island that the River Clan reigned over. Roth was right; we didn't know how to navigate this terrain, but we would have to learn fast.

"What do we do now?" I asked, rubbing my shoulder, which felt a little sore from the tumble.

"Walk," Jon said.

"A tad farther than expected," Terrance remarked.

"We'll manage," Jon told him. "It's only five miles or so."

"Won't Ash beat us there?" I asked.

"Not if we hustle."

"This is the River Clan's home. They're not going to like us stomping on it," Rocky said cynically.

"Good point," Jon agreed. "Maybe some of us should wait here in the van."

Looking around at the Halcyons, a pang of guilt vibrated in my chest. They shouldn't risk their lives for us. "Ash is my brother, so if I die trying to free him, I'm okay with that. If you want to save your skins, I get it. Take the van and go back."

They exchanged glances, considering my offer.

Jon slung his pack over his shoulder. "We're all in."

PART II

THE SOUL TRACER

12

As I stepped into the forest, I was engulfed by enchanted energy. The trees were massive and vast; this forest had to have been hundreds of years old. We were enfolded by the ancient trees. Their presence made me feel lighter, and the air in my lungs somehow seemed fresher. The moonlight was bright enough that we could still see, but not entirely. Growing on the trunks of the trees were vines that held large, heart-shaped, dark green leaves. Here and there, the forest floor was interspersed with deep red hibiscus flowers. Surrounding us, a chorus of frogs chirped. Frogs meant water.

As we took careful steps deeper into the forest, we saw fruit growing sporadically around us. A young mango tree, a few papaya plants bearing green papayas, and a banana tree with a royal purple flower in bloom. All of it grew within sight of the road. I wondered how dense the forest would become the farther we trekked into it. I allowed myself a moment to imagine what it would be like to live in this forest. Fresh water running in a stream, the ocean nearby to swim in, being surrounded by beauty and, most of all, fruit growing abundantly, independent of a farmer's hand. No wonder the Helio wanted to protect this forest and keep it all to themselves. It was magnificent, bountiful, and fertile. All the things our side of Sub Rosa Island wasn't.

"I don't see the path," Amur commented.

"Shhh," Rocky whispered, his index finger over his lips. "We're not in Halcyon anymore, darling."

Amur rolled her eyes.

Jon motioned for us to get closer, and we met in a huddle. "It's a quarter mile inland, that way," he said quietly, pointing behind me.

I looked over my shoulder to find nothing but forest. No paths. We would have to make our own way.

"I'll lead," Rocky volunteered. "Jon, you go behind me. Terrance behind you, then Amur, Bay, and Nic last. We stay in a single line, walking as stealthily as possible. If I do this"—he made a fist—"it means stop. If I do this"—he crouched down low—"you better do the same." He rose. "We'll talk again once we reach the kid's trail. Clearing the path is too loud. We're going to have to walk through the brush." He glanced at Amur. "If a spider crawls on you, don't scream. The River Clan will come, and believe me, they're more deadly than spiders."

"What if the spider's poisonous?" Amur looked at him sourly.

"Then don't eat it," Terrance said. "You mean venomous. You have to eat a poisonous animal for it to kill you."

"Keep moving," Jon said. "We want to beat Ash to the chase"—he looked at the tracer—"and he's a tad faster than us."

We moved through the jungle wherever Rocky led us. The plants and trees were spaced far enough apart to make the hike possible. There were instances when we halted at Rocky's order. The first stops were sloppy, with us bumping into one another. Each time, Rocky scanned the area for dangers, and then we would move on. We hiked less stealthily than we should. It was obvious we didn't have military training.

I wondered what I had gotten myself into—what I had gotten everyone into. We weren't fit for this type of mission.

Maybe we should have gotten more Masculines as backup. No, that wouldn't have worked. We didn't have enough time. And anyway, Rocky said they wouldn't have supported us. I was scared of what might happen to all of us, but I was more terrified of what would happen to Ash if we died before releasing him from that contraption.

After hiking for about half an hour, we finally found Ash's soul path. It was still glowing yellow, bright enough to see, though I understood what Phillip had said about it appearing like a carbon copy. Just as on the GPS function of the tracer, this path was duller than the first. If Ash didn't make it into this form, the next path would appear even fainter. Maybe we wouldn't be able to see it at all.

"Which way do we follow it?" I asked as we fanned out on Ash's soul path.

Jon peered at the tracer and pointed behind me. "That way, about another four miles."

"We can be there before sunrise," Rocky chimed in.

"Let me get a shot of you all by the path," Amur requested. "Just, everybody, go stand there and smile pretty."

Without understanding why, I heeded her words, and we huddled together. I waited for her to take a camera out, but she never did. "All right, that's good, thanks," she said, and then we parted ways.

"Can't believe I'm gonna be famous," Rocky said.

Before Amur could answer, we were interrupted by a shout. Paces away from me, Jon kicked something and it slithered into a bush. Wincing in pain, he squatted, slid off his pack, and pulled out a T-shirt. Terrance ran to him, held him in his arms, and began examining Jon's leg. Jon slit the shirt with a knife, ripped off a piece of it, and tied the fabric around his leg just above his knee.

"Damn it," he said, biting the sleeve of his jacket. His face broke out in a sweat.

"Jaguar snake?" Terrance asked.

"Lucky me," Jon said, rocking his body. "It burns like hell."

Terrance glanced around, searching for ideas. We were in the middle of the jungle, no anti-venom, no cures. The clay and herbs in my bag. *I have clay!* I ran to him, kneeling by his side. I opened my satchel and removed the pouches. I cupped my palm and mixed some of the clay and healing herbs with my fingertips. Nic came over, and I had him open my canteen to drip drops of water on the mixture. I stirred it to create a cement-like clay.

"I'm gonna smear this on the bite," I told Jon. "It will draw out some of the venom. It will only buy you time though. You'll still need anti-venom. You have that in Halcyon, don't you?"

He nodded.

"Three, two…" Tenderly, I smeared the clay over the bite, which looked insignificant for how painful it must have felt: two tiny penetration marks surrounded by inflamed pink skin. Jon flinched at my touch, biting onto his sleeve to keep from screaming. I finished applying the clay and wiped the excess off on a leaf.

"I'll take him to town," Rocky offered.

"You have to stay and protect them," Jon protested, barely able to speak; his words trailed off in a wail.

"I'll go." Nic stepped up.

"It should be me," Terrance said.

"You need to trace the kid," Jon said, weakly trying to rise.

"I'm not leaving you," Terrance said, his eyes heavy.

"Fine," Jon said, picking the tracer up from the ground and handing it to me. "You'll need this." He told me how to use the tracer, wincing in between sentences.

I was receiving a crash course in technology but wasn't fully comprehending it. We had no computers in Smallholding, and technology was a foreign language to me. Terrance pulled Amur aside and gave her his pack. Nic and Rocky took guard around us, patrolling for Helio, or more snakes, I didn't know. Our defenses were down, and we were way too loud. Once Jon finished his lesson, I pulled him in for a hug.

"Don't worry, I got this." I rubbed his back.

We separated and made eye contact. With a nod, Terrance helped Jon to his feet and supported his weight. Jon held back his shrieks of agony as they hobbled off. It would take them nearly an hour to get back to the van at that pace—if they made it there undetected by Helio. Even if they made it to the van, it would take another hour to drive back to Halcyon. Was it enough time before the venom spread to his heart? Fear entered my body and my legs went weak. *Everything will be all right,* I reminded myself. *Everything will be all right.*

It was just the four of us now: Rocky, Nic, Amur, and me. As we trekked through the jungle, guided by Ash's soul path, I thought about my mother. Her panic attacks could often last for days. Ash dying and his soul being in danger had undoubtedly set her off. She would be lying in bed, unable to do anything—unreachable, off in her own reality.

In the past, during these episodes, I mashed food for her to eat, although she would just throw it up. Kailas knew most of this from being there with me throughout the years. He knew what to do. He could take care of her. Yet I wished he was here with me. I ran my fingers across the bracelet.

It was nearing sunrise; I could tell by the way the sky turned a grayish shade of violet. After we had been hiking inland for about an hour, Ash's soul path cut back to the ocean. That's when I wondered what would happen if Ash's soul reincarnated off Sub Rosa Island. How would we follow him?

Maybe that was the reason scientists believed there was no other life left outside our island—because no souls ever left it? Many questions plagued me, but there were no scientists in our crew left to ask.

We walked atop boulders near the water's edge, and Rocky's demeanor softened, saying the River Clan most likely stayed inland.

Holding the tracer in my hands, I glanced down at the screen and followed the golden-yellow path to the end. It didn't seem far on the GPS—an inch farther west, and then inland another half an inch. In real life distance, it was still miles away. There had to be a shorter, more direct route, but I didn't want to leave the path to find out. The tracer showed that Ash's orb wasn't far behind, adding pressure to pick up the pace.

"Not too fast," I whispered to the yellow orb on the tracer.

As we continued on, I peeked over Amur's shoulder. She pulled a digital pad and a small, circular sticker from her pack. She stuck the sticker to her temple, where it adhered to her skin. Then—one letter at a time—words appeared on the screen of her digital pad. Notes or thoughts about the day's events. Amur must have felt my presence because she glanced over her shoulder at me. Blood rushed to my cheeks.

"That's amazing," I said, embarrassed by being caught.

"It's called the *Mind Writer*. My friend, Sterling, made it for me, so I don't have to write everything down when I'm working."

"I didn't realize Halcyon still made new tech," I said.

"You better believe it," Rocky shouted from ahead of us. "The science crew is addicted to their toys."

Amur shook her head. "Try it."

She pulled the sticky dot from her temple and pressed it onto mine, then passed me the digital pad. I let her hold the tracer so I could hold the pad. Then I watched curiously as my thoughts appeared as words on the screen.

Okay, it's on. When is it going to… Whoa, how is it doing that? This thing really knows everything I'm thinking. This is creepy. When I was ten, I stole a basket full of mangos from Mr. Watson's tree. Okay, no. Stop. Gosh, this is weird. I have to take this thing off.

Stripping the sticker off my head, I returned it to Amur as she passed the tracer back to me. "I don't like it," I admitted. I would rather have the privacy of keeping my thoughts to myself.

"It can be fun." She smiled. "I used it on my ex to see what he thought about my spots."

"And?"

"He thought they were ugly… too much make-up."

"They are ugly. I don't get all the face paint." Rocky paused and rotated to face us. "You look better without it."

Amur narrowed her eyes and shook her head at him.

"Where did they get the materials to make the mind writer?" I asked, happy to change the subject.

Amur faced me. "The island."

"Without imports?"

"Yeah, it literally comes from the island."

"Where on the island?"

Nic caught pace with us as we stepped from boulder to boulder. A hundred feet to the left, the ocean washed over the sand. Rocky peered out at the sea, waiting for us to catch up.

"Haven't you lived on Sub Rosa your whole life?" Nic asked, looking at me.

"Yeah. What does that have to do with anything?"

"The reason people came here in the first place was because of the island's rare elements."

"I know. My stepfather was a miner." A realization hit me

and I turned to Amur. "Did you say Sterling? A friend named Sterling?"

Amur's eyes lit up. "You saw Sterling?" Maybe I shouldn't have brought his name up. "Was he with his girlfriend?"

"No, no. I, uh, I just liked the name," I sheepishly said, not even fooling myself. We were catching up with Rocky, and I hoped once we reached him, he would change the subject.

"You saw them." Amur beamed. "In Smallholding? I have to know where they went."

"Probably not the same Sterling." I was making it worse.

"Oh, come on," she said. "You suck at lying."

Faster than I could understand it, something leapt out of the jungle onto Rocky, knocking him down on the boulder. He landed hard on his back with a giant animal standing on his chest. The creature's golden fur shone in the moon's light. Its fangs were visible as a chilling growl filled the air. A behemoth.

Within a second, I drew a throwing knife from my satchel and lined up the target. I would hit the cat in the neck. It was the best kill-shot without accidentally hitting Rocky. I sent the knife flying, but the moment it left my fingers, I knew it was off. Too high. It hit a boulder and ricocheted.

"Hey," Nic yelled, running in front of me, waving a torch. *A torch?* "Hey, cat! I haven't seen you in forever—since, what? Elementary school?" The beast raised its head to look at Nic, snarling, its fangs dripping blood. "You're looking teethier than ever."

Rocky didn't move. The massive predator growled as Nic dared to inch closer and started waving the torch.

"Go back to your nice cave or tree or where ever the hell you live," Nic told it. "Go home!"

The jungle cat removed one of its gigantic paws from Rocky's chest, and then the other, and slowly backed away into the brush. Then the behemoth turned from us and sprinted into the jungle.

Unfrozen by fear, I rushed to Rocky.

As I passed Nic, he reached out for my shoulder. "Stay close, it might come back," he whispered.

I lowered to check Rocky. He lay still as a board, his eyes wide open and unblinking. I stopped and stared at him with a sick feeling in my chest. A deep gash bloodied his neck. He looked dead.

He coughed and tried to sit up. "His damned teeth sliced through my skin like butter," Rocky managed to say, his voice weak.

By some miracle, he was alive. He sat up slowly, but I wasn't sure that was best. I didn't know what to do.

Nic kept guard for the behemoth with his torch, and Amur stayed behind us, fiddling with one of the gadgets that Terrance had given her. Rocky pressed his palm to his gashed neck wound, wincing in pain.

"He missed." He gritted his teeth. "My jugular."

Amur sat the gadget on a boulder, removed her pack, and then slid her jacket down her arms and off her body. She balled it up and pressed it hard against Rocky's bite, obviously not knowing first-aid either.

"Way to focus on the silver lining, Rock," she said. An unsettled smile surfaced on her face. Rocky's condition was dire. We wouldn't be able to stop the bleeding. The sight of the blood turned my stomach.

"Let's use the beach," Nic suggested. "Clean the wound and keep our backs to the ocean. Behemoths hate water."

"It's a plan," Rocky agreed. Amur and Nic helped him to his feet. Blood dripped from Rocky's neck and stained the rocks below him. It took some time and assistance, but we got him down the jagged path. When we reached the bottom, our feet planted firmly in the sand. I had forgotten what it was like to walk on the beach, the way it gave beneath my feet. As Nic and Amur helped Rocky to the water, I gave myself a moment to take in the ocean.

It was the closest I had been to the sea since I was a little kid. The sound of the roaring waves and the scent of the sea spray brought back memories from when I was just a girl. A hot, sunny beach day with my parents rushed me: buckets, sandcastles, waves.

The sky changed to a light bluish-purple; daylight was breaking. Concealing ourselves from the behemoth and Helio would be a challenge once the sun was up. As I moved in the direction of my remaining crew, I looked at the GPS on the tracer. Ash was still far enough away to make it to the form in time, but the pressure to get moving was mounting. I switched the tracer off and attempted to squish it into my satchel. It barely fit. Even after I rearranged the contents, it still stuck out at the top.

Ahead of me, the crew reached where the land met the sea. Nic planted his torch in the sand and together, the three of them approached the water. That's when I jogged to meet them. As I arrived, Amur removed her jacket from the wound and splashed salt water onto it. Rocky blanched. I wished we had a field medic, or at the very least, someone who knew real first-aid.

"The bleeding has slowed," Amur said as something occurred to her. "I think Ter gave me a medical kit." She unzipped the pack sitting beside her and rustled through the contents. She lifted out a white plastic box with a red cross. *Well, a first aid kit is something at least.*

"Why didn't Terrance use that on Jon?" Nic asked.

"There's nothing in here for a snake bite," she said, rummaging through the kit. "There isn't much in here for a behemoth attack either. Just some basic things to clean wounds. I wish we had some thread to stitch you up."

"I'll be fine," Rocky said, but his tone wasn't convincing.

"Wait." She pulled out a small tube. "Score. Liquid stitch."

Amur tended to Rocky as I slipped away to take a moment by myself. Looking toward the jungle above me, I contemplated what to do. Time wasn't on our side. My lips were chapped, and my throat went dry as I moved my tongue around my teeth to find any moisture left in my mouth. A dull ache started to pulse above my eyes, something water might be able to cure, if I had enough. I had learned to live with the constant pounding in my head, and today would be no different. I would get on with it.

In the jungle above me, a monkey of some kind stretched across branches, bounding from one tree to another. We were a twenty-something-mile hike from Smallholding. Our vehicle was gone. Would Terrance come back with the van to pick us up? Maybe a behemoth already ate him and Jon before they made it to the van. Years from now, would some explorer find the abandoned van by the fallen tree? Six skeletons dispersed throughout the jungle? Anxiety filled me. Everything Gemma had taught me felt futile. I knew then that I would likely die out there in the forest—by some snake, vicious wild beast, Helio arrows. Something was going to get me.

"You don't have to go alone." Nic approached me from behind. "If that's what you're thinking. Taking off to track your brother solo." He stepped forward so we were parallel, facing the jungle together.

"Not what I was thinking."

"What, then?"

"Where'd you get a torch?" I asked, changing the subject.

"Made it."

"Made it?" I twisted to face him.

"Yeah. That's what you were thinking about? The torch?"

"No, I, um…" I didn't want to answer, but I felt it coming up my throat. "I don't think I'm going to make it back to Smallholding. I think I'm going to die out here."

He wrinkled his face. "Yeah, the jungle will probably swallow you whole," he said, reaching for the key on my chest. He held it between his fingers for a second and clicked his tongue. "But we'll just have to make it worth it." He let the key go, and it rested on my chest. "Just in the nick of time, you'll save him."

His eyes were serious and sincere. I barely even knew him and he was offering me his twisted version of a pep talk in the middle of the jungle.

"Rocky is a Masculine, Jon and Terrance are science crew," I said. "Amur is… whatever she said… a documentarian. And you? I don't remember hearing what you do."

He snatched the tracer out of my satchel in a single swipe. I reached for it, but he pulled it back and switched it on. "That's enough small talk," he said. The hologram projected before us with Ash's golden orb lighting up on the map. "Let's go free your brother."

13

We told Amur and Rocky a lie: Nic and I would forage for fruit and be back soon. If they knew we were going after Ash, they would want to tag along, which Nic said would slow us down and put us all in danger. I couldn't argue with his logic.

The sun made its way onto our side of the planet, bringing dawn. Sunrise was a dreadful thing once I realized that the Helio could easily spot us hiking in the jungle. Two mutants with targets on our heads. Yet there was one benefit: behemoths were nocturnal. The light gave us a temporary safe haven from the beasts. I didn't know about Nic, but I much preferred an arrow to the heart than being mauled alive by a huge, fanged panther.

"Your mom was a mess when we left," Nic said as we hiked between trees.

"Yeah." I wasn't sure why he brought that up.

"Must be terrible to lose a child."

I looked down. "Yeah."

"But I get the feeling she's always like that. Not just last night."

"Yeah." I wished he'd stop talking.

"That's why your boyfriend stayed with her?"

I tried to figure out who he meant. "Kailas?"

"Yeah, the guy who follows you around like a lost puppy."

"What? No. He's my friend and he knows how to take care of my mom."

"Oh." He looked up at the trees. "I thought you two were a thing."

"You thought wrong."

He bit his lip. "So, your mom, she has panic attacks?"

"Anxiety disorder."

"Sounds bad."

"Anxiety disorder? It sounds horrible."

"Well, yeah, but I was talking about *you*. Seems like you've been carrying a load for your mom."

Why was he psychoanalyzing me? "Let's just listen for predators, okay?"

Up the trail by Ash's soul path, I spotted a papaya plant with ripe fruit. My hollow stomach begged me to stop for it. Nic followed and, as we got closer, I realized the fruit was too high for me to reach.

"Your favorite," Nic smiled. He pulled the trunk, using his weight, and the branch curved so that the papaya came into my reach. Hanging there were a pair of perfectly ripe, orange papayas. I picked them both.

"We'll wait to eat these somewhere safe. Up a tree, maybe," I told him.

I tried to fit the papayas into my satchel, but the tracer left no space for them. "You have room in your bag?"

"Sure," Nic said, and he turned so I could reach his pack on his back.

I unfastened the zipper and set the papayas inside, next to his water canteen. There was also a sack of supplies, and a novel he must have been reading.

"Hey," he called out, "I think we're going to have to take a detour."

I zipped the pack and stepped to the side. About a hundred

feet ahead of us, the thick jungle ended and a clearing opened up. A couple yards beyond the clearing was the ocean. Only it wasn't directly before us—no sand, no beach. We weren't even at sea level. We were, by some means, forty feet high on the mountain, and the waves roared below us down a jagged cliff in an inlet.

Worse, Ash's soul path extended beyond the cliff, hanging in the air over the inlet and cutting back into the forest on the opposite side, like a tight rope connecting one side to the other.

The two of us followed the path to the edge of the jungle. After surveying for River Clan, we emerged onto the exposed cliffside. No movement around us, besides birds hopping in the treetops. I stood at the border of the cliff, peering down at my feet. Vertigo hit as I took in the sight of the distant ocean below. Waves violently crashed against the rocks one after another.

Next to me, Ash's soul path floated onward, past where we could walk. I reached for it and my fingers went through the golden dust.

"Do we jump?" Nic asked, scoping out our possible landing spot.

"To our deaths?" I responded. "No, thanks."

I scanned the area for a plan B. There had to be another way to cross. Nothing useful to my left, but to the right: a dry riverbed.

"There." I pointed. "We'll cross the riverbed."

Nic trailed behind me as I led us through the jungle and made a path to the dry riverbed. We climbed in by using solid exposed tree roots like steps on a ladder.

When my feet hit the rocks, they slipped around on the glossy surface. Drizzles of water landed on the skin of my arm, making my hairs stand up. Inland, up the mountain, the clouds loomed dark and gray. Nic stood beside me and we both looked to the other side of the bed, which, now that we were in it, seemed more like a ravine. We moved over the boulders, but about halfway through, we hit trouble. A thick stream of water rushed through the rocks and passed our ankles. Before I could take another step, it rose to my shins.

"*Cross the riverbed*," Nic called out, "fantastic idea."

"We can still make it."

We forced our way through the ravine, pushing against the water at our knees. We clambered across the boulders, slipping and sliding. I took his lead but found myself skidding and plunging every few steps. The water rose to my calves when we were twenty feet from the other side. *You can do this*, I thought. *Move.*

I forced myself against the current, reaching out for anything I could grasp. We finally made it to the other side, and I grabbed a tree root. The river pulled my legs out from under me as I held onto the root with all my strength.

Nic slipped.

"Nic!"

The rushing river took him, and he was gone in a second.

I was able to pull myself up to the jungle floor, my elbows on the ground. I was almost out of the ravine when a zillion red spiders came from nowhere and crawled like crazy on my arms. I freaked out and tried to brush them off, but when I let go of the root, the river swept me away. I smacked into a boulder with my shoulder and flipped onto my back. The falls propelled me off the cliff and I spilled into the ocean.

The force drove me deep below the surface, my body shocked by the impact. I kicked and swam toward where I thought was up. When I finally emerged, I took in a breath, then several more until my lungs were full. Getting my bearings, I spotted Nic treading water. I swam his way, but the current was strong and pulled me out to sea. A weak swimmer,

I couldn't stay above water. The world left me as the water held me down. My heart pounded in my ears and I couldn't take the breath I needed.

Something grabbed my arm, pulled me from the force and back to the air. I broke the surface and inhaled. Nic was there. We were out past the falls now, wading in less violent waters. He was trying to tell me something, but his voice was muffled. My arms were weak and my clothes, shoes, and satchel were heavy with water. I searched for an exit, but we were surrounded by a steep rock face and tall cliffs.

Finally, Nic's voice came through. "Swim! Come on, Bay, you can do it."

We doggie paddled to a nearby pebbly beach. When I crawled out of the ocean, I took a minute and flopped onto my back, a thousand tiny rocks poking into my spine. When I mustered up the strength, I found a boulder to sit on and wrung out my shirt at the waist. Nic emptied his pack—his book was saturated, the cover breaking off into pieces, but the papayas survived.

That's when I remembered the tracer. It was in my satchel. My wet satchel! I slung it onto my lap and flipped the flap open. I pulled it out and put on my lap. Electronics weren't my thing, but I knew they weren't supposed to get wet. I pressed the power button and waited for it to turn on. Nothing. I pushed it again. Still nothing. Panic rose in me.

"It won't turn on." I held it out to Nic, who sat on a rock beside me. I waited anxiously, as he fiddled with it.

"See this light? It's green," he said, "but the screen is waterlogged."

"Waterlogged?"

He pointed up. "Ash's soul path still lights up"—his soul path was still cast above us—"but we lost the GPS."

I exhaled. "I can work with that."

My hand went to the key on my chest, realizing it might have fallen off in the ocean. I rubbed it, thankful it was still there.

"We need to keep moving." I scanned the area for a way to Ash's soul path, wherever it was. The rocks were too steep to climb, and even if they weren't, I didn't want to head back in the direction of that miserable behemoth, even if it was probably sleeping. In the opposite direction, the beach curved around the rock face.

"Let's follow the shoreline," I said, rising to my feet.

Nic and I headed down the beach, uncomfortable in our wet clothes. The morning air was cool, which didn't help. The cloud cover was thin so I hoped that, once the sun was high enough, it would warm us. My wet hair fell out of its braid, the water weighing on it. I loosened the band and allowed the locks to flow at my sides.

We rounded the mountain, and a mile-long stretch of rocky beach opened up. Usually, I'd be engrossed by its beauty, but I didn't have the time to bask. My focus shifted to the mountainside, where I searched for a trail into the jungle. Ash's soul path would be inland, and we had to find it.

"River Clan," Nic hissed and pulled me low to the ground.

Crouching, I spotted them, about quarter a mile down the beach, a group of ten or so. They appeared to be fishing or spearing, their green skin shining in the sunlight.

"We need cover," Nic whispered, nodding to the brush opposite the ocean.

We half crawled, half crouched over to the trees and hid behind them. Panic surged through me as the memory of the first attack resurfaced. I wasn't sure I could survive another fight with the Helio. I didn't know how many toddlers they had in their clan that I could rescue in exchange for a pardon.

"What's the plan?" I asked.

"I thought you were the one with the plan."

"Right," I said. "We need to find a trail that leads up into the jungle so we can find Ash's soul path."

"You mean a trail like that?" Nic said, pointing behind me.

I turned to see a clear-cut trail heading south. It must have belonged to the Helio. No animal could have made such a wide, apparent path. Taking a Helio path was risky, but so was going into uncut jungle, so we took the path.

We trekked uphill steadily, at an even pace. I didn't bother to keep an eye out for the behemoth. If it was going to pounce on me, then so be it. It was out of my control. The mosquitoes came out to eat, and I was the main course, leaving me with itchy, red blotches. About a mile into the hike, I spotted a glowing light through the dense trees. *Ash's soul path.*

"The only question is, which way do we follow it?" Nic asked. I hadn't thought of that. I pulled the tracer out and tried to get it to work, but the only thing that lit up was the green indicator light. Nothing else. There was no way of knowing which way to go for sure, but I knew what to do. I closed my eyes.

I imagined a ball of light encircling me. With my palms facing out, the wind picked up, and my hair blew behind me. Then I knew. I wasn't very spiritual but I had a good gut— intuition—whatever you want to call it. I opened my eyes to find Nic staring at me.

"What?" I asked.

He turned over his bottom lip and shrugged. "Nothing. Which way?" he asked, and I pointed left. "The ocean is behind us, so yeah, that makes sense."

We moved slowly, letting Ash's soul path lead us. I was worried we had missed him, that he had passed us already. For all we knew, he had made it to the form, couldn't enter it, and moved on already. If that happened, I had failed him. I couldn't think like that, though; it was defeatist. Anyway, the soul path was still lit. If he had reached the form, it would have disappeared, wouldn't it?

Nic hiked ahead of me, walking with a bounce in his step. He held back a branch and let me pass through.

I swallowed, but my mouth was dry. A cough escaped me, and I cleared my throat.

Nic reached into a side pocket on his pack and pulled out a bottle. Extending it out to me, he said, "I have plenty."

I shook my head and pulled my own water supply out of the satchel and drank the few drops that were left. I was still thirsty, so Nic offered me his water again, and I reluctantly took it. I hated feeling like I owed him something.

"Thank you," I said with a smile, handing him the bottle back.

"Look," Nic said, glancing to the right. About fifty feet away from us stood a tall, mature mango tree bearing ripe fruit.

It was taller than the mango trees in Smallholding. This tree wasn't stunted and thirsty like the ones back home. I found myself climbing its limbs and perching on a thick branch. A couple mangos dangled before my face. I plucked them and silently said my thank you to One. Then I pulled my remaining throwing knife out of my satchel. That's when Nic joined me, climbing awkwardly up the tree.

"You don't climb much, huh?" I asked.

He shook his head and balanced on the branch opposite me so we faced one another. He twisted his damp pack onto his lap and pulled out the papayas, handing me one and keeping the other for himself.

I cut my fruit and balanced the slices on my thighs. I handed the knife to Nic and he prepared his food. We sat in silence as we ate our breakfast, our hands growing sticky with the sweet juice of the fruits.

"You're right, papaya is good," Nic said softly, taking a bite and licking the juice off his finger.

"Wait, is that your first papaya?" I whispered.

He shook his head. "It's been a while, though."

"Halcyon gets a quarter of our papaya yield."

He looked puzzled. "We have papaya in the cafeteria."

"So, why don't you eat it?" I grasped the seed of the mango, sucking the pulp off it.

"When grilled chicken and rice with a ciabatta roll is on the menu, plain papaya seems… meh," he said with a shrug.

I tossed the clean seed into a bush. "What's a caba roll?" I asked, licking my fingers clean.

He took the last bite of his papaya and said, "Smallholding doesn't have bread?"

I shook my head. I didn't know what else to say, so I got busy eating my papaya.

"Have you ever considered a haircut?" Nic asked.

I glanced at my damp locks. They were bunched up on my lap and draped onto the branch next to my thighs. A piece of mango got stuck in them, so I plucked it off and ate it.

He looked at me funny, and I realized he might have been teasing me. "You don't like my hair?" I asked, more defensively than I meant to.

"I didn't say that." He smirked.

"Hand me my knife."

He hesitantly extended the handle of the knife out to me.

I snatched it from him and tucked it into my satchel. After chewing my papaya, I spoke again. "What're you really doing here? We both know it's not about my brother."

He clicked his tongue. "I'm—"

"If you say something stupid, I swear, I'll push you off that branch."

He took in a long, drawn out breath. "The truth is… I was

commissioned to get close to the River Clan... to take them out. I needed you because you speak Helio."

I stopped chewing and stared at him while doing the calculations. What he said made sense, kind of. Except no one had known I spoke Helio before we set out to trace Ash's soul.

"Liar." I threw my papaya skin at him. It hit his chest and plopped onto his lap. He laughed and tossed the skin out of the tree.

I was about to throw my mango skin at him, too, when I heard something. I raised my index finger over my mouth to shush him, and we both went silent. I couldn't see a thing from my branch, but Nic had a better view. When his eyes widened, I knew it was them. It was confirmed when he mouthed the words, *River Clan.*

I turned off the tracer and the bright golden path flickered out. If the Helio came across Ash's soul path, who knew what they would make of it. I pulled my knees into my chest and held my breath, trying to will myself to be invisible.

Then, slowly, one by one, a group of Helio passed under us. Mostly young men, some women, a couple elderly, and even some children. Most of the adults had bows slung over their shoulders with a quiver of arrows alongside. Their green skin glistened with drops of water. Was this the same group from the beach? Did they track us? Maybe they followed the soul path before I switched it off. Yet they weren't confused by its disappearance; they weren't looking for the path. That gave me the feeling that they never saw it in the first place.

Sitting with my chin resting on my knees, minutes passed while they walked annoyingly slowly. If they spotted us, we were dead. I wouldn't be able to save my brother. There were too many obstacles. *Stop, don't think like that. Believe in yourself. How would a spiritual person think?*

A young Helio woman stopped under the tree below us.

We were low, maybe fifteen feet from the ground. If the Helio woman glanced up, she would spot us through the foliage. My breaths remained controlled and shallow. She reached up and yanked one of the low-hanging mangos, breaking it free from the branch.

I recognized her—it was the woman I had fought in the forest two days before. Her shark-tooth necklace still dangled from her neck. Below us, she rubbed her thumb along the skin of the mango. Her clan disappeared into the jungle, their footsteps growing quiet until eventually, we couldn't hear them.

Shark Tooth looked up, and I closed my eyes. I didn't know why. It was like when I was a child playing hide-and-seek and I thought if I couldn't see my dad, then he couldn't see me. I allowed some time to pass before I opened my eyes. My heart started beating again when I realized Shark Tooth was gone. When I was sure the clan was far enough away, I climbed over to Nic and took the spot beside him.

"What's with the glowing foreheads? And no eyes? Are they blind? They can't be human. I'm calling it… they're aliens. Ugly aliens," Nic said.

"You've never seen a Helio before?" I figured Halcyons had at least seen photographs of them.

"What? And you have?"

I pulled a face. "You know, they could kill you in a heartbeat, so be careful what you say about them." I brushed my hair out of my face. "Anyway, ugly is relative. To them, you and I are ugly."

"I could take them. They don't look so tough," he said. "And for the record: you're not ugly, you're beautiful."

Blood rushed to my cheeks, setting them on fire, as a mixture of flattery, embarrassment, and anger swirled inside me. I didn't think it was possible to be filled with such a melting pot of emotion.

"This isn't a date," I informed him.

"I know."

"Good."

"This isn't where I'd take you on a date."

I groaned. "You know, I bet when you die you'll come back as a dung beetle."

"Beetles are insects, so they don't reincarnate."

"A rat then."

"I bet you'd come back as a *fox*," he said with a devilish smile. *Is he trying to flirt?*

I punched him in the arm.

"Stand down. I'm joking." He rubbed his tricep. "You really want to know why I'm here?" he asked, a serious look on his face.

"I've only asked you three times."

He exhaled and straightened his spine. "I don't have a passion." I gave him a shrug because that meant nothing to me. "It's a Halcyon thing. It's a job. We're supposed to pick a passion by the time we're eighteen, but my birthday came and went, and I never chose one. I've tried most of them, which is why I know how to make a torch, but none of them were my thing. So, my mom sent me on this tracing because she thought science could be my passion. I'm here because of my mom. It's embarrassing."

Halcyons had jobs? That they got to chose? "I don't know what to say."

"Yeah."

"I guess that would be hard," I said.

"Yeah, hard." He shook his head.

"What?"

"Nothing."

"What?"

"Nothing. It's stupid. It's not hard. Not like what you've been through," he said.

"Me?"

"Your brother died and a jerk jeopardized his soul. That's hard. Most people I know would've been broken by it, but not you. You're… you're resilient. You're confident. You know who you are and where you fit in," he said.

He got me all wrong. "You don't know me."

"I've seen enough."

"I don't know where I fit in. I've been told what to do most of my life. I never had a choice. I was raised on a farm, so I became a farmer. I hardly consider that knowing who I am," I told him.

"That's crap. You know who you are. And it's more than just a farmer." He shifted his weight to face away from me. When I didn't respond, he faced me again and continued talking. "If you weren't given the life of a farm girl, what would you be?"

"Farm girl? Is that how you see me?"

He looked at me with firm eyes. "Just answer the question."

"I have no idea," I admitted. "I don't know what I'd do if I had the choice. I honestly never thought about it. What's the point of thinking about something that will never happen?"

"Why wouldn't it happen?"

"I have to grow food for Smallholding. I have to trade Halcyon food for water. Last I checked, no one can survive without water."

Nic pointed his index finger up. "Doesn't it fall from the sky?"

I pretended to laugh. "You're hilarious. That should be your job: comedian."

"Passion."

"Whatever."

He shrugged. "You can find ways around it… work hard to get out of your situation."

"Wow, I hadn't thought of that. I just need to work hard. I'm so relieved it's that simple." I was trying to keep my cool.

"That's not what I'm saying—"

"Good, because I break my back so you and your Halcyon friends can eat. Of course I work hard."

"What I meant was that you have options. Like, you could apply to be a Halcyon citizen."

"Oh, sure, and abandon my village."

"You don't have to look at it like that. I'm sure someone would take your place on the farm."

"Even if I did apply, Halcyon is impossible to get into. I know plenty of people who were rejected. And they are way more spiritual than me."

"More spiritual? What do you think makes someone spiritual?"

I gave myself a conscious moment to think. Then I answered, "I don't know."

"Come on."

"I don't know. I'm probably wrong."

"Just say it."

"I guess… someone who has their emotions perfectly in check and feels peaceful and positive and in total acceptance all the time."

I didn't want to talk about this anymore and we were wasting time. I climbed off the branch and worked my way down until I dropped onto the forest floor.

"Aw, come on," he moaned, climbing to meet me. "Our date's not over."

I made a face. "I've changed my mind. I think you'll come back as a donkey."

He landed on the ground, pouted, and held his chest as if wounded. "Damn." He perked up. "That's a step up from rat."

I meant to glare at him with angry eyes, but I couldn't stop the smile from lifting my lips. As he smiled back at me, I got lost in his eyes. *No. No eye-gazing.* I pulled the tracer out of my satchel and turned it on. Beside us, Ash's golden path illuminated, leading the way.

14

14

I couldn't stop replaying Nic's words. *"You can find ways around it... work hard to get out of your situation."* Dawn until dusk, I labored in the fields. Tilling, weeding, harvesting. He had no idea how labor-intensive farm work was. I bet he had never truly worked a day in his pampered Halcyon life. I gritted my teeth as anger filled me. *Bitterness is bad. Spiritual people don't get bitter. Take a breath and calm down.*

Nic led as we hiked alongside Ash's soul path. Maybe I couldn't stop thinking about him because I was forced to stare at the back of his head the whole way. I was supposed to be keeping an eye out for Helio, not wandering off in angry thoughts. It would have been nice for Ash's soul path to be invisible to everyone except us. If the Helio found it—well, I didn't know what they would do, but it wouldn't be good. Nic stopped, raised an index finger, and twisted to face me.

"Hear that?" he asked, tilting his head.

I listened. Birds sang far off in the distance. "Birds?"

"Not that."

A whooshing came from somewhere close. "A waterfall?"

His smile grew. "Let's find it." He moved off toward the sound.

I glared at him. "You aren't serious."

"One hundred percent."

I followed after him. "We were just swept away by a river. I'm done swimming for today."

"This is different."

I groaned. "What about Ash? And the Helio?" How could he consider another detour after how dilatory we had already been?

"We deserve to swim in a waterfall before we die," he remarked, pushing branches out of the way to make a path.

I gripped his shoulder. He froze and twisted to face me.

"Ash could reach the form before us," I said softly.

"He won't. We're way ahead of him."

At some point, I had lost touch with my gut. Fear, confusion, stress—those were the things in my forefront. I fiddled with my bracelet, rubbing the shell, as I thought about it.

"We'll never have another chance to swim in a waterfall. Even if we survive today, there are no big pooling waterfalls on our side of the island. It's now or never," he said.

"I don't know, Nic."

"Well, I'm going. Come with me or go on without me," he said, throwing his hands in the air.

"You're leaving me?"

"You're the one leaving me," he replied as he stepped off the path. "We'll only be five minutes," he called out.

I stood there, glancing at Ash's soul path. As I focused on the golden dust, I felt the weight of it all—Ash's sickness, the farm, my mother. I deserved something more than caretaking. It would only be a couple minutes. We would still make it in time. I couldn't believe I was doing it, but I switched the tracer off and chased after Nic.

"Five minutes! That's it. I'm serious."

The waterfall was a quick hike through the dense jungle. Rocks, vines, and tall trees surrounded us as we stood in the presence of a thirty-foot-high gushing waterfall. My eyes went teary at the sight of it. So many days where I thought I would die of dehydration and here was a lifetime's worth of water just falling down the mountain.

A cool breeze from the pool blew my hair. Nic yanked off his shoes and pulled his shirt above his head. He wasn't wasting time. I shouldn't have been either. I couldn't believe I was doing something this stupid. What could Nic be thinking? What was it like to live so frivolously, without a care in the world?

Walking over to a bush, I took my satchel off and tucked it under the leaves. I stepped out of my pants and got down to my underwear. I was about to pull my sleeveless gray shirt over my head when I hesitated. Nudity was customary in Smallholding, but was it in Halcyon? I looked at Nic, who wore black briefs, nothing else. My eyes lingered, taking in his form. He was in better shape than I thought; his stomach and chest were well defined. Walking up to me, he passed me his folded clothing and his pack.

"Can you put this with your stuff?" he asked.

I peeled my eyes away from him and tucked his things with mine. Seeing how he was wearing briefs, I left on my underwear and shirt. We balanced on the rocks and made our way to the water. My feet submerged in the pool, which was freezing, but with the excitement, I didn't mind at all. Nic dived in and I plunged in after him.

The second I started enjoying myself a pang of guilt surged within me. *I should be following Ash's soul path, not taking a selfish waterfall swim,* my inner voice scolded me. *I'll be back on the trail in the matter of minutes,* I told myself. *There's nothing to feel guilty about.*

Bathing in a frosty mountain stream, I sank under the water and the world fell away, my ears and eyes oblivious to anything going on above the surface. My skin erupted in goosebumps as I glided from one side of the pool to the other. My swimming lessons from fourteen years ago all came back to me. I broke the surface and floated on my back as the sky moved through the tree branches above.

Nic climbed a ten-foot rock face, leapt off the boulder, and came crashing to the water with a splash. When his head popped up, he shook his hair out of his face.

"That thing you're feeling… that's called having fun," he said.

I gave him a sour face instead of a reply, and our eyes locked for the first time. I hadn't noticed that his were the color of honey. Something in my stomach fluttered as I took in Nic's smile, but then, the sound of distant voices caught my attention. My horror grew as Helio appeared out of a trail, one-by-one like marching ants.

We ducked underwater.

It seemed we only had two choices: stay underwater forever and run out of air, or resurface and get arrows to the head. Both of those outcomes sucked. Luckily, a better idea hit me.

I tugged Nic's arm so he knew to follow me, and we swam behind the falls. As the water turned shallow, we emerged into the air, planting our feet on boulders deep in the pool.

Behind the waterfall now, we found ourselves in a mossy cavern, hidden by sight and sound. We would be invisible to the Helio here—if they hadn't already seen us. Carefully, I peeked out at the clan, being sure to stay concealed. With their wild, lilac hair tied back in ponytails, they knelt beside the pool, filling their flasks with water. Some of them stepped into the shallows and splashed themselves with water to cool down. None of them seemed to be gearing up to kill us.

I lowered my body into the water and faced Nic. "They're filling their flasks."

"Did they see us?"

"I don't think so."

Some part of me knew that being terrified was the normal response, but I couldn't help but feel anxious. The Helio were taking their time at the pool, and Ash didn't have time for it. We were trapped and useless to the mission standing at the bottom of a waterfall. The pool was freezing and I was dying to get out of the water and let the sun warm me.

It was all Nic's fault. Him and his persuasive ways and honey eyes. My jaw tightened. *Don't get upset, it's not a big deal. Let it go,* I told myself. *Learn to let things go.* Pulling my hands into my chest, I shivered and stared at tiny streams of water cascading down the cavern walls. The only distraction I had from the cold was analyzing the hairy green moss that grew along the rocks.

Standing across from me, Nic opened his arms to let me know that warmth was just a hug away. I wanted to puke, but I shook my head instead.

"I'm fine," I said, making my best attempt to hide my frustration. I didn't need him—I would warm myself with my thoughts. *The hot sun. Working on the farm. A summer day at noon. Blazing fire. Blistering heat.* My teeth started chattering. This prompted Nic to move in closer.

"You're turning blue," he whispered, and I could almost feel his warm breath.

The muscles in my back grew painfully tight from shivering and my resolve weakened. *Smoke. Sizzling hot rocks. Boiling water.* I glided toward him, giving in. With my hands balled into fists on my chest, I pressed my form onto his. I didn't know what my plan was, but the feel of his skin on mine made the hairs on my arms stand up.

He held me, and we stayed there like that until I stopped trembling and my jaw relaxed. Warmth settled into my bones and I realized that Nic smelled good.

Against my better judgement, I looked up at him. His honey eyes had specks of amber in them. There was goodness in him and I saw it through his eyes. My spine shivered as his hand made its way to the back of my neck. Our lips pressed together. I let the tension in my arms go and wrapped them around him as he kissed me. Somehow, my reservations disappeared and I kissed him back. Actually, it was more than that—I *liked* kissing him.

Then we separated. My eyes opened, and we gazed at one another. I was hypnotized for a moment, but then I snapped out of it.

With a groan, I sank under water. *Why did I do that? No, wait, why did he do that? This is crazy. This isn't a summer romance.*

Standing up, out of the water, I punched him in the arm before he could cause me to swoon again. "Why'd you have to go and do that?" I snapped.

"Do what? Make out with you?" He smiled.

I stared at him wide-eyed and nodded.

"Because I wanted to."

"You do a lot of things just because you *want* to, huh?"

"Only when I know what I want."

I grumbled. "You can't just… there's not… ah, never mind." I didn't know what to say, so I shut up and crossed my arms with a huff.

"Should I have asked? Because it seemed like—"

"Just forget it. Let's wait out the Helio and get out of here." I moved as far away from him as I could get in the cavern and tried to forget about it. I would stare at the moss again, instead.

As I rubbed the goosebumps on my arms, I noticed the bracelet that Kailas had made for me was gone. It could be anywhere in the pool, weighed down by the shell. Lava boiled up under my skin, but I promised myself I would control my anger. Anger wasn't going to help. *This is all Nic's fault.*

After what felt like an eternity, the Helio got their share of water and went on their way. We made it back to our things, dressed, and started following Ash's soul path again. Nic trailed behind me this time as I led us through the jungle. I wasn't angry with him, not really. How could I be mad at someone who was risking his life to save Ash? I was upset with myself for getting distracted. I had made a promise to Ash, and I had risked that. Either way, I didn't feel like talking about it. *If I want to be spiritual, I have to learn to let this stuff go,* I reminded myself.

As we hiked, I focused on a walking mind-break to control my thoughts. Mind-breaks were about being present and seeing what was around you. So, I took in the colors of the jungle, the greens and browns. I let my mind go and witnessed what was happening instead of judging it. The forest surrounding me was more than just trees. It was alive. I could feel its presence. The mental abstraction I had viewed it as before disappeared. Tuning into the moment, I connected with One, to everything.

"You seem pissed," Nic said, his words dragging me away from the mind-break. "If I crossed a line, I'm sorry."

"It's fine," I blurted, abandoning the meditation, the connection flickering out. Slowing to a stop, I twisted to look at him.

I was ready to rip into him with my words, but then I saw the look in his eyes. I stereotyped him as a man—tough and emotionless—but of course he had emotions; he was human, after all. He had made himself vulnerable to me and I punched him.

"I just need to focus on Ash right now." I didn't feel like talking about it. "And I lost my bracelet in the waterfall."

After that, we hiked in silence. Other than the waterfall

setback, we were making good time. We hadn't encountered any of the same landmarks, so I must have chosen the correct path at the crossroads.

We had hiked another ten minutes when we heard voices in the forest. Instinctively, we took cover behind a tree. With our backs against the bark, we waited. The sound of a machete hacking away at weeds clued me in to who could be coming, but how could it be?

Rocky slashed through the jungle terrain, Amur trailing behind him.

I revealed myself. "Rocky! Amur!" I called out. Rocky held his machete up in striking position.

"Whoa, guys, chill, it's just us," Nic said, his hands in the air.

Rocky lowered the blade.

"Didn't think it took that long to forage fruit," Amur said as she stepped out from behind Rocky. The paint on her cheeks had gotten smudged.

"Are you okay?" I asked.

"River Clan found us," Amur told us.

My eyes searched her for injury. "No."

"They shot their damn arrows at us," Rocky said. "They chased us through the jungle. We hid in a nola, but then one found us. I had to end 'em before he could tell the rest. I tore my neck open." His hand reached for the bandage, which was spotted with fresh blood.

"It's my fault," Nic apologized. "I convinced Bay to leave you behind. I thought you'd be safer at the beach."

"Wasn't your call," Rocky retorted.

"I know."

"If I could've figured out how to use the tech weapons, we'd have been alright," Amur said.

"Tech weapons?" Nic asked.

"Terrance's pack was full of 'em."

"It doesn't matter." Rocky shook his head.

"And, Nic," Amur said as she got close to him and looked at him straight on. "I signed on to document this tracing and even if it kills me, I'm going to get this story. Don't ditch us again."

"Relax," Nic said. "You'll get the story. It's not over."

"The kid didn't enter the form yet?" Rocky asked.

"Not yet," I answered, "but it's happening soon."

"How much farther?" Rocky looked at the path.

"The GPS isn't working, so I'm not exactly sure," I told them.

"You broke it?" Amur asked, striding toward me with her hand out.

I unlatched my satchel, pulled the tracer out, and handed it to her. "It's waterlogged," I told her.

"You took the tracer for a swim?" Amur asked, raising her eyebrow at me. I gritted my teeth. Amur turned the tracer every which way, examining it. "Did you try the projector?"

"I didn't think…"

She pressed something and an aerial view of the jungle projected out before us in holograph form. A green dot indicated where we were, alongside Ash's soul path, and a white dot that represented Ash's new form. We were close, but Ash was closer.

"Man, your brother is in hyper-speed. We're going to have to book it," Amur said, wide-eyed. She switched the holograph off, and the map sucked back into the tracer.

There was no time to waste. We took off in a single file sprint, me in front as the golden path guided me. I was dashing—leaping over rocks, sideswiping between trees, pushing through brush, and breaking through spider webs.

As I focused more deeply on my mission, I thought of Ash. I imagined his face and the innocent, kind nature he emanated. Zoning into the forest, I moved through it effortlessly.

All at once, it was as if the world fell away as I spotted ahead of me the end of Ash's soul path.

The golden dust abruptly ended in the middle of the forest. No obvious form waited for him, but it was there somewhere. Still racing, I reached for the key and held it between my fingers, ready to set him free.

That's when I was tackled from behind.

The person's momentum brought them crashing into me, and I hit the ground hard, my face bashing into a protruding tree root. I managed to turn over and sit up, but she was already standing. I couldn't react in time as she kicked me in the face, and I was flung backward. I lay with my back on the dirt, warm blood dripping down my lip. The Helio woman stood over me, a leg on either side of my body. She had the same crazed look she'd had the first time we fought. The shark-tooth necklace still hung over her cold heart.

"How dare you come back," she growled in Helio.

She raised her foot and stomped on my stomach. I reflexively rolled to my side, protecting myself from more kicks as I waited for air to return to my lungs. A kick came hard at my back. I had to get up. *Get up, Bay. Get up!*

I yanked her leg and her butt slammed on the ground. I enclosed my fist around some dirt and tossed it into her face.

While she was blinded, I pounced to my feet and sprinted in the direction of Ash's soul path. My body screamed at me to stop, but I couldn't stop. I couldn't give up.

While running, I saw Rocky fighting a pair of adult male Helio. I watched as he swung his machete and sliced open the flesh on one of their arms. The other lunged forward, Rocky got him in the throat and the man fell to the ground. *If the*

Helio are here, it must mean Ash's soul will be reborn as one of them. I had no doubt that the pregnant Helio woman was around somewhere with a fetus waiting for a soul.

I was only yards away from the end of Ash's soul path when Shark Tooth caught up to me.

She tackled me from behind, and I landed hard on my chest. My nose radiated with pain as it hit the ground, and I couldn't breathe. She leaped onto my back and pulled my arms down, pressing them into my sides. Next, she knelt on them, crushing them painfully. Grabbing a fistful of my hair, close to my scalp, she used it to lift my head and ram my face into the ground. Blood gushed from my nose.

"Get off me!" I screamed. Ash would be here any second. It was my chance to save him. I had to get up. But I was pinned. I tried to break free, but it was no use. I screamed and screamed. Suddenly, a blast of white energy surged toward us, collided into the Helio woman, and threw her off me.

I pulled my arms up to my chest in a push-up and glanced to the right. Amur was standing fifty feet away, camouflaged in foliage, holding some type of gadget. There was no time to make sense of it. I sprang to my feet and darted for Ash's soul path. I was almost there when I felt it—an arrow coming from the left. I stopped dead in my tracks and it whizzed by my face. It was so close I could hear it. It sank into a tree to the right.

"Bay, duck!"

I dropped to the dirt. A sword swung over my head and lodged into the bark of a tree beside me. A gigantic Helio man with green hair and an unreadable expression held onto the handle, towering over me. He yanked the sword free from the tree. *This is it. I'm about to die*, I thought. *There's no way I can win a fight with him.* Then, miraculously, my feet rose off the ground, and I was floating. Both of us were. He mistakenly let go of his sword, and it drifted away from him, floating out of reach. As we rose higher, we separated farther apart.

Everyone hung in the air. Rocky spun in circles, grasping his machete. Nic hung upside down, not too far from the end of my brother's soul path. The Helio rose into the sky. Arrows and bows hovered among the trees and got lost in the branches. Even fallen limbs and leaves rose from the forest floor. I wondered if this was Amur again, with one of the tech weapons. I willed myself toward Ash's soul path and drifted in its direction.

As I took a fleeting look at the army of Helio surrounding me, I knew I would die. There was no way I could survive this and make it home. But I would free my brother first.

15

Before Ash fell sick with Hackle, I went with him to a weekly ball game for children in Smallholding. They played in a dirt field that had been a backyard long before the war. The yard was empty besides an old concrete shed. The game started by bouncing a kickball off an outer wall of the shed; wherever it landed, the kids took turns kicking it to the goal on the opposite side of the yard. Each kid was limited to one kick. Either they got it into the goal, or they didn't. There was no lone winner: everybody won or everybody lost.

At a glance, it seemed like an easy feat. All they had to do was kick a ball to the goal—no opposing force and no rival team. But, especially at first, the children just couldn't get the ball to the goal. They would fight over whose turn it was, the older kids would try to dominate the younger ones, some cheated by taking second turns, the little ones often wandered off the field and, most of the time, no one could remember who had already taken a turn because they weren't paying attention. Gemma had created the game to foster collaboration and cooperation, but mostly, it taught me the very real struggle in trying to get people to work together.

There was nothing I could say to make the Helio understand that I had to save my brother. If this had happened to one of their own, they almost certainly would have been sympathetic. If I looked like them, maybe they would have opened their ears and their hearts to my situation. If only words were enough.

We were suspended for no longer than a minute when, simultaneously, everything that was hovering in the air dropped. I smacked into the hard ground once again. My face couldn't take much more of a beating. Before I found my feet, I was pulled by my underarm. A gigantic Helio held me so tightly I thought my arm might burst open. He spun me around so the others could see his grip on me.

"*Jawno*," he yelled.

Nic looked over to see me being held captive and froze mid-fight. I couldn't find Rocky or Amur. Everything stopped.

All eyes were on the giant Helio man and me. I wiped my face with the back of my free hand, cleaning the blood from my nose. If I was going to die, I wanted to do it honorably. He shoved me until my back hit a tree. Pointing to another Helio man, he ordered him to grab a rope. The giant, green-haired Helio used it to bind my hands together and then tie me to the trunk.

Nic stepped forward, demanding, "Take me and let her go."

Another Helio man came up behind Nic and grabbed him. I searched for the pregnant woman and spotted her far back in the foliage, without her daughter. The woman stood with a man, presumably the father. That's where Ash would most likely go. But in front of her was Shark Tooth, wearing a cynical smile that told me she wasn't going let me near her.

Behind me, the Helio men were deciding what to do with me. They planned to make an example out of me, discussing whether or not to decapitate me. One of them had the idea to let me live but cut off my hands; that way I could go back to Halcyon and cause fear of the Helio. The giant one wondered what the purpose of the golden light was. I wondered how many others he had killed before.

In no time, they agreed a stoning would do the trick. They took their places. I wanted to be at peace when they did it. I wanted to feel calm when I went through form-death.

The giant Helio stood before me and raised a boulder to the sky. My heart pumped with adrenaline, but I had nowhere to go. Neither flight nor fight were an option. Closing my eyes, I found whatever connection possible.

Then, compulsively, I said, "*Li wanaha lucha para la resta.*" *The golden light is magic* in Helio. The impact didn't come. I opened my eyes to find the rock was stopped inches from my head. The giant man's expression was unreadable without irises, but I knew he was taken aback by my words.

"You understand me?" he asked in his tongue, lowering the stone to his side. "You speak our way?" His eyes shone like a starry universe. His beard was green and trimmed, unlike the others.

"Yes."

"How?"

"I… I learned how,"—my voice trembled, betraying me as I choked back tears.

He loosened his grip on the stone and it fell to the ground. "That is not possible."

"Why not?" I felt like I was messing up the pronunciations.

"Mutants are not capable of it," he said, his face moving close to mine as he examined me. He seemed to be looking at me sincerely, but it was hard to tell.

"Okay." Terror took hold of me and my hands shook.

"Mutants do not care to learn. They do not feel. They kill mercilessly." I couldn't say a word.

"Yet, you are here," he said. His second sentence was nothing but gibberish to me.

"I'm only here to find my brother. He is lost in this forest." It was true, mostly.

"You should not be here. Nor your brother."

"I know."

"Do your people call you something?" Tilting his head, he gently picked up a piece of my hair and then let it fall back into place.

My heart pounded with my terror. "Bay."

"Miluchas," he said, placing a palm on his chest. "Tell me what the golden light is for, Bay."

"It's, um… magic to help find my brother."

"Um magic." He said it as if trying to get his tongue used to saying an unfamiliar word. "How does um magic help find your brother?"

"It leads me to him."

"And you care for your brother?" he asked. "You feel such feelings?"

Taking a step forward, he looked at me deeply, as if trying to decide something. By some means, I felt his presence, his life force—the fact that he was a person like me. He pulled back and his expression softened. *There, see, I'm a person*, I thought.

Miluchas coughed up a mouthful of blood and it sprayed my forehead. His hand went to his chest and he collapsed to his knees before me. He balanced there for a second, and then his face planted on the ground by my feet. Rocky's machete knife stuck out from his back.

"No," I shrieked.

I trembled as I watched Miluchas die. A fight developed around me, but the details eluded me. The world spun off-axis. Some kind of time passed, but I wasn't sure how long. An explosion burst from behind me, rocking the ground and making me deaf. My reflexes kicked in, and I dropped down as ash rained on me. My ears rang loudly.

Run. I willed myself to move. My feet took off, but I was yanked backward. The rope bound me to the tree. I tugged at the line, but it was no use. The forest behind me blazed. I could feel its heat and I choked on the smoke. Rocky materialized and grabbed the handle of the machete. With one sharp tug, he released the blade from Miluchas's spine. He stepped over the corpse, smacked the tree with his blade, and I pulled away. Rocky took my hands into his and worked the knot loose around my wrists. The rope fell to the dirt.

Everything was groundless. I wanted it to stop. My head tingled, and I thought I might faint.

"Bay." Nic ran to me. "You okay?"

I looked into his eyes. No words came to me.

"I think she's in shock," Rocky said. "Get her out of here. I'll take out the last two."

Rocky turned from us and rushed off. He made it about three yards before an arrow pierced his back and he fell to his knees. I didn't see what happened to him after that because Nic maneuvered me behind a tree. Arrows sank into the trunk. Another wave of Helio had found us.

That's when a bright light shot through the jungle at us. It was a bomb of some kind that would explode and kill us any second. It soared by with golden flickers that beamed like the sun. Wait. It wasn't a bomb. It was Ash! All at once, I jolted back into my body.

"Ash." I darted in the direction of the pregnant Helio woman. All I had to do was touch the key to Ash's soul orb before the Helio killed me. I rocketed as fast as my legs could carry me. I reached for my necklace and tugged it hard, ripping it off. Arrows whistled by me on all sides as I clutched the key tightly in my palm. I prayed that none hit me. Not yet.

The crazed Helio woman appeared with an ax that she swung at my face. I slid on the dirt, gliding under the blade on one knee, and then kicked up back to running. Nothing was going to stop me. Ash's orb floated directly beside me now, progressing alongside me at the same speed. We weren't close enough to the pregnant woman to unlock the fail-secure, but we were closing in on her.

Jon was right; Ash's soul orb rocketed fast. I could barely keep pace with it at a full sprint. We were still many yards away from the pregnant woman when Ash's orb slowed and glowed a bright white. I readied my hand with the key. I knew it was time. As I sprinted, I faced the soul orb and it waved like fire.

"I love you," I whispered.

The soul orb changed from golden-yellow to completely bright white. With a tight grip on the key, I stretched it out to the light. Then, just barely, the key touched it. The pod shone a bright sapphire, then a surge of power radiated outward from it. The energy propelled me backward through the air. My back landed on the ground, knocking the air from my lungs. With my cheek in the dirt, I looked up in time to watch Ash's soul orb slow as it approached a plant.

The white light spiraled. With each spiral it shrank, until it vanished into the leaves. The golden path from the tracer faded to nothing. The path and light were gone. The pregnant Helio woman was nowhere in sight. Ash must not have gone into her baby after all—but where did he go? I crawled to the plant and stared at it. No soul had ever been reborn into a plant.

"Do it, Amur. Put up the shield!" Nic's voice boomed throughout the forest.

As I turned to face him, something hit me from behind. I couldn't breathe. Intense pain surged through my shoulder and radiated outward in waves. I ran my fingers along the arrowhead poking out of my chest as blood poured from the wound.

Nic was there now, kneeling beside me. Panic swept across his face as he took in my condition. I was suddenly light-headed.

"I did it," I said weakly. "I freed him."

Nic smiled sympathetically, then looked to Amur. "Amur!"

"I'm trying."

Shifting my eyes to find her, I spotted Amur behind a boulder, holding the silver spherical gadget she had earlier. She twisted the top and smacked a control.

"Damn it. Just work," she screamed at it, giving it another whack.

All at once, a green light shone from its core and surged outward.

"Hell yeah," she rejoiced as the light ballooned around her into a sphere. She rose to her feet and dashed toward us. The sphere moved with her as she stood in the center of it. She knelt beside us, and we entered the bubble. Amur shone a scanner from the gadget into her eyes, Nic's eyes, and then my eyes. I was temporarily blinded by it.

"Is it on?" Nic asked.

My vision returned to me, and the forest faded back in.

"I think so."

The sphere expanded and encircled the three of us evenly. A soaring boulder closed in on us. I shielded myself with my good arm, but it hit the blue bubble instead. We were protected by a force field.

"How long will it last?" Nic asked.

"A day? I don't know; I'm not a science nerd," Amur answered.

"We have a day to get back to Halcyon then," Nic said.

"What about her?" Amur asked, looking down at me.

"Ash," I managed to say through teeth gritted in pain. "He's there." I pointed to the plant.

"The bush?" Amur asked.

"No, look," Nic said, "The egg on the leaf. It's sparkling."

Amur removed a jar from her pack, clipped leaves from the plant, and dropped them in. Nic cradled me in his arms and rose to his feet, with the protective barrier enclosing us. A horde of Helio surrounded us—hurling rocks, shooting arrows, doing whatever they could to penetrate the magical shield. I peered over Nic's shoulder in time to watch an explosion send a rally of them tumbling to the ground. Then it all went black.

16

I didn't think it was possible to feel cold in a dream. Yet I knew I was dreaming, because there was a red light floating before me in the uncut darkness. Even though it shone warmly, it didn't help me to feel calm. More than anything, I was scared. My throat began to smolder until it burned so hot I thought I was breathing fire. Then, all at once, an outside force pulled me from the dark.

A fluorescent light blinded me and I couldn't keep my eyes open for long. Silhouetted, shadowy figures hovered over me. They were speaking, but their voices were muffled and my ears rang. It was as if I were half blind and half deaf. Someone stabbed my arm. I yanked it away and threw my limbs around in fight. But I was being held down. Before I could break free, my blood went cold and I trembled. Then once again, everything went black.

This time, it was a memory.

***

I was five, and a blast had woken me at dawn. I swung my feet off the bed and ran to the window in my nightgown. Barely tall enough to see over the windowsill, I stacked books on the hardwood. Standing on my make-shift stool, I slid the window open and smoke drifted in with the night air. A house was on fire down the street.

The front door slammed. My father ran past my bedroom

and into the bathroom. He turned on the faucet and water rushed into the tub. It was a strange time for a bath, I thought. My stepfather peeked in through the opening and saw that my bed was empty. He scanned the room for me.

He found me on my books. "Big fire, huh?"

"Uh huh."

"Let's have a race: who can get dressed the fastest. Shoes too. Go."

Leaping from my book tower, I dashed to my dresser and threw on a shirt and pants. As I rushed to get my shoes, my mother screamed and I went to the living room to find her.

Mother stood at our front door, facing a guy with a rifle. It was Mr. Hanson, our grumpy old neighbor. My stepfather slipped on his boots and marched over to the door with his untied laces dragging on the ground.

"What do you want?" my stepfather asked firmly.

"You're wrong," Mr. Hanson slurred. "Have you seen the news?"

"You're drunk."

"Have you seen?"

"I've seen. Now, get off my property," my stepfather said.

"You don't get it…" Mr Hanson laughed absurdly. "You were wrong." He lifted the rifle but before he could aim it, my stepfather snatched it out of his hands. Turning the gun around, he smashed the butt into Mr Hanson's forehead and he dropped to the pavement.

***

I woke. My head was too heavy to raise, but at least now I could see. I was in a room, lying in a bed. A woman with a lime-colored pixie cut stood with her back to me, sorting stuff on a table. She slowly turned to face me, and when she saw I was awake, she ran into the hall. On the table were folded blankets and what I assumed was medical equipment. My forearm was sore where a tube was inserted under my skin. I placed my fingers on it.

A tall man with gray hair and a white jacket rushed into the room with the green-haired woman.

"Don't touch that," he said. I removed my hand from the tube. "I know it's uncomfortable, but you have to keep it in for now."

I glanced around. "What's this place?" I tried to sit up, but he put his palm on my shoulder to keep me down. I smacked his hand away.

"You should rest," he said.

"Where am I?"

The man looked at the woman and then back at me. I noticed he held a clipboard. "I'm Dr. Welsh. This is your nurse, Gwen."

"Someone needs to check on my brother. Is he with my mother?"

"What's the last thing you remember, Bay?" Dr. Welsh asked.

That's when everything rushed back to me. Ash was gone. He turned into a soul orb that Dr. Phillip Grayer put a pod on as an experiment. We followed him to the west side of the island. We fought the Helio. I opened the fail-secure. Ash went into a tiny egg.

"My shoulder..." I touched it tenderly, to find it covered with a bandage.

"It was an arrow," Gwen said, "but we've healed you up nicely." She placed her hand on top of mine for reassurance. It was warm and comforting. Dr. Welsh pressed a syringe into the tube in my arm. The pain melted away, and so did the rest of the world.

***

I was about ten years old. My very pregnant mother swept the kitchen floor while I worked on a drawing at the table. We had moved into a new home on an abandoned farm. My baby sibling was on the way, and my stepfather was stressed most of the time.

He worked out in the fields that day, tilling the soil to prepare for sowing seeds. The front door swung open, and I looked up from my drawing. He lowered to the floor and sat right there in the foyer, his shirt covered in dirt and sweat. With a flushed face, he slid off his boots one at a time.

My mother leaned over to him with her big belly. "You okay?" she asked, placing a palm on his forehead.

"I feel like crap," my stepfather muttered, looking like he were about to pass out.

"Hackle?" my mother whispered, thinking I couldn't hear.

"No, it's not that. I'm going to wash up and see that doctor though," he said with a reassuring smile. "Don't worry."

***

My eyes fluttered open and I returned to the hospital bed. My stepfather and pregnant mother were gone. My head was heavy, and my form was stiff. My hand rested on the sheets, and on top of it rested someone else's. Of course, it was his.

"Hey," I whispered. He sat on a chair beside me with his head resting on the mattress, asleep. I jiggled my hand to wake him. "Kailas."

He raised his head and stared at me blankly, then a smile washed over his face when he registered it was me. He rose and I squeezed him as tightly as my shoulder would let me. I had missed him so much. He pulled back and as we locked eyes, he pushed a strand of hair behind my shoulder. "So, did you bring me a souvenir?"

I smiled, stretching my spine. My back cracked and I felt some relief. "The arrow is all yours."

Kailas placed his hand back on mine and settled into his chair. "How are you holding up?" he asked sincerely.

"Hanging in," I said, not wanting to delve into the details.

"You look like hell."

"Gee, thanks." I glanced around the room. "How long have I been here?"

"A week," he said. "You had a blood transfusion, an infection, and severe dehydration."

I ran my tongue along my teeth. It was as dry as a sponge. I cleared my throat, but a cough came out instead. Kailas lifted a cup with a straw to my mouth and I leaned forward to take a sip. When he pulled the cup away, I yanked it back and drank until the cup was empty.

"We're in Halcyon, aren't we?" I asked, relaxing back into my bed.

"What gave it away?"

"Blood transfusion, antibiotics, water... there's only one place that has those things," I replied and rolled my neck. I felt like I hadn't moved in years. Then something occurred to me. "Wait, where's everyone else? Nic, Amur, and Rocky?" But as soon as I said his name, like a blow to the heart, I remembered.

Kailas took in a long breath. "Nic was in the room next door for dehydration and exhaustion. He was released yesterday and is doing fine. Amur is fine and focusing on the documentary, but"—he hung his head low—"I'm sorry, but Rocky…"

"I remember," I whispered, trying not to replay his death in my mind. He was a skilled Masculine and good person, and what happened to him was sickening. Then I thought of Jon.

"Did Jon and Terrance make it to Halcyon?"

Kailas rubbed his neck. "A day before you."

"Is Jon okay?"

"The doctor gave him the anti-venom in time, but the tourniquet caused some problems. They had to amputate Jon's leg above the knee. They transferred him to Verve, for physical therapy and rehab."

He had to live the rest of his life as an amputee—because of me.

"What about Terrance?"

"Roth escorted him and Jon to Verve. Terrance is his support person. He's fine, if that's what you're asking."

"I thought a behemoth got them." I could see the behemoth again as if it were there, with its paws on Rocky's chest. I smelled the rusty stench of fresh blood—Rocky's blood, Miluchas's blood, my blood. There was so much blood.

"I wish I'd gone with you," Kailas said. "I hate that I wasn't there."

I shut my eyes hard and then reopened them to reorient myself. "I know." I wasn't sure what else to say because I was glad to have spared him.

"If I knew you were going to end up in Helio territory, I would have stayed with you. I would've been there. I would've gotten Brutus to watch your mother. I should've gotten Brutus. I've thought about that every day. I could've gotten him."

"It was supposed to be a short walk down the road. Don't beat yourself up about it. I'm fine. You're fine. Who knows, maybe the Helio would've killed you if you came." We both smiled, but neither of us were in a joking mood.

"You lost your bracelet, didn't you?"

I looked at him somberly. "I'm sorry."

"I'm just glad I didn't lose *you*." He sat back and sighed. "Your mother is fine, too, by the way."

I had put her out of my mind, again. "Where is she?" I asked, pulling at my hospital gown.

"In the lab. You'll see her soon."

I stretched my legs out through the covers. I took in a breath to speak, but all that escaped me was air. There was so much I wanted to tell him, but the words wouldn't come. I couldn't handle talking about it yet, not without breaking down.

"They almost killed you," Kailas said.

I looked to him. His eyes were glossy. "Almost," I whispered. Then I thought about it: *Why didn't they kill me?*

"How did I get to Halcyon?"

His eyes shifted around the room, and he bit his lip as he mulled something over in his head. "Nic and Amur got you here."

I shook my head. "How?"

"You'll see." He sighed. "Everyone else has seen."

"What are you talking about?"

"Amur's documentary premiered today. Everyone in Halcyon saw what happened. The town can't wait to meet the famous Bay Lilly."

17

The arrow wound was itchy. I kept the bandage on because I was afraid it would be gross and I would faint if I looked at it. Kailas went to find my mother, leaving me alone in the hospital room. I tried shifting my weight to sit up, but any time I put pressure on my left side, I felt acute pain in my shoulder. The rest of my form was sore, as if I were one big bruise. I was weak and tired. Panic surged through me. *What if I never feel strong again*? Before my mind took off with these thoughts, I took a breath and reminded myself that this was temporary. I *would* feel healthy again.

"Hey," I heard someone say. I looked up to find Nic standing in the doorway. He wore workout clothes with a bag slung over his shoulder. He was thinner than the last time I saw him. Overall, though, he seemed all right.

"Hey." I found myself running my fingers through my hair, searching for mats. The nurse must have washed and brushed it because, to my surprise, it was clean and soft.

"How're you feeling?" he asked from the entrance.

I felt awful, but how could I tell that to the person who had saved my life? "Oh, um, okay," I said clumsily. "How are you?"

"Great."

We had a million things we could have talked about but we both went silent. He stepped into the room and approached the side of my bed and settled into the chair Kailas was in earlier.

"I heard about—" I began, wanting to thank him for what he had done, but he interrupted.

"I brought you something." He swung his bag onto his lap, reached into the opening, and then, with care, he pulled a glass jar from it. The jar was full of thin, green leaves. They were familiar, but it took me a while to place them.

"Ash," I whispered. For the first time since I woke, I thought of him.

"I told you you'd save him in the nick of time."

I thought back to that morning on the beach; it felt like yesterday and also a hundred years ago. I sat straighter, dealing with the pain in my shoulder, to take the container into my hands, holding it before my eyes. As carefully as I could, I held the glass still and peered through.

"Where's the egg?" I asked.

"You were asleep for a while. It hatched."

"Oh," I said, trying to catch up. "So, what is he? A lizard? I mean, I've never seen an egg so tiny." And then I saw him: an itty bitty, multi-colored caterpillar. It was mostly yellow with black, pink, and white markings. It had long hairs poking out of its sides in spikes. I often found them on the weeds on our farm.

"A caterpillar," Nic told me. "The lab is going insane over it." And then, as if he realized something, he added, "We've been keeping him safe, though, don't worry. Phillip won't lay a finger on him; he's gone."

"Gone?"

"They banned him from the lab and forced him to choose a new passion. He got so angry over it that he left Halcyon altogether. We think he joined a non-alliance village."

All I knew for sure was that I was pleased to never have to see that man again.

"Anyway, the science crew is curious about Ash. They're trying to figure this out."

"Because no one has ever reincarnated into an insect before," I said, realizing what he meant.

"This complicates everything. A lot of people are advocating for a law to protect insects…" I knew Nic was talking, but I tuned him out and tried to recognize my brother's soul in the caterpillar. He was a caterpillar? It felt impossible that this was him. My head throbbed and I felt a little queasy.

"They're calling him Brotherfly," Nic said.

What a silly name. "Who's calling him that?"

"Everyone. Amur's documentary was a hit. The tickets for the ceremony are already sold out," he said, scratching his chin. "Mother Quinn will be there to reunite Ash with you and your mom. So, this never happened, by the way."

"Ceremony?"

Nic looked at my condition, really seeing me for the first time since he had walked in the room. "How's your shoulder?"

"Fine. It's my head that bothers me. I just… don't feel right."

"Is it the nightmares?" He shrugged. "I've had a few."

"No," I shook my head. "Maybe."

"They'll pass before the ceremony."

"I'm not going to be in a ceremony. I can barely talk."

"All you have to do is stand there. Minimal talking, I promise," he assured me.

"Why am I feeling like I don't have a choice?"

"Mother Quinn and Amur have already planned out the Brotherfly Ceremony. They say it will be a successful soul tracing if the audience feels connected to Ash as a caterpillar… That they'll feel invested to attend the second ceremony."

"*Second* ceremony?"

That's when Kailas and my mother came through the door. My mother ran to me and took hold of me, squeezing me tight. The jar pressed against my chest, and I groaned as I pushed her back with my good arm.

"My shoulder, Mom."

"Sorry," she said, pulling away from me. "I'm just so relieved you're all right. I couldn't watch the documentary. I'm sure you've been through hell." She looked at the jar in my hands. "You've got Ash… they showed him to you already?" She lowered herself to my cheek and kissed me there. "Thank you." She grabbed the jar with caterpillar Ash inside it and headed out.

Kailas approached the opposite side of the bed of Nic.

I looked at Kailas. "She seems okay."

"They gave her anxiety medication and therapy, and she's acting… kind of like a functional person."

"Good."

Kailas looked at Nic, and they exchanged glances. "What are you doing here? Don't you have somewhere to be?" Kailas asked him.

"I'm just checking on Bay. She and I have been through a lot *together* and we got to know each other pretty well in the jungle."

"Thanks, but I got it from here. You can go."

"It's okay, he can stay," I said.

"It's fine. He's right, I have somewhere to be," Nic said. He rose to his feet and walked to the door. "See you later, Bay."

After Nic left, I glared at Kailas. "That was rude."

"Sorry." He bit his lip. "I'll be nicer next time."

"What's the problem?"

"Nothing, forget it. Get some rest. I'll sit with you."

I was too tired to press the issue. "Okay," I said, feeling my eyes grow heavy.

Kailas sat in the chair beside me and held onto my hand as I drifted off to sleep.

***

The following days passed in a blur. The healing of my shoulder was slow. I guessed having an arrow penetrate your form wasn't a rapid-healing injury. I had trouble, at first, even wanting to use my left arm for *anything*. Nurses came in several times a day and did physical therapy with me. I asked if Gemma could come to Halcyon for spiritual therapy, but they declined. They said I was allowed two visitors: Kailas and my mother. They offered one of their therapists, but I only wanted Gemma.

My brother's new form grew quickly. He ate through every leaf Amur snipped from the plant, and someone had to go find another one for him. The caterpillar shed his skin and got bigger each day.

Technically, I wasn't supposed to be reunited with him until the ceremony. I think Nic broke some major rules when he brought him to me. And, since then, I got to see him regularly. Some part of me knew Ash was in there, but it was outlandish to look at the caterpillar and think of my brother. When I thought of Ash, I saw a freckle-nosed, brown-eyed, golden-blond-haired little boy.

The Officials forbade me from leaving the hospital until after the ceremony. No one bothered to elaborate to me on why that rule existed, though I had the feeling it had something to with a big *reveal* they didn't want to spoil. I also wasn't allowed to watch the documentary. They planned to play it during the ceremony, and they wanted it to be a surprise, whatever that meant. I had lived through the ordeal, so why would any of it surprise me?

Kailas and Nic visited me several times, separately, bringing me activities to do and books to read. We talked a little, but mostly I wanted to be alone. I processed best when I was alone.

There were no windows in my hospital room, which made me crave sunlight and fresh air more than I ever had in my life. I didn't realize how difficult it was to connect to One without nature or sunshine. Being held in the hospital gave me a new appreciation for my freedom to be able to roam outside.

Three times a day, a nice lady brought me food on a tray. There were mushy white squares, hard ovals, and every once in a while, something familiar like broccoli or strawberries. I ate everything because I had to. I had lost a lot of weight that I needed to put back on before I got back to Smallholding.

18

When the day of the Brotherfly Ceremony arrived, I had healed enough to get out of bed without pain. A young cosmetologist named Frankie met me in the early morning. She laid a custom-made and bespoke dress out on my hospital bed for me to wear. Tiny white gems shimmered on a tan material with green lace. I didn't know what the fabric was called; all I knew was that it was soft to the touch. I pulled the dress over my head and shimmied the material down my body. My shoulder was tender as I worked the strap on, but the cut of the garment concealed the wound. I wondered if that was on purpose.

Frankie had me sit on a chair across from her, and then she applied makeup. She was bigger than me, almost double my size, and taller. She had face paint like Amur's; bright orange and pink stripes along her cheeks. Her hair was dark brown, pulled back in a ponytail. She wore a tight white jumpsuit with heeled white boots. I studied her because she was the first Halcyon I had seen since I arrived besides the doctors and science crew who were always in uniform.

She had me close my eyes as she gently brushed something on them. Next, it was my face and cheeks. Last, she did something with my hair where front pieces were braided around the crown of my head. They met in the back and connected. She opened up a little basket and pulled out tiny lavender flowers, which she tenderly tucked down my braid. I immediately thought of Ash.

It was relaxing to be pampered. I couldn't remember the last time I had been taken care of like that. Frankie didn't speak the entire time she worked on me. Then, abruptly, she stood from her chair and collected her things. Turning to face me, she smiled and said, "You look beautiful." Then she opened the door and left.

As soon as she exited, another person was standing in the hall. It was Kailas. He walked through the door with a sandwich in his hands, it made it halfway to his mouth before he froze in place, staring at me.

"Wow, I expected you to still look half dead," he said, then took a bite of his sandwich.

I gave him a hard nudge with my good arm. "Shut up."

"Seriously," he said, chewing noisily. Once he swallowed, he finished his sentence. "You look, well—have you seen yourself?"

I shook my head. He turned around and grabbed the door, pulling it shut. Hanging on the back of the door was a full-length mirror. My form fell into the frame, and at first I thought it was someone else. It didn't look like me. This person was sparkling and pristine—no muddy jeans and matted locks. My hair was goddess-like as it waved out long. The braid and flowers gave me a naturally beautiful look. As a farm girl, I had never worn anything like it.

"Let's just say that you clean up well."

I gave him a look. "Thanks, but I don't know. Why not just go out there looking the way I normally do?"

He put his sandwich on the table and came right up to me. He took my hands into his and gazed into my eyes.

"What is it?" I whispered.

He exhaled. His eyes fell to the floor for a second, and then they came back to me. "I want to ask you something, but there's never a good time."

My eyes narrowed. "Ask me now."

"I want it to be a certain way, though," he grumbled.

"Why would—"

There was a knock at the door. A short man I hadn't seen before entered the room. He wore all white, like Frankie. His face paint was different, though; entirely gold.

"Bay, you're taking the stage in ten." He held out the jar with caterpillar Ash in it. I took it. "They want you to be the one to introduce Ash to the crowd," he told me.

"Aren't we supposed to be reunited in front of everyone?"

"New plan. Mother Quinn feels that's inauthentic now that she knows you've already seen him." Busted. "I'll be back in five to bring you to the stage. Be ready," he said and disappeared in the same manner in which he had appeared.

I inspected caterpillar Ash in the jar. He was even bigger than earlier that day.

"I'll see you out there," Kailas said, pulling me in for a hug.

"You were about to ask me something," I said.

We pulled away from each other and he gently smiled and shook his head. "Later."

"The only time is now," I said, repeating one of Gemma's mantras.

"Don't get all spiritual on me," he said as he walked backward toward the door, and then he was gone.

<h1 style="text-align:center">19</h1>

I sat on the hospital bed, cross-legged, a tiny, multi-colored caterpillar crawling across the top of my hand. His little suction-cup-like legs tickled my skin as he moved. His antennas wiggled about.

"We're about to meet an entire crowd of people," I whispered to the alien-looking thing. "I'm kind of nervous. I'm not sure what to expect. Everything is different here."

He paid no attention to me.

"I miss you, but I try not to think about it because it hurts." A tear welled up in my eye. "I miss your smile and your laugh. I miss playing with you in the fields. I even miss taking care of you. You were kind and funny and smart. Now, you're a wrinkly, hairy blob." The last sentence made me chuckle, but only for a second.

"Everyone said it would be easier having you here in your new form, but it's harder for me. It's harder to mourn you this way. You're here, but you're not. And everyone expects me to be happy. Which I am, don't get me wrong. I'm happy your soul isn't lost. It's everything I wanted. It's just... this is hard."

There was a knock on the wall, and the short man with the gold paint poked his head through the doorway.

"We're ready for you," he said urgently.

I carefully lowered caterpillar Ash into the jar, and he climbed onto a leaf. I secured the lid and set it in my bag. I slung the bag over my good shoulder and rose to my feet. The man and I headed down the hall. We entered a sunlit room with huge, curtain-less windows. It was the farthest I had been from my hospital bed since I came to Halcyon. It was over a week since I had seen the sun, and the light burned my eyes.

We approached an exit door and when the man swung it open, a revitalizing breeze blew in. The outside air was cool and refreshing. Finally, we walked out to a clear day. The warmth of the sun on my skin was comforting and I instantly felt better. The bright blue sky above me felt like a grand prize. It's interesting what being deprived of these simple things can do to a person's wellbeing.

The comfort that had swelled inside me shrank as I looked at the town around me. The land under my feet was hard gray cement. Smallholding only had concrete at the village center, but Halcyon had it all over the place. Tall buildings stood every which way I looked, blocking my view of whatever else the place had to offer.

The man ushered me to keep following him, so I did. He led me to the rear entrance of another building. It was much smaller than the hospital. We entered through the back door, crossed through a hall, and stepped into a large foyer near the front entrance of the building. Standing there, by the door, a crowd of people with unfamiliar faces congregated.

We approached the back of a tall woman with short, bluntly cut orange hair. She wore an off-white ensemble as well as a matching cape, with a crimson lining, draped over her shoulders. She was speaking with someone, and the short man gently tapped her on the shoulder. She glanced at the man and then excused herself from the conversation. The short man scurried away as the woman swiveled around to face me. It was her energy that I noticed first—it was luminous and alluring. Her smile was wide and welcoming. Her eyes were a piercing light blue. The face paint she wore was subtle; only a white glinting around her eyes and cheekbones. She was maybe mid-thirties.

"Bay Lilly!" she beamed excitedly, embracing me. "Just a tender hug, since you're hurt." She looked into my eyes sympathetically. "How are you, honestly?"

"I'm fine," I said, wondering who she was.

"Wonderful, that's great! I'm *so* glad you're able to keep a positive mindset through these growing experiences."

I smiled uncomfortably. "Thanks."

"How rude of me… I assumed you knew who I was," she hooted, glancing around at the others in the room, holding up a glass of pink liquid. Then her eyes met mine. "I'm Mother Quinn." The leader of Halcyon. The master guru. The most spiritual person on the island.

"I'm so sorry," I said, feeling dim, I bowed, unsure of what to do.

"Oh, don't. I should be bowing to *you* after all you went through. And we don't bow here, we *ataraxy*," she said as she placed her glass on a tray and then put her palms together in front of her face. Sensing she wanted me to mirror her, I did the same with my hands.

"Ataraxy," she said, and I repeated the word. Gemma had taught me about it once; a greeting that meant you wished the other person peace and harmony.

"You look ravishing," Quinn exclaimed. "Look at your hair. My goodness, Frankie did an astonishing job on you. Oh, and that dress. I love it for you."

"Thanks." I smiled nervously.

She looked over my shoulder. "You'll have to excuse me, dear. I have to talk to the woman over there. My son is around here somewhere. I'm sure you two can chat until the ceremony begins. Just ask around for him," she said before rushing away.

Abruptly alone, I stood there with the empty space in front of me. There were about a dozen people gathered in the foyer, chatting while holding tiny plates of food. Most of them wore face paint and neutral-colored clothing, all appearing to be brand new.

That's when a hand reached for my neck. Panic surged through me as I grabbed the wrist with my bad arm and yanked it away from my chin. With my stronger fist, I punched the person in the groin, followed by a hard elbow to the stomach. Miluchas's battered face flashed before my eyes, but then he disappeared. A man lay on the floor, moaning and holding his crotch. A silver tray with little pieces of food was scattered around him.

"Miss Lilly," Quinn exclaimed as she rushed to me. "What in the universe?"

My eyes shifted. I took in the scene around me and realized I had made a ruckus of their hors d'oeuvres. "I'm sorry. I thought…"

"We don't beat up the waiters," she scorned me. "What is it with Smallholding and fighting? We don't allow that sort of behavior here. I'm setting a boundary. I won't allow it."

"It won't happen again. I'm sorry. I don't—"

"It's not the end of the world," Nic's voice came from behind me. He materialized beside me with his hand on my good shoulder. "I'll talk to her."

"Nickel," Quinn said. "Quickly, please."

Nic nodded, and Quinn wandered off with a group of women. I tried not to get my feelings hurt, but Quinn treated me as if I were a hindrance. What was she thinking? That I purposefully tried to beat up the waiter? I knelt to the man, who had stopped his groaning, and helped him pick up bits of food.

"I'm sorry. I thought you were going to choke me." I shook my head. "I know that's crazy. I hope I didn't hurt you."

"I only tapped you on the shoulder to see if you wanted anything to eat, but it's fine, I guess," the waiter said. He took his tray through a door I assumed was the kitchen. I looked to Nic, who was only person left in the room. I had scared the rest of them off.

"You okay?" he asked.

"Physically, yes. Socially? Not so much."

"Did you have a flashback?"

"A what?"

"It happens to me too. It's like everything seems normal and then, suddenly… I'm back in the jungle, being attacked," he said. "You just have to breathe through it. You're safe here."

Before I could speak, Quinn darted from the hall, her heels clicking. She stopped in front of the entrance, paying no attention to us. Then she cleared her throat, straightened her hair, and smiled widely. She tossed the doors open and stepped out into the daylight. A chorus of cheers poured through the opening, and gravity shut the door behind her, muffling the applause.

"What was that?" I asked Nic.

"The ceremony."

Nic and I waited there for a while in silence. I lifted the jar with caterpillar Ash out of my bag and rested it on my lap. I was watching him climb up the glass when the short man appeared, waving us over. I was to go out first. He held the door open for me as I stepped outside into the bright sunlight. Totally blinded, all I could hear were wild cheers. As the world came into focus, I saw a stage before me. In front of the stage stood a crowd of excited Halcyons.

I climbed three steps onto the stage, clutching the jar nervously. Quinn stood at the head of the stage, wearing a giant smile, waving me on. I made my way to her and as we met, she placed her arm around me in a hug and kissed my cheek. We separated and stood side by side as I gazed out at the massive crowd. It was the largest gathering I had ever seen; hundreds of people. The majority of them wore face paint, some in the style of animals: frogs, birds, any animal you can imagine. Others were flowers like lilies, magnolias, or poppies. A teenage girl in the front row caught my eye. Her face was a sunflower. Two blonde braids draped over each of her shoulders.

Above us, and surrounding us, was the most majestic nola tree I had ever seen. It appeared as if twenty trees were encircling us when, actually, each perceived tree was part of the one nola. I made a mental note to explore it after the ceremony was over and the courtyard was empty.

Slowly the cheers faded, and Quinn began to speak into a microphone. "Thank you so much for your outward display of gratitude and kindness," she said, grandiloquently, to the crowd. "Next to me is the strong, brave, and beautiful sister of our Brotherfly, Bay. We all know that she deserves an ataraxy for her endurance and bravery."

Each person in the crowd raised their palms and pressed them together by the tips of their noses. "Ataraxy," their voices echoed. I think they meant for me to feel respected.

"I see you're holding your brother there," Quinn addressed me. "What's it like to know that you saved him?" She held the microphone out to my face.

The previously wild crowd fell so silent that I could have probably heard a cricket if it decided to chirp. Having all the attention on me was agonizing. *What is the perfect thing to say?*

"Good, I guess," I said into the microphone.

"I bet it does. This is the first time the town is getting to see little Ashy. It's exciting for us all."

I got lost in the part where she called him *little Ashy*—as if she knew him personally. I didn't know how to respond, so I simply smiled and held the jar high so everyone could see. A collective, awe-inspired gasp washed over the crowd as they saw my brother climb up the side of the jar in a live video feed displaying behind us.

"Please sit on the couch next to Amur, while I introduce my son," Quinn said, smiling widely at the crowd. I did as she said and found my way to the couch, taking a seat next to Amur. It was the first time I had seen her since our fight with the Helio. She looked good; great, even—with fresh face paint and rested eyes.

"Next up is someone I'm vexed with but also proud of. After going against Official orders to stay behind on the mission, he snuck off in heroic fashion to aid in saving little Ash. He soon became a faithful friend and team leader and eventually saved our dear Bay Lilly by carrying her over ten miles back to Smallholding. Let's show our love and appreciation, with cheers, as we welcome my son, Nickel," Quinn exclaimed.

The crowd applauded wildly, and Nic came bounding onto the stage. Gears in my head turned as I tried to figure out why she had called him her *son*.

I turned to Amur. "*Son?*"

"You didn't know? Quinn is Nic's mom. Like, actual birth mother."

Several things suddenly made sense: why Roth had asked Nic to stay back, why his mother would encourage him to find a passion, why he was able to go on the tracing in the first place.

Quinn and Nic embraced, and then they bantered back and forth for longer than I could stomach. The tone of voice they used, their mannerisms—all of it—was bombastic. The ceremony felt fake. A show. And the audience ate it up.

After their chat, Quinn asked Nic to sit next to me.

Lastly, she introduced my mother, who shuddered at the sight of the audience. With a bashful, red face, she took a seat next to Amur. Quinn then took the jar from me and placed it on a table in the middle of the stage. There was a camera angled at caterpillar Ash and the feed was projected onto a screen that showed him crawling in full zoom.

"This ceremony is going to be the first of its kind. It's going to be a duo-logy. Today, Brotherfly Part One and, in about ten days, Brotherfly Part Two: The Release," Quinn announced.

The screen lit up and the first video was of Ash—highlights from the *Soul Tracing* documentary. It was just him talking in an interview, but the sight of him gripped me. It was as if he were there—as if the video somehow preserved him. I imagined reaching into the screen and pulling him out, but the documentary moved on to the next scene, and just like that he was gone.

We watched my brother's deterioration on the day of his form-death. I veered away, not willing to re-traumatize myself. During Ash's death, you could hear me singing, and as I heard it echo out for all the Halcyons, I felt queasy. That song was for my little brother, not an audience. At least Amur had captured the sunset instead of focusing on him while he died. She leaned closer to me and told me it was poetic.

Next, they showed me noticing the pod and shoving Phillip up against the wall. I was mortified. They must have thought the worst of me—the least spiritual of anyone in the town. Then Amur showed us realizing Ash's soul had changed paths, and the scene cut to us in the van. I guessed that was to protect Roth. It then skipped ahead to me running to free Ash's soul from the pod. I saw myself as I, from Amur's perspective, unlocked the fail-secure, and my brother's soul went free. The arrow pierced my shoulder. The screen went blank, and then a visual of Nic carrying me unconscious appeared. I grew hot with embarrassment. I looked terrible, but worse, he sat directly beside me, and I had yet to thank him for what he had done.

The documentary showed Nic as he struggled to carry me.

The Helio followed us, screaming, attacking the force field. I couldn't peel my eyes away as I watched Nic fall to his knees with exhaustion, rise back up, reposition my body, and keep walking. I looked awful. Pale, bloody, dirty, and mostly dead. Blood was caked around the arrow sticking out of me.

At some point, Nic laid me on the forest floor, and Amur cleaned my wound with hydrogen peroxide from the first aid kit. They disagreed on whether or not they should pull the arrow out of my shoulder. In the end, they decided it might be keeping me from bleeding to death. They snapped the fletching off, making it more comfortable for Nic to carry me. To my surprise, I seemed to wake a couple times, murmur unintelligible things, and then pass out again. I had no memory of that.

The Helio finally stopped harassing us after mile nine. Nic then gathered together branches and strong leaves to makeshift a gurney he could drag me on. He laid me in a fetal position on the gurney and hauled me through the jungle. The moment we reached Smallholding, he collapsed to his knees and passed out. Kailas rushed us to Halcyon, where they admitted us to the hospital. Text illuminated the screen: *In ataraxy of Rocky Roland.* Then the screen cut off and returned to hairy caterpillar Ash crawling around and chomping on leaves.

I wanted to look at Nic and say something, but I had no idea where to start. Anyway, everyone was watching. Quinn strode up to me with her microphone and took a seat on the couch between Amur and me. She looked at Nic and I seriously.

"How did it feel to watch that?" she asked solemnly. The crowd waited for my answer.

"I…" I said into the microphone, my voice booming through the speakers. "I guess I wish I would have seen that in private, so I had time to process it."

Nic grinned as if I had said something hilarious.

"I appreciate your authenticity. What about you, Nic? What did you think watching that?" Quinn asked, handing him the microphone.

Nic scratched his chin and wrinkled his brow. "If I'm being honest, I was thinking"—he smiled wryly—"what a great job Amur did at making the documentary. Let's give it up for Amur, everyone."

He applauded loudly, and the audience followed his lead and cheered. Quinn wrenched the microphone out of Nic's hands and shot to standing. Something told me that this wasn't going according to *her* plan. She approached Amur and asked if she wanted to address the audience.

"I just want to say that I'm thrilled to be documenting our history. Once upon a time, we recorded history on walls and stone, and then in books, and now we're doing it in videos. Imagine how awesome it will be for our future generations to *watch* history unfold instead of having to read about it. I'm honored to do this work. I'm humbled that you like it," Amur said with an ataraxy, and the crowd praised her.

The audience then had an opportunity to ask questions about my brother. I found this triggering, and I excused myself from answering. They already knew I was horribly unspiritual, so what was the point in forcing myself to smile and talk about Ash? My mother's new anti-anxiety medication and therapy had worked wonders because she was able to take the lead from me. I found myself zoning out and dissociating from the ceremony.

During this time, I looked off and spotted Kailas in a reserved section in the audience. Even just seeing his face made me feel better. I shot him a smile, and he returned it with an eye roll. Behind him, a man caught my attention, an olive-skinned elder dressed in all black. Everyone else was dressed in light colors, so he stood out most amongst the crowd. We made direct eye contact, and I quickly gazed away.

After an eternity of torture, the ceremony was finally over. I couldn't wait to go back to the hospital and decompress. But then Quinn had one last announcement.

"I know this news will be heavy and hard to accept," she announced, "but we all must trust in my gift to make these tough decisions. With the recent killing of a Halcyon"—she must have meant Rocky—"I was pressed to make my hardest decision yet… to set a boundary with the River Clan." The energy of the crowd changed from its previous peaceful ambiance to cumbersome clamors and angry outbursts.

I turned to Amur. "Set a boundary? What does that mean?" I asked.

"Nothing," she said, though her eyes told another story.

A loud argument broke out in the crowd and a pair of Masculines pushed through the mob to bind the wrists of two men who had escalated into a fist fight.

"Amur," I pressed.

She exhaled and then looked me in the eye. "It means *war*. She's planning on waging war with the River Clan."

20

Back in my hotel room, I tried to process what I had heard, but my mind was going a mile a minute. *Wage war on the Helio? Is Quinn insane?* War was bloody and sick and horrible. I couldn't stand to hold it in my memory; I never wanted to experience it again. I paced the room, thinking of what terrors my future might hold and trying to come up with the perfect words to persuade Quinn to change her mind. Anxiety swirled in my stomach. I needed some air before I went full mom-panic-mode.

When I exited the hospital, it was nearing sunset. The evening air was chilly and helped me to calm down. The air was welcome in my lungs as I walked the streets and cleared my head. Just as I was feeling better, I came across a courtyard—cement covered the ground, except for a circle of grass in the middle. In the center of the lawn sat a statue of an angel. Beyond the statue, and adjacent to me, was a building with a sign above the entryway that read *Science*.

Intrigued, I wandered over to the building. Standing before the brown door, I twisted the knob and pulled it open. I stepped through the threshold and clicked the door shut behind me. The decor of the building reminded me of the hospital. The lighting was drab, and the walls were bare. As I made my way down the hall, a crash came from one of the rooms.

I walked cautiously to the open door and spied inside. A man sat on a stool, hunched over a countertop. He bent over and picked up paper clips that had spilled on the floor and placed them back into their box. I caught his side profile and recognized him. It was Sterling.

I decided to clear my throat to get his attention.

He turned and immediately recognized me.

"Bay. Come in," he said as he tossed the box of paper clips on the counter. I stepped through the door, and he motioned for me to take a seat on a swivel stool next to him. He peeled something from his temples and I realized what it was when I spotted the Mind Writer on the table.

"Sorry I didn't make it to the ceremony," he said, slipping the temple strips into a pocket on the device.

"Oh, don't apologize. You didn't need to be there. I wished I wasn't."

He laughed lightly. "Fair enough," he said. "Did you come to the lab looking for me?"

"No, actually, I was wandering around and ended up here."

He shut a book, straightened up his things, and returned his attention to me. "You know, you were kind of reckless with the tracer for it being a famous one-of-a-kind device."

It was interesting that, of all the things he could have said to me, he chose to say that. "I was focused on my brother," I explained.

"It's fine, we fixed it. Terrance and Jon got their asses handed to them, though, for letting you use it."

"As if they needed more problems." I lowered my head.

Sterling swiveled in his chair, glanced around the room, and then looked back at me. "It's kinda crazy," he said, "the way we met in the forest."

"I've been wondering what happened to you—after Kailas dropped you and Blue off."

"Oh, nothing." He shrugged. "We told the Masculines we went on a romantic getaway. They gave us a slap on the wrist."

"Where's Blue?"

"Don't know. Is it after six? She might be walking the beach."

"But she's fine? I haven't seen her at all."

"Oh, yeah, she's great."

It went dead silent in the lab, and I started to think up ways I could excuse myself from the room.

"Have you heard of False Coincidence Theory?" Sterling asked, keeping me in the conversation.

I tried to recall what Gemma had taught me on the subject. "Something like... nothing is a coincidence. Everything happens for a reason."

"Right. So, my next question is: what led you to come in here?"

I inhaled, because I knew my answer would be long-winded. "Well, I left my hospital room to get some air because I was sort of freaking out. As I was walking, I saw this was a science building and thought maybe I could get some answers to the thousands of questions that keep me up at night."

Sterling readjusted himself on his stool. "What answers are you looking for?"

"You know, the usual, I guess—am I alone? Am I crazy? Is everyone crazy?"

"No, yes, and yes."

I smiled awkwardly. I was too dressed up for this conversation.

"I'm sorry to hear of everything you went through with your brother. First him catching the virus, then his death, and Grayer's experiment. It's a lot."

"Virus? You mean curse?"

"Oh, yeah, sorry... curse."

I studied him carefully—his thick-framed glasses, love for science, his broad shoulders, and combat skills. He was a walking oxymoron.

"You know, I never pegged you as a scientist," I told him.

"Because I'm not a skinny, glasses-wearing nerd?"

"Well, the…" I pointed to his glasses.

"One out of three." He looked down at his notes. "Want to hear my theory on the after life?"

"Your theory?" There were no *theories*, we knew what happened after death.

"I'm dubbing it *Belief Theory*."

I adjusted my dress. "Okay, tell me about Belief Theory."

"It's the idea that what happens to our soul at death is determined by our beliefs. So, if we believe we reincarnate, we reincarnate. If we believe we ascend to another dimension, we ascend to another dimension. If we believe we go to a terrible place, we—"

"Go to a terrible place?"

"You got it." He pointed at me. "This can explain why people who have briefly died recount different experiences. It also gives us a logical reason for bounce behavior."

I stared at him incredulously. Human souls reincarnated at death. It was fact. Everyone knew that. No spiritual person questioned it—certainly not someone as aware as Sterling.

"But reincarnation has been proven," I uttered, "by the soul tracer."

He slightly tilted his head. "Has it, though?"

"Of course," I said, but then realized I was talking to an expert in the field. "I mean, *it has*, right?"

"Maybe, but there are still other possibilities. Endless possibilities," he thought out loud.

My head was starting to throb, and I wanted to leave, but

also, I couldn't stop talking. "You said something about *bounce behavior*?"

"Yeah... the technicians would manifest a soul in orb form—like Ash's—but then, instead of leading to another form, it would shoot into the sky, completely untraceable." He swiveled in his chair and leaned in closer to me to whisper, "Instead of investigating *why* they were bouncing, they wrote them off as failed attempts at tracing."

My heart sped up. "Did anyone figure out why?"

"Some of us in the current scientific community believe we know why. Only Quinn has forbidden us from ever testing the theory because it would create conflict—"

"And conflict is against the peace laws."

"I doubt Belief Theory will ever see the light of day."

This was unbelievable. "If bounce behavior has been hidden from us, how do we know what's true?"

"And how do we know if the soul tracer actually traces souls?" Sterling asked.

"I guess we don't," was all I thought to say. Then I considered my brother. "What about Ash? He didn't have bounce behavior."

"Actually, Bay, forget about my rambling. You saved your brother. Don't listen to my crazy theories."

He wasn't convincing. "I'll come up with worse ideas in my head. You might as well tell me what you're not telling me."

He clicked his tongue. "It's just this idea that *soul* and *energy* might be two separate entities. What we're tracing with the soul tracer may be energy, not the soul." My face fell, and he hurried to comfort me. "It's a theory that no one has been able to prove."

It was a lot to take in, but I didn't want to be comforted, I wanted the truth. "Basically, we still don't know what happens at form-death," I said.

Sterling nodded. "I'm starting to think our simple human brains don't have the capacity to understand it."

***

I exited the science building more confused than when I walked in. The irony was that I went in there for answers and left with only more questions. On my way out, I stopped and retrieved Ash, or just some random caterpillar that wasn't him. I didn't know what to believe anymore.

I decided not to over-think it. I brought him to a nearby bench under the nola tree. It was quiet there. The crowd from the ceremony had dissipated. I was alone.

Pulling off the lid, I searched for the caterpillar but couldn't find him. I pushed leaves aside with my fingertips, but he wasn't there. For a second, panic surged through me, but then I spotted something dangling from the lid. It looked like a tiny green sack—a chrysalis. Ash had bravely surrendered his caterpillar form to the unknowns of metamorphosis and was in the process of transforming into a butterfly.

The sun had set, and the stars revealed themselves in the sky. I carefully put the lid back on and then lay my head on the bench, being tender with my shoulder. I gazed at the twinkling stars through the branches of the nola tree. While I probably should have felt anguish at what Sterling had told me about the afterlife, I didn't. I was, somehow, okay with embracing the unknown, even if it was scary. If my brother could brave the unknown twice, then I was sure I could too.

A lot of unknowns were ahead of me: living in Halcyon, a second ceremony, Quinn declaring war on the Helio. Life would be unpredictable for a while but, at that moment, I chose to surrender. I chose to relax into it. I looked at the gleaming stars and marveled at the universe—its vastness, its allure, its mystery. I speculated on how we got here, where we were going, and our purpose in between.

With a wild feeling of awe, I whispered, "I wonder what happens next."

PART III

COALESCENCE

21

The jar holding Ash's chrysalis sat on my chest as I lay flat on the park bench. I gripped the sides of the glass to keep it from sliding off. For a long while, I gazed serenely at the stars, basking in the mysteries of life. The night edged on, and the temperature dropped. Goosebumps sprouted on my arms. I was still in the dress from the ceremony, and my hair was still braided into a crown around my head. Neither of those things were comfortable.

More than anything, I was dying to take a shower. A physical, emotional, and spiritual cleansing, so I could rid myself of the trauma of my brother's death, the horrible violence during the soul tracing, being struck with an arrow, and living in Halcyon away from everything familiar. I wanted to wash it all off. I was ready for it to be over. I longed to go home and sleep until I felt like myself again.

"Bay?" a voice called out.

I shifted my head to the side and spotted a teenage girl standing a few feet away. "Is that you?" I carefully moved to a seated position and rested the jar in my lap. I studied the girl, trying to figure out if I somehow knew her. She had medium-length brown hair, which she wore loose around her shoulders. Her face paint was done in blues in the shape of an ocean wave around her eyes. She wore an off-white cotton dress. The only thing I recognized about her was that she was a Halcyon.

"I'm sorry, have we met?" I asked tentatively.

"You're Bay Lilly. *The* Bay Lilly from the documentary. I can't believe you're here. You're my hero. I loved when you punched Dr. Grayer in the face. I've always secretly wanted to do that. Oh, and the part when you sang little Ashy a song as he moved on. That was *so* authentic. And, oh my goddess, your hair is to die for. You have to tell me how you got it to grow so long," the girl said in what seemed like a single breath.

I had no idea which part to respond to or what was even happening.

"Thanks," I uttered.

"I'm Shellsea," she said as she sat on the bench beside me. "What are you doing? Looking at the stars?"

"It helps me get perspective on things."

"My friend told me she saw something shoot across the night sky last week. She thinks it was a rocket from the mainland heading to other planets. How crazy is that? But I mean, that would have to mean civilization survived over there, *and* are building rockets. That's just nuts." She looked down at the jar. "Oh, my universe. Is that Ash?" She reached for it. "Can I hold him?"

I reflexively shielded the jar and pulled it closer to my stomach.

"No," I responded. It was rude, but I didn't care. I would never forgive myself if I let this girl hold my brother and something bad happened to him.

"Oh, you're protecting him," she said. "You're such a good sister. I wish I had a sister as awesome as you. Have you gotten your face painted yet?"

I shook my head.

"You just gotta. Go put Ash away and come with me."

I found myself being led to the science building by Shellsea. She waited outside as I returned my brother to the lab.

As I handed chrysalis Ash over to the scientist on duty, he scolded me and then informed me about the proper protocol. I wasn't supposed to have taken him without permission. There was a logout sheet and everything.

Once I told him that Ash had gone into a chrysalis, he freaked out and decided there was to be a Masculine guarding the chrysalis at all times. He went on to say that the jar shouldn't be moved or carried around any longer. The chrysalis was too delicate. Even though I wanted the best protection for my brother, the extra security irritated me. I mean, I didn't want random curious Halcyons, like Shellsea, wandering into the lab and taking the jar. However, the person who had nearly died saving him should have special privileges.

When I exited the science building, Shellsea was still there, eagerly waiting for me.

"I can't believe I'm going to be hanging out with Bay Lilly. This is so fire. You're the second most interesting person on the island. Sorry, first will always be the guru queen herself, Mother Quinn. She has all the answers. Ya know? But I'm still so excited you're here. I just love you. Let's get your face painted."

For the first time, I saw Halcyon from the inside, rather than from up in Smallholding. The citizens of Halcyon mostly lived on Main Street. I was vaguely familiar with it as I had been there when I was little. It was where the local shops were. Even if my memories had been crystal clear, it still would have been hard to recognize. They had converted the store fronts into apartments, and Halcyons resided in them. Tents were sporadically pitched on the street for others not fortunate enough to have a home.

"Do people still drive cars?" I asked, seeing that tents covered the road.

"Oh, no way, we walk barefoot everywhere. But we do have Masculine vans."

Deciding that I wanted to finally pick a Halcyon's brain, I went for it. "So, what's a typical day like for you?"

We passed by a group of people chatting on the street. "Let's see. I wake up in the morning. I guess I didn't need to say that part, because of course I wake up. Anyway, first I shower, and then I put on my face paint. Sometimes I get it done by Matilda, but it gets expensive, so not often. And then I get dressed. I do a morning meditation, but authentically speaking, I've been distracted lately and missed some days.

"After that, I head to my spiritual guide and we do a lesson. I go to my passion. Then it's dinner time and I eat at the cafeteria. Afterward, depending on how much *zaram* I have, I go for a beach walk. Lately, that's only been about once a week. Sometimes I visit my dad."

Shellsea pulled a small, thick disk out of her pocket.

"I can show you my dad. I have a message from him." She swiped her finger over the disk and an older man's face appeared above it as a holograph. The man starting speaking, but then Shellsea paused it. "That's him. He sent me here with my aunt for a better life. I was just a little kid."

"Oh." I wasn't sure why she was telling me all of this. "He seems nice."

Shellsea turned the holograph off and slipped it back into her pocket.

It occurred to me that I couldn't recall the conscious moment when I'd chosen to go with her. Why was I walking with her? She entered one of the shop doors and I followed. We walked into a dimly lit room with twinkling, whitish lights hung on the walls. A woman in a bathrobe sat at a table, flipping through a pile of papers.

"I've been expecting you," she said with a breathy, aged voice. Her face held many wrinkles, and her hair was long and gray. Curiously, she wasn't wearing face paint.

"You say that to everyone, Matilda." Shellsea responded lightheartedly. "I brought Bay from the documentary. I was hoping you could do her paint."

Matilda eyed me up. "Let's go into the light of the moons. That's where I do my best work." She rose from her chair and headed for the rear of the building. We followed her through what I assumed was her home.

"Do you moonbathe?" Malta asked me.

I hadn't a clue in the world what she was talking about. "Moonbathe?" I asked.

"You know, like sunbathe, but with moonlight," Shellsea explained.

Walking down the hall, we passed a table lined with fiery wicks in scarlet candle wax. The tiny flames flickered from the breeze we created as we walked by. Next to the candles were miniature statues of wild animals. My eyes caught onto the behemoth-shaped one.

"No, I guess I don't."

"Well, you should. It does wonders for the soul," Matilda told me.

Once we exited the rear door, we were in an enclosed yard with an array of delightful, tall flowers. The moon's light was nowhere near as bright as it was during my trip to the west side. Weeks must have passed since then. Matilda gestured for me to sit in a wire chair in the garden. I hesitantly settled into it.

She hit a switch on the side of the house. A light bulb fastened to the building illuminated the yard. She picked up a medium-sized cardboard box and walked toward me. Sitting in a chair opposite me, she placed the box, filled to the brim with painting supplies, on the ground by her feet.

"Your hands," Matilda said. I held my hands out to her. She flipped them over so she could see my palms. Holding my hands in hers, she closed her eyes for a long moment and took in an extended breath. When she opened her eyes, she studied my palms carefully and then let them fall to my lap.

"Passenger pigeon," Matilda said curtly. She reached into her box and pulled out a paint palette and a brush.

"Passenger pigeon?"

"It is your spirit animal," she explained.

My eyes narrowed. "Haven't heard of it."

"I suppose you wouldn't have; they're not of this time or place," she told me, pouring water from a canteen into a small cup.

"How is it my spirit animal, then?"

"Because *you* are not only of this time and place," she said softly, looking directly into my eyes. "You have a bird's eye view. You're here to carry important messages. Your type was once bountiful, and then later rare. *You*, my dear, have the energy of a passenger pigeon."

She dunked the paintbrush into the water, dabbed it into gray paint, and raised it to my face and paused—staring at me as if I were a blank canvas.

"Close your eyes," she said.

I gently shut my eyelids and surrendered. At the beginning of the day, I never would have guessed I would get my face painted by an eccentric elderly woman that night.

While she worked, I found myself naturally entering a state of mind-break. I was a bird flying through the clouds. My wings soared through the wind as I glided over the mountains. I soaked in the landscape, watching people scurry through the town like ants. Some time had passed when I started to feel like I might fall asleep right there in the chair.

"Finished."

I opened my eyes, and Matilda held a mirror to me. What I saw reflecting was my face, but she had turned it into art. Brushstrokes began at the edges of my eyes and curved upward onto my temples. The color closest to my eye began as gray and then blended into a melon orange and then violet. She dotted on white flecks below my eyes and onto the bridge of my nose. There were also dots on the ends of each brush stroke on my temples. Wings. They were wings.

"It's beautiful," I said, smiling at her. Her eyes gave off nurturing energy, but there was something else there, too; a pain that lay underneath it. "Thank you."

"You're welcome, dear," she said gently. "It's ten zaram."

Again, I hadn't a clue what she was talking about. "Zaram?"

"I'll spot her," Shellsea said and made a fist, revealing a ring with the Halcyon emblem engraved on it.

Matilda held out a long necklace dangling from her neck that had the same engraving. They moved the emblems together and, for a second, as they touched, a pulsating green light appeared and then vanished. And that was it; our time with Matilda was over. After Shellsea told me how wonderful I looked, we rose to our feet, crossed back through Matilda's home, and headed toward the hospital. As we walked, I asked Shellsea what *zaram* was.

"You've never heard of zaram?" she asked, astounded.

"No." I shrugged, feeling dumb.

"Really? That's so weird," she said, her face puzzled.

"So, what is it?"

"It's energy."

"Energy?"

"We exchange it for goods, services, experiences, food."

"You mean instead of trading?" I asked.

"Kind of. You earn zaram and then use the energy to exchange for other things."

"How does someone earn zaram?"

"You can earn zaram by doing your passion. Though usually, you also have to do other things. You can get it by being kind, inspiring others, showing authenticity, entertaining, or creating. Really, you could do anything that another person is willing to give you zaram for."

Shellsea came to a stop and slid a tincture bottle from her pocket. She unscrewed the lid, held the bottle high, and took a shot of the vibrant pink liquid. Then she screwed the top back on and offered the bottle to me.

"You can have some if you want," she said.

"What is it?" I asked, staring at the pink fluid.

"Flower nectar from the lunar plant. It has deeply reflective properties. It puts you into a higher state of consciousness. Try it… if you want."

My gaze rested on the lunar nectar as I watched it slosh around. Maybe with the lunar nectar, I would reach a higher state of consciousness than I had ever reached before. Perhaps the lunar nectar was the reason why the people in Halcyon were highly spiritual beings. Maybe it was the answer.

"No, thanks," I said, because I honestly didn't trust her.

Shellsea shrugged and tucked the bottle back in her pocket.

"Your loss," she said as she lowered herself to the street, first to her butt, and then flat on her back on the pavement. "You know, Ash reincarnating as a caterpillar is kind of lame. It's a bug. Boring. If he had come back as a Helio, that would have been flaming fire. But if you think about it… never mind. Anyway, authentically speaking, you have everything—good looks, luscious hair, a fit body—it's no wonder everyone is inspired by you." The way she thought and behaved confused me to no end. I wished I could open her brain and experiment on it as a way of understanding her madness.

"You shouldn't have let Nickel carry you. A man swooping you up into his arms and saving your life isn't a good story anymore," she said absently, her eyes unmoved from the night sky. There was something horribly off beam with Shellsea.

"It's not a story," I explained, starting to feel anger bubbling up.

"All I'm saying is… your story inspires a lot of people, but some are upset with you and how you represented women. I'm only giving you a heads up."

"Representing women?" I yelled, "I was trying to not die and—you know what? I don't need to explain myself to you. I'll see you around."

I didn't wait to hear if Shellsea would respond. I walked off and planned to get as far away from her as possible. Anger was a bad emotion and I didn't need to let myself fall into it. I couldn't let it take me over. So, leaving before I punched Shellsea in her dumb face was my way of keeping the peace. I made my way back to the hospital, changed into my nightgown, closed my eyes, and drifted into another realm.

***

My brother stood before me in his human form in an entirely white space. The silence was complete enough that I could hear my ears ringing. A gray bird with a pale orange chest perched on Ash's shoulder, and I took a moment to study it. Its eyes moved in every which direction, but otherwise it was calm and still. Somehow, without explanation, I knew it was what Matilda had called a *passenger pigeon*. Then I shifted my gaze back to my brother. Something preserved his soul here. This was where I could visit him… in my mind.

"Hey," he said, and the sound of his voice felt like home.

"Hi, Ashy," I said as a smile washed across my face. We stared at one another as if we hadn't seen each other in a hundred years.

"Do you remember what I said?" he asked. "Walks and tennis balls."

I understood what he meant.

"We're going to let you fly away." As if the word *fly* was its cue, the pigeon took flight off Ash's shoulder. The sound of its wings fluttering illogically echoed throughout the space around us. I was watching it soar when my brother's voice brought my attention back to him.

"How's Mom?" he asked. His golden blond hair fell into his face, as it always used to, and he brushed it to the side.

"Actually, she's good."

The bird circled us, and then it flew up into the whiteness and slowly disappeared. I shifted my gaze back to Ash, but he had vanished. I was desolate in the pallid space, or so it seemed. Something pulled on my shoulder.

I twisted around, and standing behind me was Miluchas with his green skin and beard, and universe-like eyes. Blood seeped from his mouth and dripped down his chin. My heart pounded as he collapsed to his knees. My eyes shot open, and I sprang awake, screaming until I realized I was safe.

It was only a dream. It was only a dream.

22

The shower spray was warm as it streamed down the skin on my back. I wasn't sure if I should wash the paint off my face or not, but I felt out of place wearing it, so I decided to let it swirl down the drain. I had never washed myself in the morning. It seemed silly to bathe before I ever got dirty, but I didn't care. I was in warm water shower bliss. The shower allotment for Halcyons was five minutes, and there was no enforcement, so they could go longer without repercussions.

As I showered, I put myself in the present moment, noticing the existence of the shampoo bottle, watching the steam rise as sunlight came in through the window. The world was spacious and bright.

The nurse laid out clothing for me on the bed: a flowing beige top with a burgundy floral design and a leafy green pair of linen shorts. It was far from an extravagant outfit; actually, it was something I would have picked out myself. I towel-dried my hair, then pulled the clothes on.

My shoulder throbbed, so before I headed for breakfast, I asked the nurse if she had a sling. She politely fetched me one and requested I bring it back when I no longer needed it. The sun was hot, but I didn't mind it. After a week inside the windowless hospital room, it was wonderful. As I walked, I soaked up the rays on my face.

It felt strange to have free time. My mind habitually

reminded me of the things I needed to be doing: tending to the farm, checking my brother, cleaning the house. That was my life back in Smallholding. I didn't know what was expected of me in Halcyon, and being idle made me uncomfortable. Though at the same time, it was freeing, as if I were unburdened by an enormous weight.

For breakfast, I ate a slice of avocado toast from the cafeteria. They let me know it cost ten zaram, but because I was *Bay Lilly, from the documentary*, they let it slide. As I was digesting my toast, I made my way to the nola tree. The rainbow bark was soft as I ran my fingers down it. I reached up and one-handedly pulled myself into the tree. I climbed onto a broad branch, which was actually an aerial prop root, and balanced on it.

With the sling, it was a challenge to keep stable, but I was determined to walk across it to the other side. For the first time in a while, I felt like myself. Once I made it halfway, I carefully lowered to sitting and folded my legs into full lotus position. That was as good a spot as any for a mind-break.

I consciously relaxed my shoulders. The tension in my body melted away. I let go of any stress I was holding. Concentrating on the rise and fall of my chest, I allowed myself to enter into a state of One. There were no thoughts, no worries, and no obligations; just breathing. Free, like a baby, to simply exist. To be.

When I was ready, I opened my eyes, completely unaware of how much time had passed.

A group of Halcyons had gathered below me in full lotus with their eyes closed. Something about the scene made me feel uneasy. I had thought I was alone. They opened their eyes and I lightly smiled at them as I found my way down from the tree. A young girl approached me. She had butterfly face paint—an orange butterfly with yellow sparkles around it.

"You're such an inspiration," she said and leaned in to hug me.

"Thank you?" I replied awkwardly. *Why am I so inspirational to these people? I'm not anything special. They are. They are the most spiritual people on the island.*

From the corner of my eye, I spotted Kailas strolling up to me. I politely parted from the girl and headed toward him. We exchanged a look that we both understood meant we wanted an escape.

"Want to go for a walk?" he asked. Obviously thrilled for an excuse to leave, I nodded. Kailas gently reached for my good hand, and we headed off. As we rounded a corner, he did a fast look to make sure we weren't being followed and then let out a breath. "People are strange here, aren't they?"

"I don't like the fuss they make about me," I said. "I can't believe I'm saying this, but I can't wait to get back to Smallholding."

"We'll be back there sooner than we know, so we might as well enjoy what Halcyon has to offer, yeah?" We were still waiting for Ash to hatch for the second ceremony.

"I guess."

"What's with the sling?" he asked.

"My shoulder hurts."

He rubbed his thumb along my hand.

"Where're we going?" We had made it quite a ways down the street. The road wasn't bustling with people as it was the night before.

"You'll see."

We walked until the buildings on our right ended, and a boardwalk began. It stretched for about a mile, and at the end were more buildings. We continued on the wooden boards until we stopped and rested our arms over the railing, looking out at the ocean before us. I stood there, taking it in.

"I've been here before," I whispered.

Kailas grinned, clearly pleased that I remembered. "Our mothers used to take us here."

Memories flooded back: learning how to swim, floating on a wave board, building things with sand.

"I thought maybe you'd like to swim," he said. And he was right. There was nothing in the world that I wouldn't love more. We headed for the stairs to the sand, but a Masculine guarded the way. With hesitation, we moved toward him. The tattoo on his forehead seemed new; the skin surrounding it was irritated and red. His initiation must have been recent.

"Hey, man," Kailas said, "we're going for a swim."

The Masculine held up his palm; in the center was a device with the Halcyon mark on it. We looked to one another and then back at the Masculine.

"Zaram," he said.

With that, Kailas exhaled nosily.

"Do you see that mountain up there?" he asked, pointing to where Smallholding was. "We haven't left that mountainside for thirteen years. We would *really* love to swim in the ocean before we have to go back up there forever."

The man blinked. "Zaram, please."

Kailas's jaw tightened. "If we had zaram, I would've given it to you already."

The Masculine lowered his hand. "Go earn some zaram and come back when you've got enough," he told us, his eyes fixed on something off in the distance behind us.

Kailas leered at the man. If we were in Smallholding, I was sure he would have fought him, but we weren't. And he couldn't.

We were about to turn away from the beach when we heard a voice call out.

"You can let Bay and Kailas through." From ahead of us, I

spotted Quinn in an ashen, one-piece swimsuit walking toward us on the beach. Her orange hair was soaked with seawater. "I forgot to give Bay her emblem device and the zaram she earned from the documentary. You can let them on, and we'll work it out later."

The Masculine nodded and stepped aside. As we passed the man, Kailas looked him straight in the eye and grinned.

"Sorry about that. Find me before dinner in the courtyard, and I'll get you set up with zaram," Quinn said, drying her carroty hair with a sarong.

"Thank you. It means a lot to us. You wouldn't believe how long it's been since we've gone swimming together," I told her.

"No worries." She smiled. "I have to be going. Enjoy the beach." And with that, she was off, up the stairs and headed to the town. If I lived in Halcyon, I would have just about lived on the beach; but we were alone in the sand. Not a soul in sight. We dashed to the crashing waves and let the seawater cool our feet.

My feet sank into the wet sand, and my worries went with it. The powerful waves crashed into my legs, and the sensation brought me to life. White sea foam washed in by my toes and bubbled up, popped, and disappeared. The tide pulled in itty bitty crabs, which dug holes and buried themselves under the sand.

A gust of salty air came from the ocean, blowing my hair behind my shoulders. I closed my eyes and raised my chin. I took in a long, deep breath and the sounds of the breaking waves filled my eardrums. Nothing seemed to exist except that moment.

Then I heard a splash in the water. I opened my eyes to see Kailas's head emerging from the ocean. He shook his head, flinging water from his hair. He looked at me with the world's biggest smile. Behind me was a pile of his clothes, briefs included.

"Come on," he yelled and dove into a wave.

Filled with excitement, I pulled the sling over my head and tossed it by his clothing. I removed my shirt and shorts and sprinted into the waves, diving into the first one that was over my head. The seawater roared around me as I submerged.

I instantaneously remembered what it was like to lose myself to the sea, to allow the vastness of it to make me feel small, to be humbled by her. The experience of swimming on the west side paled in comparison. I wasn't terrified, fighting for my life, or saving Ash. I was free.

Kailas floated on his back as the waves moved under him, his naked form exposed to the sun. I gazed away and dived back under the sea. My hands slid through the water, and my body glided effortlessly. What a unique sensation it was to swim. It was as if I were on a different planet. I re-emerged into the air and took in a breath. Kailas appeared and pressed his palm on the top of my head, pushing me back under. I held onto a breath at the last second. As I came back and broke through the water, I waved my good arm as a white flag.

"I surrender. My shoulder..." I uttered. I wasn't able to be as physical as usual, and being a renewed swimmer, I didn't want to strain myself.

Kailas stopped trying to drown me and instead stood in the ocean near me. His wet face and chest glistened in the sun. Water droplets dripped down his black, ear-length hair, and as they landed on the sea, they became one with the ocean again. The waves hit me at just the right spot where my shoulders were exposed, but my breasts were concealed underwater.

"Is it okay if I..." He gestured toward my shoulder.

I looked at the bandage still taped on my skin, covering

the wound. I gently nodded, giving him permission. Kailas moved his form close to mine, the water line at his ribs.

Tenderly, he reached toward my shoulder and placed his palm over the bandage. His touch made something jolt inside me, but I didn't shy away. His eyes moved from the wound to my face, and our gazes met. The blue of his eyes matched the blue of the ocean.

He looked back to the bandage as he carefully peeled the tape around the edges. The water had soaked the adhesive, so it came off easily. I focused on his face as he worked the bandage off my skin. I took in the muscles of his arms, the details of his neck, the curvature of his cheekbones. Gosh, he was handsome.

When the bandage was off, the corners of his mouth rose into a smile. I had yet to look at the wound; I imagined it to be gross. My impulse was to turn away, but his hand brushed along the wound smoothly and it didn't hurt. I tucked my chin to look at it. It wasn't gross at all. For the most part, it was healed, leaving behind a pink spot surrounded by light scar tissue.

Kailas's arms came out of the water and held my upper arm. He leaned over and tenderly kissed my wound. His lips on my skin made my spine tingle. Our eyes met, and he paused in front of my face. I wanted him to kiss me then—really kiss me.

But then, in a flash, something swam by us. Its egg-shaped shell glided under the surface before its scaly head popped out of the water with its big, round eyes fixed on us. It took in a breath. It was a sea turtle. Alarm left me and was replaced with joy that we had crossed paths with such a magical creature. Gemma once told me they lived to be hundreds of years old. Judging by its size, it was probably much older than me. Yet I looked at it as if it were the most adorable thing I had ever seen.

Kailas and I took to the water and swam alongside the creature. The three of us glided under the sea together as its flippers slid gracefully through the water. A sense of thrill took me over, and I entered a deep state of gratitude. The turtle seemed in complete harmony with the ocean as it swam, without a care in the world. Sure, it had to find seaweed, avoid predators, and seek out a mate. But it was less complicated than being human.

We had laws and systems. We had to exist and survive in both the natural world and within human civilization. And those things had entirely different sets of rules. I decided I would like to come back as a sea turtle.

Kailas and I eventually made our way inland. We slipped our clothes back on, and I rested my arm back in the sling. For a while, we sat in the warm sand as I told him how I would like to be a sea turtle in my next life.

"I'd come back as a saltwater crocodile," Kailas said in response.

"I don't see it."

He scoffed. "Fine, a bunny, then."

I laughed, but then I remembered something. "I ran into Sterling in the lab," I said as I picked up a fist full of sand and let it fall through my fingers. "Have you heard his theories on the afterlife?"

I recollected the conversation Sterling and I had the night before. I told him how Sterling believed human souls moved on depending on their beliefs. I explained bounce behavior and how some soul orbs shot into the sky never to be seen again. I divulged the idea that soul energy might be two separate entities and that we genuinely didn't know what happened to us when we died.

"Whoa, that's crazy," Kailas said when I finished. He flattened a mound of sand with his palm.

"You didn't believe Gemma's lessons anyway, though," I said.

"I guess not. But I always thought rebirth made sense. I believed that part." We looked out at the horizon in stillness. I pondered life and considered what Sterling had said. Kailas was most likely doing the same.

As we stared off, we watched a gull clamp a clamshell in its beak, shaking it furiously. It dropped it to the sand and pecked it. When it couldn't get the shell to budge open, it pressed it back in its beak and flew off with it. A yard away, the gull hovered over a pile of black boulders. It opened its beak and let the clamshell go. The shell smashed onto the hard rocks and shattered, exposing the clam.

The bird then swooped in, pinched the clam in its beak, and flew back to the beach, landing on the sand in front of us. It dropped the shell, wedged its beak into the fractured part, and yanked the meat out. In an instant, it had guzzled it down whole.

"Look at this," he said, holding up a shell that looked like the one from my bracelet. "I guess I can replace your bracelet now."

"I'd love that."

He smirked and then tucked the shell in his pocket.

"So, how does it feel to be back on the beach?" Kailas asked. "Haven't been here since we were kids."

I took in a breath as images from my last beach outing came to me. "I was on a beach during the soul tracing," I said. "A behemoth attacked Rocky, and we brought him there. It wasn't quite as relaxing as today, though." I looked at him wryly.

He reached out and placed his hand over mine in the sand. "I didn't know that. Amur must have cut it out of the documentary. Do you wanna talk about it?"

"Not really."

"You know, I brought you here to forget about all of that, not remind you of it," he said with apologetic eyes, and his hand made its way back to his lap.

"This was great."

Behind Kailas's head, my eyes caught something black.

I shifted my gaze until it came into focus. It was the elderly man in all black I had seen sitting by Kailas on the day of the ceremony. He stood at the shoreline, throwing stones into the water. He had a clean-shaven head with olive skin. He turned his head and looked straight at me, his lips curved up in a winsome smile.

"Who's that?" I asked Kailas, who turned to see what had caught my attention.

"Oona. The resident crazy old guy."

Something about the way Oona had looked at me during the ceremony, and then again there on the beach, was almost beguiling, as if we were meant to meet. I needed to speak to him; I felt it in my gut. I rose to my feet and brushed the sand off my shorts. My hair was sandy, too, so I attempted to shake the grains out of it.

"You're going to go talk to him, aren't you?" Kailas asked, not moving from his spot.

"Is that okay?"

"Sure. I know that when you have a gut feeling, you have to act on it."

I smiled at him. "Thank you for understanding. You're the best."

"No worries," he said, waving. "Bye."

"I'll see you back in town, maybe in the cafeteria later." Then I turned to face the mysterious man and headed his way.

23

As I sauntered towards the man in black, I had a déjà vu feeling, as if I had done it before. He faced me, still as a tree, and waited for me to arrive. As the space between us closed, I saw his face in detail. Time had taken its toll on his skin, which was wrinkled and loose. Yet he had a youthful smile and bright eyes that reminded me of a child's. I eased to a stop a yard away from him.

"Hello," he said.

"Hi."

"It's good to meet you… again."

"We've met before?"

"I've met you but you have not met me. That is… until right now."

I squinted my eyes.

"Will you look out at the ocean with me?" he asked, holding his arms out to the sea.

I stood beside him as we gazed out at the blue horizon. The sun was directly above us, creating a bright glare on the water's surface. The rays were strong and burning my eyes.

"Where are you?" he asked.

I surveyed my surroundings because it was an odd question. "At the beach?"

He let out a subtle giggle. "No, where are *you*? Your form

is on the beach, yes. But *you*, you went somewhere else...
distracted by the mind," he said, tapping his temple.

I traced my thoughts. "I was thinking about the sun
burning my eyes."

"I see," he said, then took a step away from me. "Come on,
we'll go inside. We can't talk meaningfully when your mind is
worried about the big, beautiful sun burning your eyes." He
shuffled toward the stairs. I followed Oona but looked back at
Kailas, who sat on the beach, looking out at the ocean alone.
Maybe it was wrong of me to leave him.

Oona climbed the stairs to the boardwalk, then headed to
the first building on the street. As I passed the Masculine guard,
I gave him a nod and then pursued Oona. He approached the
entryway of the building, turned the knob, and walked in,
leaving the door open behind him. I moved through the
doorway and gently clicked the door shut behind me.

He ascended a flight of stairs, and I followed him to the
top. We curved to the right, and there was a wide open room.
A queen bed sat in the back corner with a burgundy duvet
thrown over it. The floor was hardwood, and on top of it were
several sitting pillows. In the middle, there appeared to be a
designated meditation area with statues, candles, and incense.
The left wall was a series of extra-large windows that overlooked
the ocean.

"Please sit," Oona said, gesturing to the pillows. "Tea?"

I moved to a teal cushion and sat in full lotus position.
"No, thank you." I didn't care for tea. "Do you have water?"

He disappeared through a doorway to the kitchen. I
peered out at the ocean and got lost in the view for a moment.

"There you are," he said, standing next to me with a glass
of water. I accepted it, and he sat on the cushion beside me.
"This was once a restaurant. I donated the tables and chairs to
the cafeteria, redecorated, and made this my home."

I could see reminders of a restaurant. There was an exit sign over the door, license plates mounted on the back wall, and the kitchen was commercial-sized.

"Do we have to small talk?" I asked, drinking the water.

"I suppose not." He smiled. "I know you'd rather get straight to the point."

"You don't know me," I said.

"I know you have the dreams," he told me, looking through the window. I recalled the many I'd had since my spiritual test, but I couldn't imagine how he would know about them. "I rarely meet a person who has energy like yours."

I thought about my face painting experience. "I was told that I have the energy of a passenger pigeon."

"And you do," he said. "My fear is that this place will corrupt you, and you will lose all you emanate. And just as the passenger pigeon, your kind may go extinct forever."

Extinct? "Matilda said passenger pigeons are *not of this time or place*."

"And she's correct. They are not. She and I both hold the gift of divination… seeing through time."

"What have you seen?"

"I see all that happens."

"That must be weird, living life already knowing what happens."

"On the contrary; it's interesting to see the variables move," he said with a gentle smile. "I believe you are part of a prophecy that's unfolding."

"*Prophecy?*"

"Did you hear that mainlanders have survived and are headed to space? It's rumored they're searching for a new planet for humans to survive on because ours is dying. They aren't exactly wrong about that."

"How could you possibly know that?"

"I'm a seer of all things, remember?" he asked with wit in his tone.

"Then what exactly do you see?"

"Disasters beyond our control. Oceans boiling, ash falling from the heavens, and darkness sweeping the land. Hope lies in the prophecy. It tells of a person who is sent beyond the present to save humanity with a gift. A gift like the one you possess," he said evenly.

I shifted on my pillow to face him.

"Wait, you… you think I get sent to the future?"

He fluffed his pillow and adjusted to get comfortable, and then gazed out at the sea through the wide window. He yawned and, as he did, his lungs and chest puffed with air. As he exhaled, I found myself taking in a breath because it looked too refreshing to pass up.

"It will take some time to process this. So, go and when the time feels right, come back, and we will talk more."

"I don't need to process," I retorted. Oona couldn't drop a bomb like that and not elaborate. "Do I get sent to the future?" I asked, my words coming out anxiously.

He hesitated for a moment, and then responded while still gazing out at the ocean. "Only time will tell."

***

After my talk with Oona, I headed to the beach to find Kailas, but the Masculine told me he had already left. I sat in the sand and stayed a while, glancing out at the sea, processing what Oona had told me. I couldn't make sense of it. Maybe the old man truly was crazy. *Sent beyond the present?* What did that even mean?

My stomach rumbled as I entered the cafeteria. Everyone else in Halcyon must have been hungry too, because the place was crammed. A line formed, and I stepped into it. The procession gradually made its way toward the food. Eventually, I was at the front and with my good arm, I grabbed a plate of rice, beans, corn, and some type of bread. The meal appeared like magic; no tilling, no planting, no watering, no weeding, and no harvesting. It was as if the entire process never happened.

The corn could have been grown on my farm, though I had no way of knowing for certain. The cashier let me go again, because she was a *big fan*, but I told her I would come back and pay once Quinn gave me my zaram. As I left the cashier, I scanned the cafeteria looking for an open seat. I wasn't sure which table to sit at until I spotted a girl with teal hair sitting at a table of women. Trying to hide my smile, I approached them.

"Hi, Blue," I said. "Is it okay if I sit?"

She glanced up at me, apparently not surprised to see me; she must have seen the documentary and knew I was in Halcyon.

"Sure." She moved her chair over to give me space. I placed my plate on the table, a little unsteadily since I could only use one hand. I sat in the seat beside her. One of the other girls at the table had light blonde hair and light pink swirls painted on the side of her forehead. She also had a butterfly on her face.

"Nice paint," I said. "Are butterflies your spirit animal?" I asked her.

"Oh, no," she said, covering her mouth as she swallowed. "It's um—I'm surprised you don't know this—it's actually face paint in the spirit of you and your brother."

I must have made a face because Blue explained, "Anyone who is wearing the butterfly face paint is inspired by your story. It's in honor of Ash."

I gazed around the cafeteria and spotted several more with

the same paint. "Oh," I said, knowing that my eyes gave me away.

"I hope it's not weird," the light blonde-haired girl said. "We're just inspired by your bravery, kindness, and resilience. And Ash's too."

"No, no, it's… it's okay. Thank you," I said, but it *was* weird. I didn't want to make anyone feel forlorn by admitting it. They were being so nice to me.

"I'd like to come back as a butterfly," one girl said, "or a fluffy kitten. Maybe a glitter unicorn."

"Unicorns aren't…" Blue started and then rolled her eyes. "You'd make a great unicorn, Bethany."

For a while, I sat silently eating forkfuls of rice while they chatted about their Halcyon lives. Then I noticed the girl across from me was eating a chicken leg.

"Where'd you get that?" I asked.

"The meat counter," she said, pointing to a second line on the opposite site of the room.

"They keep the meat separate," Blue told me, "for the vegetarians. So they don't have to see it."

"Oh," I said, salivating at the thought of white meat.

"Remind me again why we can eat fish and chicken, but not pig?" asked Bethany.

"The Omnivore Compromise," said the light blonde-haired girl. "Remember? Years back it was written into the Peace Laws?"

"Duh, I remember." Bethany scoffed. "I was pointing out the hypocrisy."

"I'll be right back," I announced, sliding the legs of my chair away from the table.

I rose out of my seat and got into the meat line. It was shorter than the other one, and within five minutes, I had two chicken legs and was back at the table. I couldn't help but chomp into the meat. Something came over me, and I inhaled both legs faster and far more messily than I knew was appropriate for a lunch table full of girls.

"Sorry. I'm starving," I muttered, wiping my lips on a napkin. I hadn't eaten that much in, probably, years.

The girl with the butterfly face paint was named Nora. She was a healer, or training to be one as her passion. Apparently, she'd had a frustrating day trying to heal an injured cat.

"How'd you know you wanted to be a healer?" I asked Nora.

She thought about it and then said, "I found an injured baby bird that had fallen out of a tree when I was five. I couldn't help but want to save him. I think that's when I knew."

"I wonder what passion I would be if I were a Halcyon," I contemplated.

"You'd be a great creator," she said. "You're so entertaining and creative."

That didn't sound right to me. I wasn't creative, and I had no idea what she meant by me being entertaining. I was about to ask the other girls about their passions when Blue interrupted.

"It's been nice, ladies, but I have to go. Would you walk me out, Bay?"

I finished my last bite and nodded in agreement. We stood, holding our trays.

"It was nice to meet you all," I said with a smile to the girls. They said their goodbyes, and Blue led me to an oversized sink to wash our plates and trays. In the area, there was a giant trashcan with the word *compost* written on the side in bold marker. It was nearly full of perfectly fine, uneaten food. I couldn't help but stare at the sustenance being wasted. It was enough to feed my family for a week, maybe longer.

"Sorry, I just can't be around those girls for too long,"

Blue said after we washed our plates and exited the cafeteria.

"Why?" I asked, because she seemed to be friendly with them.

"They're all right." She shrugged. "I just… I don't know, never mind. They're fine."

"What is it?"

We strolled toward the nola tree. Blue's teal hair and bright blue eyes were mesmerizing, and I realized she was one of the few Halcyons who didn't wear face paint. I looked at her necklace adorned with a gem, and then met her eyes when she started speaking.

"It's just that I can't be real with them. I don't like the way I feel around them," she said as we walked in the shade of the nola tree. The branches made a canopy that shaded us from the hot sun.

"I get that," I said. "Ever since I came to Halcyon, I've started to feel like… like well, like you said… like I can't be honest. Even at the ceremony, they dressed me up in that garb that I never wear, and it all felt so… so…"

"Fake?"

It was refreshing to speak to someone who got it. "Yes."

Blue raised her chin and fixed her gaze on the branches above us. "It's quite the nola tree, huh?" she whispered. I remembered the pain she showed when the Helio didn't accept her into their clan. She had a unique quality I couldn't name.

"Promise I won't fall out of this one," I joked. She looked to the ground.

"No one knows about my gift. Well, besides Sterling. It's just easier that way. So if you—"

"I won't say anything," I reassured her.

"Thank you. I've already spoken to Kailas about it."

I exhaled, debating. "Hey, can I ask you about something?"

"Shoot."

"The food in the compost bucket—where I come from, nothing is wasted."

Blue's eyes narrowed. "Yeah, that," she said, glancing around the courtyard, considering something. "Let me show you something."

She led me to the side of the cafeteria. Peeking around the brick wall, we spotted a Masculine with purple hair, striking eyes, and a serious expression. Standing at attention, he guarded a door. Out of nowhere, his baton lifted from his holster and floated at his eye level. At first he looked dumfounded, glancing around in every direction, looking for an explanation. Then he swiped at his baton, attempting to retrieve it. Blue floated it farther away, until he was chasing it down the alley. Having distracted the Masculine, she pulled my hand and we entered through the door he had left unguarded.

"Here, this way," she whispered. We made our way through an industrial-sized abandoned kitchen. We passed a row of metal tables and a rotating oven as she led me to a metal door, which unlatched itself and swung open. Blue wasn't shy about using her gift in private. Cold, frosty air poured out from the freezer and hit my skin.

Shelves were filled to the brim with boxes upon boxes of broccoli, peas, carrots, mushrooms, tomatoes, herbs, beans, lettuce, spinach, green beans, corn, onions, garlic, turmeric, ginger, cucumber, kale, peppers, zucchini, squash, strawberries, blueberries, apples, oranges, pears, limes, lemons, and even more produce on the upper shelves. Some of the boxes I recognized: they were from Smallholding.

"This isn't the food that feeds Halcyon citizens," Blue told me. "That's in the front cafeteria. In the rear, back here, Quinn keeps her own personal stash. This… this is all hers."

I stepped into the freezer and ran my hand along the

boxes. Inside one was a bag filled with broccoli—my broccoli. It took weeks of care to grow them, days to harvest. The florets were yellowing, just as they did when they went bad. This was too much food for any one person to eat in a year, even if stored in a freezer.

"How long has this food been in here?" I asked, upset seeping through my tone.

"Long enough," she said, "but it gets worse." She had my attention. "Quinn has more freezers like this all over town, in old restaurants. Sterling and I found them, probably eight of them, and all guarded by Masculines."

"I don't get it," I said, forcing myself to take in a deep breath to stay calm. "I... People are hungry in my village. Children are... and we... we send her this food... and she... she does this with it? This is what she's doing with it?"

"It's not fair, I agree. When Sterling and I found out about this, we started a non-violent protest. After Quinn spoke, most people accepted her lovely-sounding, yet unacceptable, excuse as a legitimate reason for her actions."

"What was her response?" I asked.

"It doesn't matter," she said as we exited the freezer. As the door closed, I turned to see the food as it got locked away. "Most people here take food for granted because it's always been available to them. They have no idea what it's like to have to go without it like we do."

The back door swung open and the purple-haired Masculine returned with his weapon. There was no time to hide because he looked straight at us.

"What are you doing back here? This area is off limits," he said firmly.

I was trying to decide if we should run or talk our way out of it when Blue strutted straight up to him.

"Lux." She smiled at the guard. "How's it going?"

"What do—" he began, but then she placed her palm on his cheek and looked deeply into his eyes. A bright blue light surged from her eyes and shone into his and then dissipated, leaving behind a blue light in his pupils. He stood there motionless, staring into her irises. Blue released her hands, and the Masculine stood idly by, blankly staring into space, impervious to the outside world.

"It's time to go," she said to me.

"What did you do to him?" I asked, waving my hand in front of the Masculine's unresponsive face.

"After we leave, he'll wake up disoriented. He won't remember we were ever here."

"How?" I asked.

"I'm instructing him to forget."

"I… I thought you can't control humans because of free will and all that."

"I can't move others' physical bodies, but I found that I can get into the minds of simple-minded people when they allow me to. There was a moment when he was so mesmerized by me that he made the decision to let me in. I've been practicing since we got back from the… the fight. I needed another skill to help…" She trailed off as we both recalled the day. "I haven't worked out the kinks. There's a chance he might wake up grouchy, or with two heads or something," she said.

We left the cafeteria and returned to the nola tree courtyard. Blue asked me to keep our field trip between us, as she was on thin ice in Halcyon as it was. I reluctantly agreed, but it was going to be difficult not to confront Quinn. As I stood there, I was left to wonder if Blue had mind manipulated me, too, just like Lux the Masculine, and I didn't know it.

Before I could ask her about it, a crowd of Halcyons rushed wildly toward us as if running for their very lives.

24

I smelled it first, and then ash fell from the sky. Some of it made its way through the branches and landed on the ground, the bench, and then onto my palm as I held it up. A fire blazed so tall that I could see the smoke from behind the two-story buildings. A massive cloud billowed above and filled our lungs. Blue and I, and the others under the nola tree, stared in shock. The street filled with fleeing people and I recognized two: Kailas and Sterling.

"Kai," I yelled, "over here." I dashed toward him, and we met just outside the nola tree's canopy. Sterling and Blue were there too.

"You've gotta get inside, away from the smoke," he told me.

"What? No, not without you," I shouted.

He shook his head as people ran around us franticly. "Me and Sterling are headed to the ocean for water."

"I'm going with you then."

He gave me a firm look and then poked me hard in the shoulder. I winced and held my tender wound. "So maybe I'm not at my strongest," I said, the smoke irritating my lungs, "but I can help." What Oona said earlier came into my mind. *Ash falling from the heavens.*

"Then help. Get people into the cafeteria." He gestured toward the building. "Masculines are planning an evacuation there."

Without a good-bye, he jetted off toward a Masculine truck parked nearby. I chased after him with Blue and Sterling.

"Blue, we could use you," Sterling said. "Maybe you could help."

"But I've never been able to—"

"I know. We need you to try." He reached his hand out to hers and they interlocked fingers.

"Why does she get to go?" I protested.

"Drop it, please? Just do this for me." Kailas reached down under the truck and grabbed the key from the wheel well.

"Fine."

"Thank you," Kailas softened. "The cafeteria, okay?"

A siren pierced my ears.

"We've gotta go," Sterling yelled over the alarm. He and Blue climbed into the bed of the truck. Kailas was about to jump into the cab when I called out his name.

I didn't know why I did it. I hated seeing him go without me. He halted in his tracks to face me. *What if this is the last time I see him? What if the fire kills him?* My expression must have given away my fears because he jogged toward me.

As he closed in on me, I expected him to console me by telling me everything would be all right. But he didn't.

Instead, he just about crashed into me, grabbed the back of my head, and pulled me into his lips. The world froze as he kissed me. A tingle surged from my head, down my spine, and throughout my body. I pulled my hands around his neck and felt him—his life force, his soul. I wanted to keep him there, safe in my embrace, forever. Then he disappeared, and my hands were left in the air, searching for him.

"Cafeteria!" he yelled as he hopped into the cab of the truck. Then they sped off, leaving me in a world of smoke. After the dust settled, I stood there taking it in. Halcyons ran hysterically in the smoke-filled street. I couldn't see fifty feet in front of me. The world felt as if it were crumbling. I wanted to panic, but I focused instead. I came back to myself.

I knew Kailas wanted me to get into the cafeteria, but I couldn't help myself. I ran to the science building to make sure chrysalis Ash was okay. The Masculine on duty was preparing to evacuate the jar, but being a chrysalis, the smoke wasn't going to hurt him.

The Masculine let me know that my mother had gone to the cafeteria. I left the science building and ran toward the cafeteria, pulling my shirt over my mouth to keep smoke out of my lungs. As I ran through the street, I spotted a young boy hiding under a park bench. I knelt to meet his eyes. Feeling for him, I reached my hand out to his. "Take my hand."

He looked up at me with innocent, dark brown eyes. He reached out, and I helped him to his feet. We ran toward the cafeteria together. On the way, I found two more stragglers whom I ushered with us.

My eyes were hazy, and my head felt sluggish. The cafeteria door was stuck shut, so I banged on it with my fists. The smoke coated our throats, and we all started to hack. The door swung open, and a Masculine stood tall on the other side. We made our way in, and he closed the door quickly behind us. I took in the sight of the cafeteria. It was filled with confused and scared Halcyons. Some sat at the tables; others paced anxiously back and forth across the floor.

The windows were shut, which saved us from the smoke, but it made the cafeteria hot and stale. I saw familiar faces: Shellsea, Nora, and Bethany. Across the cafeteria, my mother sat at a table. When we met eyes, she rose to her feet and ran to me. I gave her a one-handed hug, my arm in its sling in between us. Her brown eyes reflected concern, but she seemed to be steady and not nearing a panic attack.

"Where've you been? Are you all right?" she asked.

"You don't have to worry about me," I said with a gentle smile.

"The Masculine has Ash. They wouldn't let me take him, but… but I trust them. They'll keep him safe."

We sat together in the cafeteria, waiting forever while my thoughts raced. My mother had learned a new coping mechanism: box breathing. So, she did that beside me as I tried to do the same, failing miserably. What were Kailas, Sterling, and Blue doing? Was the fire being put out? Or was it growing? I tried to breathe to steady my mind. *Shouldn't we be evacuating? What are we waiting for?* With each breath, I struggled to enter a mind-break.

"Bay," someone called. I pivoted to see Amur standing behind me with her spotted face paint and curly black Mohawk.

"Amur."

Her demeanor told me she meant business. "Where are Kailas, Blue, and Sterling?"

I nodded toward the door. "They went to help with the fire."

Amur looked disappointed. "Damn, I was hoping to catch a ride with them. I need to get to the fire to document it."

"I'll go with you," I said, even though I had told Kailas I would stay back. Besides, I wasn't helping anyone in the cafeteria, and I was itching to do something.

"Can you drive?" she asked.

I exhaled and shook my head. No one knew how to drive besides the delivery workers and Masculines. I was turning out to be pretty useless.

"Maybe we can still get there…" she said, and then her face lit up.

Her idea was to sneak into a shed and steal someone's old double bicycle. It was green and rusty and had a white basket connected to the handlebars. I took off my sling and abandoned it in the shed, breaking my promise to the nurse. Amur took the front seat on the bicycle, I took the back, and we pedaled in unison.

Before we left the cafeteria, we had wet cloths and tied them over our noses and mouths to keep the smoke out of our lungs as much as possible. The air was filled with smoke, and the streets were devoid of people as we pedaled through them. It only took about ten minutes on the bike before we approached the fire. It was gigantic; much larger than I thought it'd be. The flames were scorching and unforgiving. The trees and brush surrounding it were blackened.

There were a handful of men in old fireman suits crewing an antique fire truck. They clutched a hose as water jetted toward the flames. Out of the corner of my eye, I spotted Kailas and Sterling reloading the water tank. They had covered the bed of the truck in a tarp and had somehow filled it with ocean water. Next to them was Nic. All three men were miniature compared to the monstrous fire that blazed behind them. On top of a hill to the south, I saw Blue standing tall. Her palms were faced out, eyes aglow, and she was concentrating hard.

Amur hit the brakes, and my feet halted on the pedals. As we came to a stop, we lifted our legs off the bicycle, then laid it on the ground. Amur ran closer to get a good eye on the fire, though she hadn't brought a camera. I trailed behind her, unsure of exactly what to do. The air was smoldering, and I broke out in a sweat. The smoke was much worse this close to the fire; it was wildly thick and suffocating. I regretted coming.

Amur stared at the fire and the men at the truck. I wasn't sure how Amur planned to document it. As a matter of fact, I couldn't figure out how she had documented the soul tracing either. Then, as I approached her, I looked into her eyes and watched as her pupils retracted like a shutter. Her eyes were her camera.

"Get back!" one of the firemen shouted at us. Caught, Amur and I yielded to their commands and crouched behind a fallen tree. Kailas, Nic, and Sterling looked our way after hearing the fireman.

"Bay, go back to town," Kailas yelled. "Go!"

I didn't know what to do. I wanted to help, but I wasn't sure how. How could I leave them to fight the fire alone?

"Go back." Kailas screamed. When I didn't flee, he directed his feet toward me, ready to run. But then Nic placed a hand on Kailas, keeping him back. Kailas nodded in agreement to whatever Nic said and went back to work at the fire truck. Then it was Nic running toward me instead.

He was twenty feet from Amur and me when a bang rattled my body. An explosion came from behind him, from behind the fire truck. He tumbled to the ground as a massive burst of fire expanded and took over the rest of the brush. As quickly as he fell, Nic bounced up and dashed toward us again. The smoke took over, and I lost sight of the fire truck. I lost sight of Kailas.

I lunged forward, my hands grasping at the air, my feet dashing in his direction. My wet cloth fell from my mouth as I screamed. My feet moved beneath me. "Kai."

Someone's arms wrapped around me, pulling me away from the scorching heat, my body unwillingly dragged back to the log. Nic held me tightly as I screamed, cried, and tried to claw my way forward to find what was left of my best friend. "Kailas!"

25

When my mother went into labor with Ash, she brought me to Kailas's house, and his mother watched me for two days. My stepfather had recently passed. I was still in deep grief and scared about the baby coming without a father waiting to care for it. But being there with Kailas for a couple days gave me the strength to go on. Even at the age of eleven, he had a way of listening to me that no one else did, not even Gemma. His heart was free of judgment and he didn't offer advice; he simply listened with his whole soul.

I must have talked for hours as he sat there, creating space for me. He was the reason why I healed, and the reason why I found strength again. He was the best person I had ever known. That's when Kailas became my person, my best friend. And when my mother returned holding my baby brother, she placed him into my arms, and my world changed forever. I had two people, now—my boys.

"Kailas!" I had called his name so many times that I was losing my voice.

I was on my knees, my hands covered in cinder. The smoke was thick, but I refused to leave, even though Nic continuously tried to drag me away. Amur attempted to persuade me to go back to Halcyon. Probably because there was nothing left to film. My throat was on fire, but I couldn't go, not without Kailas.

I was still screaming his name when a drop of water landed

on my face. I shut up and looked at the sky—but all I could see was smoke.

All at once, the sky opened up, and rain poured on us. I heard something behind me and looked over my shoulder to find Blue running out of a cloud of smoke toward us. I rose to my feet as she stopped before us, her hair dripping wet, her clothes covered in dark ash.

"I… I saw it was raining offshore. So, I… um… I guess the cloud must have moved in," she said. Blood dripped from her nostrils, and her irises were black instead of their usual bright blue. She wiped the blood with her thumb. Looking around, she saw Amur and I were there, but more importantly, that Sterling wasn't. "Where's Sterling?" she asked.

"He and Kailas were by the truck when the explosion happened," I said, facing the smoke again, in a despaired daze.

Blue's expression went stony, and she marched toward the truck. The smoke surrounding her magically parted as she walked through the clearing. I sprang and caught up. Finally, someone was willing to go back for Kailas… and Sterling. Eventually, Nic and Amur followed.

We marched for only a minute until we saw the fire truck. As we neared the vehicle, we both sped into a sprint. On the ground near the front tire was Kailas's form, lying face up in the dirt. I ran to his side and shook him, yelling his name repeatedly. His head rose slightly, and his eyes fluttered open.

"Kailas!" I yelled. I had never been so happy to see his blue eyes. Tears came to me as I started helping him to his feet. I hugged him tight and kissed his face. "We have to get out of here," I told him. He only nodded weakly and gave me a weary smile. I balanced him on my good shoulder, and we began to walk.

Near us, Blue rubbed the ash off a disoriented Sterling. He was twice her size, but somehow she found the strength to help him to his feet. Nic had found one of the firemen, whom he helped to raise. Amur stared at us, which I knew meant that none of this would remain private. Her contact camera was catching all of it. We helped them into the (now empty) bed of the pickup truck, and sat with them as Nic hopped into the driver seat and drove us back to Halcyon. The cold rain bore down on us.

As we arrived back to Halcyon, an army of Masculines met us at the border. They didn't give us a problem, and instead led us to the hospital where Kailas, Sterling, and the fireman, who I learned was named Rupert, were admitted. Before I left, the nurse assured me that Kailas would be fine. She said he had inhaled a lot of smoke and she wanted to monitor him but otherwise, his wounds were superficial. He fell asleep in his hospital bed, so I left his side to find dinner.

I made my way to under the nola tree and saw that most of the smoke had been blown away by the wind. The rain saturated the ground, keeping the dust down. The downpour had stopped, and the sun reemerged. It smelled like a barbecue outside, but at least the air was breathable. I was about to head for the cafeteria when I spotted a crowd, sitting in lotus position, in the courtyard.

As Quinn came into view, I remembered I was supposed to meet her before dinner to get my zaram. I approached the circle. Their eyes were closed, and they couldn't see me. In silence, I lowered to my bottom, crossed my legs, and entered the meditation circle. Taking in a deep breath, I found my center. I stayed with myself and entered a state of no-thought.

"One," I heard Quinn's voice break the silence. "Please give us the strength to set this boundary with the River Clan. Please heal those who were injured in today's fire. Please bring peace to our lives and our minds. Ataraxy."

In unison, I heard the others in the circle murmur,

"Ataraxy." I missed the cue. It would have been weird to say it after the fact, so I let it go. The sounds of bodies rising and feet shuffling filled my ears. I gently opened my eyes to find the group dispersing. Quinn sat across from me, still in lotus position.

"I thought you might have forgotten to meet me." She stood. "Follow me to my office, and I'll get you your zaram."

We strolled down Main Street in awkward silence until she stopped in front of one of the buildings. Before us was a double door. She reached into her pants pocket and pulled out a ring of keys. As she flipped through them, I counted. There were nine keys. When she found the one she wanted, she slipped it into the keyhole and turned it.

The door swung open, and she stepped inside. I followed behind. It was dark at first, but then she switched on a light. There was a desk piled with loose papers and the lamp that lit the room. Quinn stood behind it and leaned over. I heard a drawer slide open, some rummaging, and then it slid shut. Her head popped up.

"Take a seat, sweetie," she said, gesturing to the chair in front of her desk.

I shut the door behind me and settled into the seat. As soon as I got comfortable, I remembered the freezer full of food, but I had told Blue I wouldn't say anything so I bit my tongue.

Quinn held in her hand a piece of jewelry: a ring with a Halcyon emblem engraved on it. She settled into her chair, turning it so her legs tucked under the desk. As she was sifting through her papers, she spoke.

"I just need to get the zaram transfer machine. I need to organize this desk. Please excuse the mess."

"No trouble." I was reliving the experience of the day in my mind. My throat still burned, and there was ash on my forearm. I licked the back of my thumb and rubbed at the ash.

"Here it is," she announced, pulling a black box out of her drawer. "Let me check the numbers." She rifled through some papers until she came across one with my name at the top. "This is the final report from the documentary. It looks like you inspired a lot of people. That's great, especially for you. Over a thousand people voted for you as most inspiring this week. There are only fifteen hundred people in Halcyon, so count yourself lucky. That comes to"—she entered numbers into a calculator—"ten thousand, one hundred and five zaram, plus what you got for doing the documentary: thirty-four thousand, three hundred and two. That should last more than a couple months, though you'll only be here another week or so." She pressed the ring up to the machine, and a green burst of light emitted from it. She reached out the band across the desk to me, and I leaned forward to receive it.

"Thank you for—" I began to say, but then she pulled the ring back.

"Wait. I forgot to subtract the zaram from the beach this morning. Beach passes are five thousand zaram, plus you had lunch, right?"

I nodded.

"That's another hundred. And the ring itself costs two hundred. Your new total is twenty-nine thousand and two." She refreshed the ring on the machine, another green glow, and then she handed it to me. "Welcome to Halcyon. You're welcome to stay with us until the butterfly's release. After that, you can transfer your remaining zaram to a Halcyon of your choice before you're transported back to Smallholding."

"Thank you." I smiled and slipped the ring onto my finger. I traced the Halcyon emblem engraving of a circle with an infinity symbol inside it.

"I apologize for being so distracted. You can only imagine the stress I'm under right now. The fire killed one of our best firefighters. So tragic. We got lucky with the rain coming in; otherwise it wouldn't have been long before Halcyon caught fire."

"I'm sorry about the firefighter," I said somberly. "I thought we lost everyone." Kailas.

"That's right, you were there."

"I know I wasn't supposed to be, but I wanted to help."

"I get that," she said. "I was like that at your age, but it can get you into trouble, you know. My son is like that too. I didn't even know he was at the fire today until afterward. He always wants to be the hero. Well, you know that all too well, don't you?" she asked, leaning back in her desk chair.

"What caused the explosion?" I asked, changing the subject.

"The brush fire reached our oil reserves. We keep the gas tanks in that field. When the tanks caught fire, they exploded. We have no way to extract new oil, and we were dependent on what little we had left to fuel the vans we use to transport food and water. I'm not sure what we're going to do now. Officials want to use horses to pull wagons, but we'd have to find wild horses and domesticate them. There are ethical concerns with that, though."

"It sounds like you have your hands full," I said, unsure of what to say. Mostly, after I got the zaram ring, I was happy to head back to the cafeteria.

"It's the job." She bunched a handful of papers together, held them up, and let them fall onto the desk, straightening them out. "Well, that and rejecting people applying for citizenship, because we just don't have room." She held up the papers as evidence. "These are mostly requests. I barely even read them anymore because we get so many, and we have no openings. I'm going to have to make a statement about it soon. Things are coming to a head. Can you feel it?"

I flashed back to when Nickel told me I could be a Halcyon citizen. All of a sudden, it made sense why none of the spiritual people in Smallholding got accepted into Halcyon. I didn't answer her question.

"I felt guilty at first, but now I'm overwhelmed. We can barely maintain what we have," she said, setting the papers into a drawer.

A random thought occurred to me. "Like insects," I said.

She looked at me, puzzled. "Like insects?" she asked. "How so?"

"Well, if I see one insect on the counter, like a ladybug, it's easy for me to have compassion for it. It's just one. I can see it as an individual, and I'll take the time to capture it and bring it outside instead of killing it." I shrugged. "But if I'm trying to make dinner and I find a hundred ants on the counter, it's too overwhelming. None of them seem like individuals, and it feels like an invasion. So, I do what I have to do to get rid of them."

"Right," she said with a nod. "Too many ants at the picnic." She opened a notebook and wrote something down.

"When I told my friend, Kailas, about my theory, he dubbed it the *Ant Effect*."

"The *Ant Effect*. I like that."

We both went silent, and it started to feel awkward. I tried to think of something to say.

"I met Oona today," I uttered, half wondering if she knew him.

"Oona?" She eyed me. "You'd do yourself a favor by staying away from him. He wants so badly to be admired. He goes out of his way to destroy my reputation just to get attention for himself."

Nothing about Oona gave me those vibes. He hid himself away in an old restaurant on the outskirts of Halcyon, while she lived a very public life in the center of it.

"He didn't mention you at all," I told her.

"Sure." She looked away. My cue to leave.

I rose from my chair. "Thanks again for the zaram. I should—"

"Nickel tells me you speak Helio," Quinn said, gesturing for me to sit back down.

I swallowed hard, and hoped she didn't view me as a traitor.

"Does your guide typically teach Helio in Smallholding?" she asked.

"No," I rushed to answer, "I taught myself."

Quinn licked her lips. "Well, it appears knowing the language helped you while facing execution. I'm just wondering if you would help me translate a few things?"

Impulsively, I wanted to say yes, to help the leader of Halcyon, though something in me wavered, told me not to get involved. I pictured the freezer in the cafeteria and realized there was something I wanted in return. And I could word it in a way that wouldn't compromise Blue.

"I'll translate if you return the food in your freezer to Smallholding," I said, not as commandingly as I wanted to sound. "I was looking for the cafeteria and accidentally found your stash."

She looked at me seriously. "That's not gonna happen."

"Why not?"

"It's mine."

It took every ounce of my self-control not to punch her in her stupid face, even if she was the guru of Halcyon.

"People in my village are weak and skinny and often go hungry, you could help," I explained.

"You're making me sound heartless. Those people can grow their own food. Everyone wants something for nothing. It's a major problem."

"I thought you were all about abundance? Why not share?" My voice had an unintended edge in it.

"If your village isn't receiving abundance it's because they're living in scarcity mode. They see nothing but lack, so that's what they receive. It's your village's responsibility to fix their mindsets, not mine." Quinn sat back in her chair, clearly thinking she had made an excellent point.

I closed my eyes for a second and felt my chest rise in breath. I exhaled and spoke in an even tone.

"An abundance of fruits and vegetables grow on my farm," I said—pointing to where I thought Smallholding was— "which I'm forced to give to you for water." I pointed at her. "You have what everyone needs to grow their own food in this rainless valley, but you don't share it freely. You control everything, because you control the water."

"Exactly: food grows abundantly on *your* farm because of *my* water. Why shouldn't I receive something in return? You can find your own stream if you don't like the deal." If it wasn't for the water she brought us, our crops would die and we would have nothing. There are other farming villages she could get her produce from. She didn't need us in the same way we needed her.

I rubbed my neck. "People have died hiking the valley in search for new water sources. The only ones on the island are controlled by either you or the Helio."

Quinn shook her head and smirked. "Maybe you could ask the River Clan for water, or fight for it like I had to here in Halcyon."

"You didn't fight for the stream; it was just sitting there."

"We worked hard to protect it," Quinn said.

"You mean steal it." And there it was: the truth that Quinn would probably kick Smallholding out of the alliance for.

"We can't give the same resources to everyone just because they want it. Life doesn't work like that. There's a give and a take—a balance."

I exhaled, defeated. She would never get it. "This is wrong. I wish there were some magical words I could say that would make you get it."

Quinn looked me over, placed her fingers back on her chin, and responded. "You're being a bit much." She pointed at me. "You're too sensitive. Try to think more realistically."

"Okay, realistically, you don't need that food."

Quinn blew air out of her nostrils. "All right, I see where you're coming from, and I'll meditate on it. But what you propose just won't work. I have to uphold the way I know works. But I do need your help with the translation; it's imperative to keep everyone in Halcyon *and* Smallholding safe."

I was getting no where with her, so I stopped wasting my breath and moved on. "Does this translation have something to do with the boundary you're setting?" I asked.

"It does," she said, leaning her elbows on the desk. She looked at me. "I have intel that the River Clan are the ones who set fire to the brush today. It was too strategically placed for it to have been a coincidence. The burning of our oil puts us in a vulnerable position. I believe this was a deliberate act, an attack."

It hadn't occurred to me that someone had set the fire intentionally, though it didn't make sense that the brush would spontaneously combust. As I was thinking through what she said, she continued talking. "It's been unspeakably dry here in the valley. It's too easy to set fires, and we can't afford for there to be more."

"But why would the Helio come after Halcyon? Why now?" I asked.

"Because they're savages. They want to take us out because they're jealous of us."

"That's not it," I said. "There's something else." She sat back in her chair and swayed, considering something. "I'm not going to help you translate unless you tell me the whole truth," I added firmly.

She sat up with her spine straight and looked me deep in the eye. Her blue eyes were piercing, and her short, pin-straight orange hair didn't seem to move with the rest of her form. Her mauve cape draped over her shoulders like some type of superhero.

"Translate the words, and I'll tell you."

I bit my lip. "Fine."

Quinn sat straight up and pulled a paper out of her pile. "We have someone here in Halcyon who was able to translate most of it, except these two sentences." She slid the paper across the desk. Reading Helio was more difficult than speaking it, and it took me some time to get it. I wanted to make sure I was certain before I spoke.

"This says *shooting light*," I told her, pointing to the word, "and this says *sunsets of two*."

Quinn looked seriously at the paper and bit her nail. "You're sure?" she asked. I nodded. She stared off to the side in thought. "Okay, you can go."

"Wait, you said you would—"

"Oh, right." She shook her head, cleared her throat, and reclined in her chair. "The Helio that Rocky sent to his knees with a machete in his back; do you remember him? The one that tried to kill you?"

"Of course."

"It turns out he was more than your run-of-the-mill Helio. He was important to their clan, very important. And they aren't feeling all warm and fuzzy about us for killing him."

The sight of him dying came to me and I shuddered at the memory. Rocky and Miluchas were both dead because of me.

It took a moment of breath to remember where I was and to finish hearing what Quinn had said.

"How was he *important*?"

Quinn rested her hands on the desk and leaned in toward me. "He was their chief."

That's why the Helio retaliated so strongly after Miluchas died. The way the forest seemed to turn to fury in a second. The way the Helio had pursued Nic and Amur in their protective bubble for miles trying to avenge his death. Miluchas was their chief, and Rocky had killed him, which meant that *we* killed him. It made sense now why Quinn was willing to wage war. I understood what the Helio wanted as revenge: a leader for a leader.

26

I slept in the chair in Kailas's hospital room. It was two rooms down the hall from where mine used to be. But it wasn't mine anymore. It was Rupert's. The nurse was nice enough to let me use the shower in the bathroom, and she gave me some spare clothes they had: a floral skirt and a white tank top. The top fit loosely, but I didn't have much choice other than to wear it. An Official had told me that they had sent someone to Smallholding to get some of my things, yet I remained empty-handed.

I held Kailas's hand. It was strange to think that not too long before, it was the other way around. I kissed the skin by his knuckles. His hands were beautiful in the way that a worker's hands were: rough and dexterous.

"Hey," I heard him say, and I moved my focus to his face. His charming blue eyes were staring at me. Shallow scratches cut his face along his left cheek and forehead. The nurses had washed the ash off his skin, and he looked mostly like himself, except they had put him in a rosy hospital gown that made him look delicate. I wasn't used to seeing him that way. He was my rock.

"Hey, yourself," I whispered back.

"I'm alive?" he asked, looking at me closely.

"And well." I smiled.

Kailas shifted his weight to look around the room. "We have to stop ending up in here." He glanced at our hands.

"Maybe if—"

"Will you go out with me?" he asked.

What did he just say? *Did I hear him wrong?* "Huh?"

"On a date," he said. "You know, when a boy likes a girl, and he asks her to do something special, just the two of them?"

"You're... you're asking me on a date. *Now?*"

"During the explosion... when I thought it was lights out for me," he said, his face content, his eyes fixed on mine. "All I could think about was *you.*"

My breath caught in my lungs.

"Your beautiful green eyes. The way you play with your hair when you're nervous. How ridiculously happy I feel when I'm with you," he looked into my eyes. "So, yes, I'm asking you on a date, right now, wearing a pink hospital gown. Because who knows when I'll have another chance. Will you, Bay Lilly, go on a date with me?"

After my heart stopped thudding in my chest, I searched my mind for an answer. The decision should have been easy. It was Kailas. But a date was the furthest thing from my mind. Quinn was declaring war with the Helio. Oona had told me I would go to the future. How could I think about going on a date?

I tried to speak. "You... you're... there's just so much going on."

"Don't do that," he said, pulling his hand away from mine. "Don't think about everything and everybody else. It's you and me here." His eyes were soft and vulnerable. I saw him: his goodness, his integrity, who he was as a person.

"When I thought you had died, it felt like..." I said, with a flutter in my heart, "like there was no air left in the world."

Our eyes locked.

"You're like air to me, Kailas," I said, holding back tears.

He bit his lip. "Is that a yes?"

I shook my head. "It was never a question."

"So, yes?"

I chuckled. He really wanted an answer. "Yes, stupid. It's a yes."

He placed his hand back on mine. "I just have to get out of this hospital so I can take you somewhere nice."

***

When the sun reached its highest point in the sky, the doctors released Kailas from the hospital. They told us he was lucky to have sustained only superficial wounds, and that One must have been protecting him. We decided that we would go on a date after the second Brotherfly Ceremony was over and we could go home.

As we exited the hospital, Kailas asked to see Ash's chrysalis. He hadn't seen it yet, and I wanted to visit it anyway. When we got to the science building, the front door was locked. Kailas banged on it a couple times and eventually, a Masculine opened it. When he saw it was us, he let us in and brought us to the lab where they kept my brother.

As we walked, the Masculine explained, "We had to lock up the building. People were trying to get in here to see Ash. He's very popular right now."

I thanked him for guarding my brother and for keeping him safe. That was usually my job, and while part of me felt as if *I* should have been protecting him, I guessed he was in good hands.

As we passed through the doorway, I spotted the jar on the counter.

They had cleaned out the old leaves. Ash didn't need those anymore now that he was a chrysalis. Kailas and I sat on the cushioned lab stools and looked closely at the jar. Through the glass, we saw Ash's chrysalis. It wasn't even an inch long and it was green with golden speckles. It dangled from the lid, connected by threads.

"In the hospital, I had a nurse bring me a book about caterpillars," Kailas said.

"Oh, yeah?"

"Uh-huh. I read that when a caterpillar is in a chrysalis, it turns into liquid."

I scrutinized the chrysalis. It did seem rather miraculous that a crawly caterpillar could change into a winged butterfly. I got a chill. "So, Ash is *liquid*?" I asked.

"I guess so." He shrugged.

"Weird," was all I could say.

Through the window, the lunch bell sounded. We took another minute to appreciate my brother in his new form, and then we left the science building. As we took strides toward the cafeteria, I showed Kailas my new zaram ring. He asked to hold it, and then he put it on his pinky finger and spun it around. He said that he had a pass for three meals a day, but otherwise he couldn't buy anything without zaram.

That's when I told him about my conversation with Oona. I finished the story right as we made it to the cafeteria. We paused outside the entrance, and Kailas returned the ring to me.

"Sent beyond the present?" he asked, scowling. "Seriously, the future?"

"That's what Oona said."

"And how would you get to the future?"

"He didn't say."

"That's a surprise," Kailas said with a scoff. "Well, did you tell him you're not going?"

"I don't think I have a choice. It's already happened, according to him." A crowd made their way by us and into the cafeteria.

"Of course you have a choice. You always have a choice," he said.

"I don't know."

"And he says the end of the world is imminent?" He gestured dramatically, in a mockery of Oona.

"Yes."

"An apocalypse?"

"I guess."

"Yet he thinks you get sent to the future?"

"Yeah."

"Don't you see the contradiction?" As he said it, the realization swept over me. I didn't know why I didn't see it before.

"You can't get sent to the future if the world ends."

***

The following days passed in a blur. Kailas learned of Quinn's freezers and it upset him. True to his stalwart nature, he was determined to spread the truth far and wide. I selfishly wanted him to stay silent about it, because I didn't want him to give Quinn a reason to send him back to Smallholding before the final ceremony. I needed him to be there with me.

Kailas told me Quinn was the granddaughter of the man who had purchased Sub Rosa Island before the Spiritual World War. He had acquired it to excavate its rare elements, and he ran a wildly successful business that exploited the island. He was the reason why the Helio had to leave their land, and consequently the reason there was conflict between us.

Also, more personally, my stepfather had moved to the island to work in the quarry and had brought my mother with him. I was the result of a one night stand, and my stepfather was my mother's friend at the time. As she didn't have anyone else, he was looking out for her—that is, until they fell in love and got married. If it weren't for all that falling into place, I wouldn't have been born on the island.

Quinn gave birth to Nic when she was only nineteen—nearly my age. She had conceived him with her mate. Her family and Nic's father were on a business trip on the mainland when the war started, and they were unable to find their way back to the island before all connection was lost.

Quinn rose to power because she was a successor to the most influential family on the island. She had never known a day without food or water. Even during the war, she was fully provided for. Even harder to accept were the freezers full of produce, hoarded not because she needed it or could possibly eat it all before it expired, but because she felt she had earned it. All while the outer villages went hungry.

She had never experienced what most of us had, which Kailas believed made her unfit to be a leader. "How can someone who can't relate with the majority of the island be a leader of it? We need to establish a meritocracy. Not just let the powerful maintain their status," he declared during our conversation.

I wasn't convinced Quinn was all bad until I heard the last thing Kailas had to say. There was a meeting I had missed, but Kailas showed me a recording Amur had taken of it. Quinn stood in front a crowd of Halcyons in the cafeteria as she made the announcement.

"We are at our population max in Halcyon. This is something I have been anticipating for a while now. The only street with running water and electricity is this one, and we are out of space. Once a population reaches a certain size, we can expect violence, greed, anger, jealousy, and all the other negative human behaviors to flourish. This is because of psychological duress, resource management, disconnection from One, and because of something I call the *Ant Effect*."

She went on to recount my idea, only claiming it as her own. I decided I didn't care. I didn't care about any of it. I was finished. I was going to hitch a ride back to Smallholding during one of the deliveries. Or, at the very least, make myself invisible in Halcyon.

One day, I was so frustrated with the situation that I spent the morning hiding with Ash's chrysalis in the science lab. After hours of staring at the green thing, I entered a profound state of meditation. So deep that the world around me faded into a dull background, and I drifted into a phantasmagoria. The room transformed and currents waved through the air. It was as if I tapped into a mystical force of energy. Or maybe it wasn't mystical at all; maybe it was natural. I could still feel the chair beneath me but simultaneously, it was as if I didn't have a form.

"You've done well, sweetheart," a voice said. A dark figure stood on the other side of the counter. Though I could only make out an ambiguous silhouette, I could have sworn it was my stepfather's voice.

"Dad?" I called out.

My stepfather appeared from the shadows. He looked exactly how I remembered him when he was healthy: handsome, with short, dark hair, big, brown eyes, tan skin, and a strong form like an ox. His face held a comforting smile.

A gust of wind came from behind and as if made of sand, he blew away as multihued fragments. Then there was a tug on my shoulder.

A Masculine stood at my side. "You all right?" he asked.

"I just need some fresh air."

I made my way to the nola tree, where Kailas sat with a group of young Halcyons. They wore their usual face paint and neutral-colored clothing. From a distance, I heard him lambasting Quinn. He called her inauthentic, mendacious, and vain.

"She needs to be exposed as the self-righteous narcissist she is," he told them. Kailas sounded like a parrot, repeating the same things over and over. His disdain for Quinn was growing, and it wasn't going to alleviate the building tension in Halcyon.

We only had two more days until Ash was due to hatch out of his chrysalis. My clothes had finally arrived from Smallholding, and I was able to wear something from home—tan linen shorts, white top, and brown vest. I even tied my hair in a side braid. I was trying anything to find normalcy.

Nic walked under the nola tree and, when he overheard Kailas speaking about his mother, he approached him.

"Hey, man, give it a rest."

Kailas stood eye level with Nic. "People deserve to know the truth."

"She's an imperfect person, just like everyone else. There's your truth."

Kailas shook his head, blew him off, and sat with his new students. Nic scoffed and headed away.

I broke into a slow jog and caught up with Nic. "Hey," I said.

He glanced over at me and came to a stop. As we met, he smiled. "Hey, haven't seen you in a while."

"I've been lying low. Trying to do my time and get out of here."

"Yeah, lots of rumors are going around lately. Most are about my mom," he said, gesturing toward Kailas talking about Quinn. He looked back at me. "But some are about us."

I had come across those rumors too. Girls swooned over Nic's and my tale on the west side. They stupidly saw the documentary as a romance.

"I've heard."

"Don't worry, the sheeps will move on when the next interesting thing comes along."

"Thank you," I blurted. "For saving me."

"Yeah, don't mention it," he said with a shy smile as we locked eyes. I pulled him in for a hug, but we separated when a pair of teenage girls spotted us from the other side of the park. I didn't care to fuel the rumors.

"So, Mother Quinn is your mom? I didn't see that coming."

"Right. The son of royalty."

"That's not how I see you."

"Sure."

"Why didn't you tell me before?"

"You're the first person who got to know me for *me* and not as Mother Quinn's son. It was kind of nice."

"I hadn't thought of it like that." It got awkward. "So, where are you headed?"

"Meeting Sterling." He pointed and I followed his finger under the nola tree about ten yards away. Sterling sat on a bench with Blue's head resting on his lap as he combed through her teal hair with his fingers.

"I didn't know you were friends with him."

"I'm not." He shrugged, taking steps in their direction. "You can come. I'm sure they're not gossiping about us."

I gave him a look but decided to follow anyway.

As we approached the bench, Nic stopped and turned to face me. "You know, it's not such a crazy thought," he whispered.

"What?"

"You and me."

Blue rose off Sterling's lap, and they held hands for a moment before Sterling stood to greet Nic. The pair of men walked off toward the lab and left Blue and me alone. Nic's words lingered in the air.

"Hi," Blue called from her seat. "Why don't you sit?" She gestured to the now empty space.

I settled onto the bench and pointed toward Nic and Sterling heading into the science building. "What are they up to?"

"Ah, guy stuff, I guess."

"How've you been?" I looked at her. "Your irises are back to their regular teal. They were jet black after you moved those rain clouds."

Blue looked around anxiously, making sure no one heard.

"I didn't say anything," I let her know. "But you did move the clouds, didn't you?"

She moved in closer to me and spoke in a soft voice. "I spotted a rain cloud offshore and I thought, *that's exactly what we need.* So, I tried. It wasn't easy, but I did it. I've never done anything like that before."

The wheels in my head turned. "Maybe you can end the water crisis. Make it rain more often."

Blue's shoulders deflated, and her eyes veered away.

"It took all my energy to do that; hence, the bloody nose and black eyes. It's been days, and I can still barely use my gift."

After that, the conversation idled and we sat silently for a while. I looked to the treetops when a flock of small birds landed on the branches.

"I'm embarrassed that you saw me begging the Helio to be part of their clan," Blue said. "I should've known better. I see now that they were never going to accept me. I was just desperate to feel like I belong somewhere."

I looked at her. "What's wrong with Halcyon?"

She shook her head. "Everything. Can't you feel how off this place is?"

I didn't want to talk about that. Two more days; that was it. I only had two more days.

She took in a breath and held it for a second, her eyes shifting around in thought. Then, as she exhaled, she spoke. "I'm from a small, non-alliance village that sat a mile from the top of this mountain." She pointed to the range opposite of the one where Smallholding was.

"There were only fifteen of us. We drank from Halcyon's stream; high up, where the Masculines don't guard. We survived there for years after the war, living in teepees, eating wild-growing fruit, catching fish from the stream, and gathering eggs from the hens that we kept. It was a simple and peaceful existence. Until…" Her voice cracked and she cleared her throat. "Until one by one, everyone caught… H… Hackle." Her shoulders fell and she turned so I couldn't see her face.

"Everyone is gone. My mom and dad too," she said, looking off sadly in the distance. "I'm immune; the only one. At nine years old I lived alone in the forest for weeks before Oona found me."

My heart broke for her, and a lump grew in my throat as my eyes grew teary. It was equally shocking and horrible. I had misjudged her. She wasn't a spoiled Halcyon girl; she was a homeless orphan.

"You've been through so much," I said, holding back tears. Knowing there was nothing I could say, I held her close and rested my face in her teal hair. We stayed there for a while, as long as she needed. Something about her felt familiar, like a sister I had never had. When she was ready, she pulled away and looked at me with puffy, red eyes.

"I've felt broken for a long time," she whimpered. "When I first got to Halcyon, the only person who was nice to me was Sterling. The others teased me because I was different and had blue hair. Everyone else took months to warm up to me, but not him." She looked at the lab from across the park. "But still, something felt like it was missing. So, I went searching."

"For the Helio?"

"For answers. Which I thought the Helio would have."

I fixed my hair and sat up. "Blue… you aren't broken."

She let out a pitiful laugh and shook her head in disagreement. "I am."

"Okay, well, maybe you are." I shrugged. "But whatever, that's fine, because…we *all* are."

Teenage Halcyons approached us and one by one lowered onto the ground before us. They sat in full lotus, the same way they sat in front of Kailas: ready to listen. I swiveled to face them and started again.

"We're all a little broken. No one goes through life without scars. But we convince ourselves that we're the only ones who've been through hard stuff or made mistakes or had our hearts broken. Even though sometimes it feels like we're all alone… we aren't. There are people who lived hundreds of years ago who have been through hard stuff. There are people who live right next door going through it. People who haven't even been born yet who *will* go through it. But the big thing to remember is that people make it through to the other side. Our pain is valid, but it is also temporary. We will get through it… together."

The crowd stared at me blankly. Maybe my revelation wasn't as inspiring as I had hoped. Standing behind Blue, Kailas gave me a reassuring smile.

"She's right, you know. You'll do well to listen to her." Oona's voice came from the crowd. I hadn't seen him since we spoke in his apartment. "Will you please come with me, Bay? And bring your friends; Kailas, Nic, Sterling, Blue, and Amur. There's something you need to see."

27

"I haven't seen you around," I said as we followed Oona down Main Street. Five of us were present when he requested us, but the sixth, Amur, we had to find. She was editing footage and was reluctant to join us, but she agreed to come when she saw Oona with us.

"That's because I haven't left my loft," he said, his all black outfit standing out amongst us.

I sped up for a moment to reach the spot beside him and, as we walked side by side, I asked, "All week?"

Oona's lips curved up in a knowing smile. "I've been meditating."

"All week?" I asked again, astonished.

"Yes."

"Like, the *entire* week?"

"Yes, the entire week," he responded, and then he abruptly brought us to a standstill. All of us heeded. "Nic," he called out.

Nic jogged to meet us in the front. "Yeah?"

"The van, where is it?"

Nic's eyes narrowed. "What van?"

"I have spent a week meditating and can currently see things very clearly. So, the van?"

"Shouldn't you know where it is, if you see everything?"

"I thought you'd like to be the one to bring us there. It's your van, after all," Oona told him.

"Or maybe you don't know where—"

"Next to the willow tree, behind the yellow hibiscus bushes," Oona said. "Now, will you lead us there or should I?"

We followed Nic for a quarter mile before abruptly veering off to the left in an alley, and then behind town. We hiked in tall grass for about five minutes. The hot sun beat on us, and I could feel my skin heating up.

Kailas complained about the brush bugs that jumped off the grass and onto us. Their bites itched like mad, and soon everyone was more than ready to get out of the overgrowth. That's when I saw the willow tree and hibiscus bushes. The yellow flowers swayed in the breeze. Nic parted two of the bushes, revealing an old Masculine van. He held the opening for Oona and me but then, as Kailas was about to pass through, Nic cut him off.

"Your mommy gave you a van?" Kailas called out as he pushed his way through the brush.

"I stole it," Nic responded. "She doesn't know about it, but I'm sure you'll spin it however you want when you tell your disciples."

We piled into the van, which was similar to the one we had taken from Verve. There were identical benches on either side of the van. The only difference was that this van had rear windows. It was uncanny to be in it, as if we had gone back in time.

As Amur sat on the bench, she whispered, "Déjà vu."

Dust rose in a cloud around the van as the wheels spun off. The road was rugged, and we bumped along as Nic steered around boulders. Oona instructed him which turns to take and after ten minutes, we parked. As we jumped out of the van, my feet landed in the dirt and I realized we were in the mountain valley; or, at least, almost in the valley. We were at the foot of it, with a single path leading deeper into it. The mountains above us were breathtaking—two sharp rocks covered in moss, and us mere ants.

Without uttering a word, Oona set foot on the path. I trailed behind him, and the rest followed us in a single line. The ground here was moist. Instead of dusty dirt, I walked on packed mud. It had rained recently; within the last two days, I guessed. We hiked in peace for what felt like half an hour, on a very slight upward incline.

The air was refreshing in my lungs and as I breathed, my face held a calm smile. The verdant scenery reminded me of the west side of the island. There were tall nola trees, vibrant green vines with massive leaves, fruiting banana plants, tall papaya plants, and coconut palms. Then I remembered what else lurked on the west side.

"Oona," I called out to him.

"The Masculines have removed the behemoths here, but do keep an eye out for the slithering creatures," he said, as if he had read my mind.

At first, I didn't understand why the Masculines had removed the behemoths, but then it made sense—their water source. That's where Oona was taking us. He knew how to bypass their patrol border, and we were well on our way to the stream.

Heeding Oona's warning, I took careful steps, looking out for snakes like the one that had taken Jon's leg. When we reached the top of a hill, I heard the sound of trickling water, and then I saw it—a mountain stream gliding through boulders.

"Go ahead," Oona said.

Kailas and I were the only ones who broke out into a sprint toward it. We had to maneuver down a slight decline, through a thicket of bushes, over some roots next to the riverbank, and then we were there. Kailas took off his shorts, which enticed me to do the same. I removed my shorts and vest but kept my shirt and underwear on.

Instead of jumping into the water, I paused atop a faded red boulder. The sun had warmed it, and I enjoyed the residual heat. As I stood there, I witnessed the water as it slid between the surrounding rocks, slipping down the mountain.

"What're you doing?" Kailas looked at me in his black briefs.

I grinned at him. "I'm savoring it."

"Okay," he said, but then he grabbed my arms and pulled me as he fell backward. I landed on top of him and we sank under the water. The shock of the impact went as fast as it came, and then my feet felt the rocky bottom.

I emerged into the air, taking in a breath. As I opened my eyes, I saw Kailas in the stream next to me, grinning from ear to ear. "Kai," I groaned.

There was so much fresh drinking water gliding by me, enough to share with every village on the island. I scooped water into my palms and slurped it up—it was unbelievably cold and refreshing. The deal we had made with Quinn was unfair. She received an abundance of hard-earned harvest from our farm in return for something that flowed freely in nature. If it weren't for the Masculines guarding it, I would have made a plan to come back with Kailas and scoop up our own supply for Smallholding.

Nic and Blue stood on the side of the riverbank, looking at us. Nearby, Sterling and Amur jumped in the stream wearing their undergarments. I searched for Oona, but Kailas tackled me under the water. As we emerged, I leapt on top of his head and ducked him under. Before he could rise, I ran away against the current, but he grabbed my waist and pulled me to him.

Both of us fell sideways into the stream. I pushed him away and climbed up the steep rock face about four feet. I was going to jump on top of him, but then something shone in my eye.

It was a little cascade, weaving its way down the side of the mountain. The sun must have reflected off it, which caught my attention. Hopping from boulder to boulder, I kept going until I reached it. Behind the tiny falls was a cavern, and something told me to go inside it. There was a presence behind me, and I turned to find everyone had followed me there; everyone besides Oona.

"I'm going in," Kailas said as he pushed by me and passed under the falls. I glanced at Nic, who was unlike himself; quiet.

Amur scooted by me and followed Kailas's lead into the cave. Behind me, Sterling whispered something to a distraught Blue, and then he held her hand. I faced the cascade and leaped in. The cold water from the falls pushed on my scalp, the chilly water soaking my body.

A burst of energy ran through me. It was as if I exploded into pieces and then regenerated.

***

I stood atop the faded red boulder again, completely dry and clothed. The stream flowed faster than before, the water completely whitewashed. Above me floated dark gray clouds, and a drizzle landed on my skin. The roaring of the rapids grew loud, and the stream rose over the boulder and threatened to pull me with it. I leapt onto an exposed boulder to my right. As I landed, my foot slipped, and I fell forward, my stomach smacking into the rock. The wind was knocked out of me, but I willed myself to stand. Without a second to waste, I jumped across the boulders until I landed safely by the bank of the stream.

"Kai," I yelled. "Nic?" I climbed the roots of the bank until

I found myself on the trail. I searched for my friends, but they were nowhere to be found. None of this made any sense. The rain poured hard on me, drenching my clothes. "Oona. Anyone?" I screamed desperately.

A twig snapped behind me and I twisted around. A young girl carrying a rack of bananas froze on the path. She was feral, with matted blonde hair and wearing soiled, torn clothes. She stared at me like a startled deer that didn't know which way to dart.

"It's okay," I said before she could run off. "I won't hurt you."

She dropped the bananas and fled.

"Wait," I yelled, running after her. "Wait!" I tracked her far into the forest until the canopy grew thick and dense. As I pushed aside a large leaf, I came to a much unexpected clearing.

The jungle ended and instead, I stood at the summit of the mountain. The rain that soaked my clothing evaporated in an instant, and my clothes and hair were once again waterless. I ran my hand along my dry hair, then turned around in search of the forest, but it had vanished. The trees and plants were gone. I was surrounded by rusty red rocks of all sizes. The mountain landscape rose and dipped into shallow valleys. The air was thin and cold.

An astronaut was there too, a few yards down a crater. He rebounded on the dirt but made no progress toward me. I tried to walk toward him but, as I stepped, I didn't move. It was as if I were on a treadmill. I broke out into a sprint and pushed as hard as I could, but I was stuck in place. Then, without warning, the force holding me back disappeared, and I tumbled down the pebbly landscape. I blundered, fell onto my side, and rolled down the mountain. I tucked into a ball and shielded my face with my arms.

"Hey," someone said, shaking me. "Hey, you alive?" I was no longer falling. I lay curled in a ball on the ground. I removed my arms from my face. The light was bright, and it took me a moment to focus. A disheveled woman hung over me, holding a large stick. Her clothes were ragged, her face smudged with dirt. She poked me in the leg with the stick so that it only somewhat hurt. "Who are you?" she yelled as her eyes narrowed.

We were in a lush rainforest. There was a clearing before me that held multiple shelters built of logs that were pointed at the top—teepees. There were others—men and women, dressed similarly to her—manning a fire. An ugly, bedraggled chicken ran by my face. It startled me and I sat up straight.

The woman pointed the sharp end of her stick at me. "I asked you a question."

I straightened my spine and looked at her. "Is this where Blue's from?" I asked in almost a whisper.

She looked at me wide-eyed, and then called someone over.

"I don't belong here," I whispered to myself.

Somehow, inexplicably, I knew how to get back to where I was supposed to be. I pulled my legs into lotus position and with my finger traced a circle around me in the dirt. Placing my hands on my knees, I closed my eyes and took in a deep breath.

The air shifted around me, and I could tell I had moved again, transported to a new place. My eyes shot open on their own, as if something had forced them. As I looked at my new surroundings, my breathing grew rapid and shallow. I sat in ruins. A desolated desert, covered in dusty, burgundy sand. It was an unforgiving place: no life, no growth. Death was everywhere.

A strong gust of wind blew from behind me, throwing my hair into my face. Dirt blew into my eyes, so I closed them tight. When the wind stopped, I pushed the hair away from my face so I could see.

I was in an entirely black space, floating in the air, still in the lotus position. It was the night sky, and I was surrounded by stars. The air was chilly, but then the sensation went away. All sensations seemed to go away. A tiny, bright light shone in the distance before me. As it grew closer, I recognized it. It was the moon-faced person who came to me in my dream. They wore the same robe adorned with sparkly gems. In their hands they held the glowing red light; it was as bright and entrancing as ever. They extended the light out to me.

I held my hands out to accept it. As it landed in my palms, a red aura exploded around us, and I was blinded. When the light faded, my surroundings returned to me. I was back on the faded red boulder, dry and clothed. The stream was calm as it glided by the rocks as I looked down at my feet.

"Bay," Kailas called out to me, and I looked up to find him. Far down the stream, he balanced on a rock. Behind him, Nic, Amur, Sterling, and Blue exited the cave through the falls.

Kailas bounced from rock to rock until he met me. I was as still as the red boulder beneath me. "Hey," he said, stepping next to me and grasping my hands. "Where'd you go?" The rest of them made their way to us and stood on rocks nearby.

"You vanished," Amur said, "as in *literally* vanished, like… poof, gone."

"Your hair is dry," Nic told me, "and your clothes."

I glanced down to find my clothes dry as a bone.

"Bay?" Kailas said, drawing my attention to him. I saw the worry in his eyes. "What happened?"

Then I sensed him. My head turned in his direction. He stood tall on the top of the riverbank, smiling down at me dressed all in black.

"She's been endowed with her gift," Oona told us.

At his words, I trembled and toppled to the side. The last thing I remembered was something or someone catching me, and then I fell unconscious.

28

"Not everything needs to make sense. Not every story gets wraps up in a bow. That's a very human way to think," I heard Oona say. But, I couldn't see him. I was in darkness.

"What's happening to her?" Kailas asked. Thudding footsteps crunched leaves around me.

"She's… tired. The journey isn't easy. She just needs a good rest and she'll wake up like new. Better, actually," Oona answered.

I wanted to wake up. I wanted to ask Oona questions. I wanted to feel the ground under my feet. I wanted to see.

"Since when can you float people?" Amur asked loudly, and then more quietly, "You could have told me, you know."

There was no answer from Blue. Instead, Sterling spoke. "It's the pendant she wears. It's from the quarry. It enhances the wearer's gift."

Kailas scoffed. "Right."

"How long can you float her like that?" Amur asked.

"I'm not sure," Blue answered. "Maybe until she wakes up." The group was hiking, and Blue floated me along with them.

"You don't have to levitate her. I'm sure Nic could carry her back to the van," Kailas called out.

"Yeah, I *could* carry her. Could you?" Nic retorted.

"What's that supposed to mean?"

"Smallholding doesn't eat very well, and it shows on you."

My body came to a stop. I guessed the group halted.

"Hey," Amur said.

"No," Nic said, "Kailas obviously has something to say."

"You're right. I do," Kailas replied. "You've got a thing for Bay, and I'm not okay with that."

"Hey, guys," Amur said, more urgently this time. "Look."

My eyes opened. After they got accustomed to the light, I saw everyone standing around me. Then my feet glided to the ground and landed on the path. As my soles hit the dirt, I felt it. I was different. I was changed, somehow.

Kailas approached me. "You got a little something there." He gestured toward my hair.

I looked down and saw a strand in the front was somehow dyed vermillion red.

***

As we headed back to Halcyon, Oona explained himself.

He told us that what happened to me was what he had hoped would happen to one of us. He said the cave was an ancient chamber called the Portal of Gifts by the ancestors. When a person who was worthy passed through the cascade and into the cave, through the portal, they were tested. If they passed, they were endowed with their gift.

"Does that mean the rest of us aren't worthy?" Amur asked, clearly offended. "I donate zaram to the poor."

"Being worthy isn't something we do. It's something we are," Oona said.

"Oh, great, more riddles from the crazy old guy," Kailas mused.

We were back on the main street in Halcyon. The sun was low in the sky; it would set beyond the horizon soon. I planned to count down the day at sunset, because the next day was the last day until my brother was due to hatch. Yet something was different. My intentions had shifted. Surviving a couple more days in Halcyon and getting back to Smallholding felt insignificant.

"Are you all right?" Nic asked, approaching me. "You haven't said a word since you came to."

I looked at him, taking in his features: his honey-colored eyes, thick hair, and muscular build. I wanted to say something; nevertheless, no words came to me. The act of speaking somehow felt too small a gesture.

"Can you move things?" Amur asked. "I mean, that's what Blue can do."

Curious about this myself, I glanced off to the side and spotted a lawn chair sitting on the sidewalk. I focused on it, imagining it moving, trying to will it to rise into the air. After a few seconds of trying, I gave up. I was no Blue.

"Bay's not a director, I can tell you that much," Nic offered.

"What's a director?" Kailas asked.

"It's what Blue is… It's a passion," Sterling answered. "They're leaders who influence people. With Blue, though, she has it more physical than mental, and super powered by the gem."

"They're not leaders," Oona corrected him. "Anyone can be a leader. Directors consider themselves leaders because they easily succeed at manipulating people. However, true leaders inspire others to lead, not to follow."

"Sounds like Quinn is a director," Kailas remarked.

"She's a negotiator," Nic told him. "They're gifted at conflict resolution."

"Sure, and what are you?" Kailas looked at Nic.

But Blue spoke first.

"What other gifts are there? Besides the ones we know?"

she asked pensively, her poker face on as if she didn't want to reveal her thoughts.

"As you know, Halcyon currently recognizes eight," he told us. "Director, helper, negotiator, thinker, protector, seer, creator, and healer."

"*Healer*. That's totally Bay," Amur said. "She healed Jon that day in the jungle with the clay. Oh, but then later he—um, never mind, just ignore me."

I could have done without the backhanded compliment, but she wasn't wrong. Healing wasn't my gift.

"What are *you*?" Kailas asked Oona.

Oona looked to him. "They refer to me as a seer. Matilda and I are the only two I know of."

"But what other types are there that aren't publicly recognized?" Blue asked.

Numerous Halcyons passed by us on their way to the beach. Oona gestured toward the nola tree, silently requesting privacy. We all made our way under it and gathered in a semi-circle, some of us standing, others seated. I sat on a long bench.

"Doers, fixers—" Oona continued.

"What are they?" Sterling asked, like a true scientist. "What properties are endowed? How does it work?"

"It's not something that can be studied," Oona said, seeming weary. "Let's rest and talk in the morning." He looked up at the sky. "It's getting dark."

The group fell silent. It looked as though everyone was about to disperse and go their separate ways.

"Maybe it didn't work," I whispered, my voice foreign, as if it were someone else speaking, the words stalled in my throat. I tried again. "I mean, I don't have any special power."

Everyone broke out in a chorus of reaffirming words, telling me that I was special, that it had worked, that everything would be all right. But, I didn't believe them.

Oona was quiet. He silently placed a hand on mine. It was the first time we had touched; his skin was soft and his veins bulged. Out of nowhere, an image of Oona popped in my mind; a vision of him as a child, maybe ten, throwing a tennis ball against a wall in a courtyard. More than see him, though, I could feel what he was feeling. Earlier that day he made the mistake of telling a schoolmate that he could see the future. The kid thought he was crazy, and before the end of the day he had the other kids chanting: *Oona the Know it All*. Oona never wanted to go back to school again. He felt humiliated.

Alarmed by the vision, I pulled my hand away and stared at him, wide-eyed. He just smiled. "It worked," he whispered. And then he stood and walked off. "Tomorrow morning," he called out behind him.

"Maybe it's best to rest," Kailas said, sliding to the spot beside me. "You look exhausted." A canopy of stringed white lights illuminated above us. They wove their way through the branches like vines. I hadn't noticed them before.

"What's that?" Kailas asked, looking to Amur.

"They turn them on during the nights with no moonlight. So we can still see out here," she told him.

He looked up, the light shining on his cheeks.

"Rest sounds good," I managed to say. "But I don't want to go back to the hospital. I can't sleep good there."

"You can stay with me," Nic offered, approaching the other side of me. "Take the bed."

Kailas's gaze shifted to Nic and he stood from the bench to get eye level with him. "I bet you'd love that… Bay sleeping in your bed."

"I didn't say I'd be in it too."

"Please stop." I told Kailas, hating this conversation. He looked at me seriously, his breath heavy with outrage.

"She doesn't like you like that," Nic blurted out, and

Kailas's eyes snapped to him. I wanted to go invisible. "You're just…"—he leaned into him— *"friends."*

"You know nothing." Kailas said, taking a step forward, clenching his fists. He and Nic were only two feet apart.

"Guys, please," I pleaded.

"Bay can stay with Blue tonight," Sterling said, offering a solution. But, the two of them still glared at one another for a long while. Then, Kailas turned his back and walked away.

Exhausted with it all, I decided not to chase after him. Instead, I crossed between them and headed toward Blue. This was all too embarrassing.

"Bay," Nic called out to me from behind. I faced him just as Kailas did. "When we kissed, I felt something, and I know you—" But before he could finish his sentence, Kailas knocked him to the ground, got on top of him, and punched him straight in the face.

I grabbed Kailas, trying to pull him back, but he brushed me off.

Nic got Kailas off him, and they were on their feet. Kailas swung at Nic, but Nic parried, grabbed his arm, yanked him down, and punched him in the gut with his other fist.

"Stop," I yelled. But neither of them could hear me, blinded as they were by their anger.

I wedged myself between them, forcing them apart with my palms. They lunged at each other, but then settled when they realized I wasn't getting out of the way.

With my hands on their chests, it was as if lightning struck the three of us. A strong surge of power glued us together. I couldn't pull my hands off their chests even with all my strength. It was as if we were cemented together by a powerful force. A sparkling, vermillion red light surrounded us as if it emanated from our own bodies, our irises glowing a bright red.

At first, I was terrified, but then tranquility washed over

me, and I relaxed. It was as if peace flowed into me from an outside source. What happened next was a feeling of connection, belonging, and love that warmed us. Our issues, worries, and problems melted away. All thoughts were erased from our minds as we fully merged ourselves with the present moment.

That's when the visions started. It was as if I were Kailas.

I saw the way he saw things. I felt his feelings as if they were my own. He had known he loved me since we were very young. He vividly remembered the moment he knew. My long hair swayed as I ran from him in a game of tag. He felt love for me but didn't yet have the words for it. When he was old enough to understand, he wanted to tell me but was too afraid to.

He carried deep shame from the abuse he had endured from his father. His father had told him he was *no good* so many times that he started to believe it. His mother's death was his greatest loss. He had cried himself to sleep for weeks, wishing she could hold him. Yet he knew she was never coming back. All at once, I experienced the range of emotions he had experienced throughout his life—joy, sadness, pain. Everything. Then it faded, and I had a deep understanding of what it was like to be Kailas Andrews.

In a second wave, it was as if I were Nickel.

I saw his memories. I felt his feelings. I saw life through his eyes. His feelings for me were real, and they were stronger than he had let on. He saw me for who I was and on some level, he thought he might love me. He used wit to play it off because he thought it was the best way to get me interested in him.

I also felt his embarrassment at being the leader's son. He didn't feel seen as a person, and he often felt invisible in Halcyon. Even though he would always defend his mother, the truth was that he hardly agreed with her decisions. As a child, he was lonely. He had never truly gotten to know his father before he disappeared. He missed his grandmother, who raised him, and it broke his heart when she never returned to the island. More often than not, he was lonely, but I also felt his happiness and the thrill he got from adventure seeking. Then I knew. I understood what it was like to be Nickel Copeland.

Then it was my turn to share, to let these men into my heart; to share my memories and allow them to experience them as if they were their own.

My heartbreak over my brother's death came up first. It was fresh and raw. The emotion was overwhelming. It was hard to let him go and I missed him so much it hurt. Watching Ash die of Hackle reminded me of my stepfather and I never got over it. A tear slipped from my cheek as I watched memories of Ash and me playing in a vision: him chasing butterflies, me tickling him.

Then a young Kailas was there playing with toddler Ash too. The feeling came on strong. My love for Kailas was deeper than I ever let myself feel. I carried an unconscious fear that I would lose him like I had lost my father and now my brother. I believed my love for someone sealed their fate in death or going insane, like my mother.

My mother losing grip on reality left a hole in my life that I had never been able to fill. Nic held a special place in my heart because he had been there for me when I needed someone the most—when I needed to save my brother. Nic had shown me that I could be more than I was. His bravery and kindness stuck with me, and some part of me fell in love with him on the west side of the island.

My heart opened up, and every feeling I had ever felt came into existence all at once. Somehow it was as if fireworks burst out of my chest. The climax of emotions was so intense, I thought I might actually explode. But I didn't. I calmed, and it faded. And then I knew. They both understood what it was like to be me, to be Bay Lilly.

The three of us fell into a relaxed state of total surrender. It was as if we were in a mother's affectionate embrace. We felt warmth, understanding, and connection to one another, the planet, and ourselves. It was as if we converged, as if we were in perfect alignment, in a harmonious song, with everything that had ever existed. Feminine and masculine energy came to a balance. Light and dark, positive and negative, pleasure and pain—they were all equal and right.

Then we remembered who we were under our skin. We remembered who we were before we were given a name, before we were born. We had a purpose. We were light. We were perfect in every way. We were infinite energy, more intelligent than our human minds could ever imagine. And in that moment we were restored, once again *whole, infinite, One.*

As if we were unplugged, the energy cleared away from us, and the red light faded to darkness. The three of us stood unmoving and silent. My hands were still pressed to their chests, our bodies still there even though it felt as if they had disappeared altogether. Everything was lucid at first. Then, slowly, our thoughts and personalities returned to us. But, they were less important. They held less significance. I lowered my hands to my sides, separating us physically, and took a step back to see them both. I now knew them more profoundly than anyone had ever known another person.

It was my gift.

Before the cave, my gift was dim, a seed of unfulfilled potential. Now, it had grown to its full, inherent capacity.

Blue and Sterling approached us, as well as other Halcyons who had caught the show. We stood motionless, staring at one another. Words were pale compared to the language I now knew how to speak. How could I possibly explain that experience in words? It would be like trying to explain physics to a bug.

I glanced around at the crowd who surrounded me curiously.

A young Halcyon girl, maybe twelve years old, stepped forward and reached her hand out to mine. I tentatively reached for it, half afraid I would drag her into a red current and learn her life's story. But when our hands touched, it didn't happen. There was no magic.

Instead, she led me a couple yards toward the cafeteria. We came to a stop before the oversized windows that overlooked the nola tree. I looked to her questioningly, and she gestured toward the glass. The sparkle lights that adorned the tree lit the area around us. The cafeteria was closed for the night, and it was pitch black inside. This combination created a reflection in the window, acting like a mirror.

In the mirror image was a crowd staring at themselves. It was those of us under the nola tree. I saw Blue, Sterling, Kailas, Nic, a handful of other Halcyons, and the young girl who held the hand of someone I had never seen before.

I stepped closer to the glass for a better look and the person in the reflection did the same. I raised my hand in the air, and she mimicked me again. Wait. The person wasn't mimicking me; the person *was* me. I let go of the girl's hand and went right up to the glass.

The girl reflecting back at me had long, red hair with faded white roots. Her eyes were a lustrous red and her skin as pale as powder. Raising my hands, I examined them because they didn't seem like mine anymore. I flipped them to the dorsal side, wiggling my fingers to make sure they still moved to my will. I grasped a strand of my hair and held it up to scrutinize. It was red, just as in the reflection. My skin was pale white; my freckled skin, and the girl underneath it, was gone.

29

I had never felt so tired in my life. Each time my eyes opened, I planned to wake but ended up falling back asleep. I repeated this every hour until midday, when the sun beamed through the window onto the bed and shone on me. The rays were so hot that I sweated through my clothes. That's what finally got me to rise from the bed.

At first, I was disoriented, until I remembered I had slept in Blue's apartment. I staggered around in search of the bathroom. When I found it, I leaned over the sink, turned on the faucet, cupped water into my hands, and splashed it on my face to cool down. As I raised my chin to look in the mirror, I jumped back. I had forgotten: I had white-to-red ombre hair now. Glowing red eyes. Freakishly pale skin. I squished my face, pulling my cheeks down with my fingers. *Who is this person?*

Taped to the frame of the mirror was a note. I ripped it off and held it close to read.

Bay, went with Sterling to the gym. We have news. We'll share it with you when you wake up and find us. – Blue

Realizing the sun was already high in the sky, I got on with the day. Or whatever was left of it—only one more day until Ash hatched. And then what? I couldn't guess. I showered in

Blue's tub and dressed in one of her sundresses. I didn't think she would mind; anyway, I had nothing else to wear.

Having never been there, I had no idea where the gym was. As I walked down the main street in Halcyon, all eyes were on me. Each passerby did a double-take, staring for longer than was comfortable, as if they had never seen a fiery-eyed person before. I imagined this was how Blue felt when she first came to Halcyon. After wandering aimlessly for awhile, I asked someone for directions to the gym, and it turned out it was the building beside the science lab.

As I entered, I was taken aback by the tall ceilings. The gym was full of weights, exercise equipment, an obstacle course, a climbing rope, rock climbing wall, punching bags, a wall of weaponry, and a bunch of foam mats. There were probably fifty or more Halcyons actively doing something—training, climbing, running.

In the back, I spotted teal hair. Blue stood at a target, tossing knives at it with her mind. I guessed her secret was out, and everyone knew about her gift, since she was floating objects in public. As I strode toward her, Kailas approached me in my peripheral vision.

I slowed to meet him.

"Hey, Red," he said with a grin and then shook his head. "Wow, this is going to take some getting used to."

"Tell me about it," I said. "I was afraid of my own reflection this morning."

Nic approached my other side, and I was once again standing between the two men. Silence surrounded us as we remembered the night before. Our connection could never be undone. We truly saw each other. Once they understood the other on a deep, complete level, hostility faded into the ether. There would be no fighting between them.

"You know, I think the two of you would've been friends if it weren't for me," I said.

"I don't think so," Nic remarked.

Kailas clicked his tongue, then extended his arm for a handshake. "Truce?"

Nic hesitated, but then he reached in and gave it a shake. Once they separated, they both looked over at me.

"See that?" Kailas said. "Your gift works."

"What are we calling your gift?" Sterling asked as he approached us. "I thought about it all night after hearing Nic and Kailas's testimonies. At first, it reminded me of a syzygy; so, I called it that in my initial notes. But then, what you actually did occurred to me. You weren't only aligning the three of you; you coalesced together—or your souls, or energy, or something of that nature. So, that's what I unofficially called it in my report: *coalescence*."

"*Coalescence*?" I repeated the word.

"Only if that's all right with you."

"Sure."

"There's something you should know," Kailas said, looking at me gravely. "A pair of River Clan infiltrated Halcyon a couple days ago. The Masculines caught them and took them prisoner, and they got them to confess their plans. And we finally understand what the translation means."

Shooting light, sunsets of two. That's what Quinn had me translate. "They broke into the tech vault to steal weapons, because they're planning an attack."

I stopped breathing.

"A battalion will come to Main Street tomorrow at sunset."

It suddenly made sense why the gym was full of citizens training. Tomorrow there would be a war. I wanted to end the war before it began, to make them all see how foolish war was.

But then I realized maybe I could. My gaze shifted to Blue, who was still in the back, suspending knives in the air and aiming them at a board.

I marched purposefully across the mats toward Blue. I crossed paths with someone who was practicing with a fighting stick; he didn't see me and almost whacked me in the face, but I felt it and ducked in time. I kept on track as if it never happened and in seconds, I reached her.

She didn't notice me. She had four blades hovering in the air, preparing to send them off to the target.

I reached for her crystal necklace and yanked it off.

"What the hell, Bay?" The knives continued to hover behind her.

Her eyes never left my face as the blades sped off and embedded themselves in the board, with most of them hitting the bull's-eye.

"When did you go into the cave?" I asked sternly. "This gem doesn't do what Sterling said it does—your teal hair and eyes. The same thing that happened to me happened to you, didn't it?"

Sterling was there now. I reached for his shoulder and held onto it, trying to will my gift to work, to show him my perspective. I wanted him to know why I chose to do what I did. But nothing happened, and he shrugged me off.

"It's all right, Sterling," Blue whispered.

Sterling gave her a nod and hesitantly left.

I handed Blue her necklace as the pair of us exited the gym and found a bench in the garden area outside the science building, where we could be alone.

"My given name isn't Blue," she told me. "It's Ali'i. When I first came to Halcyon, the kids called me Blue because of my hair, and it stuck."

She explained that one day, after her parents' form-deaths,

she was on her own in the forest when she spotted a Halcyon. She had run as fast and as far as she could when she came across the cave. She thought to hide in it until the Halcyon went away. As she crossed through the cascades, she was transported, just as I was. She saw visions, until eventually she was back at the cave, only when she came back, she had bright blue hair, blue eyes, and could move things with her mind.

Before the sun fell that day, Oona went into the forest and found her. He explained that her transformation had sent a vision to him. In a dream, he was told by a mystical presence to go find Blue and bring her to Halcyon, and so he did. For months, she lived with Oona and he taught her how to use her gift. Eventually, he set her up in Halcyon as a citizen, helped her meet Sterling, and then went back to meditating.

"Why didn't you tell me?" I asked. "Especially after yesterday."

"Honestly, I don't know," she admitted, holding onto her necklace, rubbing the gem with her thumb. "I've kept the secret for so long. I guess I planned on never telling it."

"You seem to be throwing knifes with your thoughts just fine in front of everyone today."

"I practiced in public for the first time today because we told them the gem powered my gift. It's not easy for me, and I'm still conflicted about killing Helio. Still, I have to protect myself and the only place I know as home. So, I have to practice. Sterling needs me to."

"Okay, I understand," I said. "So, I was right? The gem doesn't enhance powers?"

"They do. That's why he's been selling them. He discovered these gems in the quarry and they enhance the wearer's gift up to twenty percent so long as it's touching their skin."

"How's that possible?"

"He didn't know exactly. But, after seeing the cave yesterday, he thinks the mineral is what energizes the cave. The quarry isn't too far from there, just a couple miles south."

It made sense. "I need your help. I can't seem to control my gift. It just happens spontaneously."

Blue gently held onto my hands. "Show me," she said and closed her eyes.

I wasn't sure why, but I did the same. I concentrated on sending her a flash of—what did Sterling call it? Coalescence. I waited for it to happen, but there was nothing. I pulled away.

"See?" I shrugged.

"How are you trying to control it?"

"With my mind?"

"There's your problem," she said. "Your gift doesn't come from the mind. The gift is born out of your soul and controlled by your emotions. That's what Oona taught me. He said we have to embody who we are—to feel it."

What she said was nice, and it made sense though I continued to struggle. It took five more failures before Blue decided I should seek Oona's advice. I went to his beach apartment, and Oona spent the better part of an hour coaching me patiently. He didn't get impatient, but I did.

"Let's try again," he said for the sixty-seventh time.

I took his hands into mine, and we sat on the meditation mats in his studio. I closed my eyes and tried to channel my emotions, my soul. But it didn't work.

"Channel Oneness. Be yourself," Oona reminded me.

Exhausted, I gave up without Oona knowing. I closed my eyes and decided to give myself a break. I let myself relax. Then, the vision of him in the play yard reappeared. I could hear his thoughts, feel his feelings. I *was* Oona. He was sullen, sitting on the ground with his tennis ball, feeling alone. It reminded me of when my mother had neglected me when I needed her the most. I would sit like that too. Bad feelings—unspiritual feelings—bubbled up, so I turned them away.

"What was that? What did you do right then?" Oona asked. "You had it, and then it sputtered out."

"I don't know."

"You have to treat it like a fire: let it build and keep it going. You let it die."

"I'm sorry; I'm trying."

"You cut yourself off from it, from your feelings. Why?"

He didn't get it. *He* was spiritual. He a wise old man, and *he* didn't get that negative emotions were bad? "Because negative emotions cause pain and problems. They cause anxiety. They aren't spiritual."

"What else?"

Gosh, what was he getting at?

"I don't know," I nearly yelled.

He looked at me deeply and quietly restated himself. "What else?"

I spoke without thinking. "They'll make me weak like my mother. She gave into her emotions and abandoned me," I told him, feeling shaky. Tears welled up in my eyes at the admission of it all.

"I see," he said. "You're only human, Bay. No emotion is negative. Anger, sadness, regret... all are purposeful. Emotional intelligence is a great strength, not a horrible weakness. It's time to get back in touch with this part of yourself. The natural curiosity you have about the inner workings of others... let that grow. Be curious. That's the seed of empathy."

I inhaled for strength.

"Now, tell me about your mom," he said. Somehow, with Oona's listening ear, I let it all out. A rain after a long drought that just kept coming for what felt like forever. He listened compassionately the entire time. When I was done blubbering, Oona told me it was progress, and that releasing the pain was integral. He was right. I let go of something in that moment that freed me from shackles I hadn't known I was wearing. But it wasn't just pain about my mother. It was more than that—it was suffering of my own doing. It was my quest for perfection. I didn't need to perfectly control my every emotion in order to be spiritual. In fact, I couldn't perfectly control my emotions and be spiritual. The thing I thought would free me had actually been holding me back.

When I was ready, we tried again.

I channeled One, got curious about Oona, and allowed the feelings to flow.

I had access to his childhood memories, his emotions, his thoughts. It was as if we were bound together, the two of us lit up in a sparkling red aura. The serenity was beyond imaginable as I took in Oona's perspective. His meditations left him feeling tranquil even during the mundane. I thought the coalescence might allow me to use his gift of divination—to see the future too. But it didn't.

"Gifts don't transfer," he told me. "Sorry to disappoint."

I laughed. "That's all right. I don't want that burden anyway. I'm not even sure I want mine."

"Your gift is special. Learn to cherish it."

"What is my gift exactly? I mean, what does it do? I know how it feels, but I can't find the words to describe it."

"Your gift restores our connection with the force of life, with One. Once connected, the insanity of the mind is exposed. The connection to all things arises, and perspectives are shared. Usually, what is shared are the memories and feelings at the core of a person's being, the things that have shaped them in this lifetime. Sometimes, even past lifetimes. The restored connection is temporary, though. It's felt most strongly during the transfer but then, when it's over, it wears off. This is especially so as the humdrum aspects of life take over. The person will eventually need repeated restoration. They can do these themselves through meditation or by living in the moment."

It was a lot to take in, but it was also wonderful to have the words.

"Your friends are waiting on the beach for you," Oona said, ending our session together.

***

As my feet hit the sand, the bliss from the coalescence remained strong, and the ocean appeared marvelous to me, with increased vibrancy. I spotted Sterling and Blue by the shoreline, embracing as waves washed over their feet. He placed his hand behind her head and brought her to his lips. The sun behind them made them shine and their love was cast for all to see.

I approached Kailas, who was in the middle of the beach, talking with three Halcyons. The first was a young man with faded canary-yellow hair. Beside him was another man with violet-white hair, and then a middle-aged woman with bright eyes and short, lime-green hair with white streaks. They looked familiar, but I couldn't immediately place them.

"Hi," I said to Kailas, and then nodded at the others.

Kailas introduced them. "Meet your equals. This is Samuel, who is a helper, a protector named Lux, and that's Gwen, the healer. They passed the cave test, too, and got their superpowers. Oona has been training them, and they're ready to defend Halcyon."

I suddenly remembered Gwen from the hospital when I first arrived in Halcyon, and Lux from the freezers. He was the man Blue had subdued with her mind control.

"Hi," I said, realizing they must have gone through the same ordeal as me when going into the cave. They all nodded at me.

More than fifty others were enjoying the beach around us; jumping over waves, swimming in the ocean, and chatting on the sand. That's when I realized there wasn't a Masculine asking for zaram at the entrance. Quinn must have allowed for a last hurrah.

"What do your gifts do?" I asked.

I expected them to answer, but it was Kailas who spoke. "The helper can supercharge other people's gifts," he explained.

That was useful—a power boost for my coalescence.

"The protector has super strength." It was no surprise that the protector was a Masculine, then.

"Last, the healer. In everyday life, she's learning how to heal wounds instantaneously."

I wondered if that was why my arrow wound seemed to be healed in only a week. If she could heal Masculines as they got injured, that would keep each warrior in the fight and save a lot of lives.

Up until then, I hadn't realized that others had their gifts, and I wondered how many Oona had taken to the cave. For a second, I imagined what the world would be like if everyone could reach their fullest potential and use their gifts. Would we still be going to war? Would anything change? Or would we still find reasons to fight?

30

Everything was falling apart, or maybe falling together. I wasn't entirely sure. Out there on the beach, I turned away from the ocean and faced our mountain, staring at the dots that made up the houses in Smallholding. For better or worse, it was home, and I planned on going back there. Only now, with the impending war, it seemed nugatory to trek up there and... what? Say goodbye?

I felt a presence behind me.

"Missing home?" Kailas asked, his warming touch on my shoulder.

"How'd you guess?"

"My superb observational skills," he said.

"Do you think Oona is right? About the world ending?" I asked, turning to face him. His arms wrapped around my back, pulling me into his chest. Losing everything was too much to bear.

"I don't know," he said gently. "I think there's still hope."

"I wish we could go home one last time."

"Maybe we can."

I looked at him inquisitively.

"We could take a van and drive there now, be back before the second Brotherfly Ceremony tomorrow. Go on our date?"

I thought about it. "Okay," I said, getting excited at the idea. "Let's do it."

"Really?" he asked, surprised by my response. "You went for that?"

It wasn't difficult to get a van. With the Masculines busy preparing for battle, they weren't guarding the vehicles. To get across the town line, though, we had to lie. I hunched down behind the dashboard, while Kailas told them he was doing a delivery for Smallholding.

Soon after, we flew up the road and climbed the mountain. The wind blew in through the open windows, and my hair whipped around us in a red blur. We didn't speak for the entire ride up to Smallholding, but there were times I glanced over at him to check him out.

When we made it to the entrance of our village, it felt good to be home. We parked by the village center, and some nearby neighbors came to greet us. My appearance startled them at first, but to avoid spending too much time explaining, I shrugged it off as a Halcyon thing. Most of them didn't know what Halcyons looked like, anyway.

I decided I would keep my gift and the impending war with the Helio a secret. I wanted to save myself the hassle of explaining everything. Also, to spare them the fear of what was to come. After all, wasn't ignorance bliss?

Kailas and I strolled to my house. As we approached it, it gave the impression of being smaller somehow, as if it had literally shrunk in size. My world was so much bigger now. We came to a stop by the porch stairs, and a thought occurred to me for the first time since my brother's form-death.

"Ash's form," I said. "Where is it?"

"Around back," he answered, extending his hand out to me. "I'll show you."

We interlocked fingers, and he led me to the back yard. In the far right corner was a mound of dirt, and on top of it were grey rocks intentionally placed to make a circle. Directly in the middle, someone had planted a lavender bush.

A small gasp escaped my lips, and my hand went up to my mouth. My eyes grew teary. "It's beautiful."

"Brutus helped," he said. "I thought Ash would've liked it."

"It's perfect," I whispered as I walked closer to it and lowered to the ground. "And it has a sunset view."

He sat beside me, and I rested my head on his shoulder. I thought of my brother then, but I didn't have anything to say to him. I mean, he wasn't there, right? He was in the chrysalis in the science lab. We sat for a long while watching the sun peek out from the clouds. I reached for Kailas's hand and rubbed the surface of it with my thumb.

"Do you have to go see your dad?" I asked.

"Eh, maybe tomorrow. I'd rather stay with you. He'd put me to work." It was true. His father saw him more as a servant than a son.

There was a rusted metal swing with a three-person seat in my yard that we decided to sit on. The fabric on the cushion was ripped and tattered, but it was still lovely for a relaxing swing. Kailas laid his head on my lap and looked up at me as I brushed through his hair with my fingers. His knees were bent, and he barely fit on the swing like that.

His hair was soft, and the weight of his head on my lap felt comforting. We talked about the good times in our lives, the happy stories, and I realized that the majority of mine had been with him. We spent a long while on the swing, long enough to watch the sun lower.

"I've been meaning to ask you to be my mate," he confessed, "but there always seems to be some crazy crisis or apocalypse in the way."

I wasn't surprised by his confession, since I had seen it

through his perspective in the coalescence. "You still could've asked."

He sat up and shifted his weight to look seriously at me. "Oh, yeah, maybe I could've asked when you were falling out of the nola tree?" he mused. "Or when the Helio were shooting arrows at us? Or when you were kissing Nic?"

The last part stung a little.

"Fair enough," I said.

"Look," he said gently. "I know how you feel about him. I know how you feel about me. I know how you feel about… well… almost *everything*. And honestly, no offense, because I love you, but whether or not you *choose me* seems to matter a lot less. After you did your thing it gave me perspective."

A strand of black hair fell into his face, and I tucked it behind his ear. "I know what you mean." I looked at Ash's grave and then back at Kailas. "I love you too."

He reached his hand toward my face and held my cheek in his palm. His touch was everything.

"And just so you know"—I told him, placing my hand on his—"I would've said yes."

Looking profoundly into my eyes, he leaned forward and kissed my forehead, and then pulled me in for a hug.

I didn't know what was happening, but I liked being this close to him.

We rose from the swing, my feet had fallen asleep and I had to shake them to get the blood flowing. It was an overcast day, and the sun hid behind gray cumulous clouds. There wasn't much to see until about ten minutes after the sunset, when the billow lit up a fiery pinkish color.

We were gazing at it when he reached into his pocket and pulled out a necklace—a black cord adorned with the shell he had found on the beach. He moved my hair over my shoulders and put the necklace around my neck, clasping the ends together over my spine. My skin tingled.

"Thank you," I whispered, holding the shell between my finger and thumb.

His capable hands found their way to my hips. He drew me close, and then placed a hand on my jaw line. I lost my breath as a powerful surge rushed my spine. His lips connected with mine, and then we were kissing in the pink light of sunset.

When the light was all but gone, we found our way inside my house. Stepping toward my room, I passed my brother's door. Catharsis took hold of me. But I didn't want to go there and, for the most part, I was ready to let him go.

Everything in my room was how I had left it, except a dresser drawer had been left open by whoever came from Halcyon to get my clothes. I shut the drawer and made my way to the bed. Kailas followed behind me. I had no idea what was going to happen, but my heart raced anyway. I lowered myself to the mattress.

Kailas climbed onto the bed beside me and lay flat on his back. I moved forward and placed my head on his chest, and his arm curled around me. In all our years of friendship, we had never lain like that. The sound of his beating heart thumped in my ear. Right there, lying with him, I was truly at home.

Feeling safe, I drifted off to sleep. A dreamless, restful sleep.

When I woke, the sunlight was entirely gone, and the very dim moonlight came in through the window. I hadn't moved in my sleep, and my head still rested on Kailas's chest. I found him staring down at me. Shifting my weight, I pulled my body up to meet his eyes and placed my hand on his face, pulling him in to kiss me. This kiss led us into a night of bringing masculine and feminine energy together as one.

As we made love, I felt a connection to Kailas that was even deeper than our coalescence. It was spiritual *and* physical. Inconceivably and simultaneously, it was imperfectly human and yet immaculately divine. We were given a taste of what it was like to be in a state of eternal, blissful no existence. I never wanted it to end. I wanted to stay wrapped together with our warm bodies intertwined forever. I truly saw Kailas and he saw me. I didn't know a connection could feel so good. His soul entered mine, and I couldn't separate me from him. We became a single person, and I knew then that we were soulmates.

What I didn't know was that it would be the last night the two of us would be alive to share in this connection. The following day, our world and everything in it would change forever, and only one of us would be alive to see it.

31

In the morning, I lay on my bed, staring at the ceiling. Naked under the comforter, Kailas snored loudly beside me. I leaned in and kissed him on the cheek. Then I rose, found my clothes, and dressed. Before I made it to the bathroom, though, there was a loud knock. Hesitantly, I headed for the foyer and opened the front door to find Mr. Andrews standing on the other side. *What does he want?* The same stain was on his shirt from the last time I had seen him, as well as a new one. As a breeze blew in through the door, I inhaled his body odor, while trying not to gag.

"Is the boy here?" he asked with a raspy voice. "I heard he was back. Is he hiding here?"

"Mr. Andrews, he's, um—"

"What the hell happened to you? You're Bay, right? Why're you red?" he asked, obviously repulsed by my appearance.

"It's, um… just—"

"Never mind, I don't care. That son of a bitch is here, isn't he? Kailas!" he yelled. "Kailas, get your lazy waste of an ass out here."

"He isn't—"

"Kailas!" he screamed, shoving by me to get into the house. I pushed firmly on his chest. I wasn't about to let him into my home uninvited.

"What do you think you're doin'?" He groaned, smacking my hand away. "No girl gets in the way of a father and his son. You got that?" He wagged his finger at me.

Kailas was there now, shirtless, maneuvering himself between us, shoving his father back. "Don't touch her," he yelled.

"Where've you been, boy?" Mr. Andrews yelled. "There's a ton of work to do at home."

Kailas eyed him darkly. "You've been drinking nectar again, haven't you? How'd you even get your hands on that stuff when there's all this work to do, Dad?"

"That's none of your business," he said through his teeth.

I had almost forgotten. I had a new way to resolve arguments. I had my gift. I tried to remember how to channel it. *Be curious, embody who I am, connect to my emotions, remember One.* Reaching forward, I grasped both of their shoulders. I closed my eyes and opened myself up to feel their pain, their broken relationship, and the love that they inevitably had for one another despite their differences.

First, I saw how their relationship began as loving when Kailas was a young boy. They played soccer together, wrestled with each other, and Mr. Andrews taught him how to shoot a bow. But then Kailas's mother died after giving birth to his stillborn younger sister, and their relationship plummeted. My heart broke with Mr. Andrews's at the loss of his wife and daughter. Kailas was devastated and missed his mother more than anything in the world.

After her death, Kailas felt that his father stopped loving him. He felt like a hindrance to his father because Mr. Andrews would consistently shut him out. Mr. Andrews seemed heartless through Kailas's perspective, but then Mr. Andrews's view came and showed us that he did love Kailas. Only after his wife and daughter died, he was unconsciously guarding his heart. Kailas was all he had left and loving him—or anyone—became too frightening for him. He didn't think he could stand to lose another person he loved.

I disconnected from the coalescence. That was new. Confused at first, I glanced around, trying to figure out what was happening. I took a few steps back and watched the two of them standing still, surrounded by red light. For the first time, I didn't have to stay for the entire exchange. I could make the connection, fuse them, and then leave while the visions continued without me. My perspective wasn't included in their coalescence.

After a few moments, they came back to their normal states, yet I knew their relationship would be unquestionably reshaped. A feeling of exhaustion washed over me, and I had to reorient myself. Kailas and his father came together in a hug as tears streamed down Mr. Andrews's cheeks. That's when I saw the sun peek out from the mountain behind them. The second Brotherfly Ceremony was to start an hour after sunrise.

I gave them space while I went to dress for the day, taking a minute to sit and rest on my bed. I changed clothes a couple times, unsure what a person should wear to battle. Not having anything suitable, I decided on linen pants and a loose-fitting tan top. Hopefully they would re-dress me in Halcyon before the fight that night. Then I fastened my hair into a side braid. This time, the long braid was red instead of blonde.

I met Kailas outside as he was saying goodbye to his father.

I approached them while they looked at a compass.

"It broke this morning. I'm going to spend the day fixing it. It was your great grandfather's, a family heirloom I planned on giving to you one day. You'll be back again this week, right?" Mr. Andrews asked Kailas. The needle spun haywire. I wasn't sure how he planned to fix that.

"We'll be back soon," Kailas said. I guessed he hadn't filled him in on the apocalypse. They went in for a hug. "I love you," I heard Kailas say, and his father returned the sentiment. I expected Mr. Andrews to ask me about the coalescence—to ask what had happened—but he didn't. He simply embraced me, and we left.

***

We stopped by Gemma's cottage on our way out of Smallholding. I very much wanted to see her, but she wasn't home. We waited for as long as we could, but we had to leave to make it in time for the final ceremony.

As the vehicle made its way down the mountain, we watched the sunlight creep its way over the entire valley, bringing day to the island. Kailas sped to be sure we made it to watch my brother fly off as a winged butterfly. He rested his hand on mine, and our touching skin brought me back to the previous night—the memory of his body over mine. It caught my breath. Were we supposed to talk about it? Or pretend it never happened? How could I pretend that never happened?

"Last night," Kailas whispered. He must have been remembering it, too. "I don't even have words for how amazing it was."

My heart raced too much to think of a good response. "Me neither," I ended up saying, but I wasn't sure if it was enough, if he knew just how meaningful it was to me. His eyes returned to the road, and we sat in silence until we reached Halcyon. A crowd rallied around the gate at the border, trying to get into Halcyon—men, women, and children, who all weren't well groomed or face painted; they were grungy and weak.

The Masculines pushed them back several feet so we could drive through with the van.

"Who are they?" I asked Kailas.

"Non-alliance wanting to be citizens."

"I had no idea they were out here."

"Masculines usually keep them away but with most of them training, I guess there aren't enough to hold them off."

We passed through the gate and into Halcyon. Citizens moved off the road as we drove by the rainbow nola tree and parked in a lot by the lab.

Hundreds gathered at the stage that had been built the night before. The scene was in the same place as the first ceremony, and we met the others in the rear building, in the same spot Nic and I had waited the first time. Sterling brought Ash's chrysalis to me before disappearing to help Amur set up the equipment with other stagehands.

The chrysalis had turned a deep blue with golden speckles. Or maybe the shell was turning translucent and the blue color was the wings visible through the outer shell? I remembered the ugly, fuzzy green caterpillar he once was and couldn't believe something could transform so drastically.

It appeared we had made it to the final Brotherfly Ceremony just in time, as it was about to begin. Two Masculines escorted my mother to me. As I looked into her eyes, I could tell she different—changed—just as Ash had, over the last two weeks.

"I like your hair," she said.

"Thanks." I blushed, not wanting to explain. "How are you?"

"I'm… good," she said. I gave her a look. "The therapists are great here. I didn't think I'd ever feel this way again. So, really, I'm good."

She did seem good—steady for the first time in I couldn't guess how long. I embraced her, relieved that she had found herself again. After a long moment, we parted and I stood next to Kailas when Nic appeared.

"Where've you guys been?" Nic asked us.

"Visiting home," Kailas told him.

"You missed training."

"The Helio aren't coming until nightfall… We'll catch up," Kailas said.

The short, gold-faced man in white, the event coordinator for the first ceremony, reappeared. He grabbed our attention and ushered us toward the door. "Five minutes," he told us.

Quinn approached the three of us, her short, orange hair as pin-straight as ever. Her tight-fitting, off-white dress was ironed flat and pristine. Her matching off-white cape with a crimson lining flowed out behind her. She looked me over.

"Is that what you're going to wear?" she asked. "I can get Frankie."

"Mom…" Nic shook his head.

"Right, okay, well, no time for that. That's fine."

"You can cancel the ceremony and focus on the fight," I offered, knowing that would kill her. "My mother and I could release Ash in private."

"Nonsense," Quinn scoffed. "We've been anticipating this for weeks. Everyone is excited. We can't cancel events just because the River Clan is terrorizing us."

"Please tell me if I'm remembering this wrong but aren't we the ones who invaded their territory and killed their chief?" Kailas asked bitterly. I nudged him and he gave us all a look. "What? Is no one allowed to call the queen out? And by the way, Quinn, you stole Bay's Ant Effect idea."

Quinn shifted her hip. "I… It was One's idea that wanted to come into existence. It doesn't matter who expressed it, so long as it was expressed."

"Yeah, no. Your words sound pretty, but I don't buy it. You got awarded twenty thousand zaram for having an inspirational idea… Bay's idea." Kailas shook his head.

"You don't know how it works here. And I don't need zaram, I have plenty," she responded.

I had things to say about Quinn. About her hoarding food, about her stealing my idea, about the way she ran things, but I closed my mouth and swallowed the words.

"Listen," I said instead. "Coalescences take a *ton* of energy out of me. I already did one today. I don't want to have to do another on the two of you." Though I had to admit, the idea of understanding Quinn was compelling.

"He's hatching. Ash is hatching!" my mother called.

Quinn rushed to my mother, grabbed her under the arm, and led her to the stage holding Ash's jar. All of us followed awkwardly behind.

"Get him into the cameras," Quinn cried. She had my mother set Ash on a table in the front. She removed the lid and placed it on a towering mantel, which they seemed to have constructed for this occasion.

With no introductions or lavish grand entrance, the audience wasn't sure if they should applaud or not. Amur looked puzzled, too, standing on the stage, working to untangle electrical wires in preparation for the ceremony. But then Quinn pointed to the chrysalis and, when she saw Ash emerging, Amur grabbed the stage camera to focus the lens in on him. The visual was broadcast on a screen above us for the crowd to see.

The audience clamored, as everything was in disorder on the stage. It definitely wasn't going according to Quinn's plan. I shimmied my way to the front, nudging Quinn out of the way, and knelt before the chrysalis next to my mother. Kailas, Nic, and Quinn stood behind us, and we watched on.

He came out of the chrysalis little by little, letting gravity do most of the work, then, all at once, the rest of it slipped out. He held onto the chrysalis shell with his feelers and hung upside down. What emerged was a crinkled mess of legs, wings, proboscis, and antennae—all the stuff of butterflies, just in disarray. It seemed impossible that this wrinkled ball of butterfly could ever resemble a wide-winged creature. A flow of emotion went through me. Witnessing this brand new creature come into the world was precious. And this creature was my brother.

As he hung on the chrysalis, his crinkled wings fell to the space below his body. The outer part of his wings was a steel blue that faded into a vibrant electric blue toward the middle. The underside of his wings was predominantly brown with white circles, filled with black, which made them look like teeny eyeballs.

"Ash is a blue morpho butterfly." Sterling spoke into a microphone, explaining the biology to us. "He may look like a shriveled mess now but over the next twenty minutes, he will start to look more like the butterflies you know. His abdomen is swollen because it's full of a fluid called hemolymph. As he pumps this fluid into his wings, they will expand while his abdomen shrinks. Once that process is complete, he will hang for an hour to dry before taking flight."

I couldn't take my eyes off it. Quinn must have taken the microphone as I now heard her voice through the speakers, "Once his wings are dry, we will set him free to fly."

The audience applauded, and I shifted my gaze to them for a moment. They looked just as they had ten days before—wearing tones of browns and greens, with glittery face paint. Many of them had various butterflies painted on their cheeks, and I remembered what Blue's friend had told me about that. They were honoring Ash—and me. I smiled at the thought of having support and then returned my gaze to Ash.

As Ash's wings filled with fluid and settled straight, I remembered that he once told me he wished to have wings in his next life. What did he say? He wanted to flap them around in the sky? *Oh, little Ash*, I thought, *you got what you asked for.*

The hour passed quickly for me. I could have stayed there, staring at the miracle of butterfly Ash for eternity. The audience, however, was getting restless. Some of them stopped watching the ceremony and instead, sat cross-legged on the ground and chatted.

"Hey," Kailas said, kneeling next to me, talking to the butterfly. "You're going to fly high today, little dude."

"Part of me doesn't believe this is him," I heard my mother say. I twisted to face her. "I gave birth to him as a baby boy. Seeing this butterfly giving birth to itself, I keep thinking, *This can't be my Ash.*"

Ash fluttered his wings while hanging upside down, but he didn't lift off.

Sterling waved Quinn and Amur back over.

"Bay, let him climb onto your finger," Sterling said in the microphone. "He's ready."

I looked to Ash but shook my head. "Let my mother do it."

My mother stepped forward, and extended her index finger out to the butterfly. It took several seconds, but eventually, Ash crawled onto her finger, reorienting himself upright. He stayed like that as she held him out before her. The audience was captivated now, standing again, watching our every move.

Then my mother looked to me. "It should be you," she said, offering him to me.

When our fingers met, the butterfly extended one of his legs out to me, crawling onto my knuckle. The spurs tickled my skin. I studied the insect carefully, trying to feel my brother's soul. Every detail of it stood out vibrantly—the dark, furry form, the powder on the wings, the spirited colors.

Two musicians appeared onstage. One sat at a keyboard piano I hadn't realized was there, and the other brought a violin to his chin. As they began to play, the emotions of the moment were ushered to life by their song—each note vibrated through me, filling my wounds and mending them shut. As they played, I let myself drift into the feelings swirling within me, some of which I couldn't name for they went deeper than words.

Under closed eyelids, my brother's face appeared, clear as day. It was him, down to the way his eyes curved like crescents when he smiled, the unruliness of his thick, blond hair, the freckles on his cheeks. It was Ash, *my* Ash. I let the image of him fill my being. My body was warm and full, satiated with love. Then just like that, Ash was gone. His face faded as my eyes opened. The butterfly was there, on my finger before me. It was time to let him go. A tear fell as I surrendered to the grief.

My heart shuttered as he took flight off my finger. I could swear I heard the sound of his wings beating in the air. There was a moment of alarm as something inside me wished to chase after him, to bring him back—a final resistance. Then, I let him go, and acceptance washed over me.

"Goodbye, Ash," I whispered, as he flew over the heads of the audience. They raised their painted faces to watch.

"There goes our Brotherfly," Quinn beamed through the speaker.

He would be able to move on with his soul journey, live his lives, and not be stuck in the in-between forever. He was safe. I had done my job. He was free.

There was a moment of tranquility as butterfly Ash disappeared into the distance. But then, as I watched the blue butterfly flutter through the sky, my eyes focused on the area behind it. The serene moment turned ominous as I saw—only a half a mile from us—an army of more than a hundred green-skinned Helio marching toward us for battle.

“**R**iver Clan!” Nic yelled it out first.

The excited faces of the audience fell flat as they turned to see.

“Be calm,” Quinn said through the speakers. “Everyone, please walk east and up to the valley. No one goes home. Let’s all stay ataraxy. Nic, will lead the way.”

Nic nodded as the buzzing audience seemed on the verge of hysteria. Quinn whispered something into his ear, and he turned to face the crowd.

“Okay, everybody,” Nic said, casually making his way off the stage. My mother followed him, but before she left, I grabbed her hand and looked at her gravely. Then she stepped off in Nic’s direction. Amur followed along with my mom; I guessed she wasn’t documenting the war. “Let’s think of our neighbors and not push, all right?” Nic waved them on and headed away from the River Clan, up the main road.

I admired the way he kept calm. My hands were shaking.

“Bay,” Quinn called to me, this time without the microphone, “Kailas, Sterling, Amur, go take your places. The plan stays the same. Masculine back-up is coming.” Sterling and Blue nodded. Kailas and I were at a loss—skipping out on the training suddenly felt like an awful mistake.

“Places?” I asked.

“I’ll catch you up,” Sterling offered before Quinn could answer. “Let’s walk.”

The four of us moved, making our way down Main Street. In front of us, the army of Helio headed up the valley toward us. They would reach Halcyon soon. We needed more time.

"Blue will be positioned on the roof of the building closest to the fight," Sterling told us. "I'll be with her. Kailas, you stay with Bay, along with the power unit—ten Masculines assigned to protect her."

"And me? What do I do?" I asked, weary, trying to gather my strength.

"Coalesce as many Helio as you can."

Coalescences gave me a headache. There was no way I could coalesce hundreds of Helio without my brain exploding.

"You're kind of the key player. Once you do your magic they'll stop fighting us. We don't want more war. We want a resolution. That's Quinn's official stance. Avoid casualties by coalescing. If you can reach their chief, that would give us our best shot at ending this. Kailas, your job is to help Bay do that."

"Sure," I said, "I'll try."

Kailas looked to Sterling. "You sound like a Masculine."

"Jack of all trades," Sterling replied with a grim smile. As we approached a building, he came to a stop. "This is my get off. You guys go toward the town entrance. There's over a hundred Masculines there. We want to keep the Helio out of town, away from Main Street."

I started to hyperventilate. *Breathe*, I told myself, *just breathe*. I could make peace with the Helio through my gift. It was what I was meant to do.

Sterling disappeared into the building, and Kailas glanced over at me. Seeing my nerves, he looked me straight in the eye. "You can do this."

As we headed to the front line, there was a calm stillness in the air that didn't seem appropriate for the chaos whirling inside me. When the Masculines came into view, they were a sight to behold. In their black and brown uniforms, they appeared as a dark mass. As we approached the men, one of them strode up to me, his forehead tattoo glistening with sweat.

"I'm Masculine Tomas. My brothers and I are here to protect you." He motioned to the nine men behind him. One of them was Lux, the protector. He stood out with his violet hair and eyes. "We have a range of weaponry you can choose from, both conventional and tech."

"I'll take a shield," Kailas told him.

Throwing knives would be useless. I needed something to protect myself, to get close enough to connect into a coalescence with the Helio. Maybe Kailas was onto something. Tomas handed him a silver band. Kailas put it on his wrist and twisted it every which way, eyeing it up.

"Kinda small, yeah?"

"It's tech," Tomas said. Reaching forward, he tapped it. A white, disc-shaped force field, about five feet in circumference, shot out from it.

"Are you sure this will work?" Kailas asked, just as a flaming arrow struck the shield. The shield zapped as a rippling light expanded from the spot the arrow hit, and the arrow fell to the pavement.

We moved our eyes to the sky to find dozens of flaming arrows raining down on us. Somehow, I ended up underneath Kailas's shield. I think a Masculine led me there. Men surrounded me, protecting me with their lives. They hovered around me, extinguishing arrows, arranging my safety.

My eyes fixed on the mass of Masculines at attention about fifteen yards from where we stood. Those in the back weren't battling yet, though I had a feeling the front line was already in fight. A berserk Helio man came barreling through the crowd, stabbing one of the Masculines in his stomach. His irisless eyes glowed like a galaxy as he charged toward us, his attention fixed on me, his target.

I watched from behind the shield's force field while half of the Masculines guarding me rushed him. It was Lux who took him down. With his hands tied behind his back, the Helio grappled, trying to break free, but he was no match for Lux's super strength. They brought the unruly Helio to me. Kailas tapped his band, and the force field sucked into the metal plate. The Helio was on his knees before my feet.

"You're up." Tomas yelled.

Be curious, channel oneness, remember who you are. I knelt, trying to look into the Helio's eyes, but without pupils or irises, I didn't know where to gaze. Taking in a deep breath, I reached my palms out to his cheeks and, as my skin made contact with his, it happened. My eyes closed, and we came into a whirl of energy. The coalescence was strong as his perspective merged with mine. When it stopped, my eyes shot open, and I stood up.

"Mutants. They think we're mutants." I looked to Kailas and the Masculines.

"That's not exactly news, Bay," Kailas said.

"No, they think we don't have souls," I told him. "To them, we're nothing. Mutated to be less than human. No soul. No better than dead."

The Helio stood in a daze, Lux's grip loose on his arms.

"We have souls," I told him in Helio. "You can see that now, can't you?"

He was silent and still. I stared at his unkempt, lilac-gray beard. The beard was a sign of manhood. When it first started growing in, it meant it was time for him to train in their army. I knew this about them now. He was conflicted when he murdered his first mutant as a teenager. He once resisted believing we were parasites, but as time wore on and he lost loved ones to the mutants, he found himself deep in the belief, even enjoying shedding mutant blood.

"The war is already in motion," the Helio said, but it was in our language, not his.

"Will you help us, Mathis?" I had learned his name during our coalescence. "Tell your people we have souls, that we don't want war."

"It won't matter what I say," Mathis told us. I instantly knew it was true. There was only one person who could call off the battle.

"We need to find his chief."

"Why can I understand him?" Kailas asked.

"He must have somehow learned our language during the coalescence," I replied.

That's when the Helio broke through the front line. A horde of green-skinned men and women charged toward us, leaving bloody Masculine bodies on the street behind them. The Masculines surrounded me but then, with each new threat, they began to scatter, leaving me exposed. Time warped as I froze, witnessing the madness around me.

Then I spotted her: the woman with the shark-tooth necklace. She had just knocked out a Masculine and jerked her head up in time to lay eyes on me. Seeing me enraged her with vengeance. She took long, deliberate strides toward me. Without a weapon to wield, a shield, or my Masculine guards, I was dead.

Shark Tooth stopped six yards before me. In what seemed like a single motion, she pulled an arrow from her quiver, nocked it, and shot it. Before I could react, the arrow froze in the air inches from my face. My eyes fixed on the point. *Thank you, Blue.* I looked to the roof and saw her watching over us, bright-eyed. Shark Tooth looked on; our mutant magic no longer shocked her.

The arrow at my face steadily spun until the fletching

faced me. Then it took off, shooting toward Shark Tooth. Before it pierced her chest, it halted. After a pause, it snapped in half and dropped to the pavement. With no respect for Blue's warning, Shark Tooth rushed me, slamming us to the ground. A hard punch hit my nose and my eyes watered. Tomas barreled into the woman, and the two of them tumbled. Seeing him brought me back to my task: coalesce the Helio.

The thought of coalescing Shark Tooth motivated me. I got to my feet when Shark Tooth pulled a piece of tech from her sack and sent an electrical current at Tomas. He propelled backward, his spine smashing into the bricks of a store front.

"Tech," I screamed to whoever could hear me. "They have our tech!"

An explosion came from behind me, and I instinctively dropped to the ground. My ears rang. It all felt too familiar. Then someone had me. They launched me through the air, and my back crashed through an oversized glass window. I landed hard on the carpet and the wind was knocked out of me. I was in shock as I lay on the floor with shards of glass surrounding me. The pain in my body pulsated, but I was vulnerable if I didn't move. With unsteady hands, I pushed myself upright. I recognized where I was. It was Matilda's apartment.

A shard of glass dug into my forearm. Hesitantly, I pulled it out, and a cry escaped me as blood dripped from the wound.

"Your mutant friends can't help you if they can't find you," I heard Shark Tooth sneer in Helio. She stood in front of me. A Helio man was outside the broken window. She gave him a nod and then he was gone, returning to the battle. I guessed he was the one who gave me the lift.

I stood and glared at Shark Tooth straight on. Her irisless eyes were stunning—a green-and-blue painted galaxy—too beautiful for such a ruthless person.

"It doesn't have to be like this," I managed to say in Helio.

She stepped toward me. I stepped back. She took another step toward me, and I took another step back. My shoulders pressed against a wall. The space between us closed. I understood why she loathed us because I had seen it through Mathis's perspective. Blue was right: the Helio weren't savages. They were oppressed and full of anger but wrongly, they believed we were something we were not—soulless mutants.

"We aren't mutants," I told her, reaching forward to coalesce her, but her fist came at my face instead. I ducked. The punch landed on a frame hanging on the wall, and the glazing cracked. I parried and moved to the center of the room.

"Wild cat," a voice said. Matilda was there now, her long, gray hair flowing over a nightgown.

"What?" I asked, not taking my eyes off Shark Tooth.

"This one is fierce, with sharp claws," Matilda whispered and Shark Tooth looked at her. I dropped and swept my leg under Shark Tooth, and she went down.

"Stay down and just listen to me," I said, but then she flip-kicked up. We skirted around each other until her fist came at my face. I blocked it and grabbed hold of her wrist and twisted it. With our skin touching, I tried to focus on a coalescence. *Be curious.* My hand began to glow a soft white and the energy expanded outward onto Shark Tooth's arm, but then she slipped away and shook it off.

"You'll have to use the wax," Matilda said, grabbing my attention.

Shark Tooth bulldozed into my stomach until my back smashed against a wall. Even though it was hard to breathe, I elbowed her hard in the neck until she backed off. Then I grabbed a vase within reach and bashed it over her head. A mess of wildflowers and debris littered the floor.

Shark Tooth shook fragments of glass out of her hair. Enraged, she grabbed me and threw me hard against a wall in the hallway, my bad shoulder smashing into it. She grabbed me again and smashed me into the other side. I was unable to catch my breath; she dominated me. She rammed my back flat against a table and pinned me down with her forearm. A mini statue of a rhino and a candle with a flame were inches from my face.

"You *are* a mutant. Just look at you. You're disgusting!" Shark Tooth screamed at me. She grabbed the rhino statue and rammed the horn into my shoulder wound, twisting and turning it maliciously. I screamed, and screamed, and screamed, getting no relief from the searing pain. She pulled the rhino back and slammed it on the table by my face. I hoped she was showing mercy, but then she grabbed my neck and squeezed.

I kicked. I flailed. I went for her face, trying to press my thumbs into her eyes, but couldn't reach. My head was pulsing, and I couldn't breathe. The world started fading. *You will have to use the wax.* The wax!

I arched my back and twisted until a candle came into reach. I wrapped my fingers around the glass and tossed the hot wax at Shark Tooth's face. It hit between her eyes, and she loosened her grip on my neck. I pressed my heel into her stomach and kicked. She blew back and hit the wall. I hurled as many candles and statues as I could at her. This was my only shot. I gave myself one second to take in a breath, then I launched forward and grabbed onto her: *curiosity, oneness, connection.* And then the coalescence happened.

33

Miluchas was Shark Tooth's older brother. And her name wasn't Shark Tooth, it was Hannila. When she was a young girl, mutants raided their clan's village and killed five. One of the victims was her uncle, a fisherman who taught her how to weave basket traps. Since that day, she learned to hate, to fight, and to fear the mutants. The murders had confirmed to her that mutants were truly evil monsters. Then, years later, when the mutants killed her cousin, she made it her life's goal to become a respected warrior. To stop the mutant monsters from murdering any more of her beloved clan.

"Here," Matilda said, holding out a warm wet cloth to Hannila. "Clean yourself."

Hannila accepted the rag in a daze, then scrubbed at the candle wax. Parts of it had cooled and hardened and broke off in fragments.

"I…" Hannila whispered in Helio, looking up at me. "My whole life was about the fight. I'm a warrior." She fell silent and when she spoke again, it was in my language. "What do I do now?"

Matilda picked a piece of glass out of Hannila's hair. "You live," she whispered.

A loud crash followed by a desperate scream came through the door. I immediately knew Kailas was in trouble.

I darted through the apartment and leaped out of the

broken window. To my left were Masculines and Helio fighting one another in a bloody battle. To my right, fleeing Halcyons were running down Main Street.

"Kailas," I screamed. "Kailas, where are you?"

"Bay." I followed his voice and spotted him. An electrical pole had collapsed and pinned him to the street.

"Blue," I screamed, glancing up at the buildings, "Blue! Help. The pole!" I reached Kailas just as Blue lifted the pole, and he pulled his legs out. I gave him a hand as he stood to meet me. One leg was badly hurt and internally bleeding below his knee. He could barely take a step.

"Bay, you need a medic," he said, looking at me.

"Me? *You* need a medic, your leg is—"

"Your nose…" As he said it, I felt blood on my upper lip and wiped it off with the back of my hand. I thought of Blue's nosebleed on the day of the brush fire.

"I'm fine," I told him.

"Your eyes are black."

"I said I'm fine."

Kailas's glared behind me as I glanced to find Hannila coming toward us.

"She's okay. She's been coales—" A flash of light shot at Hannila and took her down. Tomas stood nearby, holding a tech weapon but just as I laid eyes on him, a Helio barreled into him. Fast for his injury, Kailas ran to Tomas's aid.

A Helio swung a battle ax at a Masculine, and it struck him hard on the side of his head. He fell to the ground with empty eyes and blood leaking from his mouth. He was one of the men assigned to protect me.

A bang broke my eardrums.

With my palms covering my ears, I turned toward the sound. It had come from Quinn's office. Nic was outside the door fighting a Helio. Quinn could be seen through the window barricading the doors inside.

How do I help? *Who* do I help? I wasn't sure how many more coalescences I could handle, but I could do at least one more.

"Hannila." I turned to her as she regained her feet.

She swallowed hard. "I'll take you to him." She extended her hand to me. With our fingers interlocked, she raised them high and shouted a command in Helio. She was signaling to her people that she was taking me to their leader, for diplomacy. She yelled the declaration repeatedly, her voice loud and commanding. Then, taking careful steps, she moved forward, and I followed her lead, next to her.

We moved through the Masculines and Helio fighting and made it through the crowd when we arrived at the front line. A slew of bodies bloodied the pavement around us. The elder with the staff stood before us. Gatoah. He was Miluchas and Hannila's father, and he was the clan's reappointed leader. He glared at us as if we had interrupted him with a horribly childish venture.

"You," Gatoah snarled. "We should have ended you in the forest long ago."

"Father," Hannila spoke to him evenly in Helio. "She needs to show you something."

If I could get him to understand, if I had the chance to coalesce him, we could end the war.

"Look at her. She's red. Mutated even more," he cried.

Helio men forced me away from Gatoah and Hannila as she pleaded with him. I had to do something. He had to give me the chance to show him. The men led me by my underarms to their base near Main Street. There was a medic, more like a healer, tending to their wounded. Once we reached their base, the Helio whipped me around to face the battle. They held me tightly by my arms while Gatoah made his way to me. Hannila was nowhere to be seen.

The surrounding war was gruesome; there was heartbreaking violence everywhere I looked. Ahead of me, a Helio sent a grueling punch into a Masculine's head. The Masculine whipped out a tech weapon and shot an electrical current at the Helio. The shot burned the man as he sputtered in place before dropping to the ground. A mob of vengeful Helio surrounded the Masculine. Outnumbered, they easily overtook him and beat him until he lay on the cement in fetal position. My chest tightened and I stopped breathing. I couldn't stand it for another second.

"Do you not wish to see what you caused?" Gatoah said, standing before me. "This is your karma."

I yanked my arms, pulling hard to free myself, but the men were strong, and I couldn't reach for Gatoah. I would never be able to show him.

"It will soon be over."

With one last hope, I searched the rooftop for Sterling and Blue but it was empty. I found them on the street, by the entrance of the building. Two bearded Helio men tied Blue's hands behind her back as she wrestled to break free. A third Helio forced a cloth bag over her head. Sterling was face down on the pavement; his arms were bound and a knee crushed his neck.

Across from them on the road, Quinn was being led toward us by a group of Helio warriors. Nic lay still on the pavement by their feet. Kailas and Tomas were battered and weak, but they fought through the street trying to make it to me.

I couldn't breathe. My throat closed up, and I let out an involuntary cry.

"Please. Stop!" But Gatoah ignored me. He turned his back and faced the fight. "If we don't have souls, and you do, then why do you treat us this way? Where is your conscience?" He wouldn't look at me.

Quinn was almost to him. He was about to get what he wanted: a leader for a leader. It would be the end of Halcyon. No more mother, no more Masculines to protect the citizens. The Helio warriors would make it into town, destroy it, and end our kind for good. I saw their plan through Hannila's eyes, and it was glorious. They set out to claim the island and to show us we were mere mutations and nothing more.

Quinn was paces away from Gatoah. She struggled against the Helio, dragging her feet in the dirt, trying to slow down the men pulling her to her death. Gatoah planned to break her neck, but if I could reach him in time, he would change his mind. *What about Samuel? The Helper. He could amplify my gift.* I searched for him through the men fighting on the street, but it was no use. There was no time to find him.

What if I didn't need Samuel? What if I could reach Gatoah from here on my own? Maybe if I used the ground beneath our feet, I could connect us. I had to at least try.

This was it—now or never.

I had to give this everything I had. I let my vision fall black as I found the connection. I let the warmth in my heart swell outward until it reached my stomach, chest, and finally, my neck. The warm energy emanated from my core as if I were turning into a ball of sunshine. It reached past my shoulders and down to my knees, and then into my feet and my head. I could feel it now. I could feel my connection to the world.

It was as if roots grew from my skin and dug into the soil under my feet. My soles warmed as they merged with the planet below me. Intense bliss overcame me, and Bay Lilly was gone. I was outside my form now, watching as a bright, red light took root underneath me and spider-webbed outward, like veins. The light traveled through the soil and to Gatoah, but I didn't stop there. I kept going and entered into the Masculines and Helio closest to me, and then farther and farther until everyone on Main Street was connected.

My form left me, and it was as if we were all formless. An alluring, radiant red light surrounded us. It came from us, and it became us. We connected. We were light. We were one.

34

I stood alone in a dark place I had never been. I couldn't remember how I got there or what I was doing before.

"Hi, Bay."

I twisted to find the astronaut standing behind me. His fishbowl helmet was propped on his hip, his arm resting on top of it. With his helmet off, I got to see his face for the first time. He was middle-aged, pale-skinned, and dark-featured.

"Hi, astronaut guy that's been haunting my dreams."

He clicked his tongue. "You're not an easy person to get ahold of."

"You've been looking for me?"

He pointed up at the night sky. "Syzygy."

Resting high in the coal-black sky was a bright, round light partially covered by a penumbra, leaving behind a glowing ring of light. "What?"

"That's a syzygy," he told me. "You wouldn't want to look directly at it in real life, though. You'd go blind."

"*Syzygy?*"

"Three celestial bodies aligning: moon, sun, planet. An eclipse." So, this was what Sterling thought to name my gift after: *syzygy.*

"Which moon is it? It doesn't look like either of them," I asked.

The astronaut had two differently colored eyes: one brown

and one blue. His hair was brown, too, and neatly kept. I'd never seen him while awake, but I felt I knew him: a familiar soul, but an unfamiliar face.

"This planet only has one moon."

I scoffed at his ridiculous answer. "What planet only has one moon?"

"You'll see," he told me. "Until then, just enjoy the phantasmagoria."

My curiosity faded as I remembered what being in a lucid dream meant.

"Wait. If I'm dreaming, and I know I'm dreaming, that means I can—" and then my feet rose, and I floated into the sky.

"It's not exactly a dream," he told me as he floated beside me. "You're in between dimensions."

I shrugged. "How's that different?"

"Maybe it's not."

Drifting away from him, I was about to fly off, to explore the night sky, when my eyes all at once opened, and I returned to my world.

<h1 style="text-align:center">35</h1>

I t was day again. Sunlight filled in the space around me. I lay on the pavement. Pressing against the ground, I attempted to sit, but even that small action proved too strenuous for my exhausted body. So, I lay back down and looked around me. What I saw had me stunned. I wasn't sure if I had woken up, or if I were still in a dream.

In my direct line of view was a Helio healer treating a stab wound on a Masculine's leg. She tenderly sewed his skin shut while chanting. Gwen, the healer, held her palm over a slash on a Helio's forehead. A green glow came from her fingers and when she pulled her hand away, his wound was healed. To the side of them, one of the doctors from the Halcyon hospital lifted a critically injured Helio man onto a stretcher. Two beaten, yet able Masculines wheeled the Helio toward the hospital for treatment.

Something in my head pounded hard, and my vision warped. I took in a breath and ignored the pain. This was all too interesting to miss. I was desperate to get up, to investigate, to understand what happened, but I was much too weak and logy. Then it all rushed back to me. The coalescence... it worked.

There was a hand on my shoulder.

"You did it," Hannila said, kneeling to me. Strangely, this woman who had tried to kill me now felt like a friend I had always known.

Kailas was there now, embracing me. There were slashes all over his body, his beautiful face was battered, and his nose was black and blue and probably broken. Quinn and Nic came up behind him, and then they were on the pavement, too, enveloping me with their care and love. Soon Blue and Sterling joined in, and in one big, broken, pained body of people, we came together in a warming embrace.

Unexpectedly, the rest of those who had experienced the coalescence joined us, and it was as if we were all brothers and sisters. We were a family, forever bonded. Our individual identities disappeared, and we remembered where we came from. We remembered why we were here. We remembered who we were. And it was bigger than anything we had ever thought.

The injured were sent to the hospital to be healed by an integration of Helio healing and Halcyon technology. Overall, ten people had been killed—eight Masculines and two Helio.

Kailas helped me to my feet, his leg wasn't as bad as I originally thought it was. He didn't even have a limp. Leaning the bulk of my weight on Kailas, we walked to the beach, where about twenty of us were ready to talk and figure out where to go from here. We had to plan our future together. We knew that the bliss of the coalescence would wear off, and our minds would again consume us if we let them. We sat silently in the warm sand, listening to the waves breaking. Eventually, an adult Helio woman named Liona broke the silence. She was Gatoah's partner, and she was there to speak for the chief as he went to the hospital to guide the injured.

"You call us the River Clan. People of water. But we consider ourselves sun people."

I sat next to her and looked at her closely. The galaxy of stars in her eyes mesmerized me, but it was the light shining from her forehead that was truly captivating.

"That's why your eyes shine the way they do," I said.

"Our third eye is made of light, yes. We are the last humans who are not mutated. This is what our ancestors' forms looked like... skin the color of the forest with eyes that hold stars and this..." She pointed to her third eye. "Do you see the big, shining sun up in the sky? That is our star, our home. It's at the center of everything. It gives life to this planet. It's what we are all made of. There's a reason why we are drawn to bask in the sun. There's a reason why we stop to watch the sunset."

"Why?" I asked, feeling the warm light on my skin.

"Because... the sun is what you call One."

One was a warm light somewhere in the universe, sure. But, we couldn't see it. She was mistaken.

"It kinda makes sense," I heard Sterling say. "We *are* made of stardust. Science has proven it. And the sun *is* a star. So, in theory, it's not impossible that we're made of the sun."

"According to our ancestors," Liona said, "all the stars were long ago coalesced as one." The Halcyon crowd broke out in whispers of disbelief. I was drawn in by her use of the word coalesce.

"As an example, think of the ocean. If, somehow, every drop of sea water separated from each other, the ocean would no longer exist; only individual droplets. If they stayed this way for too long, they would forget they were ever part of something bigger. They would forget the ocean ever existed. Think of each star as a water droplet. The stars were once together as one, like the ocean, but got separated.

"It is said that our souls come from the stars, and we return to our stars after form-death. If we can come together on this physical planet, we can come together in the stars as well. Then our universe can be whole again."

The tale gripped the Halcyons', and my, attention. This story wasn't something that came through in the coalescence. During the coalescence, I felt their secure connection to a supreme light. Their consciousness and their feelings toward One transferred. But the words, the logic behind it, didn't.

"You sound like you're describing the Big Bang Theory," Sterling said, his expression serious.

"The big what?" Liona asked.

"Nothing; I'm just thinking out loud. If you don't mind meeting me in my lab later, I'd love to hear more about this."

"I appreciate your interest in our ways," she said.

"That's how he is," Blue said, putting a hand on his chest, "He loves to understand everything with his big brain." She poked his head with her finger.

Sterling looked at Blue and kissed her on her forehead and smiled.

"So, why kill us?" Kailas asked, stealing the attention.

Liona rested a hand on her lilac hair. "We thought that by eliminating our biggest obstacle—you all—our clan would have a chance at coming together and making the universe whole again. But now, we see the error in that. It was wrong of us, and we're sorry."

"We see the error in our way too," Quinn spoke up. "You have a special way of life that we never understood… until now. I now see how thoughtless our actions have been. We made many mistakes, and we're imperfect. Please forgive us too. And, if you're in need, I have spare food I would like to share with your clan."

Liona reached a hand out to Quinn's in a tender gesture. It was as if we, as a group, let out a collective breath, a sigh of relief. We each felt seen and heard, and maybe that's all any of us ever wanted.

"Excuse me, I apologize for my interruption." It was Oona. He stood to the right of us, in his usual show-up-all-of-a-sudden way, and I looked at him over the others' heads. "May I steal Bay from you?"

"Oona"—I smiled warmly—"why don't you sit and talk with us? We could catch you up on what happened." He didn't speak. He only returned a warm, all-knowing smile. "Oh, right, seer of all things," I said. Of course, he already knew.

"I do have one thing I'd like to say to everyone, if that's all right," Oona said. I nodded, and he continued. "One of the hardest, most important life lessons is simple yet challenging. It's the task to see when *we* are the *bad guy* as you call him, and to choose differently. We all think we are the hero and our task is to understand that we aren't. We must see our own insanity and not only the insanity of others. And this is what I see you all doing right now."

We took in his words as Oona looked to me once again. "Will you come with me, Bay?"

I didn't think he would interrupt such a meaningful conversation for no good reason. "Sure," I agreed, moving to my feet.

Kailas came to my aid but I was stable enough to walk. Still, he walked beside me as we took steps toward Oona. For some reason, then, I turned and took a glance at everyone behind me. There was a beautiful diversity of Helio and Halcyons congregating in a circle on the beach. It was a sight I didn't think anyone experiencing it believed they would ever see. Nic and Quinn sat beside each other on a log of driftwood. Quinn leaned her head on Nic's shoulder, his arm in a sling. The two of them, mother and son, had strengthen their relationship through all of this.

I understood that Quinn had always done what she thought was right for Halcyon, but she wasn't perfect, just as Nic had said. It was then that I realized I didn't recall feeling her during the group coalescence. I made a mental note to seek her out later to do another one-on-one. Her lips curved in a smile when she saw me looking at her. She mouthed the words,

"Thank you." I think she meant that because without the coalescence, the Helio would have killed her. But she didn't need to thank me.

My eyes then fixed on Nic's honey browns. He returned the gaze but then, ever so slowly, he raised his eyebrows, crinkled his nose, and squeezed his face into the ugliest mug I'd ever seen him make. At that moment, I knew he would always hold a special place in my heart.

My mother sat cross-legged in the sand across from Hannila. The fact that she had even come to the beach meant the world to me. It showed that she wasn't going to hide in the shadows anymore. That maybe we could walk through life hand in hand from now on. I was optimistic our relationship would blossom.

"I'll be right back," I told them all. I rotated away from the gathering and walked to the boardwalk stairs with Oona and Kailas. Before we ascended the stairs, Oona turned to Kailas and asked him to stay behind with everyone on the beach. Kailas looked to me and I nodded in agreement to go it alone. Then Oona shuffled up the steps as Kailas and I hung behind for a second.

"You're incredible," Kailas said. "What you did today… you created world peace. You know that, right?"

I bit my lip and shook my head. "Not really. It wasn't the *world*. It wasn't even the whole island. Probably won't be long till the northern villages start a war."

"Well, if they do, we know who to call."

"Oh, not me. I'm retired," I replied.

"Yeah, yeah." He pulled me in for a hug. We separated, and I slowly backed away, not wanting to take my eyes off him yet. "I'll see you when you get back. I'll grab some lunch. What do you want?"

"Surprise me."

<h1 style="text-align:center">36</h1>

Oona and I hiked side by side for several minutes, keeping a slow pace due to my coalescence hangover. "Are the Helio right?" I asked him. "Is the sun One?"

"What do you think?"

"I think you're not going to answer my question."

"You're wising up." He smiled.

Once we made it to the willow tree and hibiscus flowers, I realized we were heading to Nic's stolen van. We jumped into the front seats, and Oona drove us down the same paths as before. It seemed we were going to the valley again, but I didn't ask. I stayed patient and present and kept my questions to myself. Oona would eventually tell me. I just had to wait.

He parked the van in the same place, and we took the same stroll through the rainforest. Before long, we hiked down the rock face and into the stream bed. I climbed onto the faded red boulder, but this time Oona joined me.

"So," I finally said, unable to keep quiet any longer, "What's going on? Why are we back here?"

Oona steadied himself on the boulder and took in a long breath. He exhaled and said, "It's time for you to fulfill your destiny."

I pulled a face. "Didn't I just do that? I coalesced over a hundred people. I stopped the war. What else do you want?" A bit of frustration stirred inside me. I wasn't even going to try to calm down. If emotions weren't bad, then I was allowed to feel frustrated over this.

"It's not what *I* want. It's what's meant to happen."

I clicked my tongue. "And what's meant to happen?"

"You, going to the future."

"That again?" I asked with a scoff. "Kailas pointed out to me how absurd that is. You told me that the planet dies, and that I get sent to *the future*. Both can't happen. If the planet dies, there is no future, Oona."

"I see how it can seem that way," he said. "Please just come with me."

After a groan, I reluctantly followed him, moving from boulder to boulder until I once again stood outside the small, cascading waterfall.

"I'm sorry, Bay." Oona's demeanor turned serious. "I have to be frank with you, because we don't have much time. In about ten minutes, the planet will be uninhabitable. It will die."

My face fell flat, every emotion sucked out of me. "What? No," I said blankly. It was impossible. The planet was fine. It couldn't be true. It was just too awful. But Oona was the seer of all things. He had been right before. "Well, if that's true, we have to warn everyone." A growing light in the sky caught our attention and we looked up as it stretched across the sky.

"There's nothing we can do for them. There's no way to preserve their human forms, but they're more than their forms. They'll be fine."

I thought of Kailas, my mother, butterfly Ash, Gemma, Smallholding, Nic, Quinn, Amur, Blue, Sterling… everyone.

"There's a chamber in this cave that will take you to the future," he said.

"What future is there if the planet is dead?"

"There's still a future for you if you go into the chamber."

"Then let's get everyone into it," I said, suddenly panicked. *This isn't happening. It's all a bad dream.* My heart hurt.

"The chamber only works for one person."

"Why does it have to be me?" I didn't mean to cry; it just started happening. "Why not you? Or Kailas? Or *anyone* else? Why *me*?" I sobbed.

"Because you're the passenger pigeon with a rare and needed gift." He was making no sense. The tears slowed, so I could speak.

"I don't understand. You said—"

"You do understand, just not through the mind. You're trying too hard to understand through the mind."

"What is my gift exactly, why is it so special?"

Oona glanced to the waterfall, then back at me. With an exhale, he said, "You're a restorer. Restorers remind people of who they were before they came to their physical form. You remind people of their soul. In the past, restorers were shunned. People often saw them as emotional, unrealistic, and too subjective. They suppressed the restorers' abilities, made them feel alienated and wrong until eventually, even the restorers forgot their souls. Then, over time, fewer restorers were born until they became extinct. Without restorers, the world forgets."

"Extinct?" I asked.

"That is, until you." Oona grinned at me.

"Are you saying I'm the last restorer?" My eyes narrowed.

"I'm saying you're the *first*," he responded, "or you will be." His eyes gave off a gentle energy. He pulled me in for a hug, and I was enveloped in his fatherly embrace. As I pulled back, he placed his hands on my shoulders. His smile fell as he looked at me seriously.

"You can do this." He placed a hand on my cheek. "You already have."

I took in a breath, and willed myself to be strong. "What do I do?"

His arms fell to his sides, and he gestured toward the waterfall. "You have to go back into the cave. Once in there, turn to the right. There will be an amber-colored, semi-precious mineral in the rock. All you have to do is touch it. If you're meant for the chamber—as I know you are—the chamber will release. You step into it, and you will transport." My eyes fixed on the falls, watching the water glide.

I looked to Oona. "Can I say goodbye to my friends?"

"There's no time."

I started to tremble. "What about you?" I asked, tears welling up as I looked at his old, kind face.

"I'll be fine."

"Oona..." A tear dropped down my cheek.

"Trust," Oona whispered.

I closed my eyes, refilling my soul. *I can do this.*

"One more thing, this is important."

I opened my eyes and paid absolute attention.

"Humans will get a second chance on another planet that they will call Earth. They will desperately need your help. When you meet these people, they will appear different than what you know humans to be. They are unlike any person you have seen, even Helio, because they've had to adapt. You mustn't be frightened of them, but know they will be frightened of you."

I tried to retain everything I heard, even though it hardly made sense.

"Here's the important part—remember this—when you tell them our story, when you tell them about all of this, they won't understand you. The world we know isn't anything like the one they know. The plants, animals, ecosystems, languages... it's incompatible. What you have to do is find the similarities and translate our world to them."

"That's impossible. How would I—"

"Use your gift. Once you use your gift, you will know their language. You will be able to communicate. You just have to use your gift."

"But Oona, the gift, won't it allow them to see our story too? I won't have to translate. Isn't that how my gift works?"

"It might," he said. "I hope it does, but I don't know. There are variables at play. Their minds are stronger than ours because they have mutated further. And the pesky human mind can fog up the clarity that even you possess. Some might be easier to reach than others. However, I'm certain there will be defiant ones who will need you to translate for them."

I took it in, trying to process. "What will the transportation feel like?"

"It's not truly a transportation—not time travel. It's more like a preservation. By the time they find you, more time will have passed than you can comprehend. To you, it will feel like you've woken up after a good night's sleep, when really many years have passed." A gust of wind blew through the valley and Oona looked to the top of the mountain at the growing light. He shot his eyes at me. "We're out of time." He placed his hands on my shoulders and pushed me toward the falls. I stopped and turned to him.

"Wait, Oona. I can't. I don't know what I'm doing."

He smiled. "Take this." He held out a small holograph disk and I took it from his hands. "None of us know what we're doing, but we have to do it anyway."

My choices were apparently either enter the chamber and fulfill a destiny or die. I pulled Oona in and hugged him tight, whispering a thank you to him. Then I took a step toward the cave, looking back at him over my shoulder. He nodded reassuringly. My body shivered as the cold water rushed over my head. With that, I let my fears go.

I was in the small cave, wet. I scanned the walls for a semi-precious mineral, but didn't see anything except moss. Running my hand along the green hairy stuff, I clawed at it, pulling it off the cavern wall. As I pulled the moss away, I saw it—the gem—just where Oona said it would be. I twisted my mouth and tried not to cry as dread swelled inside me.

Before I could hesitate, I pressed the gem. A moment passed and nothing happened. I kept my hand on the precious stone, unsure of what to do. Maybe it wasn't for me like Oona had thought it was. Maybe I could run back to the beach in time to be with everyone for our last moments—to be with Kailas. But then the gem shone bright, and the ground shook beneath me. Tiny pebbles of rubble fell from the cavern above me and landed by my feet.

The wall before me slid open, revealing a vertical hole only big enough for me to step into. I was afraid it would trap me. As I stood there, my trust in Oona wavered. I wondered if he was mistaken or if it were a cruel ruse. What if there was no end of the world and I ended up stuck in the cave with no one knowing I was there? My fears spiraled, and doom loomed around me like a shadow.

The holograph.

Holding the disk upright, I slid my finger over the activation button and a flickering light shone from the top of it. An image of Kailas appeared. My heart leapt.

"Hey, Bay," Kailas said, pressing his lips together, trying to suppress a laugh. "Oona tells me that by the time you watch this you'll be on your way to the future, and I won't be there to say goodbye. So, here I am recording this message." He looked over at what I assumed was Oona and then back at the holograph. "You go do your thing, live your destiny, and all that. Don't worry about me. I mean, yeah, I'll miss you… but honestly, I don't think you're going anywhere. I think Oona is full of crap. So, there's that." He finally let out the chuckle he was holding in.

"But, in case this is goodbye…" His eyes softened and he slowly mouthed the words *I love you.*

The holograph flickered off. But then, in an instant, it flickered back on. "I almost forgot. Oona wants me to tell you that you and I will find each other again." Kailas rolled his eyes and begrudgingly picked up a piece of paper. "He says to look for this symbol and you'll find me." It was a circle filled with a red wave at the top, a white wave in the middle, and a blue wave at the bottom. "So, I guess this isn't goodbye. I guess this is… see you later."

Kailas faded and the holograph turned off.

A tear escaped my eye.

A ray of sunlight came through the falls and landed on the gem, lighting the cavern with a yellow aura. I smiled as the beam fell on my skin. All of a sudden, I was calmed by a presence in the cavern with me, an angel or a ghost. Whatever it was, it made me feel protected and secure, as if whispering in my ear: *"You've got this."*

That's when I did it. Before I could change my mind, I stepped into the chamber. Immediately, the rock slid shut behind me, acting as a barrier. There was just enough room for me to turn around and feel the rock with my palms. It was pitch black; I couldn't even see my hands in front of me. It took every ounce of bravery in my bones not to bang my fists on the stone and beg to be let out.

"I can do this," I whispered to myself, "I *am* doing this."

That's when amber-yellow liquid seeped through holes in the rock and filled the bottom of the chamber. It was sap-like and cold. After only seconds, it filled the chamber to my knees. As it soaked my shorts, the cloth faded away until it disappeared into the sap. Even Kailas' necklace vanished. Naked now, I took in deep breaths as I battled my mind. I would drown if I didn't escape, but there was nowhere to go. The sap rose to my chin. Soon it would all be over, one way or the other.

"Everything is going to be okay."

"Who's there?" I called out.

Drowsiness took over, my head wobbled and wavered, and my eyes grew heavy and warm, opening and closing as I fought to stay awake. The sap rose over my face. It was dark, sound warped, and I couldn't hear a thing. I couldn't move. But I gave into it. I surrendered in the same way I surrendered to sleep. I let the world slip away from me and succumbed to the darkness.

37

I was in Smallholding, on my farm, on a perfect, sunny day. A blue morpho butterfly fluttered by my view, and I thought of my brother as I watched it fly off into the distance and land on a lavender flower by the edge of the property. Kneeling in the grass, over a pond, was Ash, in his human form. He had always asked for a pond, but it was too dry to ever dream of making one. Seeing him made me stall and stare.

My stepfather bounded out from our house and ran to him, picking him up and placing him on his shoulders. I was overtaken with emotion at the sight of them together. They had never been alive at the same time. The two of them twirled in a circle, smiling with glee. But then, as they spun, they faded until they were translucent and vanished altogether. I was frozen in place, staring at the empty spot they were once in.

The astronaut was there now, standing beside me, appearing out of thin air. This time, he was in civilian clothes: a pair of jeans and a red flannel shirt. I couldn't help but look at him with annoyance.

"You look happy to see me," he said with a grin.

"Why are you here?"

He shrugged. "To keep you company."

"But why *you*? I don't even know you." I looked into his brown and blue eyes.

"You know me." He smiled. "You just don't know it yet."

I tilted my head and looked at him closely, trying to figure out if I had seen him before, besides in my dreams.

"Who are you?"

"It's dying," he said, peering out over the island landscape. It appeared healthy and alive, but it was a facade.

"The planet?" I asked.

He nodded. "The shield was damaged from an impact. The core will go cold." I couldn't think of it; it didn't feel real. "This is a gift. A sort of dream to enjoy during… whatever is happening to you."

I looked around at the dream, the perfect day in Smallholding. It was a lie, the planet wasn't thriving. I knew that now.

"I'm the person who finds you here…." he said, "in a few billion years. I haven't been born yet, but when I am, I'll have an obsession with your planet. My people will call it Mars and we'll come here one day and find you."

A flock of crows flew over our heads, cawing loudly.

The entire flock crashed to the ground, smashing into the grass. Inconceivably, and all at once, the water in the pond boiled. I screamed in alarm, but no sound came out of my mouth. There was no sound anywhere at all. The light went out, and it was black. The entire island went dark. Our spectacular planet and every living being on it died—everyone except me.

I lost everything, and I mean everything. You would think I would be devastated, but I was in a state of absolute peace. One, or the mountain, or whatever it was, gave me a spectacular dream that kept me in a warm embrace while I waited. Time didn't move for me, and there was no pain. It was as if I were in a heaven dimension, waiting for someone to find me.

Maybe I was actually dead. Maybe the transportation had failed, and I was already gone. Because this was how I imagined I would feel when I reemerged with One. As if I were a bright light dancing about in a sphere of tranquil energy, and everyone I loved was there, only not how I remembered them, not in their human forms, but as their pure energy. It was an infinite coalescence.

38

THREE BILLION YEARS LATER
MARS 2088

Bingham is using a soft bristle brush to dust off a skull when Rafe pops his head through the doorway of the white anthropology room. He's wearing a casual t-shirt sporting the Pepsi logo rather than his uniform. Again. Bingham has half a mind to write him up.

"What's up, Rafe?" Bingham asks, trying to let go of his in discrepancy.

Rafe smirks. "Jim found something outside. Wanna see?"

Bingham sets the brush down and blows grains off the surface of a bone, looking at his work with satisfaction. He steps away from the table to meet the astronaut, leaving behind a largely constructed skeleton.

"Human?" Rafe asks as they stride through the white halls of the station. "The skeleton you're working on?"

"Results are pending," he says, his eyes heavy already from a long morning.

"Let me know when you know. I bet Johnson a hundred it was human," Rafe says.

"Did Jim find more bones?" Bingham asks.

"Like you need any more of those," the astronaut says as they turn into a hallway. "Isn't it crazy?"

"What?"

"We come to Mars, thinking we're the first ones here. Yet, we find all these bones." The two men approach a large, pneumatic door. Rafe presses his thumb to a scanner, the scanner sounds, and the door slides open. The room they enter is lined with space suits and, as they step inside, the door slips shut behind them.

"Outside? Seriously?" Bingham asks.

"If you want to see it, yeah."

"Great."

"I know, I freeze my nads off out there, but this is worth it. Trust me."

Rafe and Bingham suit up, test their gear, and follow the proper protocol. They radio to the team to let them know they're on their way, then they enter the airlock. Before long, their boots are in the red dirt with carabiners attached to a yellow rope, leading them to the excavation site. As they maneuver, they gently bounce-walk their way toward a cavern.

Bingham hears Rafe's voice boom through a speaker in his helmet.

"Almost there."

Together, Rafe first, they enter the large cavern the team began excavating weeks ago.

"Hey kid, we're miles from the last dig. Why'd Jim come all the way out here?" Bingham radios to Rafe.

"He had a *good feeling* about it. Very sciency, huh?" Rafe chuckles. "Oh, by the way, it's Jim's boy's birthday today. Might wanna mention it."

They approach the end of the cave, where a crew of astronaut excavators are working. The pair unhook their carabiners from the rope, their arms pressing the top of the cave. Before them stands Jim, a big smile on his face.

"Jim," Bingham radios him.

"Bingham," Jim radios back.

"Happy birthday to your son. How old is he now?"

"Two."

"Wow, time flies," Bingham radios.

"Like a jet."

"Rafe tells me you found something."

"This way," Jim says, his heterochromia eyes—one brown, one blue—visible through the glass of his helmet.

The three men in the astronaut suits maneuver their way through a chamber carved through the rock. Lights are strung along the way, keeping them from uncut darkness. An excavator works a palm-sized, amber-colored gemstone loose from the cave wall. Like a diamond in a mine, he wipes off the dust, polishing its vibrant surface. As they approach the farthest part of the cavern, something large comes into view. Cradled in the rock is a substantial slab of amber-yellow gemstone. Its height reaches well over their heads and several feet wide.

The rock is impressive in its own right, but it's what's within the amber slab that is truly remarkable: a body, a person. A woman. Her attributes look human: two arms, two legs, a torso, eyes, a nose, a mouth. Yet there are slight differences, like her hair color, which even through the rock appears to be unnatural shades of red and white.

She is conserved, her body appearing vital, not ossified. She isn't a skeleton, not bones, not something that Bingham would study. Her skin—her body—appear to be entirely preserved. It's like nothing they have ever seen.

"Whoa," Bingham says. He loses his breath and almost rips his helmet off to get a better look. He knows he'll never again see a discovery as remarkable as this one.

***

It takes two days for the extractors to remove the young

woman safely. They carve the rock-like stuff to fit into a biohazard chamber with the woman still enclosed. It isn't the perfect place to put her, like an isolation chamber, but they don't have one of those lying around. Once inside the chamber, the rock starts to soften, slowly turning from solid to liquid. They have no idea what to make of the substance, it isn't like any element on Earth.

Jim isn't filing paperwork for this excavation. He's taking a risk, but in recent years, the contractor who hired him rarely inspects Jim's findings. Even so, he's one hundred and forty million miles away. What is he going to do from that distance? Jim's the boss up here. He'll handle the fallout from the higher-ups when he gets back to Earth. It's too compelling a discovery to wait five years for permits.

After several tedious hours, the outer edges of the rock liquify. Yet the core, where her body lies, remains solid. As the gemstone softens, the three men watch over her in amazement.

"She's human, right?" Jim asks, breaking the silence.

"But how'd she get here? Stole a rocket, found her way to Mars, and stranded herself?" Rafe remarks in his most sarcastic tone.

They gather around the chamber.

"Any missing persons on Mars? Any tourists unaccounted for?" Bingham asks.

"Nope, never," Rafe replies, looking at her closely.

Jim gazes away from them. His gut is pulling at him with information that doesn't make sense. Somehow, he recognizes her. Is it possible that they met at the academy way back?

"What should we call her?" Bingham asks, looking at the girl.

"Eve?" suggests Rafe.

Bingham shakes his head. "Let's leave religion out of it," he says.

"How about Marsha—get it? *Marsha*?" Rafe jokes, feeling high from the discovery.

"That's even worse."

"We gotta nail down a name for the press. She's going to be famous. *We're* going to be famous," Bingham says with a nod. "I can see the headlines now: crew finds girl on Mars." He invisibly traces the sentence in the air with his hand.

"I guess if we don't name her, they will," Rafe says. "What about Amber? A play on words since we found her in this amber crap."

Jim presses his palm against the side of the chilly chamber.

He sighs. "You guys go back to work. When she's thawed, I'll call you." The two men pull faces but then reluctantly give Jim a nod and walk off. "Remember, keep this to yourselves, all right?"

They agree and disappear through the door.

Jim stays, settling into a chair next to the chamber. He thinks of his son—Ares. He's never met him. His wife gave birth while Jim was on his way to Mars two years ago, and he hasn't made it back to Earth since. He can't help but wonder if he'll ever meet his son. Ares has only ever known Jim's voice through phone calls. On his desk, he keeps a framed picture of Ares in his crib, innocently looking up at his butterfly mobile.

Jim wonders if they'll ever get to know one another. Will Ares have a curiosity about the universe, as Jim did when he was a young boy? Will he have the same obsession with Mars, as Jim did? Will they have things in common? But then, suddenly, he stops thinking of his son. It will be at least another year before he can meet him and the wait feels more grueling when he thinks about him.

Alone in the lab now, Jim feels the silence around him. It's somewhat uncanny, but then again, he never minded being alone. He stares at the girl he found, feeling personally responsible for her. The familiarity is eerie and he can't help but ruminate on how she got to Mars. Is she an astronaut? She seems too young, and she would have been reported as missing. What other explanation could there be? Any conclusion he can think of falls short of possible. *Amber.* He picks up a manila folder and writes it on his personal report. But then he flips the pencil around and erases it because, somehow, he knows this isn't her name.

✳✳✳

The substance is liquified, but Jim doesn't see it yet—he's asleep. His neck is crooked to one side, and his bottom jaw droops low. The pencil rolls off the folder on his lap and drops to the floor. The patter it makes on the tile wakes him. For a second, he's disoriented, but then he glances at the chamber and remembers. He instantly rises to his feet, placing the folder on the seat of the chair. He takes a step forward and sees that the girl is floating in the fluid; her face is breaking the surface.

Hesitantly, he approaches the chamber and places his palm on the glass for a moment. She's stunning, with her white and cherry red hair waving alongside her in the amber yellow fluid. Her skin is youthful now, since thawed, and she appears more like a teenager than an adult. But is she alive?

Jim leans forward for a closer look, but there doesn't appear to be a breath in her body. The sun peeks its way through the skylight above the lab, illuminating the room with its rays. A beam of light falls on the girl's face. Her eyes shoot open, and she takes in a wide, gasping breath.

Jim's first instinct is to run away but instead, he settles. He stays. She coughs a few times and blinks slowly. Then she glances at her hands, examining them, in the way a baby does when it's discovering them for the first time. She holds them out before her, wiggling her fingers.

Then, in silence, she lifts her torso forward. The amber-yellow liquid cascades down her naked body and drips into the chamber. She comes to a seated position as she twists to face Jim.

Jim knows he should be doing something—recording with the camera, radioing the crew, running for his life—but he's mesmerized.

The red-haired girl stares at him intently.

Behind Jim, Rafe appears, wide-eyed with his jaw dropped. "Holy shit."

The girl shifts her gaze to Rafe, and when she sees the red, white, and blue Pepsi logo on his shirt her eyes light up, as if it means something to her.

"I'll get Bing," Rafe whispers and then sprints out of the room.

Alone again, Jim observes the girl calmly even though he's terrified. For what seems like minutes, they stare at one another without moving. Then, ever so subtly, the girl narrows her eyes and tilts her head to the side, studying him. Delicately, the corners of her mouth rise into a smile.

She extends her hand out to Jim, placing her palm on the glass at the opening. He begins to reach toward the hole, but then he pulls back with uncertainty. What is he doing? Shouldn't he at least wear a glove? There are a million reasons why he shouldn't touch her—but irrationally, he finds himself inserting his hand into the chamber.

At first, as he locks gazes with this breathtaking girl, he's astonished by the color of her red irises. But as he journeys deeper into her eyes, he remembers where he knows her from.

And then, with a brilliant glow of light, she shows him.

She shows her little brother everything he forgot.

Turn the page to read a bonus scene from this novel.

THE RAINBOW

A PREQUEL TO
SOULS IN THE STARS

The grass beneath my bare feet was brittle and sharp, like hay, but my soles had grown used to it. Walking under the shade by the dried-out creak brought me some relief from the heat. The creek was usually dead silent, but today, I heard a sound—a trickle. Unwilling to believe it, I climbed down the rocks. Then, there! A thin stream of water. Searching the sky for proof, I found a gray cloud in the distance. Bounding out of the creek, I raced the cloud, daring it to beat me home to share the news.

In the yard, my mother sat on an old tree stump, staring off at something. I traced her line of sight and spotted a bluebird perched on a fence. As I came into her view, she glanced at me with her empty eyes and sunken, papery face. My enthusiasm flickered out in her presence.

"How was your lesson with Gemma?" she asked, her eyes still on the bird.

"Good." I rubbed the back of my neck. "I uh, I... have some news."

"Yeah?"

"The northern stream is running."

She shifted her gaze to the sky and then returned to

herself as she realized what that meant. "I'll set up the catchment," she told me. "You go get your brother."

"And bring him outside?"

She scanned the yard. "No one's around."

I didn't need more permission than that. I threw open the front door and dashed into the house. One leap at a time, I made my way to my little brother's bed, where I found him sleeping soundly. His eight-year-old face slumped to one side with drool hanging from his bottom lip. I touched his warm shoulder, gently attempting to wake him. His arm twitched as his sweet brown eyes fluttered open.

"Hey," I whispered. Ash looked at me, struggling to keep his heavy lids open. His blond hair was knotted from sleep.

Without a word, I scooped him up and put him in his wheelchair. Switching off the break, I pushed him out of his quarantine and into the light of day.

It didn't take long for the rain to arrive and bring a radiant spectrum of light. The hues of red, orange, yellow, green, blue, and purple stretched the sky above us in a perfect arc. It was a sight to see, a normality in our world that would have been better regarded as a miracle.

A thousand tiny water droplets landed on my skin as I raised my arms in the air, tilted my head back, and opened my mouth. The rain landed on my raisin-like tongue and returned the tiniest bit of moisture to my mouth. Pulling my long hair out of its elastic band, I let it loose to bathe in the shower from the sky. If it poured every day, there would be no enduring thirst, no dehydration headaches, and no muscle cramps. No trading crops with Halcyon for our water supply. The many ways my life could possibly change were unimaginable. A life with an unlimited supply of water. What would that even look like?

I lowered my arms, opened my eyes, and faced my brother

in his wheelchair on the porch. For the first time in a while, he looked like himself. Not weak, frail, or dying—just Ash. Also, dry under the roof of the porch. That wouldn't do. He needed to be showered by the rain just as much as anyone.

"It's like magic," my brother said, with his eyes on the rainbow. I slipped behind the wheelchair and paused to take in the spectrum of light. The rain beat on the porch roof, and the sound felt like comforting white noise.

As I detangled my hair, something occurred to me. "Have you learned about rainbows yet?"

"Nope."

I wrung the rain out of my hair. "They're a message."

"Message? But, there's no letters."

"Not that kind of message. They are a sign from One, encouraging us with our spiritual growth."

"Spiritual growth?"

"Kids learn this stuff during their first year with Gemma. She says our souls are invisible to the human eye, but in their realm, they have color. The baby souls start as purple. Then, as they mature, they turn blue, green, yellow, and orange, and finally, when they reach a higher consciousness, they turn red—the Old Soul. Gemma says reaching red is everyone's destiny… everyone's purpose. Spiritual growth."

"Bay," Ash turned to me seriously, "you say the weirdest things."

I ran my fingers through his blond hair and smiled at him. "Rainbows remind us that we are more than just human." My brother sat silently, staring up as it grew bolder. "At least that's what Gemma says," I admitted. "You can believe whatever you want."

Ash shrugged. "All I know is I'm happy when I see one… like I've won a prize."

"Hey," a voice yelled, drawing our attention to it. "Is she

talking about that woo woo stuff again?" Striding toward us was Kailas, my very best friend, and biggest pain. He bounded up the stairs, two at a time, and met us on the porch with his usual enthused energy. His ear-length dark hair, and his clothes, were soaked through. "You know it's just sunlight refracting off the rain, right?"

"Maybe I wasn't even talking about the rainbow."

"You were."

"How would you know?"

"My superb observational skills," he said, pointing to his noggin. I gave him a scowl as he shifted his finger to point at the sky. "You're staring at one." He moved his attention to my brother. "The rain is not gonna last. Don't you want to get out there before it's gone?" He was right. The rainbow was dulling, and the shower slowed to a drizzle.

"I'll wheel him down," I said.

"Wheel? Just pick him up and throw him in the mud," Kailas said.

Ash grinned, "Yeah. Throw me in!"

I shook my head. "It would take a lot more rain than this to churn up mud in this desert."

Kailas bounded down the stairs. When he reached the bottom, he bent over and dug his hands into the soil, scooping some up. The mixture slipped through his fingers in thick, goopy wet chunks.

I ducked just as a fistful of the stuff flew over my head and splattered on the house. Before he could get me, I rushed down the stairs and leaped onto Kailas, tackling him to the ground. The mud splattering on his back with me landing hard on his chest. Before I could smother his face, he flipped me over and pinned my arms to the ground. I hated when he did that. Mad that he dominated me again, I arched my back, released my arms, and pushed him off me. In a flash, we both stood tall, holding fistfuls of mud. "You know evasion is more your thing, right?" he teased. I wasn't the strongest fighter and he always loved to rub that in.

I hurled my mud at his head, but he bobbed down and flung his at my face. It splattered on my forehead. I bent over, grabbed fistful after fistful, and launched them at him until one finally hit his cheek. Before long, the both of us were caked in the messy stuff. We could have gone on pulverizing each other, but a small voice broke us up.

"The rainbow is gone."

Ash sat at the edge of the staircase in his wheelchair. That's what Kailas did; he made me forget. Kailas darted up the stairs. Coated in mud, he whisked my little brother into his arms and carried him to the bottom step. Ash sunk his bare feet into the stuff, wiggling his toes around and giggling. Ash's laugh was as essential as the rain in this drought. I tried to mesmerize it. The way his eyes lit up, the freckles on his nose. I tried to take a mental picture and lock it up in my memory vault to keep him with me forever.

ACKNOWLEDGEMENTS

First and foremost, I want to thank my readers. I imagine you carrying this book around, stealing time to read a few pages here and there—maybe on an airplane, in-between classes, on break at work, in bed just before sleep, or on the beach during your vacation. Maybe you're reading it on a Kindle or listening to the audiobook on your drive home from work. Where ever you are, I'm honored that this novel has traveled with you through your daily life. Thank you. Thank you.

Twelve-year-old Sara, thank you for sparking this dream. Thank you for spending your summers typing away on a clunky nineties computer, writing your little heart out. It only took twenty-three years but we finally finished and published a novel.

Thank you, Lucas, for believing in me, taking the kids out to the playground, making me food when I forgot to eat, and never once telling me that my dream of becoming an author was silly (even though I told myself that enough times for us both). You're a top-notch husband and a great man.

My daughter, Kaia, was five years old when I started seriously writing this novel. As I type this now, she is ten. I've been working on this story for half of her life. She's been patient with me, she's read parts of it with me, and she gave me her opinions on the cover. It's been a long journey, and she's been with me every step of the way. Thank you, Kaia.

Magnolia—Nolie—my second-born grew inside of me as I sent out query letters and worked on the fifth revision of this book. Thank you, Nolie, for being here and being you.

My mom and dad have always found ways to support my

endeavors. From buying speakers at Radio Shack for my band (that never got one gig) to driving me to acting classes. (I didn't become a famous singer or actor but the support is what I remember most.) Thank you.

Thank you to the eighty-six literary agents who sent me rejection letters (and the twenty-three others who never responded). You thickened my skin.

To Emily M., Pam P., Jenny A., Matt, and Kelly P.—thank you for being my test drive and reading a very early draft of this story as my alpha readers. Your feedback, and willingness to read and discuss my novel, meant everything.

Thank you to the many commenters on various FaceBook groups who offered helpful and often harsh criticisms on excerpts, blurbs, and cover concepts.

Big, endless thank you to my editors Nick Hodgson and Donna West. This book is shiny and polished because of you both.

To Danielle, your encouragement meant the world. Without you, this book would probably still be a draft in my computer. Thank you.

Thank you to Snowfire Publishing, my interior designer, Lorna Reid, and my cover artists at Get Covers for bringing my vision to life.

Thank you to my sixth grade English teacher (whose name I sadly can't recall) for telling me that I had a gift at writing. It was the first time I was told that I was good at something I loved. To my seventh-grade English teacher, Mr. Peters, thank you for doing the same. Finally, to Mr. Sabatini thanks for scaring the crap out of me in high school honors English—it made me a better writer. Also, shout out to Lois Lowery for writing *The Giver*. At twelve years old, it inspired me to become an author.

Thank you to everyone who made me who I am. Love you all.

Souls in the Stars is an action-adventure sci-fi fantasy with romance and a satisfying bittersweet ending. However, the story includes themes that may not be suitable for all readers. A scene involving the death of a young boy, mild violence, battles, insinuated (closed door) sexual content, discussions of poverty, a wildfire, and neglectful parents are all themes that appear in this novel. Readers who are sensitive to these topics, please be advised.

ABOUT THE AUTHOR

Sara Jane Triglia is a sci-fi, fantasy, and mindfulness children's book author writing from the slopes of a volcano. Sara's stories often bring us on fantastical adventures for teens or for the whole family to enjoy. She has published short story eBooks, including, *Jumping Caspian* and *The Origins of Raine*. In 2021, she published her children's book *The Littlest Magnolia* which she wrote and illustrated when her daughter was diagnosed with epilepsy. As a former YouTube vlogger, Sara loves to share her passion for writing on social media. When she is not writing, you can find her chasing around a toddler on a beach, watching early 2000's nostalgia reels, or folding a massive pile of laundry. You can follow her on Instagram @sarajanetriglia.

www.sarajanetriglia.com
@sarajanetriglia on Instagram and YouTube